Praise for the novels of
New York Times bestselling author

SUSAN KRINARD

"A master of atmosphere and description."
—*Library Journal*

"Susan Krinard was born to write romance."
—*New York Times* bestselling author Amanda Quick

"Magical, mystical, and moving…fans will be delighted."
—*Booklist* on *The Forest Lord*

"A darkly magical story of love, betrayal, and redemption…
Krinard is a bestselling, highly regarded writer who is
deservedly carving out a niche in the romance arena."
—*Library Journal* on *The Forest Lord*

"A poignant tale of redemption."
—*Booklist* on *To Tame a Wolf*

"With riveting dialogue and passionate characters,
Ms. Krinard exemplifies her exceptional knack for
creating an extraordinary story of love, strength,
courage and compassion."
—*Romantic Times BOOKreviews* on *Secret of the Wolf*

SUSAN KRINARD

Lord of Sin

HQN™

Recycling programs
for this product may
not exist in your area.

ISBN-13: 978-0-373-77398-5

LORD OF SIN

Copyright © 2009 by Susan Krinard

www.HQNBooks.com

Printed in U.S.A.

Lord of Sin

Bigotry and intolerance, silenced by argument, endeavors to silence by persecution, in old days by fire and sword, in modern days by the tongue.
—Charles Simmons

PROLOGUE

London, 1889

"I SHALL NEVER MARRY AGAIN!"

Deborah, Lady Orwell, faced her interlocutors bravely, chin up, dark hair perfectly coiffed in spite of her prolonged state of grief. She still wore black even after eighteen months of widowhood.

Nuala sighed. A quick glance about at her fellow widows convinced her that Lady Orwell's bid for membership would face less than unqualified support. Most had been out of mourning for at least two full years, and none found their grief so intolerable as this young girl who could not possibly have much experience of the world.

I shall never marry again. That was the credo of the Widows' Club, the common ground that brought them together. For her part, Nuala had few doubts about her fellow members' sincerity. But this girl—this naive girl who had married so young—would have ample opportunities to love again.

Not that her suffering should be taken lightly. Nuala still grieved for her husband of six months,

Lord Charles Parkhill, though she had known from
the beginning that their union would be of short
duration. Had he lived longer, she might have come
to love him, might have become more than a companion and nurse to comfort him in his declining days.

But never could she feel the sort of love Lady
Orwell professed. That was almost two and a half
centuries behind her.

"My dear Lady Orwell," Tameri, the dowager
Duchess of Vardon, said gently, "we must consult on
your case. Will you make yourself comfortable until
we return? Shenti will provide you with anything
you require."

Lady Orwell sniffed very quietly. "Of course,"
she said. "I quite understand."

The ladies rose. They followed Tameri out of the
Gold drawing room and into the larger Silver, where
they settled themselves in the somewhat uncomfortable wooden chairs the former duchess had commis-
sioned when she had furnished the town house in the
Egyptian style. Reproductions of ancient gods gazed
down upon them with various degrees of severity
and benevolence: gods with the heads of cats, of
crocodiles, of jackals. Not for the first time, Nuala
found herself distracted by their glittering stares.

Once such gods had presided over a potent mystic
tradition, perhaps the precursor to the magic Nuala's
own people had practiced for millennia. That which
she had once practiced, before…

Nuala brought herself back to the present and
looked at each of her fellow widows in turn. Frances,

Lady Selfridge, sat in her chair with the straight back of a lady born, but her "mannish" clothing—tailored jacket and nearly bustle-less skirt—conveyed a decided air of austerity. Lillian, Lady Meadows, was her precise opposite: dressed in flowing pastels with a modest bustle, her pretty peaches-and-cream coloring was a direct contrast to the vivid tones of the orchids she adored.

Mrs. Julia Summerhayes, who tended to dress in drab browns and grays, was a spiritualist, a follower of Madame Blavatsky. She regularly held séances in her own town house, though Nuala herself had never participated. Nuala had withheld judgment as to whether or not the young woman really possessed the powers others claimed she did.

At the moment, the young woman was looking intently from one face to another as if she were attempting to read her companions' minds.

Garbed in loose, Aesthetic dress, Margaret, Lady Riordan, was as ginger-haired as Nuala herself, with aqua eyes that might have been painted on one of her colorful canvases. A brilliant artist, she had just begun to have her works shown in some of the smaller London galleries. Her gaze was far away, focused on some interior landscape; she would doubtless hear only a small part of what was said.

Clara, Lady John Pickering, was, at the settled age of thirty-three, the eldest of the group save Nuala herself—a devotée of the sciences of chemistry and astronomy. In spite of her unusual interests, hardly considered suitable for a woman of any age, she wore a very traditional dress complete with corset and heavily draped skirts. As she met Nuala's gaze she pushed her spectacles higher on the bridge of her nose and smiled encouragingly.

Last, but hardly least, was the dowager duchess herself. Her given name was Anna, but she called herself Tameri and would answer to nothing else when among friends. In keeping with the fantastical nature of her surroundings, she wore a dress modified to suggest both a woman of fashion and the reincarnated Egyptian princess she purported to be. Pleated linen draped her arms and fell in cascades from the front of her bodice, and a heavy, bejeweled collar decorated her long and graceful neck. She possessed such a regal air and such a large fortune that few in Society dared to mock her, even in their own most private circles.

Compared to Tameri, Nuala was only a dull country mouse. For years she had taken on so many forms, so many personae, that it had been strange to fall back to what she had been when she was born: a not-unattractive woman who appeared to be no more than twenty-five years of age, with untidy ginger hair and very ordinary gray eyes. Charles, who had died in the countryside he so loved, had left her a courtesy title, a house in the city and all the money she might need to make her way in London; his mother, Victoria, the dowager Marchioness of Oxenham, had done the rest. All the appropriate introductions had been made, cards and calls exchanged, and Nuala was free to move in a society that had never been a real part of her world.

Now she was bound to pass judgment on a young woman who, in some ways, was not much different from herself…a girl who had been married a mere three years and had little experience of London. Deborah was quite alone, her husband, the late Viscount Orwell, having broken off with most of his relations long ago, and though she had a modest town house and income, she had few real friends in the city.

Tameri almost inaudibly cleared her throat. She caught up the circle of widows with her green-eyed, majestic stare and brushed the spotted cat from her lap.

"We shall take the usual vote," she said in her quiet, commanding voice. "Frances?"

Frances rose, tugging at the hem of her jacket. "Ladies," she said with a tinge of reluctance, "I vote no. It is my opinion that Lady Orwell has insufficient experience to commit herself to our way of life. I find it very likely that she will wish to marry again."

"I agree," said Lillian very softly. "She is so lovely and amiable…she is sure to find just the right husband before another year is out."

"Perhaps," said Clara. "But some of us were just as young when we made the decision to remain free."

"Indeed," Tameri said. "It is quite impossible to know the girl's mind, but she has a sincerity about her that I find admirable."

"She *must* be here," Julia Summerhayes murmured. "There is a purpose in this, though I cannot yet see it."

Tameri arched a black brow. "Indeed?"

But Julia had nothing else to say. Tameri turned to Lady Riordan. "Margaret?"

Maggie lifted her head, blinking as if she had just been woken from a deep sleep. "I beg your pardon?" she murmured.

"You must listen, my dear. What is your opinion about Lady Orwell? Shall she be permitted to join our little club?"

Aqua eyes blinked again. "I should like to paint her."

Frances rolled her own intense blue eyes. "That is all she ever thinks of," she said tartly. "Perhaps she ought to abstain."

"I agree," Tameri said. "The count is two nays and three ayes." She fixed her gaze on Nuala. "And you, Lady Charles? What is your opinion?"

Nuala knew that the matter of Lady Orwell's acceptance lay in her hands. She could not fault Frances and Lillian on their logic. But Lady Orwell's grief was deep, and she would not surrender it easily.

The companionship of a group of women both older and more experienced than she would surely have a beneficial effect upon her, as their company had done for Nuala. Tameri had been the one to approach the more experienced widows when she had formed the club; they had been meeting in one another's houses for discussion of the arts, politics and social justice for several years. But they did not forgo Society's pleasures. If Lady Orwell lacked the proper introductions to Society, the Widows, odd as they might seem to their peers, could certainly obtain them for her.

Yet Nuala couldn't help but return to the central point. Deborah was sweet, but spirited. She was undoubtedly lovely. Should the right man come along…

Nuala's thoughts began to take a dangerous turn. She imagined Frances matched with a man who shared her passion for justice and women's suffrage. Such unusual men, as unlikely as it seemed, did exist. Lillian could do wonderfully with a husband who indulged her love for her flowers and appreciated her warm and giving nature. Males of an Aesthetic persuasion were not difficult to find in London these days; one of them would surely suit Maggie to perfection.

Clara might be harder to match, but a forward-thinking man with a similar interest in the sciences might possibly be found. Julia was hardly alone in her belief in the unseen. And Tameri—

Stop. It was wrong, worse than useless to think this way. Her days of matchmaking were over. Her last attempt had hardly been an unmitigated success. Far from it. Nearly three centuries of atonement had not taught her humility. She had only grown more arrogant.

She had at last accepted that such arrogance was why her powers had deserted her. She had begun to lose them before she had left the estate of Donbridge, two years before she had gone to Lord Charles to be his nurse and caretaker. It had been like losing a limb. Like losing her family again. Like losing her heart, the very essence of what she was.

Now she couldn't so much as bring a flower into bloom, let alone two deserving people together.

Once she had possessed magic such as had not been seen in generations. And she had done with that magic what no witch was permitted. She had crossed the line from white magic to black, with no stop at gray in between.

Once you have walked into the Gray, the elders had said, *the Black Gate is only a step beyond.* But she had stepped through without thinking, without considering the price. Not only exile, but an endless span of days and years and, finally, centuries.

And guilt. The sickness of knowing that she had used her abilities for evil. The gradual acceptance of her new work for the good. The hope that one day she would have done enough.

But good works alone were not sufficient. Ultimately she had failed, and the magic was gone. As it should have been taken from her on the day of her sin.

She shook off her wretched self-pity. She had learned to live without magic. If she was no longer a witch, she could be something else.

I can be Lady Orwell's friend. Surely there was nothing wrong with that. She had not dared to have real friends in her old life. But now that she had settled in London, she must find a new purpose, new challenges to fill her empty days. She must learn to adapt to *this* world, as Charles would have wanted.

Perhaps she and Lady Orwell might do it together.

"Have you reached a decision, Nuala?" Tameri asked.

Nuala snapped out of her reverie and faced the dowager. "Yes," she said. "The girl is very much in need of peers who will not judge her decisions. It would be a kindness to let her join us."

"Even if she fails to keep the vow?" Frances demanded.

"Let us accept her as a provisional member, then. If within a year she is still resolved to remain as she is, she may be fully inducted."

The group was silent. Frances frowned and then shrugged. Lillian nodded, content to go along with the majority. Maggie popped up in her chair, her short ginger hair falling into her eyes. "I quite agree," she said.

"Then let it be done." Tameri rose, her golden earrings swaying. The widows followed her out of the drawing room. Lillian dropped back to walk with Nuala.

"You know she cannot keep the vow," Lillian said softly, placing a plump hand on Nuala's arm.

"Perhaps not. But sometimes we must think of the welfare of others above our own preferences."

"Oh, yes." Lillian smiled. "She is such a dear child. I should hate to see her unhappy."

Nuala squeezed her arm. "Perhaps she will take an interest in orchids."

"Oh, that *would* be lovely."

They walked into the corridor and continued on to the Gold drawing room, where the others were already seated. Lady Orwell glanced from face to face, her anxiety manifest in the way she clenched her hands in the folds of her black skirts.

"Please be seated, Deborah," Tameri said.

The girl sat, nervously adjusting her clothing with pale, slender hands.

"You have been accepted," Tameri said, "on a provisional basis. You will not be required to take our oath as yet, but will become fully one of us if you find you have no interest in remarriage after one year has passed."

Lady Orwell leaned forward in her chair. "I assure you, Duchess—"

Tameri raised her hand in an attitude reminiscent of the kings and queens depicted on the drawing room walls. "We do not stand upon formality here, Deborah. But in order to become a provisional member, you must put off your blacks. Half-mourning is permissible for the time being. You must not judge the interests of any of your fellow members, nor may you speak of anything you see or hear during our meetings. Is this acceptable to you?"

"Oh, yes, Duch— Tameri."

"Excellent. We shall rely upon your honor." Tameri smiled her exotic, secretive smile. "Now that our formal business is concluded, I suggest that we enjoy our tea. Babu!"

She clapped her hands, and one of her footmen, dressed in spotless white linen shirt and trousers, entered the room and bowed. He took his mistress's instructions and retreated, while Deborah stared after him.

Nuala wished she could take the girl aside and assure her that everything would be well. She would have much to learn, but among so many unusual women she was certain to find the courage to be herself, not a ghostly figure doomed to a life of widow's weeds.

And would you not give anything to be with Christian again?

Nuala let her mind go blank as the tea was served. But it was all a sham. She could not forget a single day of her long life. That was a witch's curse. *Her* curse.

For her, just as there would be no more magic, there would be no other man. And that was as it should be.

I shall never marry again.

CHAPTER ONE

THE ROYAL ACADEMY was hot and crowded, even though the Season had scarcely begun. It was supposed to be a private viewing, open only to the best and brightest of Society, but that seemed to include half of London.

St. John, the Earl of Donnington, yawned behind his hand and glanced at the paintings with only the mildest interest. He was far more intrigued by Lady Mandeville's backside. Unfortunately, she was very happily married, unlike a great many of the peerage, and her husband was a rather large man.

Sinjin strolled the Exhibition Room, seeking more amenable prey. There was Mrs. Laidlaw, whose husband was known to be involved with Lady Winthrop. She was quite acceptable in every way but her hair. It was blond, and that was anathema to him.

Lady Andrew, on the other hand, was dark-haired, and her gown was very tight in the bodice, the impressive curve of her bosom all the more accentuated by the severity of her garments. Her husband was a known philanderer, making her ripe for the plucking.

As if she felt his stare, Lady Andrew turned. Her

eyes widened as she saw him, and he wondered what was going through her pretty head.

The Earl of Donnington. Wealthy, handsome, possessed of every grace a peer ought to display. Impeccable clothing. The bearing of an Indian prince.

Sinjin laughed to himself. Ah, yes. The very pinnacle of perfection.

And London's most notorious bachelor rake.

He smiled at Lady Andrew. Her lips curved tentatively, and then she turned back to the painting. It was enough. She was interested, and when it wasn't so damned hot, he might choose to pursue the opportunity that had so readily presented itself.

Out of habit, he continued his hunting. Far too many blondes. But here, a little beauty with soft brown hair, a figure too abundant to be fashionable, and a much older husband by her side. There, an Amazon with shining black tresses and the confident manner of a woman who has been desired.

And across the room, standing before one of the new Alma-Tademas…

A mass of curling ginger hair that couldn't quite be contained in the tightly wrapped styles of the day, a height neither petite nor tall, a figure neat and fine, a dress so unobtrusive that it made her fiery head all the more striking.

Ginger hair was not fashionable. But it drew Sinjin like a roaring hearth in winter. It collected all the heat in the room and crackled with light.

"Ah. You noticed her, too."

Mr. Leopold Erskine joined Sinjin, his tie some-

what wilted, his auburn hair disheveled and his tall,
rangy body bent as if the heat were a physical burden
riding on his shoulders. The second son of the Earl
of Elston, Leo had been one of Sinjin's best friends
since their first meeting ten years ago as hopelessly
foolish and naive young men. They'd spent considerable time together since, and Sinjin valued Leo's
opinion—though in many ways Erskine had never
quite grown up. He spent months at a time either
traipsing around the deserts of North Africa and
Arabia, or with his head buried in one of his incom-
prehensible scholarly books.

He had also declined to become a member of the
confirmed bachelor set of which Sinjin was undis-
puted leader. Erskine was constitutionally incapable
of being a rake; he actually regarded women as
friends and equals.

"Quite a beauty, isn't she?" Leo commented,
squinting his curious gray eyes.

Sinjin chuckled. "How can you tell? All I see is
the back of her. And you've left off your spectacles."

"It was you who advised me not to wear them.
'Too bookish,' you said."

"So I did." He slapped Leo's back. "Someone
must look after you, Erskine. You're a little lost lamb.
You ought to join one of our gatherings…you might
even enjoy it."

"Not I. I should rather read in my library."

"Of course. How foolish of me to suggest it."

Leo began to speak again, but Sinjin's attention
had already wandered back to the fire maiden. She

had turned slightly, but her face was still not visible. Yet there was a lightness and grace about her movements as she bent her head to listen to one of the ladies standing beside her…a tall, dark-haired woman Sinjin recognized.

"I see that the lady in question keeps company with the widows," Sinjin remarked.

"Widows?"

"You haven't been living in a cave, Erskine. *Those* widows. The untouchables."

"Ah, yes. I believe they call themselves the 'Widows' Club.'"

"The Witches' Club," or so some liked to call them: a half-dozen wealthy, well-bred and eccentric ladies who had vowed never to marry again. Sinjin felt a flicker of disappointment.

"Are you acquainted with them?" Erskine asked.

"One would be hard-pressed not to be aware of the dowager Duchess of Vardon," Sinjin said. "She believes she is some sort of ancient princess."

Erskine pinched the bridge of his nose as if he were pushing up his missing spectacles. "Eccentric she may be, but she is a renowned hostess. For the past two years she has wielded considerable power in Society."

"Ha! As usual, you know far more than you let on."

"As you said, I have not been living in a cave." Leo smiled knowingly. "Even you cannot scorn such a formidable lady, Donnington."

"I won't kowtow to any woman, not even a former duchess."

"It would nevertheless be unwise to let her know that you despise her, or her chosen companions, because of their sex."

Sinjin ignored Erskine's comment. With increased interest, he let his gaze wander over the other women standing near the fire maiden. There was another ginger-haired girl pressed so close to the painting that her nose almost touched it; she wore one of those odd Aesthetic dresses without bustle or stays. It would, he reflected, be a good deal easier to get a woman out of such a garment, especially if one were in a hurry.

But his gaze passed over her, pausing only briefly on the stiffly upright young woman in the severe gray suit, the plump blonde, the brown-haired girl in an unbecoming and out-of-fashion dress and the older woman with a good figure and what might accurately be called a "handsome" face. He lingered a moment on the very young girl with black hair and dull gray dress: she must be still in mourning. *Too young, in any case.*

And that brought him back to the fire maiden. If she didn't have a horse's face or spots, she would be nearly perfect.

You may have vowed not to marry again, my dear, he thought. *But that does not preclude a little entertainment on the side.*

"What do you know of her, Leo?"

Erskine didn't ask which "she" he meant. "Lady Charles, wife of the late Lord Charles Parkhill."

"Parkhill? Charles is dead?"

"Two years ago, of a longstanding illness."

Sinjin shook his head. "I'm very sorry to hear it. I knew him at Eton…even then he was often in ill health."

"Yes. Poor fellow—after so many years of isolation at his estate, he had few people but his family to mourn him when he passed on."

"I didn't know he had married."

"Only six months before his passing. Lady Charles cared for him until the end. She was completely devoted to him and never left his side. Even after she was widowed, she remained in the country until this Season."

"She is newly come to London?" Sinjin asked, surprised.

"Yes. The dowager Duchess of Vardon and the dowager Marchioness of Oxenham have been introducing her around town, but I understand that she has remained somewhat reclusive."

"Who are her family?" he asked.

"That, I have not heard." Erskine frowned. "Are you thinking of pursuing her?"

"I might have done, if not for Charles. I owe him a certain respect in light of our time together at Eton."

"You owe *him* respect, but not his widow."

"She does not seem particularly stricken."

"You know nothing about her except what little I have told you."

"Have *you* an interest, Erskine?"

"I need not be a member of your set to decline the pleasure of marriage," Erskine said.

"And you would consider nothing less."

"I am hopelessly old-fashioned, as you have so often reminded me."

Sinjin snorted. "Someday your virtue will take a tumble, my friend."

"And one of these days, old chap, you may find a woman who is your equal."

"If such a creature existed, I would marry her on the spot."

"May I take you at your word, Sin? Shall we make a friendly wager of it?" Leo suggested.

"You aren't a gambling man."

"The study of human nature is one of my favorite occupations."

"I don't know that I wish to be an object of study."

Leo produced his wallet and counted out twenty pounds. "Surely you can afford this much. But if you are afraid…"

"Afraid of a woman?" Sinjin thrust out his hand. "Done."

"Then I shall leave you to it," Erskine said, smiling with an artless warmth that made Sinjin remember why they were friends. The tall man stalked away like an amiable giraffe and was lost in the crowd.

Throwing off a peculiar chill of unease, Sinjin returned his attention to the fire maiden. She was gone. He moved closer to the line of people observing the paintings and followed the flow.

There. She had stopped again and was examining a Frith with her head slightly cocked and her profile clearly visible.

No horse's face, and no spots. Sinjin didn't need

to see the rest of her features to know she was lovely. He realized that her profile was familiar; he must have met her before he went to India, but he couldn't remember the place or time. How could he not have noticed her then?

He began to move in her direction, walking parallel to the queue of observers. The second ginger-haired girl was expounding on some aspect of the painting, her hands animated. The plump blonde nodded. The fire maiden suddenly turned around to face in Sinjin's direction, exactly as if she had felt his stare.

Summer lightning broke through the ceiling and pierced the center of Sinjin's chest. He ducked behind a pair of amply bustled women and waited until she had turned back to her friends.

Nola.

That had been the name she'd called herself four years ago at Donbridge, the Donnington estate in Cambridgeshire. He had never learned her surname, or if she had been acquainted with polite society. He had never ascertained how she had been able to pose as an ordinary chambermaid, barely out of childhood, only to transform into the mysterious beauty she had become just before she had fled Donbridge…this same beauty who stood before him now.

But she had introduced him to a world most men didn't know existed: Tir-na-Nog, a mystical plane ruled by the Fane, a race of magical beings who were prone to interfering in mortal affairs.

Just as *she* had interfered.

Sinjin locked his hands behind his back, calming

himself with a few long breaths. Why was she here? How had she managed to snag the son of a marquess?

He laughed under his breath. She could do anything she chose, couldn't she? If she could change her very face, paralyze a man with a flick of her fingers and deceive those she claimed she wanted to "help," she could certainly trick a dying man into marrying her. Her professions of "fading powers" had not rung true; she had certainly lied to Sinjin about her weakness, even as she revealed her true nature.

A witch. Not a crooked-nosed, hump-backed crone, but *this*. This female any man might desire. A creature neither Fane nor completely human. A woman whose motives were not to be trusted for a moment.

If he had been possessed of less discipline, Sinjin might have confronted her then and there. But he would have been walking into a situation he knew nothing about. She might very well have heard he was in Town; she obviously didn't fear the prospect of meeting him again.

And why should she? She had used him just as she had the others. Yes, Mariah and Ash had found their happiness, but Giles was dead. And Pamela...

"Have you seen that girl?"

Wiping the scowl from his face, Sinjin turned. Felix Melbyrne, his latest protégé, was grinning like the fool cub he was, his gaze fixed on the very point where Nuala had been standing. Sinjin's hackles began to rise.

"Which girl?" he asked.

"Which girl? Are you as blind as Erskine?"

Sinjin began to wonder how many of his friends were going to turn up to disturb his thoughts. "Enlighten me," he said.

"That girl, right there, beside the ginger-haired one."

His aching lungs reminded Sinjin to breathe again. "The dark one?"

"Who else?" Melbyrne's blue eyes glittered. "I've already asked around. She's a widow, Donnington, and well out of mourning."

"She looks it."

The boy frowned as if he'd noticed the girl's drab gray dress for the first time. "Poor child. It isn't right for such a lovely girl to suffer so."

Sinjin passed over Melbyrne's amusing reference to the young woman as a child, when the boy was scarcely out of leading strings himself. "What is her name?" he asked.

"Oh. I suppose you wouldn't know…she's been in seclusion for the past year, and before that she—"

"Her name?"

"Lady Orwell."

"As in the Viscounts Orwell?"

"Precisely. Hardly anyone knew anything about the late viscount's bride, since he had been living in Paris for a number of years and seldom crossed the Channel."

"I never met the man."

"Most knew him only by reputation. How that old curmudgeon could catch a beauty like this one…"

"Orwell was deuced rich, wasn't he? Who are her parents?"

But Melbyrne wasn't listening. "Isn't she glorious? All that black hair. A man could drown in it."

It was ginger hair, not black, that Sinjin was envisioning.

"I should say," Sinjin said, "that she would not be the easiest lady to conquer."

"Why not? She isn't in seclusion now. She—"

"She is with that flock of widows who have vowed never to marry again."

Felix blinked. "That girl? Preposterous. And who said anything about marriage?"

Sinjin smiled cynically. The boy was still green enough to think of binding himself to a female before he reached the age of forty. One misstep, and he might fall. And *that* Sinjin was determined to prevent.

"Perhaps you ought to set your sights a little lower," Sinjin suggested. "The younger they are, the less likely that they will be able to conceal any…indiscretion. There are any number of experienced women who would be happy to accept your attentions."

"But where is the challenge in that? You always say a good challenge makes it all the more satisfying when one is victorious."

So he had. But Melbyrne might easily bite off more than he could chew…especially since it was clear from Lady Orwell's attitude that she regarded Nuala as a friend. The girl was near the age Mariah had been four years ago, and, to judge by her eager reception of Nuala's speech, just as trusting.

Don't get tangled up with her, boy. No pretty young widow is worth the trouble.

But how could he tender such an opinion without explaining what Nuala was? The real events at Donbridge remained a secret, and would never come to light.

Best if he simply distracted the boy, pointing him toward a less perilous partner who would teach him what he needed to learn.

"Come, Melbyrne," he said, gripping the young man's arm. "Don't make any sudden judgments. There are many other pretty pictures to see."

Felix sighed. "If you insist, Donnington."

Sinjin didn't look behind him as he led his protégé away from immediate danger. He suggested several suitable partners, at least one of whom returned Melbyrne's polite smile with a coquettish one of her own.

"Mrs. Tissier is an excellent prospect," Sinjin said. "She is still young, a courtesan of the first water."

"A courtesan? What is she doing here?"

"The prince has been known to favor ladies whom Society would ordinarily ignore. Mrs. Tissier is one such lady. As such, she enjoys a certain caché."

"Have you had her, Donnington? Is that why you consider her such a prize?" Felix snorted. "Of course you have. You've had all of them at one time or another."

The implied insult missed its mark. "You aren't likely to find a married woman in our set who hasn't taken at least one lover," Sinjin said. "If a matron has borne the necessary offspring, she can always pass an additional child off as her husband's. His own infidelity makes it unlikely that he would raise an objection even if he suspected the truth."

"I know all that, Sinjin, but—"

"Of course your prospect need not be married at all. Mature widows are generally intelligent enough to recognize the danger of having their *amours* confirmed by an unexpected birth."

"I know how to take precautions," Felix said with a flash of uncharacteristic irritation.

"Precautions or no, there is always a risk. *You* must convince the lady that you have such matters under control, and then keep your word."

"Which you always manage to do."

"I have produced no children, to my knowledge," Sinjin said mildly. "I avoid naive young widows just as I do girls who have yet to take their marriage vows. I urge you to follow my example."

"I'm not so certain I belong in your dashed club."

Sinjin yawned. "That is entirely up to you. But if you make a mistake and find yourself forced to marry the chit, don't come running to me."

Frowning, Melbyrne gave Mrs. Tissier a second look. "If you wouldn't mind, Donnington, I'd like to do my hunting in peace."

"As you wish." Certain that he'd made his point, Sinjin walked out of the Academy and breathed in London's not-so-fresh air. At least here, away from the crowd, he was able to think.

He'd told Melbyrne that a challenge was always most satisfying, and he'd faced more than a few himself. But there was one woman in the world he wouldn't pursue for all the tea in China. Except to make her explain…confess…

He didn't know what he wanted of her. He only knew that he couldn't let her go until he finally understood who and what she was. Until *she* knew what it was like to be the one truly without power.

DEBORAH CLUTCHED at Nuala's hand.

"Did you see him?"

Nuala looked away from the Frith. The prickle of awareness she'd felt earlier returned with a vengeance.

"See whom?" she asked a little too sharply.

"That young man who was staring at us."

Nuala turned fully in the direction Lady Orwell was looking, her heart beating much too fast. "I don't see any young man," she said. "Can you point him out?"

Deborah stood up on her toes. "He isn't there now." She met Nuala's gaze, her own filled with surprising disappointment. "He was…quite handsome, with fair hair and blue eyes."

The sharp ache in Nuala's chest eased. Not *him*. She had heard that he was recently returned to London from India. She knew their meeting was inevitable, but she was not ready to face the Earl of Donnington.

She forced her thoughts back to Deborah's young man. Lady Orwell's description might indicate any number of gentlemen in Society, and both she and Nuala were as yet unfamiliar with many of them. But Deborah's tone was most interesting, most interesting indeed. It was almost as if she were amazed by the fact that she might be the object of a handsome young man's attention.

"He must have noticed *you*," Nuala said, relieved that her own feelings of being watched had proven unfounded. "Who would not?"

"Oh, no. It must have been you he was looking at."

"You are by far the greater beauty, and I am past my prime."

"But surely he noticed that I am in mourning."

"Half-mourning. And even that will not prevent a man's admiration."

Deborah flushed. "Perhaps I ought not come out so often."

"It is good for you, Deborah. Grief does not make the world go away, as much as you might wish it."

"I wish that I might crawl into a black pit and never come out again."

"No, you don't." Nuala took Deborah's arm and linked it through hers. "You are not alone now. You will always be with one of us, wherever you go."

"I feel safest with you."

After much soul-searching, Nuala had taken on the role of a kind of mentor to Deborah. There was, of course, some risk; though Nuala's magic was gone, she might conceivably live for many more years before she was granted the release of death.

It is only for Deborah's sake, she reminded herself. *Soon enough she'll have no further need of me.*

"I suggest that we continue to enjoy the paintings," she said. "The others are well ahead of us."

"Oh, yes. We should catch them up."

Deborah hurried toward the beacon of Tameri's gold collar. The Widows were laughing about something or other, drawing a few mildly disapproving stares. After all, truly well-bred women merely tittered, if they laughed at all. But in spite of her severe suit and upright bearing, Frances cared nothing for the opinion of Society. Nor did Clara, who had joined in her hilarity. Maggie was simply oblivious to the judgment of others. Their enjoyment of their joke even affected Deborah, who all but grinned in delight.

Yes, there was hope for the girl yet.

Clara smiled at Nuala. "Well," she said, "we wondered where you had gone."

"Deborah and I were merely watching the crowd."

"Fascinating, isn't it? The study of human nature is a most vital subject that has long been neglected."

"Perhaps you ought to take up the study yourself, Clara."

"Not I. I'm content with my microscope and telescope."

Tools she would not have been permitted to use when Nuala had been a girl. In those days, mortal men had done far worse than scoff at women who held such lofty interests. Any female who stepped out of her proper place of humility and obedience, let alone show skill in pursuits that might conceivably cross the boundaries set by the Almighty…

"Are you ill, Nuala?"

"I'm quite well," Nuala said. "Have you seen the new florals in the next room?"

Lillian's round blue eyes lit up. "No, I have not. Shall we visit them?"

Allowing herself to be guided into the adjoining room, Nuala quieted her memories. Memories she had once been able to set aside so easily. Why were they returning now with such potency, when she least desired them? Was this to be yet another punishment?

She glanced at Lillian's laughing eyes and reminded herself again that she had not been completely abandoned. There might yet be answers. And perhaps, when she finally met Sinjin again, she could lay at least one of her ghosts to rest once and for all.

CHAPTER TWO

THE HYDE PARK PARADE was in full swing. Nuala, Deborah and Victoria, the Marchioness of Oxenham, sat comfortably in Lady Oxenham's sparkling landau, which—in spite of its team of handsome grays—moved no faster than a walking pace and frequently came to a complete stop amid the crush of carriages and horsemen and women.

On any given afternoon—or mornings on Sundays—Rotten Row was the place to see and be seen. Countesses, baronesses and ladies of every description mingled with gentlemen and peers in their riding clothes and top hats, smiling as the constant swirl of dust settled on their parasols and compelled them to cough most discreetly behind their lace handkerchiefs.

Nuala didn't mind the dust. She watched the comings and goings of the lords and their ladies, superb horsewomen in snug riding habits, young bucks driving their own phaetons, the more staid matrons showing off their equipages and dipping their heads to those who were privileged to know them. Each of them had a story. Sometimes Nuala imagined that she felt the spark that had always guided her in choosing who most needed her help: here a lonely young man whose shyness made it impossible for him to approach the woman he loved from afar; there a young spinster whose plain face concealed a keen intellect and loving heart.

She stopped such speculation before it could proceed any further and returned the greeting of a horsewoman to whom she had recently been introduced. The marchioness's progress had been interrupted many times by such admirers; she had many friends. Her musicales and parties were much admired by both members of the fast Marlborough House Set and the more conservative followers of the Queen. She had a pleasant word for everyone, and frequently pointed out the leading lights of Society to her two guests.

"Look! Isn't Lady Rush's hat extraordinary?" Lady Oxenham asked, peering through her lorgnette. "I shouldn't have the nerve to wear it. But of course she never gave two straws for the dictates of fashion."

"I rather like it," Deborah said in a tentative voice.

The marchioness chuckled. "It is just the sort of thing any young woman of imagination might fancy, I suppose," she said. She smiled at Nuala. "And are you enjoying our outing, my dear?"

Nuala laid her hand over Lady Oxenham's. "If it hadn't been for you and your patronage, I wouldn't be here at all."

"Oh, pish. You are the wife of my son. You made

his last days the happiest of his life. It is we who owe you our deepest thanks."

An unaccustomed flush warmed Nuala's cheeks. "If only I had been able to do more for him...."

"Never reproach yourself, dear Nuala. Charles loved you."

"A poor vicar's daughter."

"A woman of great compassion and sensibility is not to be dismissed merely because of rank. And now you are Lady Charles Parkhill, and shall be until you marr—" She paused and waved her fan vigorously before her impressive bosom. "I did not mean to offend, my dear."

Nuala squeezed her hand. "Of course not, Lady Oxenham."

The older woman beamed at Deborah. "And you, Lady Orwell? What think you of our grand city?"

"Sometimes I think it can't quite be real," Deborah said, giving her own fan a quick shake.

"Indeed, at times I wonder the same thing myself." The marchioness settled in her seat with a sigh of satisfaction. "Of course, Paris is nothing to sneeze at. You must have seen such sights there. Ah, Lady Bensham is riding alone. No doubt she's quarreled with her husband. Those two quite unfashionably adore each other, but one must expect..." She pursed her lips. "Ah! Here are a pair of gentlemen you might like to meet. You share much in common."

Nuala followed her look toward the approaching riders. "What would that be, Lady Oxenham?" she asked, her breath catching in her throat.

The marchioness glanced at her slyly. "They have sworn not to marry, just like you."

Deborah sat up and shaded her eyes with one gloved hand. "Truly?"

"Indeed. They call themselves the 'Forties,' because they have vowed to remain bachelors until they have passed the age of forty."

"Is that so very unusual?" Deborah asked. "My own dear husband…"

"Not terribly unusual in younger sons, at least," Lady Oxenham said. "But eldest sons must look to producing heirs of their own. And these young gentlemen have…something of a reputation."

"What sort of reputation?"

The marchioness had no opportunity to answer. The gentlemen were drawing their horses alongside the landau, the elder on a black stallion he held under remarkable control, the younger on a bay mare. Deborah's eyes grew very wide. The younger man tipped his hat and returned her regard, his fair hair falling across his brow.

But Nuala gave him no more than a passing glance. She stared up at the taller man, who had also raised his hat to Lady Oxenham. He seemed to be completely unaware of Nuala's presence.

"My dear Lord Donnington," the marchioness said, extending her hand. "How pleasant to see you again."

The earl took her hand and kissed the air over her fingers. "Lady Oxenham," he said. "I trust you are enjoying the afternoon."

She allowed him to hold her hand a little longer

than was strictly necessary. "Indeed I am," she said, and turned to her guests. "Lady Orwell, Lady Charles, may I present the Earl of Donnington."

Deborah continued to gaze at the younger man as if she hadn't heard the introduction. Lord Donnington bowed stiffly over his saddle.

"Lady Orwell," he said, "Lady Charles."

Nuala met Sinjin's hard brown eyes. She had never forgotten for an instant how handsome he was, how lean and graceful, how utterly masculine in his coat, breeches and riding boots. Nor had she forgotten the scorn in his eyes four years ago, when she'd admitted to being a witch. A witch who had posed as a maid at his brother's estate, Donbridge, and who had made herself an essential part of the events that had resulted in Giles's death, and the disruption of everything Sinjin had known and believed.

She clasped her hands to keep them from trembling. "Good afternoon, Lord Donnington."

He ignored her greeting and gestured to his friend. "May I be permitted to present Mr. Felix Melbyrne."

Lady Oxenham inclined her head. "Mr. Melbyrne. I understand that you are but recently come to London."

"It is true, Lady Oxenham," Melbyrne said, nervously shifting his reins in his hands. "I am most honored to make your acquaintance." His gaze wandered back to Deborah. "And yours, Lady Orwell, Lady Charles."

Deborah blushed, bobbed her head and smiled. "I...I am happy to meet you, Mr. Melbyrne."

"And I," Nuala said. She searched the young man's eyes. "Lady Orwell and I are also recent arrivals."

"I…I see." Mr. Melbyrne continued to fidget in a very telling manner. "There is so much to see and do."

"Yes," Deborah said, "I agree."

"And you, Lady Charles?"

Sinjin's voice was as harsh as his gaze, drawing a start of surprise from the marchioness. Nuala didn't smile. She was compelled to concentrate entirely on making certain that her distress was not visible to him or her companions. That Deborah should not guess that she and the Earl of Donnington had met before under the most painful of circumstances.

"It is very different from the countryside Lord Charles preferred," she said.

A flash of what might have been chagrin passed over Sinjin's face. "Permit me to offer my sincere condolences on the loss of your husband."

"You are very kind, Lord Donnington."

"The earl was also kind enough to offer me his condolences," the marchioness said, more brusquely than was her habit. "Having been out of the country so long, he did not learn of Charles's passing until very recently. But then again, my brother-in-law was very reclusive. Many forgot his existence entirely."

"Not I, I assure you," Sinjin said. "We were together at Eton. I was deeply grieved."

The marchioness inclined her head. "You have been much occupied since your return from India."

"Oh," said Lady Orwell quickly, as if she were

eager to change the subject. "You have been in India? How fascinating."

Mr. Melbyrne said something about having visited some other exotic clime, but Nuala wasn't listening. She watched Sinjin without quite looking at him, taking him in with her senses as well as her eyes.

He had changed. Oh, not so much in appearance, though there were a few more lines in his face and a deep tan gained from several years in India. He had lost none of his handsomeness. No, the greatest change was within him. He had always been somewhat cynical, a man who had a reputation as a lover and a gambler. But he had shown compassion toward his former sister-in-law, Mariah, when she had been in trouble. He was capable of great feeling and unflinching loyalty.

That Sinjin seemed to have vanished. His face revealed no expression, even as he conversed easily with Lady Oxenham. His dark eyes were shadowed, as if he seldom slept, and his mouth was tight.

There was no mistaking his coldness toward her. They had parted so abruptly at Donbridge, and that was her doing. Her cowardice. Had his brother's death and Lady Westlake's subsequent madness turned him into the man she saw before her?

You knew it might be like this. Yet his unspoken hostility was much worse than she might have imagined. A part of her had hoped for something different, a neutral meeting, some way she might explain without having to face his mistrust and obvious resentment.

He finds you in London, a lady at least in name, a stranger he never had any real reason to trust. I told him so little. Is it any wonder...

She had thought of laying ghosts to rest. But now, suddenly, she was afraid.

"We must go," Sinjin said, touching the brim of his hat. "I shall look forward to seeing you again, Lady Oxenham, Lady Orwell." He paused. "Lady Charles."

He wheeled his horse about and started away, dodging a town coach and four. Melbyrne lingered, his horse shuffling nervously beneath him, opened his mouth and bowed from the saddle before riding after his friend.

"How very interesting," Lady Oxenham murmured. But she didn't elaborate, and soon the landau was moving again. Nuala found it impossible to keep up her part in the conversation.

He is suffering, she thought. *Because of me.*

And he had judged her, just as the witch-finders had judged her family.

"It was he," Deborah whispered, leaning close to Nuala's ear.

"I beg your pardon?"

"The young man I saw at the Academy!"

Nuala took herself in hand. "Mr. Melbyrne?"

"Yes. He *is* handsome, is he not?"

"Yes. Very handsome."

"And that man with him...Lord Donnington—" She shuddered. "He was quite intimidating. Very courteous in his manner, but so distant."

"Perhaps he had important things on his mind."

"Oh, most important," Lady Oxenham put in. "What suit he ought to wear tomorrow, where he might spend a stimulating evening playing at cards, what new bit of horseflesh he might choose to buy. All very pressing matters."

"But I thought you liked him!" Deborah protested.

"I do. He has certainly kept up the family's interests in the East and has done well by his tenants at Donbridge. But he has only been in England three months, and already he is influencing the most fashionable young men…not necessarily for the better."

"The Forties?" Deborah asked.

"Quite so. Sinjin seems to take a rather dim view of women, as well as marriage—it is obvious that he was once hurt badly by one of our sex."

Nuala knew just how badly Sinjin had been hurt, but she said nothing.

"Unfortunately," Lady Oxenham continued, "Mr. Melbyrne is obviously in Lord Donnington's thrall. A pity. Such a promising fellow. Possessed of rather a good income, I believe."

Deborah fell silent, biting her lip. Nuala sighed. Not even a blind man could have failed to notice how intently the two young people had studied each other.

Sinjin must have noticed, too. He had obviously not approved….

Stop, stop, stop!

Desperately Nuala tried to distract her mind. But all she could think of was Sinjin's face. The way it had looked the last time they'd been together at Donbridge four years ago.

"I don't need the help of a witch," he had said. Such anger. Such contempt…

"My dear Nuala," Lady Oxenham said.

"Forgive me," Nuala said, snapping back to the present. "I wasn't listening."

"The marchioness is to give a ball," Deborah said. "We are both invited."

"A ball?" Nuala repeated stupidly.

"A fancy-dress ball," the marchioness said. "It is rather short notice…only four weeks from Tuesday…but my youngest son is returning from his service in Africa, and I wished to celebrate properly. He is very fond of fancy-dress balls." She gave Nuala a direct stare. "You shall attend, of course."

"I ought not—" Deborah began.

"You shall wear something bright," Lady Oxenham said. "There is no time for one of the Paris modistes, of course, but I have a dressmaker who is just as skilled and almost as inventive. I shall send her to you."

"Thank you, Lady Oxenham," Deborah murmured, overcome by the old woman's determination.

"Of course, your friends shall all be invited, as well," Lady Oxenham said. "I am quite certain that the dowager duchess will have chosen her costume even before she receives the invitation."

Deborah laughed behind her fan. Nuala was in no mood for humor.

Will he *be there?* It would be rude to ask Lady Oxenham such a question, but the very thought made her hands begin to tremble. After all these years, a man had such power over her emotions.

But she would not let emotion rule her. Before Donnington, she had been successful in her work by keeping her head and maintaining some distance from those she helped. Celebration came only after the work was completed to her satisfaction.

Every time but the last.

As the afternoon advanced, the strollers, horsemen and coaches began to disperse for home. Nuala caught no further glimpse of Sinjin or his protégé. Nuala's own modest carriage was waiting at the marchionness's residence, as was Deborah's. Nuala thought of the handsome town house her husband had bequeathed to her, of its emptiness and the loneliness that stalked every room.

"Have you given the matter we discussed any further thought?" she asked Deborah as they stood on the pavement. "There is no need to maintain two separate households when we might so easily share one without the least inconvenience."

"I have thought about it," Deborah said. "I think I should like it very much."

Nuala restrained herself from embracing the girl. "Which house shall we take?"

"Why not yours? Mine is much too large, and I can easily find a tenant for the Season."

"If you are quite comfortable with the choice…"

"I am. I am certain that we shall enjoy it immeasurably," Deborah assured her.

They exchanged light kisses on the cheek in the Parisian style. Deborah took her footman's hand and climbed into her carriage. Nuala watched the vehicle clatter down the road and turned for her own carriage.

"You are good for the child," Lady Oxenham commented, coming up behind her.

"I hope I am," Nuala said. "I hope that we can learn from each other."

"What has she to teach you, my dear?"

Humility. Innocence. All the things Nuala had lost without realizing it.

"Thank you, Lady Oxenham, for the pleasant ride," she said, avoiding the question.

"You are welcome at any time," the marchioness said.

Nuala smiled and stepped up into her carriage. Her coachman snapped the reins, and the victoria jerked into motion. Instead of going directly home, she instructed Bremner to drive toward Kensington and Melbury Road for her appointment with Maggie. When she arrived, Maggie herself came to the door. She was dressed in an oversize man's shirt and trousers rolled up to her ankles, both garments liberally splattered with paint.

"Nuala!" Lady Riordan said, waving Nuala into the vestibule. "I didn't expect you until later this evening."

"I'm sorry, Maggie. I hope this is not too great an inconvenience."

"Not at all. Come in."

Nuala gave her cape to the rather odd-looking footman, whose melancholy face somewhat resembled that of a mule. His livery was less than spotless, but Maggie seemed not to notice. She never noticed such trifling things, and Nuala suspected that her servants took terrible advantage of her negligence.

I was a servant many times. I have no right to judge.

Without observing any of the usual niceties and small talk, Maggie led Nuala upstairs to the first floor, where she kept her studio. What might have been a large drawing room had been given over to everything a painter might require: easels, canvases, brushes, paint and many varied and curious objects Lady Riordan had found of interest.

Maggie rushed to a large, blank canvas and stood before it, staring with a sort of ferocity as if a picture might magically appear by the sheer force of her will. "It will be marvelous," she said, brushing an untidy curl away from her forehead. "Please sit over there, Nuala."

Lifting her skirts to avoid the suspiciously wet-looking smears of paint on the once-handsome floor, Nuala took the chair Maggie had indicated. The young woman hurried over, posed Nuala as if she were a doll, stood back, then readjusted Nuala's position.

"There," she said, and without another word began to paint, her tongue pushing out from between her teeth. For the next two hours Nuala sat quietly. Her unoccupied mind continued to drift toward thoughts of Sinjin: the handsome but weary lines of his face, his superb seat on his black stallion, the way he had looked at her as if she were an enemy.

I must explain. But how?

"That's enough for today," Maggie said, standing back from her canvas with an air of satisfaction. She glanced past the painting and frowned. "You're very tired, Nuala. Shall I get you some tea? Biscuits?"

"I've merely been lost in thought," Nuala said, rising. "I believe I shall spend a quiet evening at home."

"Hmm," Maggie murmured, her attention focused one again on her painting.

Nuala smiled, retrieved her things and walked toward the door, making no attempt to see Maggie's work.

"Nuala?"

She half turned. Maggie was wiping her hands on a rag, her air still distracted.

"Tameri told me to remind you about the garden party next week," she said. "I almost forgot, myself."

The garden party. Nuala *had* almost forgotten about it, though Tameri had issued the invitations over a month ago.

"Of course," she said. "Thank you, Maggie. I'll be there."

The young woman gave a most unfeminine grunt and began to clean her brushes. Nuala was escorted to the door by the doleful footman. She waited for her carriage to be brought round from the mews and closed her eyes.

It must be soon. The next time she met him, she would make everything clear. Then, if he chose to continue to hate her, she would understand.

LADY CHARLES.

Sinjin bit down with such force that his cigar nearly snapped in two. *Lady Charles Parkhill.*

"Good God, Donnington," Lord Peter Breakspear said, blowing out a long stream of smoke from his own cigar. "One would think you had just learned that Poole had gone out of business."

Sinjin turned to look at his friend, letting his mouth ease into a cynical smile. "I've no fear of that," he said. "My patronage alone would keep them solvent for another century."

"Ah," Lord Peter said, nodding sagely. "Then it must be a woman."

A sharp and entirely unjustified retort came to Sinjin's lips. He bit it back. "I never have trouble with women."

"Did I say anything about trouble?"

Breakspear arched his brows. Sinjin ignored him, walked to the sideboard and stubbed out his cigar, glancing around the drawing room. Six of the Forties were present at this meeting in Sinjin's town house: Breakspear, a gentleman in his midthirties who held a strong attraction for the ladies; Melbyrne; Harrison, Lord Waybury, a staunch Tory of traditional convictions; Mr. Achilles Nash, the most cynical of the group, ever ready with a quip; Sir Harry Ferrer, portly and often ill-tempered; and Ivar, Lord Reddick, as much a devoted Liberal as Waybury was a Conservative.

Nash was regarding his glass of brandy with his usual bored expression; Ferrer was already drunk. Reddick was intently conversing with Waybury on the subject of politics and Melbyrne was in a corner, his face suspiciously blank. Watching everything with a curious eye, Erskine, who had refused full

membership in the club but was welcome nonethe-
less, remained in the background as he always did.

"I say," Waybury said, stabbing the air with his
cigar, "you're wrong, Reddick. Salibury is doing an
excellent job with his Irish programme."

"It isn't the same as Home Rule," Reddick insisted. "When Gladstone returns—"

"He'll never be reappointed," Waybury said
with some heat.

"What is your opinion, Donnington?" Reddick
asked, strolling across the room to join him and
Breakspear.

"I doubt he's ever bothered to consider the issue,"
Waybury said. "He may occasionally join us in the
Lords, but his interest in politics is minimal at best."

Sinjin turned his smile on Waybury. "I happen to
support Gladstone's policies," he said. "I believe he
will eventually be vindicated."

Waybury waved his hand in disgust. "The Liberal
Party will do this country in."

"I doubt it matters who holds the reins," Nash said
from across the room. "What do you think, Erskine?"

Leo folded his arms across his chest. "I prefer to
remain neutral."

"As neutral as you are on the subject of marriage?"
Breakspear asked.

"I am not eager to tie myself down, as Donnington will attest," Erskine said mildly. "I simply have
no objection to a man marrying before he reaches
middle age."

"Perhaps Erskine is less stuffy than he appears,"

Nash said with a cynical smile. "After all, it is not as if marriage need hamper one's appreciation of other women."

"*Some* of us prefer fidelity after marriage," Waybury said.

Breakspear laughed. "And before. You've been pretty faithful to your current doxy. Do you think you'll avoid temptation once you've found yourself a worthy wife?"

"I should think it depends on the wife," Erskine said before Waybury could reply. He poured himself a glass of water from a crystal decanter on the sideboard. "With the right woman—"

"There is no female in the world who can tie me to her apron strings," Sinjin snapped, remembering Erskine's mocking wager at the Academy.

The other men exchanged glances. "What is it, Sin?" Nash asked.

"I asked him the same thing," Breakspear said. "Woman trouble."

Ears pricked and nostrils flared as the pack closed in. Reddick chuckled. "Has Adele demanded a few too many fripperies this month?" he asked Sinjin. "Has she found a more generous patron? If not, I shall be more than happy to take her off your hands."

"Adele," Sinjin said between his teeth, "is free to make her own decisions. I suggest we change the subject."

"But why are we here if not to talk of women?" Nash asked. "If it's not Adele, who is it?"

Leo set down his empty glass. "Have any of you been introduced to Lady Charles Parkhill?"

"Erskine…" Sinjin growled.

"We saw her at the Academy," Leo continued. "Sin quite admired her."

"Ah, yes," Breakspear said. "She has only just come to London this Season. Never been before, I hear. Parkhill hid her away on his estate." He shook his head. "At least the unfortunate man had a fair companion to comfort him in his final hours."

"Is it true that she is a country curate's daughter?" Waybury asked. "Poor Lord Charles wouldn't have had many opportunities to meet potential wives, especially the sort who'd be content to give him constant nursing. Do you suppose he hoped to obtain an heir before he—"

"Enough about Parkhill," Sinjin said. "Let the man rest in peace."

"I wonder if his little widow is resting peacefully," Nash said. "If she had so little enjoyment of her marriage, she might be—"

"*Enough.*" Sinjin felt the irrational desire to plant his fist in Nash's face. He must be going insane.

And all because of *her.*

"I see that we have struck a nerve," Breakspear said in a loud whisper.

Sinjin poured himself a brandy, splashing the liquor over the sides of the glass. "Melbyrne!"

The boy looked up, his eyes dazed. "I beg your pardon?"

"Are you going to sit in that corner all evening?"

Felix got up hastily, smoothed his coat and joined the others. "I'm sorry. Were we discussing Salisbury? I think—"

Breakspear laughed. "The subject is the ladies," he said, "and Sin's nasty mood." He peered into Melbyrne's eyes. "I say, what's going on in that head of yours, boy? Have you finally been stricken by some pretty face?"

"I was never convinced that the initiation took with our junior member," Nash said. "Perhaps we ought to repeat the exercise."

Felix drew himself up. "I may be young," he said, "but I am not a fool."

"Perhaps you've also admired Lady Charles?"

The boy flushed. Sinjin downed the brandy in one swallow. He knew exactly what Felix had been thinking while he'd been sitting alone, looking like nothing less than an habitué of an opium den.

Lady Orwell. When they'd met Lady Oxenham and her friends in Hyde Park, Melbyrne had sat on his horse with his mouth agape, as tongue-tied as a girl at her first dance. He hadn't listened to the advice Sinjin had given him at the Academy; to the contrary, his introduction to the lady in question had obviously increased his admiration.

"It is not Lady Charles," Melbyrne said with a false air of indifference.

"Out with it, boy," Nash said. "We have sworn to be brothers and keep no secrets amongst us."

Melbyrne looked at Sinjin and dropped his gaze. "Mrs. Tissier!" he blurted.

Everyone laughed. "Was that your idea, Sinjin?" Nash asked.

"Why should it be?" Sinjin said, his equanimity restored. "As Melbyrne said, he's no fool."

"She's already agreed, then?" said Breakspear. "It's all arranged?"

"She'll take you on a long, sweet ride…won't she, Sin?" Nash said.

"One might ask you the same question," retorted Waybury.

They launched into a testy but civilized quarrel. Sinjin took Felix aside.

"*Has* it been arranged?" he asked.

"I haven't asked her yet," Melbyrne said, meeting Sinjin's gaze stubbornly. "But from all you've said, it should not be difficult to win her."

"There are ways to go about this sort of thing. I'll speak to you about it tomorrow, before the parade."

"Yes. Of course."

Sinjin slapped the young man's shoulder. "You've made an excellent choice, Melbyrne."

Felix attempted a grin, turned to the sideboard and reached for a bottle. Sinjin left him to it. One by one the men departed, called to some dinner or other amusement. Melbyrne was last to leave, all studied nonchalance as if he were set on proving to the world that he was far older than his twenty-two years.

Sinjin lit another cigar and sat in his favorite chair, alone with the empty glasses and overflowing ashtrays. In a moment the parlor maid would cautiously knock on the door and enter to clean up the mess. Sinjin was in no hurry to summon her.

Though there had obviously been some reluctance on Melbyrne's part, he had finally chosen a wise course of action. Tissier would take him in hand, and when they parted, as they eventually must, he would no longer play the mooncalf with naive young widows who would only bring him grief.

Sinjin's unwilling thoughts drifted to Lady Charles, and instantly his cock hardened. There was no reason for such a reaction, none whatsoever; he had certainly felt no attraction to her when she'd posed as a maid at Donbridge, and their dealings after she had shed her disguise had not been cordial.

But when they'd met again in Hyde Park, something had come over him. Something that flew in the face of every feeling he had nurtured since he'd seen her at the Academy.

He closed his eyes and imagined Adele waiting for him, sprawled across her bed in the little house on Circus Road, her breasts creamy mounds, her nipples stiffening at his touch. He might forget his evening obligations and spend the night with her. Her skill would silence even the memory of Nuala and this new identity she had claimed for herself.

But not for long. Lady Charles would still be there when he rolled out of bed.

Sinjin stubbed out his cigar and got to his feet. The time for putting off their meeting was over. He went into his study, opened the drawer of his desk and glanced through the invitations he had received in the past several weeks.

The dowager Duchess of Vardon's garden party. He had intended to tender last-minute regrets, but no longer. Lady Charles was one of the eccentric dowager's cronies. She would certainly be there. And in such a crush, no one would notice if he drew the lady aside for a friendly conversation.

CHAPTER THREE

"Are you certain you wish to do this, Deborah?" Nuala asked.

The girl nodded, a brief jerk of her head that seemed more an act of defiance than agreement. "I wish to help," she said, "not spend all my time attending frivolous entertainments."

Frances looked at her curiously. "Did you not enjoy such pleasures in Paris?"

"We preferred museums and the opera to balls and grand dinner parties," Deborah said.

Nuala wondered if the girl were speaking the entire truth. She had probably never thought to consider her own preferences at all; she had been a great deal younger than her expatriate husband, carried almost directly out of a sheltered childhood into the world of marriage. She'd had little opportunity for companionship from young people her own age, in her own country.

If she were not yet prepared to admit that she might enjoy such companionship, she was beginning to change in spite of herself. Her undoubted interest in young Mr. Melbyrne was proof enough of that.

He is not overly bold, Nuala thought, *and seems quite amiable of nature. Deborah would do very well to call him her friend. Or perhaps, in time...*

"I'm ready," Deborah said, interrupting Nuala's thoughts. "Shall we go?"

Realizing how close she'd come to slipping back into her matchmaking ways again, Nuala focused all her attention on Deborah. "You do understand that we will be entering the rookeries where the murders took place?" she asked.

"I am not afraid of the madman who killed those poor girls."

In truth, she had little reason to be. The man who had committed the horrible crimes had never been caught, but he had thus far attacked only prostitutes. Yet it took a great deal of courage to venture into a part of the city with which very few aristocrats were acquainted, and which even fewer would ever visit for any reason.

"Stay close to me and Frances," Nuala said. "Do exactly as we tell you."

The sun was only a little above the horizon as they climbed into Nuala's carriage and left the clean, quiet streets of Belgravia. Nuala's coachman knew the way; she and Frances had begun the work in Whitechapel two months ago, as part of the Widows' ongoing scheme to carry out charitable activities that most ladies in Society would never think of attempting.

As the coupé rattled along toward the East End, Frances picked through her surgical needles, bandages and bottles of carbolic acid while Deborah

clutched the sack of patchwork cloth dolls she had
made during the past two weeks. Nuala knew they
had not brought nearly enough food; there was never
enough, and never would be. But it would stave off
the hunger of a few desperate children for one more
week, and soon the new school would be ready. The
children could be fed more regularly there, even if
their hard lives would make learning a challenge.

The coupé brougham continued through Cheap-
side and finally drew up at Whitechapel High Street.
It would go no farther. Nuala always left Bremner at
the border of Whitechapel, where he would less
likely be disturbed by those desperate enough to risk
approaching the horses. She didn't want to see
anyone hurt, including the poor folk who would feel
the bite of Bremner's whip if they came too close.

She, Deborah and Frances left the carriage, and the
footmen, Harold and Jacques, removed the hampers
of food from the boot. They were heavy, but Nuala
didn't mind the weight, and slender Frances hefted
the baskets like a circus strongman lifting a barbell.
Jacques and Harold managed four each, though
Harold's grim expression announced his opinion of
the work for which he had been conscripted.

Deborah took the remaining hamper and followed
as they ventured onto Whitechapel High Street. The
squalor was already evident. Deborah sniffed—
struck, as any newcomer must be, by the stench of
unwashed bodies, offal, human and animal waste,
and rotten food. Featureless faces peered out from
grimy windows, and children dressed in little better

than rags ran alongside the three strangers, their small, gaunt faces as intent as tigers on the prowl.

But the worst was yet to come. Frances led them onto a narrow side street, and they entered a world that might have belonged in some tale of medieval horror. The dwellings could not properly be called houses; they leaned against each other like the inebriates who staggered in and out of the alehouses, any color they might once have possessed long since erased by rot and filth. Nearly all the windows were broken, and the bare patches of ground left where buildings had once stood were littered with dead animals, shattered glass and refuse.

The people themselves might have emerged whole from the infertile, rotten ground. Desperate, garish prostitutes waited on every corner, their faces withered under the paint. Unemployed men, young and old, looked up from under battered caps and stared at the intruders. Urchins, many parentless, crept from shadow to shadow, prepared at any moment to accost the toffs with cries and open hands.

Deborah must have felt many terrible emotions in the face of what she saw, but she gave no sign other than a slight quiver of her chin. A tiny girl in a badly torn dress crept up to her and grasped her skirts. Deborah almost stopped, reaching for her purse before she remembered the rules.

No money; that had been part of the agreement. Once coin was produced and given, the lost souls of Whitechapel would see not benefactors but fleeting salvation that must be obtained at any price. They were not evil, these people; Nuala had known hundreds, even thousands like them. They no longer had the luxury of gentleness.

She took Deborah's arm, and the three of them picked up their pace. They made a final turn into a noisome alley. A crowd of men, women and children waited at the empty doorway of an abandoned building; more followed Frances, Nuala and Deborah until the alley was nearly full.

Without a word, Frances pushed past the men blocking the doorway. They stood aside for Nuala, Deborah, Jacques and Harold to enter, as well. The room was barren and far from pristine, in spite of Frances's diligent scrubbing, but there were a few cots along the wall, left intact against all expectations, as well as several chairs and a rickety table.

Nuala set her hampers down, and Deborah dropped her bag on the nearest cot. Harold and Jacques faced the door, their arms folded across their chests.

Frances laid a clean cloth over the table and began setting out the bandages and medical supplies.

"Now," she said briskly, "we will begin with the food. There will always be men who attempt to force their way to the front, but they must be ignored despite any threats they may make. What we have is for the most needy, the women and children."

Deborah swallowed. "Have you ever been attacked?"

"Even the men have respect for courage and determination," Frances said. "And Harold is quite strong…is he not, Nuala?"

Harold quickly hid a grimace. Nuala prayed that he and Jacques would be willing to continue the work…and that meant there must be no trouble.

She rearranged the food in her hamper and took it to the door. There was a rush as the hungry and destitute fought to be first.

Nuala raised her hand. "If there are any orphaned children, let them come in."

Grumbling followed her announcement, as well as several curses. But after a moment a half dozen children appeared and crept inside like the most timid of mice, their eyes far too large for their grimy faces.

Nuala removed wrapped slices of bread, cheese and spring fruit from the hamper and gave packets to each of the children in turn. Deborah urged the children toward the cots, where they tore at the food with their teeth. Deborah laid a doll on each girl's cot.

The routine was always the same. Harold, Jacques and Nuala stood guard at the doorway as the women came forward with their children, hollow eyes brimming with hope. They received their packets according to the sizes of their families and scurried away before they could be robbed of their precious burdens. Even so, there was barely enough food for those who had come.

"Word is spreading," Frances said in a low voice. "We must soon find men willing to deliver wagons of provisions."

"We shall," Nuala said. "There is much that men will risk for money."

Frances cast her a grim sort of smile. "That is one

thing we have in plenty." She glanced at Deborah. "How much have you left?"

"Only a few slices of bread and a wedge of cheese," the girl whispered. "It isn't enough for all of them."

Frances moved toward the door. "Gentlemen, we ask that you send forward any women and children who have not yet received their ration."

Stony faces stared back at her. A man shoved his way to the fore, a thin fellow in a patched velvet coat. His surprisingly broad shoulders filled the door frame, and a permanent leer seemed etched into his cold, scarred features.

"Wot's aw this?" he growled. "Haven't enough fer aw o' us, then?"

"You know we do not," Frances answered, giving not an inch of ground. "We do what we can."

"She does wot she can!" the man mocked, turning to face the remaining crowd. "If she wos doin' wot she can, she'd gi' us the clothes off 'er back, wou'n't she?"

"That's enough," Harold said. "You've no right…"

"An' who're yer, then? One o' them's fancy boys?"

"It's all right, Harold," Nuala said. She joined Frances and looked from one hostile face to another. "We will be back again with more as soon as possible. Are there any among you who require medical treatment?"

"It's our bellies needs fillin'!" the troublemaker shouted. But he was not supported by all the onlookers. Two men and a boy squeezed through to the door and hovered there, uncertain. Nuala put her hand on the boy's shoulder.

"What hurts?" she asked simply.

The boy raised his arm, where a torn sleeve revealed an infected dog's bite. Nuala cursed her lack of power to soothe his distress, but she comforted him as best she could. His fear somewhat relieved, the boy continued on to receive Frances's ministrations.

The next was an elderly man complaining of pain in his joints. Nuala knew that there was little to be done for him, though once she might have eased his pain. Now all she could do was send him to stand and wait behind the boy.

The third was a lad in his early twenties, only a little older than Deborah…not tall, but wiry with muscle, his hair very black under his cap. As soon as he spoke, Nuala recognized him as a Welshman, an outsider among outsiders.

Tipping his cap, the young man held up his hand. Two fingers had been badly broken at some time in the recent past and had not been set.

"Can ye help, madam?" he asked in a soft-spoken voice.

Deborah came up behind Nuala and sucked in her breath. "It must hurt terribly," she said.

The Welshman looked into her eyes. "Not so bad as all that, madam."

"I'm certain that Lady Selfridge can assist you," Nuala said, gesturing to Frances. "Please join the others."

The young man did so, moving with a loose,

upright stride in spite of his pain and poverty. Deborah stared after him.

"It doesn't seem as if he belongs here," Deborah said.

"He probably came to London from Wales, seeking a way out of the mines," Nuala said quietly. "The city doesn't always welcome those who are different."

"If only there were more we could do," Deborah murmured.

"Yes. Once we have the drivers and more volunteers, we—"

"Oy! Wot's a wee gal loik yer doin' 'ere, missy?"

The troublemaker had been ignored too long, and now he'd found fresh prey. Before Nuala could tell Deborah to ignore him, the young woman turned to face the man.

"If you are only here to cause trouble," she said, "you should leave."

The man burst out laughing, his spittle flying in Deborah's face. "Quite th' bold un, ain'cher?" He bent to peer more closely into Deborah's eyes. "Yer looks roight familiar, a' that. Sure yer ain't never been spreadin' yer legs fer them wot can pay?" He rubbed greasy fingers together. "I got a pence er two ter spare…."

"Enough." The Welshman, his hazel eyes flashing, pushed his way between Deborah and the lout before Nuala could do so. "It's all jaws ye are, Bray, and we've no desire to hear more of your foul talk."

"An' wot'll yer do abou' i', wif yer crippled hand?"

"I've another," the Welshman said, raising his left fist.

It almost seemed as if Bray would back down, but instead he reached into his frayed coat and withdrew a knife. He sliced the air in front of the Welshman's face, then lunged toward the younger man's injured hand. He withdrew the blade in a blur of motion, leaving a red line across the back of the Welshman's knuckles.

Deborah gasped. Without thinking, Nuala concentrated on the knife and made a light gesture with her fingers. Snarling an oath, Bray dropped the knife and shook his hand as if it had been burned. He cast an evil, speculative glance in Deborah's direction, turned and barreled through the diminishing group of waiting men.

Nuala stared at her own hand in astonishment. Surely it hadn't really happened. Pure chance that Bray had dropped the knife just after she had chanted the spell. Mere coincidence…

Deborah rushed back to the table to fetch her reticule and returned with a handkerchief. "Oh," she said to the Welshman. "Oh! Your poor hand."

He glanced at the blood seeping from the wound. "It is nothing, madam."

"Nothing! You saved my life."

The boy's jaw locked. "He would never have hurt you."

But Deborah was in no mood for argument. She seized the Welshman's hand and pressed her handkerchief to the laceration. He tried to withdraw, but she kept a firm hold.

"Do not struggle so," she scolded. "You must let Lady Selfridge bind it, and splint your fingers."

There was a look about him that suggested he wished only to flee the scene of what he very likely regarded as his humiliation, but when Frances came forward to chivvy him toward the table, he didn't resist.

Reluctantly, Deborah returned to distributing the remainder of the food. Nuala watched over her while Frances finished cleaning and stitching the first boy's infected wound, gave the old man a liniment for his joints and went to work setting the Welshman's fingers. He didn't flinch as she snapped them into place.

"You're fortunate, young man," Lady Selfridge said as she splinted and bound the fingers together. "A longer wait, and you might have lost the use of them."

"It's grateful I am, madam," he said.

"You must change the bandages daily—here, take these—and keep the wound clean. It is not deep, and should heal quickly."

"I shall do as you direct, madam."

She muttered under her breath and began packing her supplies. The Welshman headed for the door.

"I beg your pardon," Deborah called after him.

He turned, his eyes shaded by the brim of his cap. "Madam?"

"I only wished to thank you again."

"It is not necessary, madam."

"What is your name?"

"Ioan Davies."

She offered her hand. "Deborah...Lady Orwell."

After a moment's hesitation he took her hand with his left and made a little bow. "Lady Orwell." He released her hand quickly and was out the door before she could speak again.

Clearly distressed, Deborah turned to Nuala. "Perhaps I shouldn't have come," she said.

"What happened was not your fault."

"But that man…" She wrapped her arms around her waist. "Did he actually call me a…" She trailed off, flushing. Nuala took her hand.

"They were only words, Deborah." Only words. As Nuala's little spell had been "only magic."

It was not real. It couldn't have been.

ALL THE WAY BACK to Belgravia, Deborah was very quiet and lost in thought. Nuala could well understand why. She had seen ugly things in Whitechapel: the worst sort of misery and poverty, pain, hatred. She would see it again. Her previously sheltered life was coming to an end.

"Do you suppose we'll see Mr. Davies again?" she asked Nuala as Frances descended from the carriage.

"Only if he breaks another finger," Nuala said. "That young man has pride."

"Surely some measure of pride is something to be admired in a place like that. He has nothing, yet he behaved like a gentleman."

"One is a lady or gentleman by nature, Deborah, not only by birth. There are true gentlemen in the rookeries and brutes in Mayfair."

"But most people are something in between."

Yes, Nuala thought. *Very much like Sinjin Ware.* And herself.

We are none of us innocent.

If she had indeed used magic in Whitechapel—if it had not been a figment of her own imagination—it was no cause for celebration. She had come very close to the Gray. And that was not how she would wish her abilities to return. Better she remember that she had earned their disappearance, and wish them away again.

She let Deborah off at the girl's house and continued to her own home on Grosvenor Street. Once in her boudoir, she sat at her desk and laid out a sheet of stationery. Pen poised above the paper, she wondered how to begin.

> Dear Lord Donnington,
> It has come to my attention that you and I must…

She scratched out the words and selected another sheet.

> Dear Lord Donnington,
> Much to my regret, it appears that there have been certain misunderstandings…

With a soft curse, long antiquated, but not inappropriate to the situation, Nuala crushed the paper and placed her chin on her palm. It simply would not do. They must speak privately, face-to-face.

She selected a third sheet and began another letter, folded it, sealed it and sent it with a footman to Tameri's town house. It was very likely that a socially prominent—if controversial—gentleman such as Lord Donnington would be invited to her garden party. And there, at last, they might have a chance to talk in a relatively safe environment.

As if she could ever be safe again.

MAYE HOUSE was all that a duchess's should be. It had been the Duke of Vardon's second house in London; the first was now occupied by the current duchess, the wife of the dowager's brother-in-law. But the former duke had seen his widow well looked-after, and so the stately mansion—named, it was said, after a distant relation of a previous century—was a model of luxury.

Luxury in the ancient Egyptian style. Towering statues of the goddesses Bast, Hathor, Sekhmet and Isis greeted the visitor in the entrance hall; the walls were painted with murals of kings and queens giving audiences to their subjects and exotic foreign vassals. In concession to modern tastes, the chairs along the walls in the ballroom, as well as those at the table in the dining room, had been constructed in a more comfortable style than the hard chairs the dowager Duchess of Vardon favored in her more private quarters.

None of these sights were unfamiliar to Society. Eccentric the dowager might be, but she held considerable influence when she chose to use it, and had a great deal of money to spend on her entertainments.

The garden party was no exception. Maye House had an exceptional garden and a conservatory that was the envy of every botanical enthusiast in the capital. Exotic plants crowded against the glass, vast rubbery leaves nodding over each other, brilliant flowers popping up in unexpected places. In the center, a cleared space allowed room for chairs and conversation. If one could tolerate the heat, it was a very pleasant venue.

The party spilled out onto a neatly kept lawn, edged with shrubberies clipped into the reclining canine form of the god Anubis, where tents had been set up to provide additional shade for tables displaying a selection of delicacies. Every sort of drink was provided, leaving no guest an excuse to go thirsty. Heaps of flowers had been beautifully arranged in vases on the surrounding walls. Doors stood open to a palm-bedecked reception room, available for those who found the clement weather too taxing.

Deborah and Nuala walked together, arm in arm, while the younger woman chattered incessantly in a manner quite out of character. Nuala thought she knew the reason. According to Tameri, most of the Forties had been invited—they were popular guests, in spite of their contempt for the state of holy matrimony—and though she didn't expect all of them to turn up, she had received notice that both Lord Donnington and Mr. Melbyrne planned to attend.

The way Deborah's gaze darted from face to face, searching for one in particular, suggested that Nuala had not been mistaken in her guess at the park. There had definitely been a spark between Deborah and Melbyrne. A rightness in their coming together.

Nuala shook her head. It was none of her business. If it was meant to be, they would find each other without her help.

At least not of the magical sort.

"Ah," she said, spotting the young man in question. "I believe I see Mr. Melbyrne."

Deborah craned her neck and almost immediately resumed a more prudent demeanor. "Oh? I did not know he was to come."

"Perhaps we ought to greet him," Nuala suggested.

"Surely it would seem a bit forward, would it not?"

"At a party such as this? Not at all. We have already been introduced."

"Well…if you really think it the polite thing to do…"

"You like him, don't you?" Nuala asked, unable to help herself.

"He…he is most personable."

"Let us go, then." Nuala gently steered Deborah toward the open doors of the conservatory, where Mr. Melbyrne was engaged in light conversation with a man with whom Nuala was not yet acquainted. Melbyrne noticed Deborah's approach and beamed.

"Lady Orwell," he said, bowing. "Lady Charles."

"Good afternoon, Mr. Melbyrne," Nuala said into Deborah's tongue-tied silence. "How very pleasant to find you here after our meeting in the park."

"Indeed. A great pleasure." He glanced at Deborah. "Are you enjoying the party, Lady Orwell?" he asked, his voice pitched a little high.

"We are only just arrived," Deborah said quietly. "And you?"

"Yes." He remembered himself and gestured at his companion. "Lady Orwell, Lady Charles, may I present Mr. Leopold Erskine."

Mr. Erskine, a tall and lanky man with a pleasant face, bowed with a charming touch of awkwardness. "Ladies. It is a privilege to make your acquaintance."

Nuala offered her hand. "I have heard your name, Mr. Erskine. Are you not an archaeologist and scholar of ancient languages?"

"Some have said so, Lady Charles."

"Mr. Erskine is entirely too modest," Melbyrne said. "He knows more than the rest of us put together."

"Are you a member of the Forties, Mr. Erskine?" Deborah asked innocently.

Nuala kept her teeth locked together. If Deborah had any real interest in Melbyrne, it had been the height of foolishness to remind him of his club's vows. But he seemed not to notice, and Erskine was already answering.

"I am not, Lady Orwell," he said. "I have never been prone to joining such institutions, but I do count several of its members as friends."

"And we are privileged by his condescension," a deep voice said from behind him.

Nuala's spine prickled. Sinjin had arrived.

CHAPTER FOUR

MELBYRNE SEEMED TO SHRINK a little, but Erskine raised a satirical brow. "Good afternoon, Lord Donnington."

"Erskine. Melbyrne." He turned immediately to the ladies. "Good afternoon, Lady Orwell, Lady Charles. It seems only yesterday that we met in the park."

Nuala didn't offer her hand. It was trembling far too much, and she feared that Sinjin might feel the beating of her heart through her fingers "Time moves very quickly during the Season, don't you agree?" she said.

He studied her intently. "Perhaps too quickly. Matters of importance may be so conveniently forgotten."

"Perhaps such matters ought to be dealt with as soon as possible."

"Business of that nature might best be conducted in privacy," Sinjin said.

"It is amazing how much privacy may be found in the midst of a crowd."

Sinjin snorted and glanced toward Melbyrne, but the boy was already walking away…with Deborah on his arm.

"Such black looks, Lord Donnington," Erskine said.

"One might think you fear that your young protégé might actually be tempted to forswear his oath."

"Melbyrne? Nothing of the kind. He must claim a fair companion while he can. I note that there are more gentlemen than ladies present today."

As if to refute his claim, an expensively dressed, middle-aged woman approached at a fast pace, her unmarried daughter in tow. Nuala recognized her, though she didn't know the woman well. She knew that the poor daughter was in her third Season and as yet unmarried, a disaster of unprecedented proportions for her family.

"Lord Donnington!" the woman cooed. "How very charming to find you here."

Sinjin's face instantly took on a pleasant but cynical cast. "Mrs. Eccleston," he acknowledged.

The woman tugged the hand of the blushing girl behind her. "You have met my daughter, Miss Laetitia."

The woman's forwardness didn't seem to trouble Sinjin, though her intentions were painfully obvious. He smiled and bowed to Mrs. Eccleston and the young lady, who was half-hidden behind her mother's skirts.

"You are acquainted with Lady Charles, I believe," he said pointedly, "and Mr. Erskine."

"Yes, indeed. Charmed." Mrs. Eccleston gave Nuala a narrow-eyed glance, doubtless considering the nature and qualities of a possible rival.

Nuala stifled a laugh at the improbable thought. "Good afternoon, Mrs. Eccleston, Miss Eccleston."

Laetitia almost mustered a smile. "Good afternoon, Lady Charles," she whispered.

"Are not the flowers lovely, Lord Donnington?" Mrs. Eccleston said. "Laetitia is most fond of flowers. She quite adores arranging them…don't you, my dear?"

The poor girl went white at being put on the spot. "I…"

"Perhaps Miss Eccleston might enjoy touring the conservatory," Sinjin interjected. "If you can spare her, Mrs. Eccleston."

"Of course, of course! You are too kind, Lord Donnington."

With a gesture Nuala might almost have called gracious, Sinjin offered his arm to Laetitia and smiled. The girl's hand was trembling when she took his arm, but Nuala recognized the flash of gratitude on her small face. Not gratitude that Sinjin meant anything by his offer of escort, but that he had provided a means of escape from her overbearing mama.

Mrs. Eccleston could hardly conceal her triumph. "Do forgive me, Lady Charles, Mr. Erskine. I see a friend and must speak to her."

She bustled off with no thought to her lack of courtesy. Erskine chuckled.

"Quite a dragon, isn't she?" he remarked.

"She has a daughter to provide for," Nuala said, watching Sinjin walk away with the most troubling of mixed emotions. "Laetitia is in an unenviable situation."

"The remarkable thing is that Miss Eccleston seems to think her daughter has a chance with Lord Donnington."

Nuala swallowed. "Are you quite sure she would not?"

"You are obviously a sensible woman, Lady Charles. What is your opinion?"

"He is highly eligible."

"Quite. But there is more to matchmaking than mere eligibility."

"Indeed. His reputation must be known by every woman in Society," Nuala said. "Perhaps some don't believe the strength of his commitment to his chosen way of life." She noted Erskine's discomfort and added, "I mean, of course, his refusal to marry before the age of forty."

Erskine clasped his hands behind his back. "He once told me that if he ever found a woman his equal, he would marry her immediately. I doubt he will discover such a paragon, and will have to settle for less when he is finally compelled to do his duty."

"Yet I have no doubt that he will do his duty in the end," Nuala said, her throat tightening around the words.

Erskine gave her a penetrating look. "How long have you and Donnington known each other, Lady Charles?"

"We met in the park less than a fortnight ago." She moved a little closer to Erskine, as if he might somehow quiet her distress. "He seemed quite put out when Mr. Melbyrne left with Lady Orwell."

"He guards his friends' virtue as savagely as Cerberus guards Hades." Erskine's cheeks took on a hint of color. "I beg your pardon."

"Not at all. I believe you meant that the earl is determined to see that his friends avoid the snares of marriage as assiduously as he does."

"Exactly," Erskine said, looking relieved. "And Melbyrne is still vulnerable, young as he is. Perhaps not entirely convinced that he wishes to remain unattached for another two decades. Nevertheless, I hope that Lady Orwell…"

"Lady Orwell has a great deal of sense for her age," Nuala said, hoping it was true. "She knows with whom Mr. Melbyrne associates and what that entails."

"I am relieved." Erskine glanced toward the tent that sheltered the refreshments. "May I fetch you a glass of lemonade?"

"I will come with you, Mr. Erskine."

They proceeded to the tent, and Nuala contrived to speak as if not a thing in the world could discompose her. She genuinely liked Erskine and thought they might have become good friends under other circumstances, now that she was in a position to make friends of a more permanent sort. But she had the strong suspicion that Sinjin would object to her association with Erskine as much as he obviously did Melbyrne's with Deborah.

He has no control over whom I wish to see, she thought. *Nor has he any power over Deborah. I shall see to that.*

She enjoyed a glass of lemonade with Erskine, excused herself to speak with Lillian and Tameri, and had fallen into conversation with Lady Oxenham when Sinjin reappeared, quite alone.

"We meet again," he said very pleasantly.

"How did you find your tour of the conservatory, Lord Donnington?" Nuala asked, feeling her skin begin to warm with the beginnings of anxiety.

"Most illuminating. A very fine collection."

He said nothing about Miss Eccleston, but it would not have been polite for him to do so, even had he anything good to say about her. He glanced at Mr. Erskine.

"Mr. Erskine, you will have no objection if I claim Lady Charles for a few minutes. That is, of course, if the lady is willing."

It was much more a command than a request, and Nuala's annoyance almost submerged her concern about what was to come. Still, she had wanted to speak to Sinjin, and here was her chance.

"Of course, Lord Donnington," she said.

He touched her shoulder, steering her toward the house. The contact was electric, sending currents of awareness through that now-empty part of her that had always been the source of her magic. She stepped out of his reach and continued on through the French doors and into the reception room.

"I believe we will have more privacy here," she said, gesturing toward a door leading off the reception room. The door led into a cloak room, hardly more than a closet. Nuala made certain that the door was left partly ajar after Sinjin entered. She moved to the small window looking out over the garden and faced him again.

For a moment they simply stared at each other. "I

know you have many questions for me, Lord Donnington," she began, unable to bear the silence.

"Do you?" he asked. His gaze swept from her shoes to her hat. "Strange to be calling you Lady Charles. I should never have thought to see you in London. How quickly you've risen...Nola."

"That name was a temporary one," she said, refusing to be intimidated by his deceptively casual manner. "My true name is Nuala."

"I remember." He looked over her shoulder at the window, as if the view beyond it held some great fascination for him. "You left Donbridge very suddenly."

"Yes."

"I wonder why? What were you afraid of, Nuala?"

"My work at Donbridge was finished."

"Your *work.*" His lips curved in a chilling smile. "The work that led you to deceive all of us. The work that resulted in my brother's death."

There would be no beating around the bush, no benefit of the doubt. Nuala closed her eyes, remembering how it had all begun—when her powers had called upon her to aid a young bride, Mariah Marron, wife of Sinjin's elder brother Giles, the Earl of Donnington. A wife who had been left a virgin on her wedding night, for Giles had plans for her that few mortals could comprehend: he intended to deliver her to Cairbre, a lord of the Fane, the unearthly denizens of the Faerie realm Tir-na-Nog. Cairbre had intended to use Mariah, unknowingly part Fane herself, as a means of taking power from the rightful king of Tir-na-Nog.

In return for Mariah, Cairbre had promised to give the avid hunter Lord Donnington the greatest prize of all: the unicorn king known as Arion. But Cairbre quickly learned that Mariah could not be forced through the gate to Tir-na-Nog by one she did not love.

Arion, exiled to earth in human form, had been deceived into believing that he would be permitted to return to Tir-na-Nog only if he could win Mariah's love and lead her through the gate. Lord Donnington had left his estate, Donbridge, immediately after his unconsummated wedding, intending to throw Mariah into Arion's path and simultaneously removing any obstacle to their love.

But his plans had not gone as expected. Mariah had not only fallen in love with Arion, he—called Ash in the human world—had fallen in love with her. Nuala, who had posed as the maid Nola in hopes of helping them defeat the evil plans of Giles and Cairbre, had not foreseen the complications that would ensue. Giles's mother, the dowager countess, had wished to break up her son's marriage to Mariah. She had conspired with beautiful, blond Pamela, Lady Westlake—Sinjin's mistress—who loved Lord Donnington and thought only of destroying Mariah. Pamela had used Sinjin, while setting out to ruin Mariah's reputation in Society.

But no one, least of all Nuala, had anticipated that Giles would unexpectedly return to England, confront Ash and break his deal with Cairbre by claiming Mariah for himself. Or that, in the chaos that followed, Arion would prepare to sacrifice his life,

Mariah would give up her freedom, and both Giles and Pamela would meet tragic ends because of their own hatred, jealousy and betrayal.

The guilt that surged in Nuala's chest nearly choked her.

"I did not kill your brother," she whispered.

"No. But his death could have been prevented. You could have stopped it."

"I…" She paused to whisper an instinctive and surely useless spell meant to quiet her racing heart. Naturally it had no effect, neither on her profound discomfort nor on her physical awareness of Sinjin's masculine power. "I did not have the ability to control or anticipate everything that happened," she said. "My purpose was to—"

"Save Ash and Mariah. 'They are destined to be together,' you told me. What happened to anyone else was of no concern to you."

Her fingers trembled. She hid them in her skirts. "That is not true, Lord Donnington. I merely observed for nearly the entire time Ash and Mariah were together. My powers—"

"Your *powers*." His eyes were dark with unspoken pain. "You claimed they were fading. Yet you maintained your illusion for months. You traveled to Tir-na-Nog twice on Ash's behalf…oh, yes, Mariah told me. You helped heal Ash when he was dying."

"Nevertheless, I—"

"You instructed me to ride after Giles, to stop him from hunting Ash. You knew that Pamela had helped my brother and was willing to do anything to protect him, yet it never occurred to you to consider that she was mad."

"You knew her far better than I."

He flinched. "*I* never claimed to hold superhuman abilities. You knew of Pamela's earlier conspiracies, did you not?"

"I could not be everywhere at once."

"Then you chose to begin something you could not hope to finish."

Anger, however unreasonable, gave Nuala a sliver of courage. "Would you have let your brother betray Mariah and kill Ash?"

"Not if I understood what was going on. You could have approached me at any time, and I would have helped you before things got out of hand. You assumed that you could interfere in our lives without consequence."

All he said was true. She had attempted too much. Even before Donbridge, she had known that her power had gradually been growing weaker, though she had not understood the reason. She should have taken heed of her limitations. Only *she* was to blame. Yet to do as she had intended, to admit her mistakes to this man who so despised her…

"I deeply regret what happened," she said, meaning it with all her heart. "But Lord Donnington chose his own path."

"Perhaps you *wanted* Giles dead."

The accusation took her breath away. "You are wrong," she said. "I would not wish to see anyone—"

Would you not, Nuala?

She turned her back to him, clasping her arms across her chest. "I wished no one such a fate," she said. "Not even a man who would sell his wife for the chance to hunt and kill a unicorn."

The silence fell like smothering snow. "My brother made many mistakes," Sinjin said at last, his voice thick with emotion. "But he planned to defy the Fane and keep Mariah."

"At the cost of Ash's life."

"You couldn't even help Ash in the end. You left it all up to Mariah."

"Because she had become strong enough. She didn't need me anymore."

"You were so certain of that, yet so ignorant of everything else?"

She couldn't answer. She couldn't explain what she didn't fully understand herself: how she had always depended upon her witch's instincts to tell her when to take direct action in the lives of those she watched over, and when to leave them to determine their own ultimate fate. It had always been a fine balance, and she had utterly failed to find it at Donbridge.

Sinjin's footsteps moved about the room, the tap of his heels beating out an agitated rhythm. He clearly wanted much more from her than an apology.

For his guilt was almost as great as hers. It simmered beneath his righteous anger and grief for his brother. He and Giles had never been close; to the contrary, both Giles and their mother, the dowager, had been cool and distant with Sinjin since his childhood.

And that made matters all the worse for him. He had to convince himself that he had not sacrificed a lifetime's closeness to his only sibling because of his own choices. He wanted to prove to himself, and to her, that he had not betrayed his brother by loving Lady Westlake, for refusing to recognize the depth of Pamela's obsession and determination to claim Giles for herself at any cost…even the former Lord Donnington's life.

Yet Nuala had no power to ease his pain. She could not fight his battle for him; she could scarcely fight her own. She hugged herself more tightly.

"Why are we here, Lord Donnington?" she asked. "Is it your intention to punish me?"

"And how should I do that, Lady Charles? By exposing you for what you are? Informing Society that they have a witch and former chambermaid in their midst?" He barked a laugh. "Even if I were to attempt it, you might summon up a spell to turn me into a toad."

"I have never possessed such an ability," she said, staring at the window glass without seeing anything beyond it.

His footsteps came to an abrupt halt. "You admitted that you were a witch when you first revealed yourself to me," he said, his words measured, as if he feared to expose his own suffering. "If I had not seen the impossible with my own eyes, I would not have believed such creatures existed. But you never explained what that means, where you came from, or how you knew that Mariah needed your 'help.'"

No, she had not. There had been no time…and then she had chosen the coward's way out rather than face just such questions as these.

But there were things she simply couldn't tell Sinjin, part of her past that, if revealed, would only make him despise her more….

And she was not prepared for that. Not when she had yet to find her own redemption. Not when she couldn't hate Sinjin, even when he made her face the weakest part of herself.

She turned back to him, assuming a calmness she was far from feeling. "If I answer these questions," she said, "will there be peace between us?"

"Peace!" He laughed under his breath. "Is that what you want, Nuala?"

"We will doubtless meet many times during the Season," she said. "You may believe what you wish of me, but I see no reason to trouble our friends and acquaintances."

"Indeed not. It would be criminal to cause Society the least discomfiture."

Nuala started for the door, intending to pass Sinjin as quickly as possible. He stopped her with a strong hand on her arm.

"I want to know," he said, the words husky with something very like pleading. "What are you?"

She tried to relax in his grip, trusting that he would let go when he realized she would make no further attempt to escape. Once again his touch gave her a jolt, as if he were not her adversary, but something else entirely….

Someone passed by the half-open doorway. Sinjin released her. She retreated deeper into the room again, rubbing her arm where Sinjin had been holding it.

"It is no wonder you don't understand," she said. "Folklore claims that witches are evil hags who wish only ill to the world, that they cast spells meant to create pain and havoc."

"And is folklore so wrong in its definition?"

She felt his challenging stare, but refused to meet it. "There might have been such people... surely there have been. But witches have been living in England for centuries, most in perfect harmony with..." She hesitated. "With nonmagical humans."

"Humans? At Donbridge, you told me you weren't Fane."

"We—my people—are human in every respect but our magic. It is a gift passed down from one generation to the next, not gained through bargains with the devil or dark rituals."

"There are more of you? God help us."

His bitterness burned her like a white-hot brand. "Once there were many of us, yes. Enough to insure that our gifts were not completely lost." She took a deep, shuddering breath and released it slowly. "We were bound by our magic and our traditions, many families scattered all over England, sometimes in small villagers where we were accepted and valued." She dared to look at his face. "You wonder why they might value us. Many of us were healers, capable of doing what no ordinary physician could. Others were more proficient at casting spells over corn to make it grow thick and hearty."

"You make these witches sound like paragons of virtue."

"Oh, we were not. Nor did we claim to be."

To her surprise, he said nothing to mock or berate her. "You are talking of things that happened in the past."

"Yes." It became very difficult to speak. "We are not as numerous as we once were. There are very few of us left in England, and most keep to themselves."

"You didn't."

"Some of us…could not help but use our gifts when they were needed. I was able to…*see* when two people were meant to be together."

"You've used this 'gift' before you came to Donbridge?"

"Many times."

"And no one died?"

Nothing she'd said had made any sort of difference. There would be no way to satisfy him, no way to make him forgive her, even if she wanted his forgiveness after the accusations he had made.

She closed her eyes. "No. I cannot say that there were no problems.…"

"You always posed as someone else to help these people?"

"Most never learned who or what I was." She opened her eyes, though she could not seem to see anything but the past. "I used magic for small things—spells of concealment, or of distraction. Often these were all that were needed to see that the match was encouraged."

"The matches *you* determined should be made."

She said nothing. He began pacing again. "And now?" he said. "Will you continue to utilize this magic?"

"I cannot…" The image of the vicious knife-wielder in the rookeries stopped her answer. What she had done to him, however mild…

She took a deep breath. "I did not lie when I said that my powers were fading."

"Did you arrange your own marriage?"

New accusations. She felt anger building again. "I did not."

"You didn't cast a spell on Parkhill to win his love?"

"I went to his estate to nurse him, with no intention of doing anything more."

"Yet here you are, *Lady* Charles."

Laughter sounded in the reception room. Nuala thought of Deborah and Melbyrne, of the wry and gentle Mr. Erskine, of the widows who were her unquestioning friends.

"Have you heard enough, Lord Donnington?" she asked.

The storm in his eyes belied the stillness of his face. "What haven't you told me, Nuala?"

"I have told you everything." She moved again for the door.

"Nuala."

"Sinjin?"

"Promise me that you will no longer interfere in the affairs of other people."

It was almost a request. She gripped the doorjamb. "Is that your condition for ending this…this conflict between us?"

"It is." He caught her gaze, and she could not look away. "You'll forgive me if I don't quite believe that your magic is gone. If you swear not to use it as a tool for your matchmaking, I will be satisfied."

Satisfied. Satisfied to relegate her to the list of his conquests, even though there had never been anything remotely physical between them.

Yet would it be such a sacrifice? She had seen no evidence that her flare of magic in Whitechapel had been more than a fluke. She had accepted that she would never again use her abilities for the purpose to which she had put them for more than two centuries.

"I agree," she said. "Goodbye, Lord Donnington."

She swept from the room, praying that she wouldn't stumble. If he followed, she didn't hear him. But there was a painful tightness in her chest, as if she were near tears. As if some sort of thread had been stretched to the breaking point…a thread connecting her and Sinjin, spun by some careless weaver who had mistakenly joined two pieces of mismatched wool.

All illusion. She intended to have nothing to do with him from now on. And he would certainly avoid her just as assiduously.

CHAPTER FIVE

SINJIN DIDN'T FEEL VICTORIOUS. To the contrary: he felt as if he had been one of the contestants in a bare-knuckle fistfight, trading gut-wrenching blows with an able and dangerous opponent.

But Nuala had promised. For what such a promise was worth. He didn't know if he believed her. He didn't know if it would make the least bit of difference in his feelings about her, or about Giles's death.

His feelings about her. It was so simple to let himself believe that he despised her. He'd told himself when they'd met again in Hyde Park that he'd never felt the slightest interest in Nola the maid. But Nuala had revealed herself to him before the final confrontation between Arion and Giles. She had asked for his assistance then, though it had already been too late.

He'd thought he'd felt nothing but anger toward the beautiful witch, so very different from the quiet, mousy girl she had been. He'd certainly treated her with hostility, just as he had since they'd first spoken in London. Far easier to hide behind contempt and resentment when the alternative was something even less palatable.

Attraction. He could not deny it any longer. He could not seem to take his eyes from her slender but eminently womanly figure, that astonishing ginger hair, those lush lips.

Even at Donnington, for all his determination to resist her influence, he must have felt the same. And when she had disappeared without a word…

He hadn't forgotten her. Not for a single day, though he had worked to make her the villain, the instigator of all that had gone wrong at Donnington.

It wasn't fair. And he'd told himself it didn't matter. *Bloody hell.* It was over. Finished.

Damn her.

Sinjin walked into the garden. He saw no sign of Nuala. The crowd had thinned as some of the guests went on to other entertainments; soon it would be time to dress for dinner. His gaze swept over the lawn and hedges and conservatory. Erskine was in conversation with one of the widows: Lady Meadows, the cultivator of rare orchids. The two were very different, one tall and lean, the other short and plump. They seemed to be getting on very well together. Idly Sinjin wondered how suited they would be if they…

Good God, man. He was no matchmaker, even if he was happy enough to recommend suitable mistresses for his friends.

And that reminded him of Melbyrne, who had last been seen with the highly eligible Lady Orwell.

He strode across the lawn, keeping a sharp eye out for the naive young man. He was compelled to pause a number of times to exchange empty pleasantries with various guests, those who still didn't consider him beyond the pale, and another anxious mama with an unmarried daughter who was considerably bolder than Miss Eccleston and had not been put off by his reputation.

Women. Young or old, timid or bold, they were all the same at heart, eager to drain a man dry…of money, of manhood, of self-respect.

At least he might save Melbyrne for a few more years.

With a scowl Sinjin circled the grounds and returned to the conservatory. He found Melbyrne and Lady Orwell together behind one of the tropical plants with leaves that resembled the ears of an elephant. They were not touching, but only a fool could fail to recognize how much they were enjoying one another's company.

"I beg your pardon, Lady Orwell," he said.

The young people started and almost leaped apart, as if they had been engaged in actual lovemaking instead of undoubtedly unexceptionable conversation.

"Lord Donnington!" Lady Orwell stammered. She flushed a bright crimson.

He executed a brief bow. "If you will forgive me, Lady Orwell…Mr. Melbyrne and I have a dinner engagement this evening."

She glanced at Felix as if seeking confirmation. "Of course, Lord Donnington." She offered her hand to Melbyrne. "I have enjoyed our talk, Mr. Melbyrne. It was most instructive."

Felix took her hand and quickly let it go again. He bowed as stiffly as a hussar on review. "I wish you a good evening, Lady Orwell." He spun about and marched out of the conservatory.

"May I escort you to your friends, Lady Orwell?" Sinjin asked.

"It is not necessary, I assure you." She brushed past him, upsetting the leaves of the exotic plants in her path. The young widow was badly flustered, which suited Sinjin very well indeed.

He strolled from the conservatory, located Melbyrne, and cornered him near one of the jackal-shaped shrubberies.

"I see you have found a method of staving off the boredom of a party such as this," he said with a faint smile. "It is not, however, a method I would recommend."

"We were only talking," Melbyrne said, shifting from foot to foot.

"In convenient solitude."

Melbyrne laughed. "For God's sake, Donnington, nothing happened."

"If you are well-disposed toward Lady Orwell, you would not wish her reputation to be compromised by being seen alone with you...particularly if it is not your desire to marry her. In the case of Mrs. Tissier, you will be free of all such constraints except those of rudimentary discretion."

Melbyrne looked up from the well-groomed lawn. "Were you constrained when you took Lady Charles into the house and failed to emerge for nearly an hour?"

Sinjin allowed his eyelids and mouth to relax in a knowingly bored expression. "It was not a pleasurable interlude, I assure you."

"Discussing 'matters of importance'?" Melbyrne asked with emphasis.

"Matters of no concern to you."

"I hope that no one else remarked upon your abrupt disappearance."

"I have seen no indication that Lady Charles is incapable of looking after her own reputation." He frowned at the unexpected burst of desire he felt when he recalled Nuala's fiery hair, the strands coming loose from beneath her hat, and the curves of her body that could not entirely be concealed by her stiff, binding garments.

"These widows," he said sharply, "may want the world to believe that they are uninterested in marriage, but I am convinced that their motives are quite the opposite. They merely wish to increase their fascination for the opposite sex. Beware prevarication veiled in innocence."

"Are you saying that Lady Charles is pursuing you?" Melbyrne asked, the laugh still in his voice.

"Even if she were, she has chosen an immovable object." He clapped the boy on the shoulder. "We should be going. Reddick will be expecting us."

With a shrug Melbyrne fell in beside him. They tendered their thanks to the dowager duchess, took leave of several acquaintances and proceeded through the house. As they descended the stairs to the entrance hall, Sinjin caught a glimpse of Nuala.

She was with Erskine, the two of them engaged in earnest conversation. Sinjin stopped so suddenly that Melbyrne nearly ran in to him. Catching himself, Sinjin continued before either party could notice his consternation.

Let them talk. For all that Sinjin had called Erskine a "little lost lamb," he was not a complete fool. And Nuala would never choose him. Surely not.

Grimacing in annoyance, Sinjin sent a footman for his carriage. At the moment, his only concern should be putting the witch out of his mind. They would meet again, of course, just as she'd said. Indifferently, coolly, as he had implied when he'd demanded her promise.

Later that night he retired somewhat more at ease, and fell asleep quickly. He woke to the feeling that something was terribly wrong.

Heat. Fire. The flames licked at him, burning, savaging him without touching his flesh. The heat was real, and the pain, but there was no smoke, no gasping for life's breath, no blackening of the flesh.

Only rage. The rage of something long desired denied, removed from the realm of possibility. The rage of lust unsated. And a voice. A voice, faceless, that warned and berated him, that shouted and pleaded.

Nuala.

The image changed, and she came to him. Naked, wreathed in fire, her hair a flame that danced on the hot wind. Magic, dark and bright, gleamed on her silken flesh.

Evil! the voice cried. But the word was laced with

that furious desire, throbbing need that made Sinjin gasp with a hunger so powerful that he knew himself capable of pushing Nuala to the scorched earth and taking her without tenderness or mercy.

Take her. Destroy her. And part of him wanted it with all the savagery of a wild beast. But she only smiled with sweet sadness, fell to her knees and lay down before him, offering herself, thighs spread and arms outstretched. And he very nearly went to her, knowing as he did so that his very soul was in peril, that she was deceiving him as surely as Satan himself....

He sat up, his breath sawing in his throat. The room coalesced around him, solid, familiar. Nuala wasn't there.

Sinjin stood and went to the washstand, splashing cold water on his face. He had never in his life had a dream like this one. And never, he prayed, would again.

What in hell's name had it meant? The rage, the hatred, had been far more savage than anything he'd ever felt for Nuala, even at his worst.

And the lust...

The sheets were soaked through with perspiration. The very notion of lying in that bed again tonight was repulsive to him. He toweled himself dry, put on trousers and a shirt and fell into a chair. That was where his butler found him.

"Your lordship?" the old man said in a whisper.

Sinjin sat up, his eyes gritty and his mouth foul. "Be so good as to bring me coffee, Hedley," he said.

"Are you…quite all right, your lordship?"

Quite all right. Oh, yes. He would be. One way or another.

DEBORAH STOOD in the entrance hall of her nearly empty town house, listening to the echoes of incipient abandonment. Soon this place, which she had inhabited for so little time, would be rented out to some other family…would be filled with other voices, other activities. Happy ones, she hoped.

Only her maid and head footman remained with her now. Tomorrow she would move to Nuala's house on Grosvenor Street, where there was plenty of room for two quiet women. Deborah had made certain that her minimal staff had found good employment elsewhere—again, excluding Stella and Jacques—and she had no regrets at the departure.

Jacques took her coat, and she retreated into the last furnished room besides her bedchamber, the forward drawing room. The sofa and table and two chairs were worn and completely lacking in any distinction; she hadn't bothered to replace them since she'd moved in. Lawrence hadn't cared about such things, especially since he hadn't lived in England for over ten years.

Saddened by the renewed memories of her husband, Deborah sat in one of the chairs and stared into the empty grate. It would be very easy to become melancholy again, after the unexpected pleasures of the garden party.

She closed her eyes, envisioning Mr. Melbyrne's very pleasant features. Oh, yes, he was handsome. Much handsomer than Lawrence. She tried to suppress the disloyal thought, to examine Melbyrne as dispassionately as if she were an artist like Maggie, about to begin a new portrait. But no matter how much she tried to distance herself, she could only admit that Felix Melbyrne, with his fair hair and blue eyes, was very nearly any woman's ideal.

She smiled a little, thinking of his boyish enthusiasm for all sorts of sport, particularly racing and shooting. In spite of his belonging to the notorious Forties, he had been most respectful in his behavior, even when he and Deborah had been alone in the conservatory. She had listened while he talked, seldom attempting to speak, allowing herself to bask in his sunny good nature.

Deborah frowned and pleated a bit of her skirt between her thumb and forefinger. Yes, she had to confess that she'd enjoyed Melbyrne's company very much. There had even been times that she'd felt completely lifted out of her grief…a prospect that aroused both bemusement and guilt. If she had reacted a bit strongly when Lord Donnington had found them, it was only because she would never have done anything to stain her husband's reputation by appearing the hussy.

Lawrence would never have wanted you to spend your life in mourning. But *she* had made the decision not to marry again. She had spent three happy years with a husband who had never been anything but a perfect friend. How could any other man provide such loving companionship?

Stella brought in the tea tray. Deborah smiled and assured her that nothing else was needed. Only time to think. To test her feelings and try to understand what they meant.

He likes me, she thought. He wasn't attempting to mislead her, she was certain of it. But he had given no indication that he had developed a real partiality for her. Surely she was quite safe.

Deliberately she picked up her teacup and took a measured sip. Yes, she quite liked Mr. Melbyrne. But more than that…

She allowed her mind to wander again, finding her way back to the rookeries where she had witnessed so much suffering. She had done very little that first visit; now that Frances and Nuala had formed more ambitious plans for founding a school and delivering additional food, along with hiring new employees to help carry and distribute it, Deborah was determined to contribute all the funds, time and work such a worthy project required. If she had been a bit frightened by the man with the knife…why, she would overcome that fear. And it wasn't as if all the men in Whitechapel were like him. One only had to remember young Ioan Davies.

Another sip from the cup proved the tea to have grown cold, but Deborah didn't pour herself another. She set down the cup and leaned back in her chair.

Ioan Davies. A most unusual fellow. She remembered his hazel eyes very well…the steady, proud

way they'd met hers even as he showed her the
respect due a lady, their sharpness when he'd confronted the troublemaker, Bray. He had been quick
and light on his feet, courageous, gallant in spite of
his worn workman's clothing.

He'd had no reason to defend her. No reason but
simple decency. Decency; yes, that was a word that
suited him very well. He was not particularly tall, not
nearly as handsome as Melbyrne….

She started. The very idea of comparison between
the two men seemed most odd. It wasn't as if they
were in any sort of competition. And they came from
very different worlds. One Welsh, one English. One
wealthy, one poor. One merry and loquacious, one
sober and serious.

*And why shouldn't he be, given the life he must
lead?*

A twinge of guilt brought Deborah up out of her
chair. Lawrence had always been generous to the
poor of Paris, but he had known he couldn't solve the
world's problems. Ioan Davies was certainly not the
sort of man who would accept charity from her, or
any woman. Aside from helping with Frances's
work, there was nothing she could do for him.

Why did that knowledge make her feel so very
inadequate?

With an effort she climbed the stairs to her bedroom. Save for the bedstead, a small armoire and her
dressing table, it was completely bare. She called
Stella to help her change from her afternoon dress
to one more suitable for a casual dinner with friends.

This evening she could look forward to viewing Nuala's portrait and meeting with the other Widows, whose company she always found stimulating and diverting. No more thoughts of men, poor or otherwise.

Stella finished hooking her bodice and stepped back. "The blue suits you, your ladyship," she said with satisfaction. "Shall I pack the grays away?"

The question startled Deborah. Pack them away? She studied herself in the mirror. The "blue," as Stella called it, was really more a sort of gray...wasn't it? It certainly wasn't a bright blue. She touched her hair, still safely caged in its severely simple style. Ought she to change again? She wouldn't wish anyone to think...

No. The color was well enough, though she must watch her choices in future. She would not put the grays away, even though the other Widows had given up mourning. Not that all of them favored bright colors. Julia and Frances both preferred browns and other sober tones. Nuala's dress was always just a little reserved, as if she preferred not to attract the attention of anyone in Society, let alone that of men.

Yet she *had* attracted them. Deborah hadn't failed to notice the sparks that flew between her and Lord Donnington. It had seemed very odd. And the earl had stared and stared at Nuala in such a way that Deborah couldn't decide whether he loathed her or wanted to take her in his arms and kiss her.

Deborah pressed her hand over her mouth as if she had spoken the thought aloud. Lord Donnington, interested in Nuala? He certainly had no *liking* for her, nor she for him; their meeting in Hyde Park had made that clear enough. Everyone knew *he* had only one use for women.

And yet...there must be *something* between them. Something not entirely pleasant. Still, even if they liked each other, Nuala would never respond to an approach by Lord Donnington. She had no interest in a purely amorous relationship with any man.

Relieved at her conclusion, Deborah rose, thanked Stella and went downstairs again. Presently Nuala's carriage arrived, and Deborah climbed in. She noticed immediately that Nuala was distracted, and that there was a certain hectic color in her cheeks.

"Are you well, Nuala?" Deborah asked, laying her hand on Nuala's arm.

Nuala smiled. "Very well, thank you. Did you enjoy the party?"

"Yes. Though I should not like to attend such events every day."

"Nor I," Nuala said. "I understand that you and Mr. Melbyrne had much to talk about."

"He is quite entertaining."

"As you said, a most personable young man." Nuala seemed about to say more, but stopped and turned her attention to the view outside the window. Deborah thought again of Lord Donnington, and almost asked Nuala what she thought of the earl. Basic courtesy discouraged her. If Nuala wished to speak of him, she would.

They arrived at Maggie's house a little before time. Maggie's footman opened the door with a bow and escorted Deborah and Nuala upstairs to Maggie's chaotic studio.

As Deborah had discovered on a previous visit, it was no simple matter to negotiate the paint-spattered floor. But her attention was soon caught by the covered canvas propped on an easel near the windows. Nuala herself seemed nervous, as if she'd rather not see the painting at all. Maggie, not she, had been the one to insist that Nuala would be a perfect subject.

"It is finished," Maggie said with a modestly satisfied air as she wiped her hands on a cloth and pushed her thickly curled red hair out of her face. "I think it may be my best work."

"Might we see it?" Deborah asked.

In answer, Maggie went to the easel and carefully lifted the covering from the canvas.

Deborah gasped. It was nothing like she had expected. Oh, it was nearly a perfect likeness of Nuala in every respect; long, graceful neck, rather grave, gray eyes, even features and fair skin. But there was something very odd about it, too, and it took Deborah a few moments to recognize the nature of the oddity.

The clothing was all wrong. Whatever Nuala had been wearing during the sitting, it surely hadn't been this. The dress was a deep mulberry in color, sober and almost forbidding. Every inch of skin above the bosom was covered with a wide, very plain white collar, which matched the cuffs at the ends of the full, stiff sleeves. Over her bright ginger hair she wore a snug linen cap.

Deborah remembered seeing just such clothing in a painting at the Louvre, one of those rather dark Dutch works depicting a domestic scene of the seventeenth century. The Puritans had dressed like this. It was as if Nuala had posed just before leaving for a fancy-dress ball.

If Deborah was surprised, Nuala was shocked. The color had drained out of her face. Deborah was astonished at the change in a woman who so seldom lost control of her emotions.

Maggie appeared totally oblivious to the reaction her work had provoked. She frowned at the left bottom corner of the painting and picked up one of her small brushes.

Aware that Nuala was trembling, Deborah guided her to one of the rickety wooden chairs scattered about the studio. She pulled a second chair alongside the first.

"It isn't what you expected, is it?" she asked.

Nuala tried to smile. "It…it is a very fine portrait."

"But you weren't wearing those clothes when you sat for it, were you?"

Confusion and alarm disappeared behind a mask of calm that Deborah didn't for a moment believe was genuine. "No," Nuala said. "I imagine that Maggie chose to change the appearance of my dress for artistic reasons of her own."

"I wonder why." Deborah examined the painting a second time, paying greater attention to the detail. "Even the style is a bit odd. It's as if she had deliberately painted the portrait as an artist might have done several hundred years ago."

"Yes." Nuala's hands knotted in her lap. "I shall have to ask her why she chose that particular style."

And so shall I, Deborah thought. Just as she had felt that there might be something going on between Nuala and Lord Donnington, Deborah sensed that there was more to Maggie's choices than met the eye.

"There," Maggie announced, straightening from the painting with her brush triumphantly raised. She turned to Nuala and Deborah with a grin. "Do you like it?"

"It is lovely," Nuala said warmly as she rose. "Quite breathtaking."

Maggie chewed on the end of her brush. "There is something missing," she murmured. "I shall know what it is after a day or two. And it must finish drying. But I shall be able to deliver it to you in a week."

"I shall be very honored to give your gift pride of place in my house," Nuala said.

"Hmm." Maggie's eyes had taken on that glazed look so typical of artists immersed in their work. Nuala smiled at Deborah, and the two of them left the studio.

"If you don't like it," Deborah said once they were in the carriage again, "you needn't display it except when Maggie calls or the Widows meet at your house."

"Oh, I truly do like it," Nuala said, too brightly. "I am sorry if it appeared otherwise."

Deborah was still far from convinced. But soon the carriage had drawn up in front of Frances's on Wilton Crescent, and they were being greeted at the door by her parlor maid. Frances kept no male servants in her home.

The other Widows—all but Maggie, who would doubtless be late—had already gathered in the drawing room, which was as neat and sensible as Frances herself. The few select pictures on the walls were all of prominent women of the past: Boadicea, Queen Elizabeth, Joan of Arc.

"What a day!" Lillian exclaimed, vigorously plying her fan. "I had such difficulty with my orchids, especially the Chysis bractescens. She was extremely naughty and uncooperative when I attempted to repot her. I only hope she will perk up again."

Clara gave Lillian an indulgent smile. "I'm sure your loving hand will soon put her to rights," she said.

"And how goes your latest experiment, Clara?" the dowager Duchess of Vardon asked. "Does it progress well?"

"Very well, Tameri. And I must say that your party was elegance itself. Lady Winthrop was most envious of your garden."

As always, Tameri accepted the praise as her due, though she nodded graciously. "Lady Winthrop is most prone to envy. It is not an attractive trait."

"She is also prone to simpering at every man of position she meets," Lady Selfridge said acidly. "And to lying with as many of them as she can take to her bed."

The room fell silent. No one was really shocked by Frances's candor; she was unfailingly blunt when it came to the relationships between men and women, at least when she was among friends. During the first few days of Deborah's acquaintance with the Widows, Nuala had attempted to shield her from Lady Selfridge's more astonishing pronouncements. She had long since abandoned the effort, though she now cast Deborah a probing glance.

"There is one man she will never have," Julia Summerhayes said, startling everyone. As all eyes came to rest on her, the shy young woman ducked her head as if she might disappear into the ill-fitting gown she wore.

"Who is that, Julia?" Maggie said, walking into the drawing room. She plopped into one of the chairs, rubbed at the smudge of paint on her chin and gazed at Julia curiously.

Julia didn't answer at once. Instead, her gaze fell briefly on Nuala, and her brown eyes grew opaque. Nuala appeared not to notice.

"Let me guess," Lillian said with a teasing smile. "Mr. Erskine. I have heard that he absolutely detests the woman."

"So you do occasionally notice what goes on in Society," Clara said.

"Far more than does Maggie, I assure you," Lillian said with a bubbling laugh.

Maggie glanced about, half-bewildered. "More than I do what?" she asked.

"Maggie is fortunate that she has more enriching work than gossip to occupy her thoughts," Frances said.

Nuala shifted uncomfortably. *The portrait,* Deborah thought.

"Julia has not told us who this man is," Deborah said. "I suspect that it must be one of the Forties."

"Why?" Frances asked. "I imagine that most of *them* have already enjoyed Lady Winthrop's favors."

Lillian tittered in a way that was far less annoying than endearing. Tameri, her arms jingling with golden bracelets, permitted herself a smile. "Julia," she said, "you must finish what you began."

But Julia only shrank deeper into her chair. "I...I am very hungry. May we not go in to dinner now?"

Clara laughed. Frances smiled and shook her head. She summoned her butler and soon the ladies were in the dining room, applying themselves to a hearty meal. Frances refused to let any of the Widows pick at their food like frightened sparrows, nor did she hesitate to enjoy her own after-dinner port and cigar.

Tameri left soon afterward, protesting weariness. Maggie simply drifted away, an almost ghostly vision in her loose-fitting Aesthetic gown. Soon Lillian retired, as well. Nuala remained in the dining room, talking with Frances and Clara. Julia sought solitude in the drawing room, where Deborah found her. She chose a seat close to Julia's.

"What did you mean when you said that there was one man that Lady Winthrop could never have?" she asked.

A good meal had brought some color back into Julia's cheeks, and she didn't shrink away at Deborah's question. "It was only foolish speculation," Julia said. "I was wrong to speak of it."

"Why? There is no harm in gossip among friends conversing in a private home." She leaned closer.

"It wasn't just speculation, was it? It was one of your visions."

Julia flinched. "I don't have visions, Deborah," she protested.

"But the spirits speak to you. Clara told me about your last séance. Even she was convinced by it. It is not as if any of us refuses to believe—"

"Why should the spirits inform me about so unimportant a matter as Lady Winthrop's affairs?" Julia said, her eyes snapping with sudden spirit.

"Because it really wasn't about Lady Winthrop at all." Deborah forged ahead, knowing that her own suppositions rested upon the most slender of threads. "I saw you look at Nuala immediately after you spoke."

Julia hesitated. She and Deborah didn't know each other well as yet, nor had Deborah seen evidence of Julia's gifts with her own eyes, but there was no earthly reason why she and Julia shouldn't trust each other.

Mrs. Summerhayes seemed to reach the same conclusion. "You must not share with anyone what I am about to tell you."

"You have my word."

"I am worried about Nuala."

Then I wasn't entirely mad, Deborah thought. "Why are you worried about her, Julia?" she asked.

"I don't know." Julia shook her head. "It is only a feeling, really. Sometimes I glimpse what is in other people's thoughts." She gave Deborah a long look, as if waiting for her reaction. "Does that frighten you?"

Deborah swallowed. "Can you see into my mind?"

"Not now. It usually only happens when someone feels very strong emotions. And I try very hard not to intrude."

Deborah tried to imagine what it must be like to actually know what someone else was thinking, and saw at once how extremely unpleasant it could be. One might hear the ugliest secrets, glimpse the darkest sins that existed among men. How could one live with such intimate knowledge?

"You understand," Julia whispered. "I'm afraid few others would." She smiled, an expression so rare on her face that it turned her from plain to pretty in an instant. "I wish..." She sobered again. "Something is troubling Nuala. Something about her past. People dressed in strange clothing—"

"What sort of clothing?"

"Dark, very plain, with wide collars. And there are people crying. Screaming."

"How horrible! When did you first...hear these thoughts?"

"Just when Nuala came into the room."

And she and Deborah had come directly from viewing Nuala's portrait. The portrait in which Lady Charles had been wearing a dark, plain gown with a wide collar.

"You can't see anything else?"

"Not about that. And I won't force myself into her thoughts. That would be very wrong."

"Of course." Deborah frowned. "What has this to do with Lady Winthrop and the man who won't have her?"

Julia bit her lip. "Have you met Lord Donnington?"

Deborah suppressed her excitement. "Yes. He was at the garden party today."

"I know."

"You were there? But I never saw you!"

Mrs. Summerhayes shrugged. "I am seldom noticed."

"Why did you not tell us you were coming?"

"That isn't important. Lord Donnington did not see me, but I was near him several times. His feelings were so strong that I could not avoid his thoughts."

"And he was thinking of Nuala."

"Yes. In the most violent terms."

"Violent? You mean he wished to harm her?"

"No. At least not…" She took a breath. "Even when he was with other ladies, he did not see them. Only her."

"Then Lord Donnington was the man who would not be interested in Lady Winthrop!"

"It was a foolish thing to say. I have no evidence of this. It was, as I said, only a feeling."

"Perhaps you're right." Deborah placed her hand on Julia's. "Was Nuala thinking of him, too?"

"If she was, I did not sense it." She met Deborah's gaze. "It is none of my business what goes on between them. I shall endeavor to shield myself more effectively next time."

"I am very sorry that it was so unpleasant for you."

Julia smiled again wanly. "One never does get entirely accustomed to it. That is why I seldom go out, you see. I shall not soon attend another party."

"Oh, Julia."

"It's quite all right, Deborah." She glanced up sharply, and after a moment voices sounded in the corridor. By unspoken consent she and Deborah fell into bland conversation, which was soon enlivened by the others who remained…especially by Nuala, who was uncharacteristically voluble. She seemed reluctant to leave Frances's house even after the others had gone.

"It is strange," Deborah said as the carriage clattered toward Grosvenor Street, "that this will be my last night in my husband's house."

Nuala emerged from her reverie and touched Deborah's shoulder. "Does it trouble you greatly?"

"No. Lawrence wouldn't have wanted me to live alone." She hesitated. "Nuala…do you ever wish that you might marry again?"

"The thought has never crossed my mind." She looked more carefully at Deborah. "Has it entered yours, my dear?"

"If it had, I should not belong to the club."

"Deborah…if you find someone to love again, you must not let anyone stop you. All of us know that you are young…."

"And so I cannot know my own mind?"

"Of course you do. No one can doubt it." Nuala leaned back in her seat. "What brought you to broach the subject of marriage?"

"It is hard to avoid it during the Season." She looked sideways at Nuala. "I saw several girls and their chaperons pursuing Lord Donnington at the party."

Nuala showed no signs of agitation. "Ah, yes," she said. "I do not envy the young lady who finally wins him."

"It does not seem as if he would make a very devoted husband."

"He most certainly would not." Nuala seemed to recognize the sudden harshness of her tone and smiled. "But that is neither here nor there."

Isn't it? Deborah thought. But she held her tongue, and soon they were at Deborah's house.

She was very tired as she entered the entrance hall and handed her coat and hat to Jacques. She was prepared to go immediately up to bed, but Jacques stopped her before she reached the stairs.

"Your ladyship," he began, and hesitated.

"What is it, Jacques?"

"Your ladyship, there is a man waiting in the yard. He claims to have a package for you, but has refused to leave it with me. Shall I summon the police?"

"Why should you summon the police? What sort of man is he?"

"He is not a gentleman, your ladyship. If you will pardon my boldness, he is of the sort one might expect to encounter in the rookeries."

The rookeries. Deborah's heart began to beat a little faster. "What does he look like, Jacques?"

"Not tall, your ladyship. Dark. His clothing is not of good quality. I believe he is not English."

"I shall see this man."

"But madam…"

"I believe I may have met him when I accompanied Lady Charles and Lady Selfridge to Whitechapel."

"But for such a man to come here…"

Deborah knew that Jacques's concern for her was real, but she had no patience for it now. "Please ask Stella to meet me in the servants' hall. Should I have any difficulty, she will be within call."

"Very good, your ladyship." He bowed and, with a slight frown, left her. Scarcely waiting for his departure, Deborah dashed downstairs to the basement, paused to smooth her hair and continued on to the servants' hall. She opened the door to the yard, her hand not quite steady on the latch.

CHAPTER SIX

IOAN DAVIES LOOKED UP. He hastily removed his cap, ran a hand over his hair and bowed.

"Madam," he said, "I am sorry to disturb you."

"You are not disturbing me." She smiled. "How are your fingers, Mr. Davies? Improved, I hope?"

He raised his right hand, displaying clean bandages and the splints still in place. "They do very well, madam."

"The wound? It is healing?"

"Yes, Lady Orwell." He cleared his throat. "I came to return this."

He held out his left hand. In it was a brown paper package tied with a bit of string.

"Mr. Davies," Deborah stammered. She took the package without thinking, holding it between numb fingers. "What is this?"

"Your handkerchief, madam." He cleared his throat. "It is not in the same condition as it was when you gave it me, but I did not wish to…" He straightened and held her gaze. "I thank you for the use of it, Lady Orwell."

Deborah looked down at the package. The handkerchief had been soaked with Mr. Davies's blood the last time she had seen it. She knew full well that the stains could not have been entirely removed, especially given the limited resources available to him, and she would not shame the Welshman by unwrapping it here.

"However did you find…how did you learn where I lived?" she asked.

He held his cap in both hands, turning it round and round. "There are many tradesmen who deliver their goods to your door, madam. I am acquainted with one of them."

"Then you do not live…you do not spend all your time in Whitechapel?"

"I was not always without employment," he said, lifting his chin. He returned his cap to his head. "I shall leave you to your rest, madam." He bowed again and turned to go.

"Wait!" She took a step after him, realized what she was doing and stopped, flushing with confusion. "Mr. Davies…"

He faced her again. "Madam?"

"If you are in still in need of employment, perhaps I can make inquiries. We are still seeking men to purchase and transport food and other goods to Whitechapel on a regular basis."

Davies's expression, already so serious, went blank. "I thank you, madam," he said, "but you had better give such employment to those with little ones to feed."

"Mr. Davies…" She swallowed, wishing herself several feet under the earth. "I did not mean to offend."

"Indeed you did not cause any offense, madam." He touched the brim of his cap again. "Good night."

This time when he walked away Deborah made no move to follow. She touched the back of her hand to her face. It was so hot that she longed to duck her head in a bucket of cold water.

How dare he speak to her so? Not only rejecting her offer, but doing so with such rudeness, such...

She sighed. She could almost hear Lawrence gently chiding her for thinking such arrogant thoughts. *"Just because he is poor and a commoner does not make him less worthy of respect."*

"But that does not excuse his discourtesy!" Deborah said aloud.

"Your ladyship?"

Stella ducked her head through the servants' door, her face screwed up in concern.

"It's all right, Stella. I shall be in directly."

The maid went back inside. Deborah slowly untied the twine and opened the neatly wrapped package.

Her handkerchief was stained, just as she had expected. But it was evident to her eyes that Mr. Davies had taken great pains to remove as much of the blood as he could.

She folded the handkerchief and pressed it to her cheek.

NUALA ADJUSTED the wide, flowing sleeves of her crimson medieval gown and paused at the door to the ballroom. She, Deborah and Clara had arrived relatively early to Lady Oxenham's ball; there were few couples on the dance floor, and the dowager Marchioness of Oxenham had not as yet been accosted by the hordes about to descend upon them.

She glanced at Deborah, who was so enchanting in her Georgian gown, all bows and pastels. Clara had chosen the unconventional costume of a Japanese princess, complete with elaborate kimono and a stylized black wig.

"I do not see how you intend to dance in such an ensemble," Deborah said teasingly. "You will be quite hobbled by that robe."

The older woman arched a brow. "But I don't intend to dance. I much prefer observation."

And that, Nuala thought, was what she would have preferred, as well. If it hadn't been for her desire to show her appreciation for Lady Oxenham's friendship, she might have avoided the ball entirely. She had a strong feeling that the earl of Donnington would put in an appearance tonight, in spite of his general disdain for any social event that would compel him to keep company with women in search of husbands.

Over two hundred and forty years, and you are still as nervous as a schoolgirl at her coming-out. The very notion made her angry. She and Sinjin had come to terms, and that was that. She must live with her mistakes, but she had no desire to have them constantly thrown in her face by Lord Donnington.

"Shall we go in?" Clara asked. Without waiting for their agreement, she hobbled into the room and bowed, Japanese-style, to the first woman she met. Nuala and Deborah followed.

Once again Nuala noted the high color Deborah's cheeks. The girl had pretended to have mixed feelings about the ball; though she had left off wearing the usual subdued colors of half-mourning tonight, she projected supreme indifference to the men who noticed her fresh, innocent beauty. Nuala was far from convinced by her display.

Three weeks ago, the girl had spoken almost heatedly of her opposition to the prospect of remarriage. At the time, Nuala had wondered if Deborah had begun to suspect the strength of Nuala's interest in her relationship with Mr. Melbyrne and had been determined to refute any speculation on the matter. Certainly the two young people had only met a few times since the garden party. They had spent no significant time together.

But then again, Lord Donnington was almost always with Melbyrne. That might give any young lady pause. What had Mr. Erskine said? *"He guards his friends' virtue as savagely as Cerberus guards Hades."*

Perhaps Deborah had been discouraged. Perhaps Nuala should have been more supportive. Nevertheless, she had far from given up hope. If Sinjin came to the ball, so would Melbyrne.

Deborah scanned the room with its half-pillared, mirrored walls. Before she could take another step, Lieutenant Richard Osbourne begged the honor of Lady Orwell's hand for the second dance set. Deborah politely agreed.

"It will not be long before every one of your

dances is taken," Nuala said. "You'll spend very little time sitting tonight, I daresay."

Deborah smoothed the wrinkles in her long white glove. "I don't expect that *you* will spend much time as a wallflower, Lady Charles."

Indeed, before another half an hour had passed, Deborah had been approached by a half-dozen male acquaintances, and Nuala by nearly as many. Deborah stayed close to Nuala until the swell of music signaled the first dance, though her gaze continued to wander about the room.

Where was Mr. Melbyrne? Nuala smiled at her first partner, the plump Lord Manwaring, who looked greatly encouraged. "You dance exceptionally well, if I may say so, Lady Charles," Manwaring said.

"As do you, Lord Manwaring. It is always a pleasure to dance with a partner so light on his feet."

The viscount, obviously surprised by the directness of her compliment, looked as if he would have liked to return the favor, but he thought better of it and applied himself to the dance. When it was finished, he escorted her back to her chair, thanked her effusively and offered to fetch her punch.

Nuala agreed absently, her thoughts on something far more important than refreshments. She searched for the pink Georgian gown and found it, situated at a proper distance from a handsome, fair-haired young man wearing the doublet and trunk hose of an Elizabethan gentleman. There was something in Melbyrne's attitude that more than hinted at his pleasure in seeing Deborah again, and *she*...

An older man with thick black side-whiskers came to claim Deborah, and she glanced back at Melbyrne as the distinguished gentleman led her back to the floor. There was no doubt as to the longing in Melbyrne's expression. Deborah's true feelings were shielded by the smile she gave her partner, but Nuala sensed that the girl's mind was not on the dance at all.

The next few sets passed quickly. Nuala's partners were uniformly pleasant and undemanding, though Mr. Hepburn seemed particularly intent on charming her. As odd as it seemed, a few gentlemen seemed to believe that Nuala might be amenable to courtship, or perhaps even a less respectable liaison.

Nuala did nothing to encourage them. She was grateful for a chance to sit out the sixth dance by secreting herself in the corner of the room, where she could watch as Melbyrne and Deborah whirled across the floor. The boy held Deborah a little closer than was quite proper, and Deborah gazed into his eyes with such intensity that she forgot the requisite bland smile.

"Hiding, Lady Charles?"

Mr. Erskine smiled conspiratorially, his easy manner belying the seeming mockery of his question. Nuala let herself relax again and expressed her admiration for Erskine's desert robes.

"It isn't actually a costume," Erskine said. "It was given me as a gift by a sultan in Morocco."

"I didn't know you traveled, Mr. Erskine."

"A trifle, here and there…though I daresay I don't look the type."

"It's always a mistake to judge anyone by appearance," Nuala said.

"You are a perceptive woman, Lady Charles."

"It's only common sense."

He made a little bow. "Would you care to dance, Lady Charles? Or are you perhaps waiting for someone else?"

"Not at all, Mr. Erskine. But I would prefer to talk, if that suits you."

"Would you care for punch?"

By now Nuala was thirsty again, and she accepted Erskine's offer. He had no sooner left her than she heard the familiar voice sounding in the doorway, and her heart skittered into the soles of her dancing shoes. She darted behind a large potted shrubbery just as Sinjin and his companions entered the ballroom and stopped almost directly beside her.

SINJIN COULDN'T FIND HER.

He knew she must be somewhere in the room; she would have been one of the first guests invited by her sister-in-law, and it was unlikely that she would refuse her friend and patroness.

Perhaps she had taken ill. The thought made Sinjin distinctly uncomfortable. He should be thanking Providence if she were absent; he had still not determined how he should respond to her when they met again.

Her supple body, writhing beneath his...

He pulled his hand across his face and remembered the real reason why he had come. It was only a precaution, of course. Melbyrne had seemed wholly indifferent about attending the ball; he had agreed to go at Sinjin's urging, if only to prove that he was done with Lady Orwell once and for all.

"I swear to you, Donnington, I shall not see her again." Melbyrne had made the promise immediately after the dowager duchess's garden party, and then again that very evening. He had listened attentively to Sinjin's repeated warnings that any further marked attention to Lady Orwell would convince Society that he was about to request the young lady's hand in marriage.

Scowling at the very thought, Sinjin looked for the boy. He caught sight of the former Duchess of Vardon, dressed in full Egyptian regalia and gazing out over the crowd with remote approval. Across the room, Lady Meadows—in a costume smothered in flowers made of ribbon and lace—chattered happily to an overwhelmed gentleman of middle age who found it impossible to contribute a single word to the conversation. Lady John Pickering, bound up in a crimson kimono, seemed to challenge the other guests with her blatant lack of convention. As if determined to outdo her friend, Lady Selfridge—whom Sinjin never would have expected to find at a ball— wore the draperies of a Celtic warrioress, complete with crested helmet and golden bands wrapped about her firm, bare arms.

He forgot them all when he saw Lady Orwell. Dressed in a high-waisted gown as frothy as foam, she stood talking with Melbyrne, her fan raised coquettishly, her gaze fixed on his face as if he were the only man in the room. Melbyrne was laughing; his skin was flushed, and he leaned toward his fair companion in such a way that no one could mistake his partiality.

Sinjin permitted himself a single brief moment of disbelief and laughed shortly. After all his years of experience observing the ridiculous posturings of deceitful women and the men they sought to impress, he had nevertheless chosen to believe in Melbyrne's sincerity.

"Look at her," Sir Harry Ferrer said. "She believes she is the superior of every other person in this room."

Sinjin turned to the others, his patience stretched to the breaking point. "To whom are you referring, Ferrer?"

The baronet, looking none too slender in his buccaneer costume, lifted his glass of punch, gave it a sour look and drank. "The dowager Duchess of Vardon," he said. "Sitting in her chair as if it were a throne, putting off every gentleman who has the temerity to request a dance."

Achilles Nash laughed, the metal of his breastplate creaking. "Why the bitterness, Ferrer? Did she refuse your romantic overtures?"

"As if I would have her," Sir Harry said. "But perhaps her kind is more to your taste…if she'd deign to stoop so low."

"Well," Waybury said, "I find Lady Selfridge to be far worse than the dowager. *She* believes that women should have all the rights of men…even the vote."

"Waybury," Sinjin warned. "You will be heard."

"Since when have you cared for the opinion of polite society, Donnington? Or are you getting soft?"

"Pity poor Adele if he is," Nash said with a soft guffaw.

The others chuckled. Ferrer, who was visibly inebriated, gestured with his glass toward Lady Meadows. "And that fat one. She is ridiculous. How any man could ever have wanted *her*…"

Sinjin didn't even begin his intended rebuke. There was movement behind a potted shrubbery less than three yards away. Nuala suddenly emerged, her gray eyes smoldering. She lifted one hand. Her fingers fluttered. The baronet took another sip of his punch, gagged and spat the mouthful all over Waybury's fine silk waistcoat.

There was some fuss afterward, and many curious and censorious faces turned their way as Ferrer cursed and Waybury berated him. Sinjin, never taking his eyes from Nuala, bent to pick up a piece of the broken glass. It smelled strongly of vinegar. While the others were still distracted, he strode to Nuala and stopped so close that she could not hope to get around him.

"What did you do?" he snapped. "What sort of magic turns punch into vinegar?"

She met his eyes without the slightest hesitation. "Perhaps you did not hear what your friends were saying."

"Ferrer was drunk. He didn't know what he was—"

"He knew very well. He obviously shares your contempt for my sex."

"I said nothing!"

"That is precisely the point." She stepped aside to pass him, and he blocked her way again with a sweep of his black cloak.

"You swore you wouldn't use your magic."

"I said nothing of the kind. I promised that I would not use it for the purposes of matchmaking."

"And have you kept *that* promise?"

The music started up again, a Strauss waltz that soon had many couples on the floor. Sinjin bowed sharply to Nuala and, without waiting for her consent, half dragged her out to join them. Her face was red with anger, the color bringing out the dusting of freckles across her nose.

Sinjin had known she would not start a row in public, and she didn't. He took her right hand with his left and clamped his other hand around her waist. He noted at once that her corset had not been tightly laced; she was breathing easily, and there was a suppleness to her movements not encumbered by a woman's restrictive undergarments.

The thought of Nuala's undergarments momentarily distracted Sinjin from his purpose. Though their gloves prevented their skin from touching, he could feel her warmth and the slender strength of her fingers. Her blush had reached nearly to her breasts, small but ripe under her bodice. Her breathing was rapid, the way a woman's might be during the act of love.

She was lying beneath him, her legs wrapped around his waist, her moans like music....

He missed a step, and Nuala nearly stumbled. He righted her again, losing his composure when he could least afford to do so. He squeezed her hand more tightly.

"How often have you used your magic since we last spoke?" he demanded as he guided her into a sweeping turn.

Her jaw was set, and she took her time about answering. "Tonight was the first time," she said.

"And what else have you done tonight besides wreaking revenge on Ferrer and Waybury?"

"I have done nothing."

The music came to a stop. Sinjin heard it as if from a great distance; all his attention was focused on the sea-mist-gray of Nuala's eyes. Only the movement of others away from the floor prompted him to take Nuala to the chairs along the wall.

"Nothing?" he repeated, bowing automatically as he waited for her to be seated.

She remained standing. "What am I supposed to have done?" she asked.

With a hand at her elbow, he turned her to face the far corner of the room. Melbyrne and Lady Orwell were still engrossed in their conversation.

"This evening," he said, "Melbyrne swore to me that he would have nothing further to do with Lady Orwell. Tonight I see him spending so much time with her that it is likely to cause a scandal if he does not propose. What have you to say to that?"

She smiled. "You are angry," she said. "I was told that you guarded your disciples most assiduously.

Does it trouble your pride that Mr. Melbyrne has slipped the leash?"

He had not meant to reveal so much, but perhaps it had been inevitable. "He's far too young to know what he's doing," he said. "I won't have him caught in the snares of one of your 'widows.'"

"You can't bear the prospect of losing one of your pupils to love."

"Love? The world would be a better place if the people in it gave up on the notion entirely."

"You are wrong, Sinjin. You and I may be perfectly content without it, but we have no right to impose our choices on anyone else."

"Impose *our* choices? Did you bring them together, Nuala? Did you work your spells to subvert young Melbyrne?"

Her breast heaved with outrage. "I did not. I did nothing to discourage Lady Orwell, but she and Melbyrne found each other without my assistance. Perhaps your judgment of your friends is not as accurate as you should wish."

Sinjin fumed. He could not bring himself to call her a liar. That she was capable of some sort of magic was no longer in any doubt. How she used it…

Could she bring a man dreams? Could she make him loathe and desire her at the same moment, burn him alive in the ravenous flames of her own dark creation?

Someone cleared his throat behind Sinjin. "I beg your pardon," the young man said, "but I believe I have the honor of this dance, Lady Charles."

Nuala smiled brightly at Mr. Keaton, took his hand

and swept past Sinjin. Sinjin was not so far gone as to try to stop her. He shook himself, taking a firmer grip on his senses. He was a rational man. A dream was a dream, no more. She had no control over *him*.

But she was still quite capable of making considerable mischief. She was determined to cause trouble, and he couldn't be sure of the extent of her resources. He must bring his own to bear as forcefully as he might lest she begin to believe she had the right to meddle further.

Pasting a bland smile on his face, he found one of the prettiest girls in the room and asked her to dance. She was like a bit of flotsam in his arms, weightless in both body and mind. He took her back to her chaperon and watched as Lady Charles walked out onto the floor with another partner. She was grace itself, almost as if she had worked a spell meant to keep her feet from ever touching the ground.

His cock grew hard. He willed it to subside, but it refused to cooperate, and he was obliged to sit out the next dance.

Damn the woman. Damn her to hell.

CHAPTER SEVEN

DEBORAH WATCHED NUALA and Lord Donnington as they conversed at the side of the ballroom. It was the first time she'd noticed the earl's presence; he was dashing in his highwayman's costume, complete with black domino, but she would have recognized him anywhere.

Melbyrne, claiming his second dance, spun her about the floor. She was glad of the diversion. For the past fortnight her mind had been disturbed by thoughts of a man she'd scarcely met. Mr. Melbyrne drove all such inappropriate distractions from her mind.

Almost.

"I notice," she said to Felix as he led her in another neat turn, "that Lady Charles and Lord Donnington have been spending some time together."

Felix, who had been gazing into her eyes, glanced around the room until he found the couple in question. "I say," he said. "That *is* amusing."

"How is it amusing?" Deborah asked casually.

"Because Donnington keeps claiming to dislike her."

"Isn't it often true that dislike conceals quite the opposite emotions?"

"Such a possibility had occurred to me. Still, Donnington…" He shook his head.

Indeed. If Deborah hadn't been fully convinced by Julia Summerhayes's feelings on the matter, she would still be doubting that Lord Donnington was capable of really appreciating a woman of Nuala's intelligence and somewhat reserved nature.

"I can't think of two people more ill-suited," Felix continued. "Sinjin mistrusts your friends, you know. He believes they are all intent on catching new husbands. In fact, he has told me—" He broke off, flushing deeply. "I beg your pardon, Lady Orwell. I spoke out of turn."

"Not at all. We have been frank with one another on many subjects, have we not?"

Relief washed the tension from his face. "It is very odd that Donnington would spend so much time with Lady Charles, who certainly does not appear to be the sort—" He broke off again, stammering in consternation.

Deborah was not particularly embarrassed by Felix's gaffes. There was something rather endearing about his tendency to forget that there were some subjects one must never broach with a proper young lady.

But what he'd said was correct. Society might interpret any show of partiality between Nuala and Lord Donnington in one of two ways: they could focus on the earl's dubious reputation and assume that he was testing the waters with the young widow, or they could speculate that he had given up his vow to avoid marriage for as long as possible.

Nuala must be just as aware of the danger as Lord Donnington. In the past few days, Deborah had heard rumors that the two had been seen going off together at Lady Vardon's garden party. Certainly Nuala had seemed somewhat agitated after she and Deborah had left the party. But it did not appear to Deborah that Nuala had made a concerted effort to escape Donnington's company.

Deborah had known that she herself ran the same risk of provoking gossip by spending so much time with Melbyrne. However, since the onus would be on him should Society expect an impending union between them, he must be the one to place limits on their friendship. And *he* obviously had no concerns about giving the wrong impression.

He was just what she needed now. She had even toyed with the possibility that she was falling in love with him. It seemed highly unlikely, but she was not prepared to cast the notion aside just yet. She was increasingly certain that Nuala would like nothing better than to see her and Mr. Melbyrne together on a more permanent basis.

But is that what I want?

The very fact that she was considering it was proof that she had changed greatly in only a few weeks. Perhaps the change was due to her getting to know Felix Melbyrne so well.

Or perhaps it had been engendered by something—some*one*—else entirely.

She beamed at Mr. Melbyrne and laughed brightly. "Let Lord Donnington look after himself," she said. "We have better things to do!"

NUALA COULD FEEL Sinjin as if he were part of her.

She felt him as he danced with the pretty young debutante who gazed into his face with blind adoration. She felt him when he took another young lady to the refreshment table and plied her with punch, as gallant as a knight out of Sir Walter Scott. She felt him as he spoke in leisurely tones to his fellow Forties...excluding the awful man who had spoken so ill of the Widows. *He* had retreated to repair the damage to his clothing, as had Lord Waybury.

Nuala felt no regret about what she'd done, though she was well aware what her success portended. First there had been the event in Whitechapel, and now this. When she had called up the spell, she'd had no idea that it would work. When it had, no one could have been more surprised than she.

Still, it was much too soon to assume that her abilities were actually returning, not in any reliable fashion. It *was* a matter of concern that once again the magic had come because of her anger, always a dangerous motivation in the use of a witch's power, even though she had used it in response to some offense to her friends.

Sinjin had been quick to assume that she had

broken her word to him and had used her abilities to bring Deborah and Melbyrne together. But that accusation was not what had disturbed her most. In confronting her with such a claim, he had reconfirmed her belief that he was deliberately trying to keep the two young people apart.

Only half aware of her current partner's dull conversation, she watched as Sinjin led another unmarried girl to the floor. It was almost as if he were mocking both them *and* her, knowing full well he would never give any of these children a second glance. Yet the young women continued to melt in his arms, as if each one believed that she alone would win his love and fidelity.

Nuala smiled, nodded at her escort's compliments and was about to summon up a suitable reply when Mr. Erskine arrived. He nodded to Mr. Roaman, bowed to Nuala and begged her hand.

Nothing would have given Nuala more pleasure. She felt the warmth of Mr. Erskine's hand lightly resting on her back. His company, unlike Sinjin's, was entirely comfortable.

The orchestra struck up a polka. They began the dance without speaking; it was vigorous enough to silence most of the dancers, save for the occasional brief comment. But it wasn't long before Erskine overcame the breathless pace and addressed her.

"Did you enjoy your dance with Donnington?" he asked.

The question startled her. It was an odd thing for Mr. Erskine to ask, though his tone suggested indifference.

"He is an excellent dancer," she said, "though I understand he seldom attends such entertainments."

"That's quite true," Erskine said after a pause for breath. "What makes his attendance tonight so peculiar is that his behavior for the past fortnight has been very odd. He's often in a temper, irritable with his friends and acquaintances."

"I beg your pardon, but I have not been much impressed with his temper in general," she said bluntly. "I wonder that his friends and acquaintances put up with it."

Mr. Erskine's face took on a thoughtful expression. "I assure you, Lady Charles…whatever you may think of him, he is ordinarily a gentleman in every respect."

"*Every* respect, Mr. Erskine?"

He squeezed her hand. "I would be greatly honored if you would call me Leo."

It was a rather forward request, given the brevity of their acquaintance, but Nuala liked him too much to refuse.

"Leo," she said. "You may call me Nuala."

"Excellent." He smiled and rubbed the slightly dented bridge of his nose. "And in answer to your previous question…until recently, I have never seen him behave discourteously towards a woman."

"Oh, I promise you…" She broke off, realizing what she was about to reveal. "I must take your word for that, Mr. Erskine. You know him far better than I."

"Yet he sought you out to dance," Erskine mused.

Nuala pretended not to be distressed by his open

speculation, decidedly wrong as it was. She took the opportunity to gather her thoughts as the dance spiraled toward its triumphant climax.

Mr. Erskine had not forgotten the trend of his conversation. "You said you had first met Donnington in Hyde Park several weeks ago," he said as he led her away from the floor. "Yet I cannot help but wonder…"

"We are not friends, I assure you," she said. "If you will forgive me, I find Lord Donnington's habits and preferences a tedious subject. If he is irritable, perhaps it is because he has not practiced his favorite hobby frequently enough of late."

The words were out of her mouth before she could take them back, but Leo didn't seem overly disturbed by her allusion. "It's true," he murmured, as if to himself. "I don't believe he has seen much of Adele lately."

Now that the delicate subject had been broached, Nuala couldn't contain her curiosity. "Adele is his…current companion?"

"Hmm." Erskine seemed to remember that she had asked him a question and hesitated, searching her eyes. "You would not know her. She does not generally run in the best circles. But she has been with Donnington for some time."

Nuala's skin grew a little warm. *In for a penny, in for a pound.* "I was given to understand that Lord Donnington is disinclined to be faithful to anyone."

"Oh, it is not entirely an exclusive arrangement…." He paused again. "I should not wish to offend you, Nuala."

"You have not."

"Mrs. Chaplin is well compensated for her tolerance of his other interests."

In other words, he couldn't even be satisfied with the woman he paid for his physical ease. Nuala shivered, remembering the possessive pressure of his hand at her waist. She had thought it might burn through bodice and corset and chemise, leaving her gasping and naked on the dance floor.

Erskine smiled. "I find it very refreshing to speak to a woman free of the missish qualities so prevalent in our society. A woman who recognizes the world as it is."

Nuala thought it better not to speak, but Leo wasn't finished. "You weren't really just a nurse to Lord Charles, were you? Or a vicar's daughter, as the rumors claim."

"I have been many things, Leo. I have lived in many places. Coming to Lord Charles was the end of my long journey. I was happy to be his wife for the short time we were together."

"Ah. I suspected as much."

"What did you suspect?"

"That you were not quite of this world. In the best possible sense."

"You aren't troubled by the possibility that I may not entirely belong to the realm of good Society?"

"Why should I be? I find your company most stimulating."

Nuala parsed his words for a deeper meaning and decided that he was not indicating a desire for anything more than friendship. She smiled warmly and glanced around the ballroom, looking for Deborah and Melbyrne.

She couldn't see them. But she did see Sinjin, who was staring at her and Erskine with such an evil look that, had he been a witch prone to black magic, would have struck the subject of his attention dead on the spot.

"I think I should like more punch," Nuala said.

Erskine glanced the way she had been looking. "May I escort you, Nuala?"

She took his offered arm with a deliberation meant to defy Sinjin's glare. When Erskine returned her to her chair, Sinjin had vanished.

Her disappointment made no sense at all. She was *glad* to see him gone. When she looked for Deborah, she found the young woman standing at the landing, gazing down at the cavernous entrance hall.

"Where is Mr. Melbyrne?" Nuala asked.

Deborah glanced up, her usually open expression unreadable. "He has left," she said, "along with Lord Donnington."

"Did the earl compel Mr. Melbyrne to leave?"

"He…he respects Lord Donnington a great deal."

In other words, yes. Nuala could picture the scene all too clearly. She closed her eyes and silenced her almost violent thoughts. "Was he in any way discourteous to you?"

"No. Not to me."

Of course not. He was a "gentleman," at least where some women were concerned. He would have been coldly but quite properly polite as he wrenched the two young lovers apart. "I am sorry, Deborah. I could see that you were enjoying your time together."

When Lady Orwell didn't answer, Nuala opened her eyes and searched the young, guileless face. "You will see him again," she said, placing a comforting hand on Deborah's arm. "The earl will not always be present to…inhibit your conversations with Mr. Melbyrne."

"Oh, but I… You must not think…" Deborah's cheeks flamed, and she appeared genuinely distressed.

"You need not hide your feelings from me, whatever they may be," Nuala said.

Deborah's pretty mouth opened, but she thought better of whatever she had been about to say. "It is nearly time for supper," she said at last, "but I am not hungry. Mightn't we leave early?"

"I should be glad to," Deborah said, accepting the change of subject. She asked a footman to summon their carriage. She and Deborah took their leave of Lady Oxenham, with thanks for the lovely evening, and then set out for home.

They were both too preoccupied to talk when they arrived. Deborah went up to her room. Nuala followed more slowly, considering everything she had observed that evening.

There was no doubt that Donnington was a formidable opponent, but Deborah was a girl of considerable spirit despite her reticence. Had she been more conventional, she would never have insisted on accompanying Nuala and Frances to Whitechapel. And she would not have spent so much time talking with

Melbyrne in a public venue. Surely she was capable of ignoring Lord Donnington's disapproval where her heart was engaged.

But she could not do it alone.

Unable to quell her speculation, Nuala allowed Booth to undress her. But as she stood half-naked in her stays and drawers, her imagination was at pains to prevent any consideration of sleep.

Curse the man. There, she could say the words without any fear that they might take real shape and form, could she not? She could rationally calculate how best to counteract his interference without breaking her promise to use magic she was not even certain she possessed.

She rubbed at her bare arms while Booth slipped from the room to fetch a light supper. Nuala's reflection in the mirror seemed to belong to some other woman: generously curved, full of bosom and hips, thick auburn hair falling to her waist. But her body had not really changed. Only her perception of it.

It was as if she were seeing it through Sinjin's eyes. Sinjin, here in this very room, gazing at her with naked lust, his strong hands ready to strip the remaining clothing from her body.

Nuala laughed in chagrin. Patently ridiculous. Though she had not been able to help but notice that some men in Society did seem to admire her appearance, Sinjin did not, *could* not want her. Nor could she want a man like *him*, no matter how long it had been since she had experienced a man's intimate touch.

She felt a gush of wetness between her thighs, an

ache of desire, treacherous sensations so overwhelming that she feared she might actually swoon. Until very recently—until she had come to London, in fact—she had nearly forgotten that her body had its own demands, too long neglected.

Charles, of course, had been unable to engage in physical intimacies; when she had agreed to marry him, after months of living at his estate as his nurse, she had known there would be no sexual aspect to their union.

Christian had been different. He had been a sensitive, gentle lover, generous with his own magical gifts, working alongside her for the brief time they had been married—so long before Donbridge, before Charles had come into her life. And he had been a truly good man, not like—

She tried not to think at all as Booth relieved her of her corset and left her to put on her nightdress. But now that the floodgates had opened, it was impossible not to imagine what it might mean to become a woman again, in every sense.

The bed creaked under her weight as she sat on the edge of the mattress. It wasn't as if she had *never* experienced sexual pleasure since her marriage to Christian. There had been that one time, a century ago, when she had sought and given comfort, without guilt or regret, and known that Christian would not have disapproved.

A century ago. That single encounter had seemed enough for so long. Close involvement with any man would have compromised her work, and so she had simply shut down that part of herself. Charles had certainly demanded nothing of her, had been quite unable to do so. She could have gone another century quite happily devoid of any sexual feelings whatsoever. But that was no longer possible.

Nuala crawled under the sheets, returned Booth's murmured good-night and drew the counterpane up to her chin. If her body's arousal was becoming an annoying distraction, surely she could find a way to dispose of it. London society was certainly not devoid of opportunities to do so.

True, she thought little of the Forties and their determination to use women as mere objects of pleasure; she might even look askance at those women, already possessed of husbands and children, who chose to ignore their vows of fidelity. But she was no prude. She had witnessed sexual congress in all its variations, and she knew that human nature could not always be constrained by law or custom.

No…she had no rational objection to giving her body what it demanded, if such an act would permit her to think clearly again. The trick was to do so without emotional entanglements beyond those of mutual pleasure and goodwill. There were certainly decent men who didn't share Sinjin's contempt for women. Mr. Erskine, for one.

Leo. A gentleman, frank and honest. Could he be interested in such a liaison? She had not thought so before, but if she were to make the approach… Would it ruin their new friendship? That was a prospect Nuala couldn't bear to contemplate. And she simply could not think of him in that sense, even if he might find her desirable.

That sense. Once again Sinjin leaped into her mind: the feel of his strong body pressed to hers, the grip of his hand, the heat of his dark gaze…

She cast desperately about for another candidate. Lord Manwaring, who had seemed to enjoy her company so much at the ball? Would she shock him with such a proposal, and would he broadcast it about? She didn't know him at all. And it was the same with every other man of her brief acquaintance she considered.

The counterpane became uncomfortably warm. She shed it, only to become even more aware of the shape of her body beneath the thin lawn of her nightdress. The solution would come to her eventually, and until then she would simply have to bear with the discomfort. She had certainly endured much worse in the past.

Nevertheless, her sleep was restless and her dreams, formless as they were upon her awakening, no little disturbing. She was up early, downstairs before Cook had done more than light the stove in preparation for breakfast.

DEBORAH DIDN'T MAKE an appearance until breakfast was ready, and remained preoccupied after the usual exchange of pleasantries. Despite her desire to draw the girl out, Nuala kept her own council. She bent her mind to considering the day's obligations: the social calls to be made, consultation with Frances over the new scheme for Whitechapel, the engagement of skilled workmen to install modern plumbing in the upstairs lavatory.

And if that didn't keep her busy enough, she could shop in Regent Street, or ride in Hyde Park or indulge herself in any number of the frivolities necessary to maintain her position as Lord Charles would have wished.

Deborah assured her that she had her own plans for the morning, and would see Nuala that evening at Lady Selfridge's house. After the girl had left, Nuala asked Booth to help her dress in a modest morning gown and dashed out of the house with almost feverish eagerness.

Nevertheless, when she returned from her errands, she did not feel in the least refreshed. In spite of her best intentions, resentment still seethed in her chest. Resentment against the man so bent on ruining Deborah's chances out of his own selfish spite.

How *dare* he. How dare he believe Nuala to be a liar. How dare he play these foolish games with the innocent hearts of others.

She came to a halt halfway down the stairs. Did he think he could defeat her so easily? Did he actually believe that this petty revenge for what he perceived as her past sins would go unchallenged? Did he want a war?

She gripped the banister. A war? Was that how low she had sunk?

It is not about my feelings. It is not.

A little dizzy, she continued into her study to read

the morning mail. There were a few bills, and the usual invitations. But there was also a letter marked only with her direction. She opened it with an odd start of anticipation.

My dear Lady Charles,
Having become aware of your keen interest in the friendship of Mr. Melbyrne and Lady Orwell, I thought it prudent to inform you that Lord Donnington intends to keep young Melbyrne away from London as long as required to end any partiality he might hold for the lady.

The note was not signed, but Nuala immediately guessed who might have sent it.

Leo Erskine. Perceptive, observant, well aware of the earl's scheming nature. Clearly he, in addition to proving himself a true friend, did not feel obliged to abet his other friend's interference in a promising relationship between two good-hearted people.

Then again, perhaps he only intended to suggest that Nuala warn Deborah away from any hopes of a lasting connection with Felix Melbyrne. But if that were the case, why tell Nuala at all? The boy's extended absence would speak for itself.

Nuala considered going to Leo for further details and decided against it. There was but one logical place Sinjin would go, a place he would scarcely expect Nuala to follow even were she inclined to pursue the matter.

To Donbridge, of course. The very house where

Nuala had brought Mariah and Ash together. Where she had seen her most devastating failure.

She set the note down on her secretary and stood very still. He would get away with it. He would bet on her fear of confronting him where she would be forced to relive her mistakes.

And she *was* afraid. The very idea of returning to Donbridge made her mouth go dry and her hands tremble. But she would not retreat, even knowing her resources to be more limited than at any other time of her life. She'd been a fool not to demand some concession from Sinjin when they'd struck their "bargain" at the garden party. Now Melbyrne had only the devil's voice to persuade him of the proper course, without an angel to show him an alternative path.

Nuala laughed at the idea that she was or ever had been an angel. But Sinjin was attempting to stop what was in essence an act of nature. In doing so, he was no better than she, with her magic and matchmaking.

The fulfillment of Deborah's love required no magic whatsoever. Only steadfast friendship, and a little courage. No less than the courage she had demanded from those she had guided through the centuries.

She locked Erskine's note in a drawer and sent immediately for Harold.

CHAPTER EIGHT

MRS. TISSIER SPARKLED UP at Melbyrne with the most delicious look in her eye, lifted her glass of champagne and saluted her new conquest.

"To Mr. Felix Melbyrne," she said, sipping the champagne with a coquettishness as unconvincing as a tiger's smile. "Many happy returns of the day!"

Everyone followed her lead, though Melbyrne's answering salute was annoyingly halfhearted. By all the gods, Sinjin thought...the boy ought to be grateful for such a present on his twenty-third birthday. One of the loveliest courtesans in London had just been thrown in his lap, ready and willing, and he couldn't even muster more than a polite interest, let alone healthy lust.

Sinjin wasn't the only one of the Forties who had noticed Felix's inexplicable reticence. Achilles Nash regarded him with a satirical eye, Sir Harry Ferrer was sneering, Lord Peter Breakspear looked from the boy to Jennie with a raised brow and Lords Waybury and Reddick had been engaged in a low-voiced conversation almost since Mrs. Tissier's "unexpected" arrival.

Even Jennie was puzzled, though not yet put out. She turned her smile on Sinjin, rustled to the sideboard and asked him to refill her glass.

"Are you quite certain the boy is up to this?" she asked in a low voice. "You assured me that he would be…eager to begin his education."

"He is," Sinjin said, trying to keep the annoyance out of his voice. "This will be his first time, Jennie."

"Astonishing." She twirled the stem of her glass in her fingers. "Such a personable young man, and he has never…" She gave an exaggerated sigh. "Still, I do like the young ones. Their naive enthusiasm is so very gratifying."

"I have no doubt that he will prove most satisfactory."

"Are you quite sure *you* wouldn't prefer to take his place?" Jennie purred, leaning into him so that her ample breasts filled the crook of his arm. "We did have such good times together."

"You will remember that I am otherwise engaged," Sinjin said gruffly.

"As if that ever stopped you!" She glanced back at Felix and raised her glass. "There has never been one like you, Sin. You fill a woman in a way she can't forget. A night or two…and I wouldn't ask for anything but your company."

Remarkably, in spite of the heat of Jennie's body and the suggestive dart of her tongue between her rosy lips, Sinjin felt no stirring. His body was usually eager to respond to any offer of sex, or even the hint of a possibility, but it lay dormant now.

It's Adele I need. It had been too long, and he required…

Bloody hell. He didn't *need* a reminder of his manhood. It was Melbyrne who seemed to have forgotten he had parts other than a pair of mooncalf eyes.

Parts. Breasts with nipples erect, round thighs parted, the moist pinkness of lips never meant for speech—

Unaccountably and without warning, Sinjin's cock began to swell. It had nothing to do with Jennie's nearness, and everything to do with the dreams.

The dreams that had only grown stronger since the night of the ball. The dreams of fire, and lust and hatred. They had come nearly every night, and in each one of them Nuala had appeared, naked and shameless, offering herself to him when he would have taken her in violence.

And there was the voice. Disembodied, alien, urging him to vanquish the witch, to humiliate her, to destroy…

I am going mad.

"Sinjin?"

Jennie's voice was laced with concern, and he snapped out of the false memories, feeling the heaviness of the perspiration beaded on his forehead and the weight of his aching cock. He pushed Jennie away gently, but with a firmness she could not mistake.

"You should return to Mr. Melbyrne, madam," he said hoarsely, "and work your considerable charms on him."

Her gaze dropped to his trousers, and her eyes

narrowed. "If you insist," she said, mockery ringing in her words. She flounced away and took Felix's arm, as rosy-cheeked and adoring as any debutante. Melbyrne flushed.

"You may have pushed a little too hard this time, Sin," Breakspear said in Sinjin's ear. "The boy seems paralyzed. Jennie's too experienced by half for a lad of his...modesty."

Sinjin uttered a soft expletive, as much at himself as at the situation with Melbyrne. "He was perfectly fine until—" He broke off, but Breakspear was ahead of him.

"Lady Orwell." Breakspear chuckled. "From what I've been hearing, it appears that she is no more committed to the Widows' creed than Melbyrne is to ours."

It was just as Sinjin had feared. The gossip mills were already hard at work speculating over the excessive time Felix and Lady Orwell had spent together at the ball. The damage would not easily be undone, but now that Melbyrne was away...

"I've also heard it said that you and Lady Charles have been seen in company on more than one occasion."

"Lady Charles!" Sinjin turned his immediate scowl into a scornful smile. "I spoke with her at the dowager duchess's garden party and danced with her at Lady Oxenham's ball. It was no more than a matter of common courtesy. I have no liking for the woman, nor her for me."

"Such vehemence, Sin. One might almost think—"

Hedley all but burst into the room, his air of dignity spoiled by the strands of gray hair askew on his head and the slight breathlessness with which he spoke.

"My lord," he said, hastily straightening his coat, "there is a caller at the door. I have attempted to detain her, but I fear…"

A chill caught hold of Sinjin and shook him as a dog shakes a rat. "Who is it, Hedley?"

The poor man had no chance to answer. Lady Charles Parkhill swept into the room, elegant in a deep green carriage dress and a smart velvet toque. She stopped just inside the doorway to the drawing room, glanced from face to startled face—lingering on an astonished Mrs. Tissier—and settled her stare on Sinjin. She performed a brief and very shallow curtsey.

"Lord Donnington," she said. "I pray you will forgive this intrusion. I had not realized you had company."

Sinjin was thunderstruck. His tongue refused to move. He saw her not as she was now, respectably and unremarkably dressed, but as she had been in the dream…naked, glistening with power, opening herself to him. Threatening to suck him down into her very depths. Lust and rage took hold of him again, and he spent the next minute battling it to a standstill.

Achilles was the first to break the stunned silence. "My dear Lady Charles," he said, "I am certain that Lord Donnington will welcome such a charming addition to our little gathering, as will the rest of us."

Still no one else spoke, though Waybury was clearly scandalized and even Breakspear wore a frown. There were scarcely words enough to describe the social conventions the lady had broken by coming alone to a bachelor's country establishment in such a fashion, without showing even so much as the courtesy of waiting to be invited.

"Lady Charles," Sinjin said in his iciest tone, "it is a pity I was unaware of your intention to visit Donbridge. You find me quite unprepared to provide the hospitality a lady such as yourself deserves."

The insult did not go unnoticed. Reddick made a faint sound of protest. Ferrer snickered. Felix started from his paralysis and spoke with scarcely a glance at Sinjin.

"Lady Charles," he said, "you must be tired from your ride. Would you care to be seated?"

Everyone looked at Sinjin, who had every right to be incensed at the boy's usurpation of his privileges as host. But he recognized that the battle was at least temporarily lost.

"By all means, Lady Charles. Pray make yourself comfortable." He turned to Hedley, who remained as frozen as the rest. "Kindly see to suitable refreshments, Hedley."

The butler bowed and hastily exited the drawing room. Sinjin's words freed the others; several moved generally in Lady Charles's direction, awaiting introductions. Nash—who had little regard for the niceties of protocol—already seemed overly attentive to the female intruder. Melbyrne's face had regained its color. Even without a supportive word from Lady Charles, he'd already surmised that he'd acquired an ally.

But there would be no further pleasantries beyond introductions, no encouragement to support Felix's rebellion or Nuala's outrageous behavior. The very fact that the woman had dared to come to Donbridge at all had temporarily set Sinjin back on his heels, but no longer.

Lady Charles was perfectly charming as Sinjin did his duty, expressing her pleasure at meeting each of the gentlemen, though Waybury was still a bit stiff with disapproval. But Breakspear continued to give Sinjin probing looks…and in light of what Lord Peter had said of recent gossip, Sinjin knew that his own reputation as one of the Forties was in very grave danger.

So was Lady Orwell's, but in an entirely different manner. Her actions would almost certainly be judged "fast" by sticklers in Society, and it would take only a casual word from one of the Forties to make those actions known. As a widow, she was granted more latitude than an unmarried girl, but she was herself young and childless.

Lord Donnington was the last person she ought to be visiting alone. And she must know it.

Deliberately Sinjin went to Mrs. Tissier, took her hand and led her to Nuala.

"Lady Charles," he said, "May I present Mrs. Jennie Tissier."

Jennie blanched a little. Very little could faze her, but a formal introduction between a lady and a courtesan was simply not done. Reddick murmured another belated protest, and Jennie clutched at her skirts.

Nuala must have heard of Mrs. Tissier; she must

have known that the woman lived beyond the pale of polite society. Had she acted in her own best interest, she would have returned a cool nod and walked away, as any true lady would. Instead, she offered her hand.

"Mrs. Tissier," she said.

With a smile of rare humility, Jennie took Nuala's hand. The contact was brief, but telling. Since Lady Charles's arrival, the Forties would have been madly speculating on the nature of her relationship to Sinjin. Now that she had shown a willingness to associate with a known courtesan, her intention in coming to Donbridge alone must be clear.

If it were too late, as it surely was, to convince the Forties that he and Lady Charles were no more than acquaintances, Sinjin still had the means of protecting himself…and driving Nuala away once and for all.

While general talk continued, Mrs. Tissier retreated into another room and the Forties hovered about Lady Charles in a haze of uncertainty. Her presence suppressed the usual blunt conversation of men safe from the constraints of "good" female society, but her ambiguous position gave her an aura of fascination that brought Waybury under her thrall.

Magic. Just as she had done to Sinjin his dreams, she was working her spell on men who should have been wholly immune. If they regarded her as fair game…

Sinjin was alternately tempted to scatter the men with a roar or wring Lady Charles's slender neck. He was considering how best to get her alone without engendering more mistaken assumptions when Nash solved his dilemma with a suggestion of his own.

"I don't know about the rest of you gents," he said, drawing the men's attention, "but I'm up for a good ride. What is the point of rustication without a show of horsemanship?"

The Forties exchanged glances. It was late afternoon, several hours before dinner, and the conversation had dwindled to stilted discussions of the weather.

"I think that an excellent idea," Sinjin said. "Would you care to join us, Lady Charles? Or are you too fatigued by your journey from London?"

In answer, Nuala rose and brushed out her skirts. "To the contrary, Lord Donnington. I should be perfectly happy to join you."

"Then, unless you have brought your habit, I am certain that Mrs. Tissier will be delighted to lend you hers."

The Forties held their collective breath, but Nuala merely inclined her head.

"If Mrs. Tissier agrees, I shall be glad to accept the loan."

A sigh swept through the room. Sinjin imagined that it was made up partly of approval for Lady Charles's broadmindedness, and renewed interest in the increasingly likely prospect that she was indicating her availability for certain pleasurable connections.

Whatever their thoughts, the Forties threw themselves enthusiastically into the promise of a ride, retiring to their rooms to change. Melbyrne was nearly bouncing with renewed energy. Sinjin knew there would be no chance to confront Nuala before the outing, but that wasn't necessary. The ride itself would provide the opportunity.

As expected, Mrs. Tissier declined to join the others and freely offered the use of her habit. Though she was a little taller than Nuala, the habit proved a surprisingly good fit, as Sinjin had cause to notice when Lady Charles emerged from the room hastily prepared for her in the wing opposite that inhabited by the Forties.

The men had loosened up considerably now that a certain informality had been established, and there were jests and a few indiscreet comments flung about the stable while the horses were assigned. Sinjin had no notion of the extent of Nuala's riding abilities; he instructed the head groom to provide Nuala with a sedate mare who would never throw her or balk at a reasonable jump. He didn't want Nuala discomposed in any way. He wanted her fresh and alert when he faced her down, under no disadvantage when he finally defeated her.

Nuala proved herself to be an excellent horsewoman. She rode with back erect, her hands light on the reins. It seemed at first that she would resist any attempt he made at separating her from the rest. But she provided the opportunity herself. After an hour of riding, when her attentive escorts were distracted by a particularly fine view of the river Ouse, Nuala abruptly turned her mount away from the others at a fast clip.

Sinjin was close behind her. She made no attempt to escape him; once they were beyond the view of the

Forties, she slowed and allowed him to catch her up. He reined Shaitan to a halt in a copse of hazel, prepared to help her dismount. She was already down before he could take two steps in her direction.

Her hair had come partly undone, ginger strands flowing around her face. Her posture was as bold as it had been in the house, but there was a vulnerability in her face that momentarily caused him to hesitate in his attack.

"How dare you come here," he said softly.

Her breast rose as she drew in a breath. "How dare *you* take Melbyrne away?"

They stared at each other. Sinjin's cock, which had relaxed during the ride, was at full attention again, and he despised his loss of control.

Flames curled around her like a lover's fingers....

"Since you are here," he said harshly, "would you care to see Giles's grave?"

Her cheeks turned paper white. She closed her eyes and took a half step sideways, as if she might fall. Sinjin closed the gap between them and caught her arm. Fire licked at his palm.

"Sit," he commanded, throwing his riding coat on the ground. She was stubborn; she didn't give way until he compelled her.

He released her arm as soon as he could safely do so. An apology hovered on his tongue, but he swallowed it. He owed her no such consideration. Yet he knew by her trembling that she did had not come to Donbridge without great trepidation, for all her boldness. She did not wish to be here at all.

"It won't work," he said, setting a careful distance between them again.

She seemed to recover a little, the color slowly seeping back into her cheeks. "Are you so certain that your scheme will?"

"I have no scheme."

"You stole Mr. Melbyrne away just to keep him from spending time with Lady Orwell."

There would have been no purpose in denial even if he had felt inclined to offer one. "I did as I thought best."

"Then you do believe I am a liar."

"I believe you will do whatever you can to encourage Lady Orwell."

The mist-gray eyes held his, warming with anger. "It was as I told you. I did not and will not use magic in this matter."

"Perhaps you can't help yourself."

She gathered her feet beneath her and tried to stand, her legs becoming tangled in her skirts. It was more than habit to assist her, to take her arm again and let her lean upon it until she was on her feet.

This time she was the one to shake him off. "I am in perfect command of myself," she said. "But I will not allow you to hurt Deborah by manipulating Felix to satisfy your own need to hurt me." She searched his eyes. "Can you deny that that is your true motive, Lord Donnington? Or is it indeed a matter of power over those weaker than yourself? It is either one or the other, for you certainly do not have Mr. Melbyrne's best interests at heart."

Her words should have been no more than the

bites of midges, minor irritations at best, and yet they burned like a hornet's sting. "You know nothing of Melbyrne's best interests," he snapped.

"I know more than a man who refuses to see what is before him…or chooses to ignore it entirely."

The danger was very evident to Sinjin then. If he let Nuala win even the tiniest of victories now, she would see his weakness and go in for the kill. Melbyrne would be lost to her machinations, and he…

Open thighs and outstretched arms. Devil's curses hidden behind smiling lips. A woman's fair shape concealing corruption that could suck a man's soul into Hell.

"I see what is before me," he said, half-blinded by the visions of terror and lust. "Get thee gone, witch!"

She flinched, her mouth opening on a gasp of shock. He touched his own throat as if he might catch the words and destroy them before they could be spoken.

For they had not been his words. The voice had not been his voice. It was the one from the dream, harsh and full of rage. Of hate.

Sinjin pushed his palms into his forehead. Sparks and streaks of red danced behind his eyelids.

"Is that how it is to be?"

So soft, her voice. So steady, as if she hadn't glimpsed what smoldered within his heart.

He opened his eyes. Though nothing in her appearance had changed, he could feel the armor she had wrapped around herself. For all the bitter words between them, these had been different. Deadly in some way he couldn't comprehend.

What the hell had come over him?

"Is it a war you want?" she asked in that same, almost gentle voice. "I would never have chosen it, Sinjin. I had hoped for your forgiveness, as I had hoped one day to forgive myself. But I see that is impossible." Her modest height seemed to grow, until she stood as nearly as tall as Sinjin himself. "By what rules shall we abide? How shall we decide the winner?"

As if it were all a game to her. As if the lives she'd trifled with were merely pawns on a chessboard.

"War," he said, though his throat still rasped with the acid of that other voice. "You will lose, Nuala."

"Perhaps. But I will do so knowing that I have done all I can to stop a blackguard who'd rather see his friend destroyed than let him fall in love."

CHAPTER NINE

WITHOUT A THOUGHT, without so much as a breath of hesitation, Sinjin strode to her and grabbed her arms. She had no chance to struggle. He brought his mouth down on hers without any concession to gentleness, and felt her lips part on a cry she never made.

Heaven. And Hell. Both all at once, the feel of her in his arms and the desire that ate at him from within. He backed her up against a small oak, spearing his fingers through her hair until it came undone and splashed around her shoulders.

Not once did she fight him. He was so lost that he didn't care what she thought or what she wanted. He simply took, and if her mouth softened under his for a fraction of a second, it was unyielding again by the time he came back to himself.

He released her and staggered away. She remained where she was, her back against the tree and her arms still at her sides. His vision cleared enough to see that she had tears in her eyes.

Tears he'd put there with his savagery. Never in his life had he taken something a woman wasn't willing to give. He had launched the first attack in the war, abusing her with his greater strength and contemptible lack of self-control.

"Nuala," he said hoarsely. "I didn't…I didn't mean—"

But she was already striding away. He didn't follow to beg forgiveness. She wouldn't want to hear it, even if he were capable of speech.

He never learned how she'd managed to mount her horse without assistance. When he found Shaitan, she was gone. He sat in the saddle, his fists gripping the reins, and fought to regain his composure before the others could guess how badly he'd betrayed his own principles.

The sound of muffled hoofbeats roused him from his dark thoughts. His heart gave a jagged lurch, and he turned Shaitan to meet the rider.

Melbyrne drew his mount to a stop and stared at Sinjin, his mouth drawn down in a rare frown.

"I saw Lady Charles," he said. "What have you done, Sin?"

"Melbyrne, it isn't what you—"

The boy pulled on the reins and spun the bay around, tearing off toward the house at a gallop. Sinjin hesitated a few moments longer and followed. He reached Donbridge after the others had already left their horses with the stable hands. A brief inquiry at the carriage house assured him that Lady Charles had abandoned the premises.

When Sinjin entered the house, the men were still in their rooms changing for dinner. Felix was nowhere to be found.

"Melbyrne?" Ferrer said as he met Sinjin at the foot of the staircase. "Haven't seen him since we got back. Why? Have you lost him?"

The man's tone grated on Sinjin. "I am not his keeper," he snapped.

"He needs one, if what I hear is true. And you, Donnington…what goes on between you and that toothsome little piece Lady Charles?" His lips curled in a sneer. "You were gone off together a rather long time."

"Nothing happened, Ferrer."

"Pity. I would have been happy to keep the lady company. Nothing like a fast ride on an eager filly to—"

He gave a grunt of surprise as Sinjin's punch connected with his jaw and he sailed to the floor. Sinjin rubbed his knuckles, wishing that Ferrer would get up and offer him another chance.

"I say, what's all this?" Reddick said from the top of the stairs.

Mrs. Tissier joined him, and soon all the Forties were crowded at the landing. Ferrer picked himself up, the sneer replaced with a look of angry calculation. He felt his jaw and smeared the blood on his lower lip.

"Well, well," he said. "How very gallant of you to defend the lady's honor."

Sinjin flexed his fingers. "You won't speak of her again, Ferrer."

"Shall I assume that Adele is now at liberty?"

He flinched a little as Sinjin offered a view of his fist. "You may assume that I will be prepared to continue our conversation at any time you choose," Sinjin said.

Ferrer barked a laugh. "Listen to him, chaps. When may we expect the happy event, Donnington?"

The fire in Sinjin's dreams was no hotter than his face. "I would not advise that you wait for it at Donbridge," he said.

"Then I shall be going," Ferrer said, brushing off his trousers. He glared up at the others and charged up the stairs.

"One more thing," Sinjin called after him. "I should be very sorry to hear that you have spread scurrilous rumors about Lady Charles's visit to Donbridge."

Ferrer paused, his hand gripping the banister. "They would hardly be rumors."

"It would be unwise to mention it, nevertheless."

Ferrer's gaze swept the observers on the landing. "Don't make the mistake of blaming me if such tattle spreads," he said. "I have no control over the behavior of your new conquest." He pushed his way past the Forties and strode out of sight.

Mrs. Tissier and the men were silent, waiting for Sinjin's next move…a general warning to all of them, perhaps, or a blustered explanation.

Sinjin gave them neither. "Shall we go in to dinner, Mrs. Tissier? Gentlemen?"

Glances were exchanged, and someone coughed. No one offered a single comment as Sinjin gave Mrs. Tissier his arm and the Forties proceeded into the dining room.

The mood gradually relaxed, and conversation settled into the somewhat ribald tone typical of the club's gatherings. Mrs. Tissier was as active in the exchanges as any of the men, though she occasionally glanced toward the door as if she wondered where Melbyrne had gone. Ferrer left without fanfare, his departure briefly noted by Hedley as the dessert course was served.

Mrs. Tissier retired early, and the others gathered in the billiard room for a game and cigars. No one found the nerve to question Sinjin further about his row with Ferrer or Melbyrne's absence. Sinjin put off going to bed as long as possible, keeping the men engaged until, one by one, they staggered up to their chambers.

Sinjin had already sent his valet to his own bed, and was grateful for the solitude as he undressed. He was just inebriated enough to feel the weight of unfamiliar self-pity.

He had told Nuala that she must lose any war between them. But he knew those words to be no more than a child's whistling in the dark. He was already well along the road to losing the battle all on his own.

She had some strange power over him. He saw that now. It wasn't merely her body, her intelligence or her spirit that drew him. She had cast a spell on him, even if she didn't know it herself.

Fool. She'd done nothing of the kind. It was the kiss that had clinched it, no mystical enchantment.

He climbed into bed, aware of every inch of naked skin against the sheets. He could almost feel Nuala lying beside him, touching him with her fiery hands. Whispering promises of ecstasies no woman had ever given him before. He was so hard that one brush of a woman's fingertips would make him come.

Adele. Tomorrow he would go to her and take his fill of her, even if he had to remain in her bed for three days running. If that didn't cure him, nothing would.

But the voice returned in his dreams. *You will never be free of her.* And the flames licked over his body until nothing was left of him but ash.

"SHE IS NOT COMING," Frances said, consulting her watch again. "I suggest that we proceed without her. This is, after all, the opening day of our new charity house."

Deborah nodded, though she cast one last glance up the street as she climbed into Lady Selfridge's carriage. It had all been very strange. Nuala had suddenly dashed off to God-knew-where two days ago, leaving only a vague note by way of explanation, and had as yet failed to return. She had known that today was the day that they would officially open the new warehouse in Whitechapel, and had expressed continuing enthusiasm for the project.

But she hadn't come. Deborah was certain in her heart that Nuala's absence had something to do with her exchange with Lord Donnington at Lady Oxenham's ball. More, she knew that Nuala had been furious at Lord Donnington's whisking Felix away from the ball. Nuala had been less than subtle about her hopes that Deborah and Mr. Melbyrne's acquaintance would evolve into a more permanent connection.

No, Nuala's absence was surely no coincidence. And neither Felix nor Lord Donnington had made a public appearance since the ball…not in Hyde Park nor anywhere Deborah might have been apt to see them.

Deborah gnawed on her lower lip and sank back in the seat. If she could but make up her own mind about Felix. He had not yet proposed, but she was increasingly convinced that such a proposal would soon be forthcoming. Nuala certainly wanted to see it happen, but what would the other Widows say? Her confusion only seemed to grow worse by the minute.

Worrying at a ribbon on her dress with nervous fingers, Deborah closed her eyes as another face rose in her mind's eye. Dark hair and a straightforward gaze. An earnest, serious face, so unlike Felix's pleasant handsomeness.

Today she might see Ioan Davies. He lived in Whitechapel. He had become involved with the charity project when he'd confronted Bray, and he might feel bound to lend his protection again. He was that sort of man.

And he had returned her handkerchief.

That means nothing but that he is a courteous young man, in spite of his situation and station. There could be no significance in their meeting again.

The drive to Whitechapel was completed almost before Deborah had realized the carriage was moving. Most of the carts had already arrived and were being unloaded; a rapidly growing crowd was forming around them, jostling people of all ages eager to be given their rations. While Clara, Maggie and the few other society women Frances had recruited wrapped up the food, the men Frances had hired as guards kept a watchful eye out for those who might attempt to claim more than their due. The guards themselves had been found in Whitechapel and were willing enough to do the work for a generous wage, though Lady Selfridge had insisted that their cudgels be used only as a last resort, and only against men who used violence to bully or impede their fellows.

To Deborah's secret surprise, the distribution went smoothly. The small warehouse Frances had acquired was much more suited to organizing the apportionment of rations; only a few could enter the door at one time, and the more needy women and children could be kept apart from the men. Bray never put in an appearance.

Nor did Ioan Davies. Deborah found herself watching for him even as she wrapped fresh food in newspapers and passed it to grateful women, or laughed with little girls as they received their rag dolls.

"What is it, Deborah?" asked Frances during one of their rare intervals of rest. "You seem distracted."

"Not at all," Deborah assured her with a smile, and returned to work with renewed vigor. But when she caught a glimpse of black hair at the rear of the thinning crowd, her heart rolled over in her chest. She stood, murmured a request that Clara take her place for a few minutes, and made her way through the men and women clustered by the warehouse doors.

No one impeded her, but Ioan had disappeared.

She stood in the filthy street, clutching her hands together as she examined every figure who passed.

I must see him. It was a foolish idea in the extreme, but she knew if she did not, she would continue to think about him at the most inopportune moments, and in the most inappropriate ways. For some reason she could not comprehend, she had built up some sort of romantic fantasy about him that must be dispelled.

Hesitantly she walked a little distance away from the warehouse. The decrepit houses seemed to lean toward her, whispering of the suffering and poverty they contained. The stench of fetid alleys clogged her nostrils. The very sky seemed to grow darker, but she continued on, trying to forget the tales of the White-chapel killer.

She had gone perhaps two blocks when she saw the dark-haired figure rounding a corner.

Resolutely she set off again. A woman in a gaudy, cast-off gown, leaning against a peeling wall, shouted an obscenity as Deborah passed. A pair of men emerging from a tavern paused to follow her progress with narrowed eyes. She walked a little faster, her skirts sweeping through the rubbish that littered the pavement.

The corner was just ahead. She dashed around it and collided with a man stinking of old sweat and strong drink.

"Well, if i' ain't the li'l tart from Mayfair," he said, gripping her arm before she could back away. "ncy findin' yer 'ere." He leaned into her, nauseat-er with his breath. "Slummin', are we?"

Deborah struggled, clenching her fist against the need to strike. "I would advise you to release me," she said with her best attempt at cool disdain.

He laughed. "Jus' loik yer ma. Aw high 'n' migh'y, as if she 'ad th' roight."

She stared at him in astonishment. "My mother?"

"You 'eard me." He smiled, giving her another view of his rotten teeth. "I were wonderin' wot i' was wot were so familiar 'bout yer."

"Let me go."

"But we ain't done wi' our conversation, missy. Yer do want ter know abou' yer real ma? Wot she did fer 'er keep afore she gave yer away?"

The filthy words coming out of his mouth erased any traces of Deborah's fear. "You never knew my mother," she said. "She would never have had anything to do with a man like you."

"That so?" He fumbled inside his wretched coat with his free hand, grunted, and withdrew a soiled and creased bit of paper. "Then why'd she gif me this?"

The bit of paper was a photograph, so stained that Deborah could not make it out at first. She drew back, but Bray thrust the photograph into her hand.

The face was darkened by time, the right half of the lower jaw obscured by a smear of dirt or grease. But there was no mistaking the woman's beauty: the fullness of her lips, the softness of her eyes beneath gentle brows or the thick, dark hair arranged simply on her head.

"I weren't wrong," Bray growled. "I see i' in yer eyes."

Deborah turned her head away, afraid she would vomit. The woman might have been her twin save for the stark simplicity of her dress.

"Where did you get that?" she whispered.

"I tol' yer, missy. She gave i' me." He chuckled indulgently, as if Deborah were a favorite niece. "Only roight t' let yer know the truf. She were a whore, yer ma. A good 'un, roight enough. But she coul'n't keep a brat, could she?"

The world tilted sideways, but Deborah managed to keep her head. "My mother was Lady Shaw, wife of Sir Percival Shaw. She was never in Whitechapel."

He nodded sagely. "'At's wot they tol' yer, ain't i'? Yer was too young ter know different. Barely ou' o' the womb afore yer fine Sir Percy offered t' take yer off Mary's 'ands."

Now she knew he was lying. The resemblance Deborah saw in the photograph was no more than a coincidence that this man used to hurt her for inexplicable reasons of his own.

"I was born in Baden, Switzerland," she said, meeting his gaze. "A doctor, a wet nurse and my father witnessed my birth."

"Yer wants more proof, missy?" Bray called after her. "I c'n find them wot'll be 'appy ter tell yer aw abou' 'ow yer real ma sold yer ter them nobs, th' ones wot claimed ter be yer real fam'ly. 'Ow yer 'igh 'n' migh'y Sir Shaw used ter know Mary, in ev'ry sense o' th' word."

She jerked her arm free. "I do not believe you!"

"Then believe this, missy. I'll be askin' yer fer a li'l baksheesh very soon. A friendly l'il loan so's I don' decide ter tell th' papers abou' yer dear ma."

Deborah squared her shoulders and walked away. The man's evil words clawed under her rib cage and refused to be dislodged, no matter how quickly she walked. The picture of the woman burned behind her eyes. The voices calling out to her from alleyways and sagging buildings could not drown out the voice in her own head.

You aren't Lady Orwell, daughter of Sir Percival Shaw. You're the child of some backstreet prostitute named Mary....

"Lady Orwell!"

The calm, familiar voice brought her to a halt. Only when Ioan Davies came to her side did she truly begin to tremble, her legs threatening to drop her to the cracked pavement.

Ioan saw her distress. He held her up, his earnest hazel eyes sweeping her face.

"You ought not to be here, your ladyship," he said, holding her much too close to his chest. "What has frightened you?"

Deborah tried not to let him see the tears pooling under her eyelids. She had what she wanted; she had found Ioan. At the worst possible moment.

"It's nothing, Mr. Davies," she stammered.

He shook his head. "You've had a rare shock of some kind, madam. Let me escort you to your companions."

"Really, I'm all—"

But it was useless. She badly wanted Ioan's support, as shameful as she found her weakness and her need for him. She leaned on his arm as he led her back the way she'd come, to the warehouse where Lady Selfridge was speaking urgently to her hired men.

Frances turned sharply as one of the men pointed toward Deborah. She picked up her skirts and strode to meet Deborah and Ioan.

"Where have you been, child?" she demanded. "I was about to send the men out to search for you!" Her gaze flicked to Ioan. "Mr. Davies! What has happened?"

He touched his cap. "That I don't know, madam, but Lady Orwell has not been harmed." With what Deborah almost might have termed reluctance, he released her arm. Lady Selfridge took his place.

"Are you ill, Lady Orwell?"

"No. Only...I should not have gone out."

"What possessed you to leave us?"

Deborah stared at the ground. She could not possibly tell Frances the truth, either about why she had left the warehouse alone nor why she now seemed so ill.

"I...I only wanted a little fresh air," she said. Frances snorted, but she was obviously well aware that they were in mixed company and a full interrogation must wait. She nodded to Mr. Davies.

"Thank you once again, Mr. Davies, for your assistance," she said. "I am certain that..."

"Deborah!"

A fresh wave of light-headedness nearly undid

her. Felix Melbyrne ran up to join them, profound relief in his expression.

"Thank God. I've been searching everywhere for you. When Lady Selfridge told me…" He stopped, glanced at Ioan, and resumed more slowly. "Are you well?"

Somehow she managed to focus on his face. "What…what are you doing here, Mr. Melbyrne?"

"I was told by your footman that you had come to Whitechapel with Lady Selfridge. I was concerned for your safety."

Deborah tried to laugh. "I was never in any danger, Mr. Melbyrne. I am hardly a hothouse violet to be kept out of the sun."

No one could have been convinced by her dismal attempt at levity. Felix looked at her with something very like disapproval.

"You are ill. You must tell me what happened!"

"She's not ill, Mr. Melbyrne," Frances insisted.

"Did someone abuse you?" Felix asked as if Lady Selfridge hadn't spoken. "Tell me where to find them, and I shall see to it that the blackguards never do so again."

"The lady has given her assurances," Ioan said, his voice so soft that it commanded everyone's attention. "Perhaps she would be best served by returning to her home."

Felix stared at Ioan, his judgment of the other man's station plain in his expression. "Lady Selfridge, may I be introduced to this…gentleman?"

"Mr. Felix Melbyrne, may I present Mr. Ioan

Davies," Frances said without the slightest hesitation. "Mr. Davies was kind enough to escort Lady Orwell back to us."

"Mr. Davies," Felix said stiffly, briefly touching the brim of his hat, "if you were responsible for aiding Lady Orwell in any way, you have my gratitude."

Ioan gave a shallow bow. "Mr. Melbyrne, it was my pleasure to do so."

The exchange was so coldly formal that Deborah felt as if the pavement beneath her feet had frozen. "I should very much like to go home," she said.

"The sooner, the better," Frances said. "Mr. Melbyrne, if you will see to the carriage…"

Mr. Melbyrne's reluctance was manifest, but he did as he was asked. Deborah found the presence of mind to smile at Ioan.

"Thank you again, Mr. Davies," she said. "I am sorry to have caused so much disturbance."

"You could never do so, madam," Ioan said, his grave expression barely giving way to a smile. "I trust you will soon be well."

She dropped a curtsey, one she might have reserved for a duke. "Goodbye, Mr. Davies."

Lady Selfridge bustled her into the waiting carriage. Felix mounted his horse and took up a position next to the door. Deborah forced herself to look ahead and not back at Ioan.

Perhaps he could have told her why Bray would say the things he'd said. He would surely know most everyone in this part of Whitechapel, or at least be able to guess at what might motivate such an evil man.

But then she would have to tell Ioan the unthinkable, and she would rather never meet him again than reveal even the gist of her conversation with her tormentor.

Never see him again...

"Well," Frances said, "you are still white as a sheet. Will you tell me what really happened?"

"Nothing," Deborah said, trying to meet Frances's gaze. "It was as Mr. Melbyrne surmised. There were...men who spoke to me. I was not prepared—"

"Good God, girl, have you no sense? Had you wished to see more of Whitechapel, I and one of the men would gladly have accompanied you."

"Mr. Davies found me before any harm was done," Deborah said. "I was never in any real danger."

"Hmm." Frances tilted her head like a hawk sighting a field mouse. "Mr. Davies has a keen regard for you, I see."

"That is nonsense! He was merely present when I—"

"And you have a similar regard for him."

"He is a kind man, but—"

"Of course he is of a different station than you, but I am firmly of the belief that such outmoded attitudes have no place in our modern society. Under other circumstances..." She shook her head. "I know that Lady Charles has encouraged your interest in Mr. Melbyrne, and his in you. But I caution you, Deborah. This is not a game."

"Is that what you believe? I did not join the Widows under false pretenses!"

"I know you did not. But if you do not wish to

marry again, guard your heart, and do not trifle with
the affections of those you admire. Men and women
can become extremely foolish when they believe
themselves in love."

"I am not in love with anyone!"

Frances sighed. "None of us will disavow you
should you choose to leave us."

"But I do not wish to leave you!"

"You must make your own decisions. Only be
certain that you know what you truly want."

What I want. The same question Deborah had
asked herself a dozen times since Ioan's visit to Belgravia. Nuala would not for a moment believe that her
protégée could look twice at Mr. Davies when she had
attached Mr. Melbyrne, even if Nuala shared
Frances's disregard for Society's strict separation of
the classes.

Would she and Frances feel the same disregard if
they knew what Bray had said of Deborah's parentage? If they believed it to be true? And what of Felix?

"I am very tired, Frances," Deborah said, sinking
back into her seat and closing her eyes. "I would
like to rest."

"Of course," Frances said. She kept her opinions
to herself for the remainder of the drive. When they
reached Nuala's house, Mr. Melbyrne was at the carriage door before the footman could perform his
office. He and Frances personally saw Deborah into
the care of the housekeeper, Mrs. Addison. Felix lingered in the hall until Frances persuaded him to leave
Deborah to her rest.

Deborah allowed Mrs. Addison to coddle her and gave herself up to Stella's ministrations, but she couldn't relax. Bray's contorted features, and the gentle face of the woman in the picture, whirled about in her brain like a child's pinwheel.

What the man had said was impossible, of course. Bray had developed an irrational dislike of her— perhaps because she had been born into a life of privilege, perhaps for some other unfathomable reason—and he had only meant to hurt her.

But no one could mistake the woman's— Mary's—perfect likeness to Deborah. She had never resembled either her mother or her father.

Flinging herself out of bed, Deborah pulled back her heavy bedroom curtains. It was just four o'clock, but she felt as if the calm and civilized London scene below were somehow unreal, part of a life she could barely comprehend.

She had come late into her parents' lives, born when her mother was nearly past the age of child-birth. There had been no other children. She had been told the story of her birth at Baden many times, because the pregnancy had been difficult for Lady Shaw and—as Sir Percival Shaw had so often said— they considered Deborah their "little miracle."

Had it been a miracle? Or had it been a transac-tion with a woman who was willing to sell a child she did not want…a transaction carefully concealed from the world? Had Deborah married Lawrence under the worst of false pretenses?

Foolish, foolish. There was no proof. Bray had

implied that he could produce witnesses, but how could one trust anything such a man's friends might say? Surely his implied threat of blackmail was no more than empty bluster.

Her best course would be to ignore the entire matter, and perhaps avoid returning to Whitechapel for a few weeks. Once Bray knew he could not frighten her, he would surely leave her alone. Yes, she ought to occupy herself with the many pleasant diversions available in Mayfair and Belgravia.

But when she recalled Mrs. Saunterton's soirée tomorrow night, her heart sank. She could not imagine going back to her regular social routine. She would constantly be wondering if she really belonged in good Society at all.

Deborah let the curtains fall and returned to her bed. She tried to sleep again, falling prey to ugly dreams of being cast out, mocked, despised. Sometime after midnight she put on her dressing gown and went downstairs. The house was dark and silent; there was no more comfort to be found in the lower rooms than in her own.

If only Nuala were here, she would set Deborah's mind at ease. She would gently but firmly assure Deborah that she'd let her imagination run away with her.

Feet dragging with every step, Deborah returned to her room. She had no sooner lain down again than she heard a rattle on her windowpane.

Starting up, she ran to the window. Another pebble struck the glass and bounced off. She opened the sash and stared down into the yard.

A man stood beside the small kitchen garden…a man whose compact figure Deborah recognized at once. She backed away from the window, shrugged into her dressing gown and flew down the stairs.

CHAPTER TEN

IOAN WAS STILL WAITING when she slipped through the door from the servants' hall. She didn't demand to know why he had come. She simply flung herself at him, felt the warmth of his arms close around her, let the tears spill over without any thought of shame.

He held her for perhaps a dozen seconds and then released her, his breath sighing into her hair. "Lady Orwell," he said with his usual formality.

The reminder immediately brought Deborah back to her senses. She retreated, breathing quickly, and turned her head to hide her embarrassment.

"I...I beg your pardon, Mr. Davies," she whispered.

He cleared his throat. "Please, Lady Orwell..." His boots shuffled in the grass. She felt his gaze on her face. "Are you...quite recovered?"

"Oh, yes."

"I think you are not."

She couldn't seem to find the will to contradict him. Her gown blew close to her body, and she was keenly, devastatingly aware of her undress. "I am...I am in no state to receive visitors," she stammered. "I am sorry, Mr. Davies." She turned to rush back into the house.

"I care nothing for your state."

The snap of anger in his voice startled her into immobility. She forced herself to meet his eyes. They had a peculiar light in them, as if he had been holding something inside for far too long and had finally determined to let it out.

"I know you are as far above me as the moon, your ladyship," he said, "but I cannot allow you to suffer." He flexed the stiff fingers of his right hand. "I took the liberty of learning who had assaulted you. I had little difficulty in finding the villain, or in discovering what he had done."

What he had done. The gorge rose in Deborah's throat.

"You must think nothing of what he told you, madam. His vile purpose is to give pain to anyone he can. But I think he will not do so again for some time."

For the first time Deborah noticed the cuts and bruises on Ioan's newly healed knuckles and the swelling on his left cheek. She gasped and started toward him again.

"You're hurt," she said. "You must come into the servants' hall and—"

"Please do not trouble yourself, madam. I have had worse."

His rebuff kept her where she was. He *knew.* He knew everything, and yet he stood here and looked at her as if nothing had changed.

All common sense and propriety demanded that she bid him leave at once. But she was no longer entirely in control of her own mind or body, and when she spoke she realized the full depth of her despair.

"Did you believe him?" she whispered.

"Ach-a-fi!" he exclaimed, his expression losing every last scrap of detachment, "I would no more believe him than I would the Devil himself."

Absolution. That was what he offered her. Freedom from the nightmares that had haunted her whenever she'd closed her eyes.

It was not enough.

"You saw the photograph?" she asked faintly. "Did you know her?"

He was as fierce now as he had been composed before. "I never knew her, the poor lass. But she—"

"You must learn the truth for me."

His shock was so mingled with befuddlement that Deborah almost laughed. She covered her mouth with her hands and prayed she wouldn't begin to weep again.

"I meant what I said, Mr. Davies," she said, lowering her hands. "You know the people of Whitechapel. You can search where I can never enter." She took a step toward him. "Bray implied that he could produce witnesses to confirm his claims. I *must* know if there is any truth to what he told me. I cannot…I cannot simply behave as if he never showed me the photograph."

A deep compassion brimmed in Ioan's eyes. "He is a liar."

"And until I am certain of that, I will always wonder. Can you understand, Ioan?"

The sound of his name rebounded in the air like a gunshot. "Madam..." he began, very slowly.

"My name is Deborah."

He swallowed. "Madam, I would do as you ask. It would be no trouble to me. But it is a door which, once opened, cannot be closed again."

So he did think it possible that Bray had told the truth. There was a kind of relief in the thought, that he believed she could be a prostitute's daughter and not flinch from her company.

But she knew nothing of his background. He might have come from similar origins. He might be anyone.

And she didn't care.

"Will you help me?" she asked.

He stared at the ground between his boots. "Aye, madam. I will."

"Thank you." She fought the impulse that demanded she fly into his arms again, feel his warmth and complete acceptance. "Thank you, Ioan."

He lifted his head. Gazed at her. Swallowed a second time. "When shall I come again?"

"Whenever you have information." Dear God, let it be soon. "I shall never forget this kindness."

"It is no kindness, madam." He bowed. "Good night."

Then he did what she should have done minutes ago: he fled, his stride swift for one of such modest height, and vanished into the darkness.

Deborah backed up until she reached the wall of the house and let it take her weight. Surely none of this had been real. Nothing had been real since yesterday morning.

"Mr. Davies has a keen regard for you, I see." Lady Selfridge's words, which Deborah so hotly denied.

And you have a similar regard for him.

Hadn't she proven the truth of Frances's words the very instant she went to Ioan in the yard?

It was too much. Too much for her mind to hold. She hurried back into the house and up the stairs to her room.

Nuala came in before dawn. She sat beside Deborah's bed and smiled, though there were lines around her eyes that Deborah didn't remember seeing before.

"How are you, my dear?" Nuala asked, laying her hand on Deborah's forehead. "Frances tells me that you had an unpleasant experience in Whitechapel."

Deborah pushed herself up against the pillows. "I'm so glad you've returned. Where have you been?"

"Seeing to some business that could not wait." She was silent for a moment. "I should have been with you."

"I am quite all right." Deborah leaned forward, wrapping her arms around her knees. "You do not look well yourself."

"Oh," Nuala said with a short laugh, "merely a few minor complications. Nothing that will not quickly be resolved."

So Nuala was not prepared to discuss the reasons for her own obvious distress. But Deborah felt as if some veil had been lifted from her eyes...not a veil of ignorance, but one tightly woven of rules and custom and expectations, all designed to create as many "complications" as possible.

"Is it Lord Donnington?" Deborah asked quietly.

Nuala started, then quickly composed herself again. "You might as well know, as it will doubtless become gossip soon enough. I went to visit Lord Donnington at his estate in Cambridgeshire."

"But why?"

"For reasons I prefer not to divulge at present."

Of course she did not. Yet Deborah's thoughts tripped over the possibilities, following the paths her own bewildered mind had opened up to her.

Lord Donnington and Nuala were in love. And they would do anything to keep the world from finding out.

"Have you seen Mr. Melbyrne while I was away?" Nuala asked with a casualness that not even a fool would believe genuine.

Deborah rested her chin on her updrawn knees, wondering how she could answer without either prevaricating or leading Nuala to the wrong conclusion.

"Yes…at Whitechapel," she said. "He had heard we were doing charitable work there."

"Then he was there to help you? I'm so glad." She pressed Deborah's hand and rose. "I will leave you to rest. Do not hesitate to send for me if you wish to talk."

"Nuala?"

The older woman turned, smiling with a serenity that did not quite reach her eyes. "Yes, my dear?"

"When two people care for each other, it is not only a matter of their own hearts' desires, is it?"

Nuala sank into the chair again. "What do you mean?"

"There are so many things that can get in the way. Misunderstandings, mistaken assumptions…"

"Such challenges exist in all relationships, especially those of love. They can always be overcome."

"But what if there are other obstacles? Questions of wealth and position and birth. The opinion of Society."

"Wealth is transitory. So is position. And as for the opinion of Society…" She gestured with her hand as if sweeping dust away with her fingertips. "It cannot stand in the way of a true match." She leaned forward, brows knitted in concern. "Why such questions, my dear?"

"It is only that…what I have seen in Whitechapel…it is so unjust. I wish everyone shared your views."

"Many do. Lady Frances…all of the widows, I am quite certain. The time will come when the artificial barriers between people will fall."

"I hope you are right."

Nuala touched Deborah's hair. "You are part of a new generation, Deborah. You will see the world change." Her eyes grew sad, and then she smiled again. "But you will have no such obstacles to face. Of that I am quite sure."

She rose again, walked to the door and quietly left the room. Deborah slid under the sheets, wondering what Nuala had really been thinking when she spoke of artificial barriers and the changing of the world.

Perhaps the world *would* change. But not today or tomorrow. For the time being, she must live with the world as it was. Until she heard from Ioan, she would remain at home as much as was realistically possible without attracting too much attention from well-meaning friends or Society at large. She would not encourage Felix in any way.

Only when she knew the truth would she be able to determine her future course.

For the first time that night, Deborah was able to close her eyes and see nothing but Ioan's steadfast, compassionate face.

SINJIN SPRAWLED ON the sheets, his body bathed in perspiration. He stared at the ceiling, wondering if it might be possible to bring the building down around him with a sufficient application of sheer will.

Adele curled up beside him, her expression all sympathy and good humor. "It isn't so bad as all that, Sin," she said.

Oh, it was every bit as bad as all that. One of the most glorious examples of the naked female form lay in his bed, and he could not serve it as it so richly deserved. As *Adele* deserved.

She twisted a lock of his hair around her finger. "I am in no hurry, darling. I shall brew you a nice pot of tea, and we shall enjoy a nice afternoon together. It has been so long since we have simply talked."

As indeed it had. Sinjin had seldom been interested in merely "talking" with Adele when there was so much better sport to be had…sport in which she enthusiastically participated.

"You are kind, Adele," he said hoarsely. "But I think it best that I not waste more of your time."

"Time?" She sighed and laid her small hand on his chest. "I should rather spend an hour here with you, just as we are, than an eternity of delight with anyone else."

He finally looked at her, prey to the pathetic sort of gratitude he'd never wished to owe any woman again. He staunched it quickly. "You were always very good at flattery, my dear."

He rolled up out of bed before she could respond, tossed on his dressing gown and went to the window. A thrush fluttered about in the half-wild garden splayed out against the high wall that protected the cottage from the street beyond. Adele crept up behind him, though she had more than enough sense not to touch him again.

"What is it, Sin?" she asked softly. "What is it really? If you've grown tired of me…" She gave a soft laugh. "You seem so ferocious and forbidding, but I know you. We are both grown-up people. I will not be offended if—"

"It isn't you." Sinjin took a breath and lowered his voice. "You've done nothing but please me, Adele."

He heard her leave the room and reappear a few minutes later with a steaming pot of tea. "Come," she said. "Sit down and tell me all about her."

"There is no 'her,'" he snapped.

"Oh, Sin. Give me a little credit for eyes to see and ears to hear with."

The sweat chilled on his skin. "Gossip, Adele?"

"Even if there were not, I would know."

Grudgingly, he recognized defeat, followed her into the small drawing room and sat in the chair she offered. He allowed her to pour and then stared blankly at the cup. Adele rose, swept away with her lavish dressing gown trailing behind her, and returned with a bottle of whiskey and a single snifter.

Without comment, Sinjin took the glass and poured himself a measure. It was early in the day for drinking, but he felt in dire need of the fortification.

"It is no use fighting it, you know," Adele said.

Sinjin finished his drink, brooded over the bottle and decided against another. Shakespeare had made it plain enough: drinking would in no wise improve his ability to perform.

Not that he would wish to attempt it. He had no desire to repeat the humiliating and unfamiliar experience of failure.

"We have had a good run together," Adele said. She tentatively rested her hand on his shoulder, a touch lacking all sensuality. "But every good thing must come to an end."

"I don't wish to end it."

"Do you really have any choice?" She laughed, sadness in her voice. "You need not be concerned for me. I always land on my feet. But you will never be free until you acknowledge what your body and heart desire."

"My heart isn't involved."

"Of course not." She squeezed his shoulder and let

him go. "She is a woman of good reputation, your Lady Charles, but she is also a woman."

He got up abruptly, crossed the room, spun about and faced her again. "What do you advise, Adele?"

But she only smiled, picked up the tea tray and walked from the room. Sinjin was left standing there like a fool, remembering the way Nuala had felt in his arms, the way her lips had given under his.

Adele was keen in her insights, but her assumptions were flawed. He might want Nuala. Not might...he *did* want her. But his inability this morning was not natural. Nuala had sunk her claws into his flesh and would not let go. *She* had caused this to happen, whether or not she realized it.

The dreams...

He laughed at himself. Did he really think she'd worked some nefarious magic on him in vengeance for his treatment of her at Donbridge? He hadn't even seen the witch since his return to London, nor had he wished to do so.

Now, it appeared, he had no other option.

Aware that Adele had deliberately granted him his privacy, he dressed and left the cottage. He didn't think. Thinking was anathema to his plans. He rode hard back to Queen's Gate Terrace, dropped into his club for luncheon, engaged in a furious game of billiards, ignored the pointed glances of the Forties and returned to his town house to change for dinner.

He could not be sure, of course. There was always a possibility that Nuala wouldn't be present at Mrs. Saunterton's soirée. But even if she entertained the fear of gossip about her visit to Donbridge, she would not very likely let it keep her in seclusion. She was not that sort of female.

What she was was a thorn in his side, one he intended to pluck out with all necessary force.

Mrs. Saunterton's drawing room was as hot and crowded as any good hostess might wish. Sinjin spoke to the other guests with only half his attention, just sufficient to maintain a reasonable level of courtesy. He noted the glances cast his way and could easily guess the subject of conversation as he passed. Doing his best to ignore the buzz of speculation, he maneuvered himself so that he could watch the door and the advent of latecomers.

Nuala, accompanied by the ever-effusive Lady Meadows, didn't see him when she arrived. Her air was distracted, her gaze darting about like a bird's.

Looking for *him*.

With finely balanced nonchalance he made his way in her direction, pausing strategically to share a quiet joke with a male acquaintance or to compliment a blushing young lady on her gown. It required the most exquisite timing to be in the right place just when Lady Charles was alone, temporarily unnoticed, and near a promising closed door.

Without giving her the slightest warning, Sinjin bore down on her, grasped her arm and opened the door. He pushed Nuala into the unlit space beyond and closed the door.

The space proved to be a gentleman's library, but Sinjin wasn't paying attention to the furnishings. He backed Nuala up against the desk, trapped her there with his body and kissed her.

NUALA'S SHOCK passed in an instant.

In her final moments of sanity, she reflected that she and Sinjin seemed to be in a sort of play, where the same scene repeated over and over again. They hadn't spoken, hadn't so much as seen each other since she'd left Donbridge, and yet here they were, as if no time had passed. He was kissing her as if she were the last woman in the world.

And she was letting him.

She worked her arms around his neck, clutching at his hard shoulders as he thrust his tongue between her lips and ground his hips into hers. Her body was no longer subject to her mind. It had a will of its own, and it demanded the satisfaction she had tried to deny it for far too long.

Sinjin moaned as she opened her mouth to accept his invasion, deepening his kiss. He worked his long fingers into her hair, loosening the pins, raking through the curling strands until they escaped their bindings and fell about her shoulders. Every nerve in her body was on fire, so sensitive to his touch that a series of electric shocks coursed through her at every brush of his hands.

"Nuala," he murmured against her mouth, his erection making itself very plain even through the multiple layers of her skirts and petticoats. He kissed her neck, the hollow of her shoulder, the place where her pulse beat so fast under her skin. She let her head fall back as he ran his tongue over the swell of her breasts, rising and falling frantically within the abbreviated confines of her bodice. He worked his tongue into the narrow vee between them, an act that made her shiver with images of that same tongue between her thighs.

Her skirts were heavy, not made to be lifted and pulled and bunched higher than her knees. Sinjin was not deterred. He continued to hold her against the desk with the weight of his body while he worked at her clothing, raising her skirts inch by inch, exposing her ankles and her calves and her knees, spreading her thighs apart with a push of his hips. Only his trousers and her thin drawers stood between his hard body and hers.

A burst of laughter outside the door was like a gunshot in Nuala's ears. Sense returned with a vengeance. She pushed as hard as she could, furious against Sinjin's resistance, dragging her skirts down as soon as her hands were free.

Sinjin persisted a few seconds longer, but the tide had turned against him. He jerked away almost violently and faced the door with fists clenched as if he might assault whoever had so unwittingly interrupted them. But the voices had gone silent. He paced across the room and stopped before the bookshelves, cursing under his breath.

Nuala was scarcely more composed herself. She shook out her skirts with unsteady hands and pressed her palm to her bodice to make certain that Sinjin had not disarranged it, as well. Her heart and lungs conspired to keep her from catching her breath, and her legs would not stop trembling.

She knew she could go. Sinjin would not try to stop her. She could simply leave, knowing that this…this thing between them would remain unresolved. The war would continue.

And she would continue to pretend that her long-neglected body would be satisfied with any man.

"Why are you waiting?" Sinjin demanded, his back rigid and his head bowed. "Go. Get out."

Strange how her first impulse was to go to him, lay her hand on his shoulder and comfort him in his defeat. "Do you want me to go?" she asked quietly.

He half turned, his profile stark in the faint light that spilled under the door. "It was a mistake," he said.

"To assume that you can have any woman you choose?"

"I can." He finally faced her, his body radiating his unsatisfied lust. "Or do you believe you don't have your price?"

His new attack left her breathless all over again. "Not everyone can be bought," she said over the racket of her heartbeat, and started for the door.

"Nuala."

The anger was gone from his voice. If Nuala had not known better, she might have imagined she heard a note of pleading.

"What is it?"

"Your hair."

Belatedly she remembered the state of her coiffure and how its dishevelment would look to the guests. She found just enough pins to secure it on top of her head.

But her armor had been breeched. Surely everyone would see and know....

"Nuala."

She felt him come up behind her, longed to lean back into his arms and feel his breath on her neck. "I...I must—"

"I want you."

CHAPTER ELEVEN

HER KNEES SOFTENED, and cascades of fire flowed into the pit of her stomach.

"I want you," he repeated.

She might have asked him why, if she could have answered the same question of herself. "It is not possible."

"You want *me*."

The lie came to her tongue and died there. "What difference can it make?"

His fingertips brushed the back of her neck, lifting aside the hair she had failed to secure. "All the difference in the world," he murmured. "You've won this round with Melbyrne, but he is still one of us. Perhaps you can persuade me..."

Nuala spun to face him, her hand raised. The magic came to her without thought or effort. A mark appeared on Sinjin's cheek, the imprint of a small hand where no flesh had touched flesh.

He staggered back, more stunned than hurt, and lifted his hand to his face. Nuala's arm went numb.

"Forgive me!" she cried. "I didn't mean..."

His lip curled in familiar mockery. "Oh, you meant it," he said.

"It was a mistake. A…a fluke."

But it wasn't. Not after the first two instances, in Whitechapel and at Lady Oxenham's ball. All small magics, to be sure. But this one, like the one at the ball, had been meant to punish.

Dark magic, no matter how mild. The sort of magic she had fought so hard to quench.

"It will not happen again," she said. "I swear…"

His gaze was fixed on her face, his eyes so dark that they made the rest of the room seem cast in bright daylight. "Perhaps you don't intend to use your power," he said without emotion, touching the fading brand on his cheek. "Perhaps it goes no further than these…small tokens of your displeasure. But even if it doesn't, I will continue my campaign to stop Melbyrne unless you agree to my terms."

A thrill of premonition turned her bones to ice. "I will not surrender to—"

"I do not think you'll find them onerous," he said. "I want you in my bed, Nuala. I want you naked under me, moaning as I take you. I want to see you helpless with desire." He took a step toward her, his raw masculinity stealing the air from the room. "If you give yourself to me, tonight, I'll leave Melbyrne alone."

Nuala was already wet and wanting. She could feel him…pinning her to the bed, moving inside her as her legs wrapped about his waist….

She gasped and turned for the door.

"What matters most to you, Nuala?" Sinjin said behind her. "Your virtue, which has so little meaning in our world, or Lady Orwell's happiness?"

Nuala closed her eyes. She knew what she valued most. And she was no virgin. There were already indications that her visit to Sinjin's estate had provoked comment. She had little virtue to lose.

You desire him. Once you have shared his bed, you can be free of him completely. In every way.

"What you are doing is wrong," she said, clinging to what was left of her principles.

"We are all guilty of some sin or other."

"Do you use such wooing techniques on other women?"

His voice became a purr. "Only on you."

She released her breath. "You will make no further attempts to influence Mr. Melbyrne?"

"None."

"Then…" She turned around, resting her back against the door. "Then I agree to your terms."

"Tonight?"

"Yes." She could not meet his eyes. "Where?"

"I have a cottage in St. John's Wood."

She knew what men of means kept in St. John's Wood. "Is it not already occupied?"

"Not any longer."

She looked up, speaking before she could think. "You mean that Adele is…"

"That is none of your concern."

"I am not taking her place."

He laughed. "You couldn't. I want quit of you, Nuala."

"Then we are truly in agreement."

They stared at each other. Nuala reached behind

her back for the door latch. Sinjin took one long step toward her, grabbed her around the waist and kissed her hard enough to sting.

"A reminder," he said. He eased her away from the door, his sudden gentleness a conundrum. "I'll go ahead and clear the way. Wait five minutes and then come out."

"Why bother? Your new conquest will be revealed soon enough."

He caught her chin in his fingers. "Oh, no, Nuala. This will be our secret."

Moving around her, he opened the door a few inches, peered out and left the room. Nuala counted five minutes by the clock on the shelf and followed.

Sinjin had kept his promise. There was no one in this part of the house, though she thought she heard Sinjin's voice, laughing, in an adjoining room.

She leaned against the wall. She must excuse herself as quickly as possible, calm her mind, prepare for this final skirmish.

"I want to see you helpless with desire." Well, she would not give him the satisfaction. She would be in control of her mind, if not her body. And when it was over, she could turn her attention to caging these small but dangerous remnants of her magic so that they could never escape again.

SHE WAS FIVE MINUTES LATE.

Sinjin checked his watch again and resumed his pacing. Five minutes after midnight, and she still had not arrived.

Perhaps she wasn't coming. Perhaps she had decided that Deborah wasn't worth the price he had demanded of her.

He paused again to twitch aside the curtains and stare out at the drive. Five minutes more. Ten. A half hour at most, and he would assume she had chosen to defy him.

What then? He remembered the supple, half-resisting feel of her body beneath his as he'd trapped her against the desk. He would have taken her then if circumstances had permitted. If she'd have let him.

And she would have.

But she'd lost her nerve. And he would have to pay his own price in lost sleep, violent dreams, a body that refused to obey his will....

The sound of wheels on gravel yanked him out of his thoughts. The carriage was making the final curve toward the cottage, as dark and silent as such an equipage could be. There was no footman at the footboard; only the driver, anonymous in dark livery.

Sinjin restrained himself as the carriage pulled up to the door. He walked slowly down the corridor to the modest entrance hall and waited until he was certain that Nuala had left the carriage. Only then did he move close enough to answer her very quiet knock.

His heart jumped against his ribs. He opened the door, carefully setting a neutral expression on his face.

"Lady Charles," he said. "Welcome."

She stared at him, her lovely face as unreadable as the Sphinx. She wore the plainest of gowns, almost severe of cut and design, as if she were on her way to a funeral.

"Lord Donnington," she said. She glanced back over her shoulder; the coachman was already driving the carriage back the way he had come. Evidently Nuala was no more enamored of having a third party present on the grounds than Sinjin was himself.

"Please, come in," Sinjin said, stepping back from the door. Nuala nodded, walked over the threshold, paused to take in the stark entrance hall and began to untie her pelerine. Sinjin hastily moved to help her out of it, took her gloves and hat as a gentleman ought in the absence of a servant. She thanked him quite properly.

It was a sort of dance, he thought…each partner knowing his or her place, going through the motions by rote. It would not be so once they were in bed. But he knew the rules as well as she did.

Why, then, was he so damnably nervous?

"Would you care for refreshment, Lady Charles?" he asked. "Tea and cakes, perhaps? A light supper? I have—"

"That will not be necessary, thank you."

So easily she put him in the position of getting directly to the point of her visit. He should have been grateful. Instead, he was annoyed. More than annoyed. He was angry.

Very well. She had set the tone for their liaison. He would honor her wishes.

Without giving her the slightest warning, he seized her shoulders and kissed her.

There was no give in her lips, no easing of her stiffly upright figure. She simply endured his attentions as if he were some common rogue mauling her for his own pleasure.

And are you not?

He released her. "Do you wish to leave, Lady Charles?" he asked in a voice he hardly recognized as his own. "I can ride home and summon a carriage...."

"No." She met his gaze, her own clear and unafraid. "We have struck a bargain. I intend to keep my part." She started away from the door at a firm walk, paused and turned.

"If you will show me the way," she said.

He strode ahead of her, leading her to the stairway. There were but four rooms on the upper floor, one seldom used, one relegated to his female guests, one his own and one set aside for but a single purpose.

He led her directly to the latter. And hesitated, his blood boiling from his head to his loins.

"There is no going back once we cross this threshold," he said.

In answer she put her hand on the latch, opened the door and entered.

Any woman not accustomed to such a room might have been startled by its decadence. Nuala was not, though she paused to take it all in: the walls adorned with hangings and carpets from the Near East, India and Northern Africa; the snarling tiger-skin rug, made of the pelt of a man-eater; the chairs overflowing with pillows of brocade and velvet; the vast bed, its coverlet already turned back, the silk sheets gleaming in the low light.

Sinjin had designed it to appear like the bedchamber of a Turkish pasha or Indian raja, a sensual realm awaiting the arrival of an houri or odalisque. He moved a little closer to Nuala, close enough to hear the rapid sigh of her breathing and note the flush in her cheeks.

He was an expert in reading the signs of a woman's arousal. She was far from indifferent to the place he had chosen for her initiation to his lovemaking.

"Do you like it?" he said, placing his hands lightly on her shoulders.

"I… It is most unusual."

"That is what I intended." He began rubbing his hands up and down her arms, feeling the tension beneath her unadorned sleeves. "Nuala…"

Her breath caught. He bent to her neck and kissed her, ever so lightly, above her high collar. The small hairs at the nape of her neck rose in response. Such a little thing, but it brought his cock to instant attention.

Functioning, thank God. Ready and more than willing.

He slid his hand to her waist. She was not wearing a corset or a bustle. He began to ache to the point of real pain. He could detect the fragrance of Nuala's excitement, feel her trembling as he moved his hands to her hips. And turned her around, slowly, slowly.

She would not look at him. Like a virgin preparing to accept a man for the first time, she gazed at the bare skin revealed by the open collar of his shirt.

"Are you afraid, Nuala?" he asked softly.

Her chin jerked up. "No."

"Has it been so long, then?" He cupped her face in his hand, feeling as if he held a bird struggling to take flight. "Lord Charles...did he please you?"

It was the wrong thing to say, and he knew it even before the words were out of his mouth. She pulled back sharply.

"My husband," she said coldly, "is none of your concern."

His anger returned, quite irrational, slipping inexplicably from his control. "He wasn't enough of a man for you, was he?" he demanded. "It wasn't a real marriage at all."

He fully expected her to leave then. But she remained where she was, fists clenched at her sides.

"Such words are beneath contempt," she said. "I was happy with him, and he with me. And now he is dead."

The hot flare of rage went out like a snuffed candle. Unfamiliar shame bade him drop to his knees and beg her forgiveness.

He could not go so far. But he wet his lips, forced his thoughts past the muffling cloud of lust and bowed his head.

"I beg your pardon," he said. "I spoke rashly, and stupidly."

Her silence could have felled an American buffalo. But once again she stayed when she could have gone.

"Lord Charles was a good man," she said. "Our

relationship was one of friendship and mutual support. I did not feel deprived. I still do not." She sighed. "If you are done with questions regarding my past, we may proceed."

CHAPTER TWELVE

PROCEED.

Sinjin wanted to laugh, but he'd done enough damage already.

Nuala had as good as admitted that she had not been with a man since she'd married Lord Charles; what she had done in the year and a half following her "service" at Donbridge was anybody's guess.

But Sinjin knew in his heart that she had been chaste since the first time he'd known her as Nola the chambermaid. Years of celibacy for a woman who was, from all he had experienced of her, fully capable of enjoying the sexual act.

Nevertheless, he must move carefully until he had reawakened the passion within her, and…

She is still your enemy.

The thought came out of nowhere. Yes, they had been enemies. She still regarded him as an opponent; her use of magic against him was proof of that. But after tonight, she would not be *his* enemy. She would not be a source of needs and hungers he could not master, hungers that robbed him of his manhood.

She would simply be another woman who had been in his bed.

He took great care as he cupped her face in his hands, lowered his head and kissed her. This time her stiffness lasted only a few seconds; abruptly she surrendered, her lips softening, her body relaxing. She had fully accepted her responsibility in meeting her obligation. But she wasn't helping. She was merely letting him have his way, yielding to his lusts like a whore entertaining yet another rutting male.

Sinjin almost stopped. *A whore? For God's sake, Sin, what's wrong with you?*

Nothing that bedding her wouldn't cure.

He slipped his tongue between her lips and touched hers. She gave a little, muffled gasp, whether of protest or pleasure he couldn't determine. He drew her tongue into his own mouth. There was no mistaking her soft moan, and the movement of her lips as they blossomed beneath his.

Sheer discipline prevented him from carrying her to the bed, lifting her skirts and entering her there and then. He was disgusted to find that his hands were shaking as he raised them to her hair and began working at the pins, loosing the flame-colored masses around her face.

Sinjin had learned to find many things attractive about Nuala, but none was so fascinating as her hair. It was a glory of autumnal hues, like a tumble of leaves drifting through his fingers.

"You are lovely," he whispered, burying his face in the fall of fire and earth.

Her lips parted as if to refute him, but he silenced her with another kiss. He set his fingers to the tiny hooks fastening the high collar of her bodice. He held the kiss, trying to ignore the unbearable pressure of his cock against his trousers as he undid the uppermost hooks to reveal the pale, slender column of her throat.

She held very still, allowing him to kiss the angle of her jaw, the tender skin beneath her ear, the side of her neck. He could feel her rapid pulse beneath his lips. He undid a few more hooks, revealing the lace neckline of her chemise.

He had been right. No corset, only the boning built into the bodice. He trailed kisses from the fluttering hollow at the base of her neck to the uppermost swell of her breasts, and paused to look at her face.

Her eyes were closed, her head slightly thrown back in a pose of abandon. Sinjin fought back the swell of triumph that threatened to overwhelm his senses. He unhooked the remainder of her bodice, exposing the entire upper portion of her chemise. Underneath lay only her naked flesh. Her small, youthfully firm breasts begged for his touch.

Yet he lingered, letting his breath bathe her skin, drawing out the moment when he would unbutton the yoke of her chemise and taste her.

"Sinjin," she whispered.

"Hmm."

"Ought we not… Ought we not go to…to the—"

His pleasure in hearing the husky yearning in her voice momentarily confused his understanding. He cursed himself for an idiot, lifted her and carried her to the bed.

She lay back almost limp, as if, having decided to let down her defenses, she had gone too far in the other direction. That would change soon enough. He tossed his smoking jacket across a chair and knelt beside her, hearing the familiar sound of the mattress creak under his weight. One by one he removed her shoes, leaving her stockings in place. The erotic effect was nearly overwhelming.

"Is there anything you would like me to do?" he asked, each word torn away from his impatience.

She shook her head against the pillow, locks of her hair catching on her moistened lips. He brushed them away, leaned over her and began a second descent from her mouth to her breasts. He paused just long enough to help her remove the bodice, leaving her pale, slightly freckled skin covered only by a thin layer of fine cambric. Her brown nipples were erect, pushing boldly against the fabric.

The blood throbbed in Sinjin's cock. He bent to Nuala's right breast and covered it with his mouth, drawing her nipple in along with the cloth. She shuddered. He flicked his tongue over the tip of her breast, sucking gently until the lawn seemed to dissolve.

He paused, looking up to gauge Nuala's reaction. Her breath came in little, excited puffs. She would be begging him to take her once he had made a thorough exploration of the body he was finally permitted to touch.

With painstaking thoroughness he gave her left

breast the same attention as he had the right. There might as well have been no barrier at all between his lips and her flesh. Unbuttoning the delicate pearl buttons of the chemise, he eased the yoke down until he could slip her breasts free.

They were like delicate fruits in his hands. He cupped them and massaged her nipples with his thumbs, then circled his tongue around each aureole. Nuala moaned.

Gratified that his skill had not deserted him, Sinjin pressed her breasts together and dipped his tongue into the valley between as he continued to rub his thumbs around her nipples. She arched her back as if she were demanding even more. He gave it to her, taking as much of her breast into his mouth as he could hold, suckling first gently and then with greater force.

It was still not enough. Not for either one of them. Sinjin reached beneath her waist, searching for the hooks that fastened her skirt. Her lack of a bustle and voluminous underskirts and petticoats made the removal easy. In a matter of moments he had discarded the overskirts, let them fall to the floor and was crouched atop a marvelously slender yet very womanly figure clad only in the chemise and a pair of simple drawers.

Her body was as he had imagined in his waking dreams, and yet far more arousing than he had anticipated. He had in the past preferred women of more prominent attributes, but her slenderness was no less stimulating. It revealed no signs of over-delicacy or fragility; there was strength beneath the pliant softness of her skin.

"Beautiful," Sinjin murmured, running his palm over her ribs and stomach, stopping only inches above the heat between her thighs. He lifted the chemise above her waist and higher still, exposing her torso.

For just a moment Nuala raised her hands to touch the hem of the chemise, as if she might pull it down again. But she gave up the attempt as soon as she had begun, gathering folds of the sheets between her fingers.

"Yes," Sinjin purred. "Give yourself over to me, Nuala."

Her lips parted, her tongue darting out between them in unconscious provocation. Sinjin caught her tongue in his mouth before she could withdraw it and sucked it gently, muffling her low cries. He trailed his hand over her breasts and down again, cupped her hips and slid his hand beneath to her lovely round bottom. Then he released her mouth and followed the trail his hands had laid, kissing her nipples, the underside of her breasts, the hollow under her ribs, the slight rise of her belly.

A few inches lower and he would taste the arousal he smelled so keenly. He could already feel her juices burning on his tongue.

But he knew she wasn't ready. Perhaps no man had ever kissed her so intimately. He must bring her to such a state that she would be unable to object to anything he chose to do. Her pleasure, her helplessness in the face of his lovemaking, gave him power that he would savor.

"Shall I stop?" he asked, squeezing her bottom gently.

The short jerk of her head was answer enough. He let his hand drift lower, across the little mound of downy hair, still shielded by her drawers. Lower yet, until he found the open hem that gave him perfect access.

A flood of moisture spilled from her engorged lips even before he began his exploration. He slid his finger over her folds, dipping it into the quivering valley where her body wept with joy. She gasped a word, whether protest or encouragement he couldn't tell and didn't care. He stroked her tiny nub with his fingertip; the moment he touched it she heaved against him as if her body could no longer be confined by the forces of gravity that chained it to the earth.

Sinjin smiled in spite of his own considerable pain and rubbed ever so gently, circling round with his thumb. Nuala's breath came fast now, her excitement a living presence in the room. When he felt her swollen lips begin to quiver, he withdrew his thumb, slipped his finger between her folds again and teased his way into her delightfully tight entrance. Her wetness made the movement easy, but he was slow and careful in his work, making certain that she would not come before he was ready. Before he was inside her.

"My sweet Nuala," he said, sliding his finger a little deeper, "has no one ever give you such pleasure before?"

Sinjin's question was a distant ringing in Nuala's ears, almost lost beneath the drumming of her pulse.

All her attention, all sensation was centered on the part of her no man had touched for a century…and it might as well have been as if no man had touched it in the whole of her life.

Unable to maintain even a modicum of modesty, she let her thighs open to his persuasive caresses. That part of her still capable of rational thought knew that there was little time remaining before her bargain with Sinjin was sealed.

And she wanted it sealed. If she had desired him in Mr. Saunterton's library, that desire had been a pale imitation of her feelings now. His finger had penetrated her, but it could never satisfy the aching emptiness where his hands had touched.

So she held back. She didn't allow her body to let go completely, though it fought for sweet release. She was almost relieved when he drew back and began to unbutton his trousers. She sensed that he had meant to continue slowly, compelling her to experience the unparalleled skill and breadth of his lovemaking. But his impatient lust seemed to seep into her very flesh, a hunger that left him as vulnerable and needy as she.

Nuala was not entirely certain when the warmth of his fingers was replaced by the weight of his hips between her thighs. First there was only heat, and then the head of his shaft grazed her inner thigh, probing, seeking its way home.

Everything they had said and done, all the angry words and recriminations, had led inevitably to this moment of joining.

The end of the war. The beginning of something

else, something Nuala didn't dare define lest it slip away like a gambler's luck.

She reached up to clutch the bunched muscles of Sinjin's shoulders, standing out in sharp relief through the fine linen of his shirt. He bent his head over her, kissed her almost roughly, eased himself closer so that his shaft nestled against her, awaiting its final office.

"I have you at last," he growled in her ear, his voice almost unfamiliar. "All these years I've waited to get you under me, witch. Now there will be no escape."

His words made no sense. The haze of pleasure clouding her mind began to clear. All these years? Did he mean since their last meeting at Donbridge? But he had not desired her then. He hadn't even really known her, and when they had met again in London he had hated her.

Witch. It was as if he hated her still. As if this were a long-anticipated revenge, and he intended to take more than what she was willing to give.

Instinctively she began to press her legs together, all to no avail. He would not be moved. Something was very wrong. There was no gentleness in him now, no effort to secure her ease and pleasure. His teeth grazed the lobe of her ear, nipping with too much force. He pinned her wrists to the bed, stretching her arms out to the sides as if he would bind her with iron manacles.

"Do you remember?" he whispered, running his tongue from her chin to her cheek. "You ignored me. You reviled me because of my father, though I was innocent."

"Your fa—" She tried to speak, but he smothered her with his mouth.

"I know how to stop you," he said when he let her breathe again. "I know how to drain you of everything you possess, all the evil that lies within you."

He moved his hips, and the head of his penis slid to the hot, wet mouth of her entrance. Panic blinded her, numbed her to all sensation but terror.

Terror gave her the power. Terror shaped the spell before she could think of the proper incantation, the gray magic that robbed him of his potency within a few brief seconds. Fear gave her the very strength his confusion stole from him. She bucked, snapping her legs together as he rolled away. She tugged her chemise over her body and jumped from the bed.

Sinjin lay on his back, his face pale and stunned. He made no attempt to rise and stop her as she dragged her skirts up over her hips and fastened them at her waist. He didn't even look at her when she snatched up her bodice, shrugged it on and somehow managed the tiny hooks.

The door seemed a hundred miles away. She reached it safely, yanked it open and half turned, bewildered and breathless, bracing herself to see a man she didn't recognize.

But she did. Sinjin hadn't changed. He lifted himself to his elbows, shook his head sharply, stared at her with an expression of utter bafflement.

"Nuala?"

His voice was groggy, as if he'd just awakened from a deep sleep plagued with nightmares. Nuala hesitated. She almost returned to him, to ask if he were ill or suffering some mental impediment.

She could not. She stepped through the door, nearly ran down the stairs and fled through the entrance hall with no thought as to how she might return to Belgravia. She had asked Bremner to return at half three, estimating that three hours would be sufficient time to…

The thought of what she and Sinjin had almost done was suddenly unbearable. Unbearable because of what she had seen and heard. Unbearable because of what she had lost.

She continued to walk at a fast pace, striding for the gate to the cottage grounds. Circus Road was empty save for a single carriage in the distance, the light of its lamps nearly lost in the mist. Half a mile on, she recognized the lanky figure hunched over the reins of the brougham. She stopped to catch her breath as Bremner pulled up to meet her.

"Your ladyship?" he said, his ordinarily sleepy eyes widening in surprise. "Have I come late?"

"No, Bremner. Let us go home." She said nothing more as he leaped down from his perch and handed her into the carriage, offering her a blanket to cover her knees. She settled back in the seat as the strength drained out of her legs.

Her thoughts racing, she barely noticed the ride home. In what seemed like mere moments Bremner was at the carriage door again, ready to help her down.

She rushed into the house, grateful that she had made clear that none of the servants were to wait up for her return. Deborah must be safely in her bed; only the ticking of the long case clock in the drawing room gave a sense that the house was inhabited at all.

The climb to her bedroom seemed to require every last ounce of effort Nuala could muster. She undressed and lay down, though the cotton sheets seemed to rub her skin raw.

He wasn't himself. Could there be any doubt of that? His voice, the way he had spoken…

Just as he had spoken at Donbridge. *Witch.* Such hatred. Such gloating satisfaction.

He was ill. Some trouble was weighing on him too heavily, driving him to speak and behave as he never would if he were in his right mind.

I should have stayed. I might have helped him.

At the cost of accepting him into her body without pleasure, without tenderness, without…

She captured the half-formed word in her fist before it could escape her mouth. Attempting to analyze what had happened would be a useless exercise now, when she was so weary and discouraged and afraid. Best to sleep on it. The morning always brought clarity. The world would look very different then, and she could sort out her tangled memories.

Nuala closed her eyes.

The fire.

It seemed to be everywhere, consuming the trees, the people, the world.

Hands bound behind him and collared with a coil

of rope, Christian gazed down from the gallows at those who had sentenced him. Not many men were among those condemned for heresy and witchcraft, but he had been denounced by a woman whose deathly ill infant he had failed to cure with his healing powers.

The child had been too far advanced in its disease. The woman had waited too long. But she must have someone to blame…and who better than a witch?

Nuala watched from the alley, her empty stomach clenched with horror. No matter her own modest powers, she could not escape Uncle Turner's iron grip. He would not let her go to Christian, share his fate.

If she had only returned sooner, she would have been beside her husband. Where she ought to be.

Let me go, she begged silently. The words went unspoken. Uncle had cast a spell to silence her lest she cry out and call attention to herself and the three witches with her.

For she, like all her family, had been denounced and would have been slain after a perfunctory "trial" by the town magistrates and the soberly dressed, self-righteous jurors who looked with satisfaction upon the bodies dangling from the gibbet. So many had died before this terrible day. So many who had worked only for the good, healing and helping the crops to grow and the cattle to thrive.

But we are different. And that was enough.

The witch-finder faced Christian, a Bible in his hand, and began to deliver his final sermon of condemnation. His voice was deep, commanding, without a thimble's worth of compassion or regret.

Hatred was an emotion Nuala had never felt before these past few weeks of terror. But she had learned to hate very well indeed. She stared at the witch-finder's back, wishing upon him the same fate he had decreed for his victims.

"Quiet, child," her uncle whispered. But he could not silence her heart.

One of the men waiting for the hanging looked toward the alley. Uncle Turner shrank back, but the young man did not see them. He glanced about the square, his brows drawn and his mouth pressed in a thin line. Had Nuala not known what he was, she might have believed him to be no more than a youth longing to be anywhere but in this place of evil.

But he had stood by his father throughout the trial, approved of the witch-finder's heinous acts, made no protest when Christian and the others were condemned to death.

Nuala had gone to him. She had pleaded, promised, begged on her knees. She had offered him everything he had demanded of her. Her body, her obedience, her respect. All but the one thing she could never give...her love.

He hadn't listened. He had hardened his heart against her, knowing she could not love him. He would do nothing to stop this travesty of justice.

Martin Makepeace. There was only one man she despised more than him...the man who now stood upon the scaffold and placed the noose around Christian's neck.

She screamed, though the cry went no further than

her chest. Uncle's grip tightened. He stroked her hair, murmuring calming chants that had no effect. Aunt Turner and Sally began to sob.

Nuala's eyes remained dry. All the fluids in her body had turned to ice. The witch-finder finished his speech on a triumphant note. The mayor, who had presided over the trials, gave the signal, and Christian was set in place. He raised his eyes to the heavens. If he prayed, he did so without words, without cries for deliverance.

The judges and their sycophants watched, unmoving. The crowd of villagers bunched behind them were equally still. They had done their work well. Did they regret their denunciations of those who had helped them?

Nuala turned her gaze to Christian's face. His skin was flushed, sweating, but there was still no sign of fear. Perhaps the spells had succeeded. Perhaps his body would release his spirit without suffering.

Save him, Uncle. Oh, please, save him.

Uncle Turner did nothing. Sally wept.

And Martin Makepeace watched.

Nuala reached into herself, into the deepest reaches of her abilities. She had never used them in the way she meant to now. Never worked to influence a man's body or mind. Or to kill. But hatred gave her a new strength. She spoke the words in her heart, willing to give her life to lend them power.

At first she thought it was only the smoke, or the shock of the torments to which Christian had been subject during the interrogation. But he closed his eyes and sagged beneath the rope, head lolling, as the life leaked gently out of his body.

Sally's muffled sobs grew louder. Aunt hushed her. They knew.

Christian was dead. Beyond suffering. Beyond the reach of Comfort Makepeace and his despicable accomplices.

Nuala collapsed in Uncle Turner's arms. But the strength had gone out of him, as well. She slumped to the ground, her mind a blank, her body fruitlessly attempting to empty her hollow stomach.

Christian is dead.

Her head was a blacksmith's anvil, but she lifted it. She looked once more at Christian's face and sent her love after his fleeing spirit.

And then she looked at Comfort Makepeace. He was speaking with the hangman now, disappointment and anger in the set of his narrow shoulders. The punishment had been circumvented, as if by an act of God. Christian Starling had not adequately paid for his sins on this Earth.

"He will suffer in Hell," one of the sober, righteous magistrates said. There was a low chuckle. Someone in the village crowd seconded his comment.

Nuala was hardly aware that she rose to her feet. Uncle Turner tried to take her arm. She had no difficulty in shaking him off. Her skirts dragged around her ankles, but it was as if they anchored her to Mother Earth, drawing the very powers of soil and stone and life to fill the emptiness in her body.

She darted forward before Uncle could even think

to stop her, dashed out of the shelter of the alley and into the square. A score of startled faces turned toward her.

Martin Makepeace gaped, his face going pale. His father's expression held surprise no more than an instant, then hardened with hate that almost matched Nuala's own.

"Witch!" he snarled, pointing. "God has brought you to us at last!" He gestured to his men. "Seize her!"

They hesitated, almost as if they sensed what was about to happen. Nuala lifted her hands. She called upon the Dark Powers, those her people shunned as they shunned all violence. Lightning prickled in her fingertips with a heat so intense that she would have felt agony had she been able to feel anything at all.

Uncle's voice spoke in her mind, as was sometimes possible in times of great trouble. She ignored his pleas. A black cloud surrounded her. She completed her incantation. For a moment there was no response. And then, with an almost comical look of surprise on his face, Comfort Makepeace clutched his chest.

Even had she wished to halt her revenge, Nuala could not have done so. The flames burst from the center of Makepeace's body, engendered from within, fed by his flesh and bones and internal parts.

He screamed, pawing uselessly at his chest as his doublet melted away. Martin Makepeace started toward his father, his horror limned in hellish light. He retreated again at the heat of the flames, helpless, his voice hoarse with wordless cries.

Comfort Makepeace fell to his knees, no longer capable of speech. The flames consumed his ribs and spine, his groin and his thighs. Yet still he lived. His dying body collapsed like a building neglected for a hundred years. The stench was so choking that the watching people hacked and coughed and stumbled, a herd of sheep without a shepherd.

Nuala lowered her hands. The black sorcery deserted her, and this time she had nothing left of will to keep her on her feet. She fell, her vision going dim as Martin Makepeace knelt beside his father, his hands clasped as if in prayer.

Then he looked up. He wore a mask instead of a face, a mask so distorted and hideous that no human hand could have carved it.

"Hear me, witch," he snarled. "I will hunt you down. Wherever you go, no matter how many years it may require, I will find you. And you will suffer."

"Hurry, child!" Uncle Turner had emerged from the alley, his eyes wide with shock and horror. He hooked his hands under Nuala's arms and dragged her away. No one dared to interfere or follow.

Uncle and Aunt took Nuala up between them and began to run.

As her useless feet bumped over the unpaved lane, Nuala heard nothing of the scuffle of her kinfolk's shoes or their rasping breath. It was Martin's threat she heard. It was his face she saw, a monster's face, pitiless and shaped by a monstrous kind of joy.

She would remember that face to the end of her days. No matter where she fled, no matter how many

good works she might to do atone for her terrible
crime, she would always see his face.

Sinjin's face.

CHAPTER THIRTEEN

NUALA WOKE WITH A START of terror as the bedsheets smoldered at her feet. She leaped from the bed and snatched up her dressing gown, beating at flames that had just begun to lick at the cotton.

But there was no fire. The sheets were damp and cool with perspiration, whole and clean.

Nuala was too ill to reach the lavatory at the end of the hall. She heaved into the dustbin in the corner of the room and remained there on her knees, trembling with distress.

For so many years she had buried the memories. Nearly everything but the sickening recollection of how she had unleashed black sorcery to kill, the most awful sin any witch could commit.

And she had been cast out for that sin. Oh, no one had cursed her. No one had punished her. Martin Makepeace had never found her. She had not lost her powers. But she had not aged. She had not died, even as her surviving family grew old and passed on. Instead, she had been compelled to make amends for her terrible mistake by helping others find love. And though she had come to see her work as her true mission in life, a blessing born out of tragedy, she had hoped that one day the Light would find her worthy of forgiveness and release her.

But it was not to be. If she had been forgiven, she would not have relived every ugly detail of that day. She would not have been compelled to witness Christian's death again, experience the savagery of Martin Makepeace's hatred.

And her own.

Slowly she rose, felt her way to a chair and collapsed into it. *Sinjin's face.* It had been the one wrong element, the one false note in an otherwise accurate memory of pain and suffering. Now that she was fully awake, she understood that seeing him had been only an invention of her crippled imagination.

But he had called her "witch." He had spoken of stopping her, draining her of all the evil that lay within her.

She moaned behind her hands. Her own fears had spun those words, twisted whatever he had really said into something cruel and distorted.

Surely that, too, was part of her punishment. Just when she had permitted herself to recognize the strength of her attraction to Sinjin, she had been robbed of any chance at pleasure and reconciliation. Her very thoughts had betrayed her.

Dawn light was beginning to show through the small crack between the draperies. Nuala lifted her head. She would not permit fear to rule her. She must see Sinjin again. She would see that what she had heard and felt in Sinjin's bed had indeed been an illusion, a construction of her own guilt.

She sat very quietly until Booth arrived with a tray of tea and toast. Perhaps the young woman had sensed that Nuala was of no mind to speak to anyone, not even Deborah. Making her best effort to nibble at the toast, Nuala left most of it untouched and rang for Booth again.

It must be a formal call. She would take Booth, so that no one might assume she was visiting Sinjin for a private interview. She would look into his face, his dark eyes, and know…

She barely reached the dustbin in time to be sick again. When she had recovered, she recognized that her brave intentions were no match for the memories she could not escape.

There was only one place to go…a place she had avoided for most of her long life. The place where she had been born, where Christian had died. Only there could she face these newly powerful visions and rid herself of her mad delusions about Sinjin.

She asked Booth to begin packing comfortable, practical clothing for an impromptu visit to the countryside. She would be making no calls on friends there; she had none. As far as she knew, she had no living kin in Suffolk. The train would carry her to Ipswich; from there she would locate an inn and hire a carriage.

Nothing more remained to be done but to see Deborah.

The young woman was ensconced in her room.

Her suite was large and included a sitting room with a desk and comfortable chairs, and she seemed perfectly content to remain there rather than join Nuala for meals or engage in social calls.

It has only been five days since her visit to White-chapel, Nuala reminded herself as she paused before Deborah's door. No matter how shaken the girl had been by the experience she still refused to discuss, she was young and resilient. Certainly Nuala could be of no help to her until she herself had firm control of her emotions again.

Perhaps it was best if she didn't disturb Deborah now. A note would be sufficient. Nuala did not intend to be gone more than three days, four at the most.

Nuala went downstairs and wrote out a brief note, informing Deborah of her plans and her general location in case of emergency. She waited for Bremner to bring round the brougham, ticking off the interminable minutes.

When she returned from Suffolk, she would know how to separate her past from her relationship with Sinjin. If there was even a relationship with Sinjin at all.

THE MIRROR REFLECTED the same familiar face: the dark eyes and hair, the same nose and lips and jawline.

Sinjin rubbed his hand across his mouth, feeling the stubble that had grown since yesterday morning. He knew he must shave, dress, go about his business. Spend safely masculine time with the Forties, find a pliant female...

Nuala had been pliant. Until something had happened…something he still couldn't begin to comprehend. He couldn't forget the terror in her eyes.

What did I do?

He slammed his fist on the washstand, nearly upsetting the basin. All he remembered was lust… black, seething lust tinged with anger as inappropriate as it had been unexpected.

Witch. He remembered speaking the word in a tone filled with rage and contempt. It was as if he'd returned in time to the first moment he'd seen her in Hyde Park.

But he wasn't the same as he'd been then. Nuala was far from innocent, but…

You are as much to blame for what happened at Donbridge as she ever was. At some crucial moment during the past weeks, he had fully accepted that fact, acknowledging it instead of dodging the admission whenever it entered his mind.

He looked away from the glass and stared at his untouched bed. He had abandoned the love-nest as soon as he had regained his sense, choosing the Spartan comfort of his own bedchamber. But his head had been full of images of fire, pain, death. And it had been those images that had twisted him into someone who could come so very close to taking a woman against her will.

Good God.

With a groan, he paced around the room looking for something to smash. But there was nothing worth destroying, even if he had been so childish as to wreck some inoffensive object merely to soothe his conscience.

If only he could remember the words. The exact words that had so frightened Nuala even before he had tried to do the unthinkable.

She would never forgive him. The thought of never seeing her again made the bottom drop out of his stomach.

Because you still want her. Want her more than anything you've ever wanted in your life.

Numb and sluggish, he dressed without his valet's assistance, declined breakfast and went directly to his club. Leo was comfortably settled in an oversize leather armchair, reading some scholarly work.

"Sin," he said, looking up. "Up and about early, I see." He frowned as Sin sat in the chair beside his. "What is it? You look like a man standing at the mouth of Hell."

Sinjin laughed. "Very perceptive of you, Erskine."

Leo closed the book and leaned his elbow on the armrest. "Anything you'd care to discuss?"

"No."

"Ah. Lady Charles, I presume?"

Sinjin signaled a waiter. Much too early to drink. He didn't give a damn.

"Bad indeed," Leo remarked as the waiter returned with a glass of whiskey. "I should think a man of your experience would be able to ignore the rumors."

Forgetting the glass in his hand, Sinjin stared at Leo. "What rumors?"

"That Lady Charles has set her cap at you, and you're about ready to abandon your oath of bachelorhood."

"Ha." Sinjin snorted so loudly that the few other club members present glanced inquisitively in his direction. He beat back the panic that had taken him by the throat, remembered his liquor and gulped it down. "What can possibly have led to such rumors?"

"You don't know?"

Of course he knew. Someone must have reported Nuala's visit to Donbridge, or a servant had gossiped about her going to Sinjin's cottage on Circus Road. He had become aware that rumors of some sort were already circulating, but he would never have guessed that they would tend in this direction.

Marriage...

Sinjin set down his glass with the greatest possible care. "There was nothing said...about Lady Charles's reputation?" he asked in a low voice.

Leo leaned back, his expression unreadable. "Are you so concerned for her reputation?"

The room was very quiet. People were listening while pretending not to, and Sinjin didn't intend to give them any more fodder.

"Not at all," he said. "Neither she nor I have anything to conceal."

Leo rubbed his thumb over his book's leather binding. "Nevertheless, it might be best for you to avoid any hint of partiality toward Lady Charles in the near future, for both your sakes."

That, Sinjin reflected bitterly, should present no difficulty. He rose, deliberately foregoing the temptation of another drink. "Thank you for your company, Erskine. And your advice."

"Gladly given, Donnington."

Sinjin left, running the gauntlet of those too-knowing stares. He considered calling on Melbyrne. They had scarcely spoken since Sinjin's return from Donbridge, and Sinjin had no idea what the boy had decided to do about Lady Orwell.

After last night, Sinjin hardly cared.

He wandered aimlessly about, visited his favorite haberdashery, purchased a new tie and went for an early ride in Hyde Park. But he could not silence his thoughts. Who could have put it about that Nuala was pursuing him with marriage in mind? Someone in the Forties? Ferrer, quite possibly…save that Ferrer would surely have preferred to suggest that Nuala was more interested in sexual liaisons than marriage.

Certainly Nuala might have wished to ruin his reputation as the founder of the Forties and the principal rake in London. But *marry* him?

He tried to brush the ridiculous notion aside, but by midafternoon he realized that he had to see her again. To set things right between them, even if he must humble himself as he had never done before in his life.

If all Leo had said about the rumors were true, Sinjin's calling on Nuala would only encourage them. But it was far better to meet her openly than attempt to arrange another private rendezvous, which Nuala would surely refuse in any case. And she would have Lady Orwell's company to lend respectability to the visit.

The time for social calls had nearly expired by the time Sinjin had made himself ready. He left his card with a parlor maid and wondered what he might do if Nuala wouldn't see him. Beating down the door would certainly attract attention and do nothing to regain Nuala's trust.

To his surprise, the parlor maid returned and invited Sinjin to enter. He was kept cooling his heels in the entrance hall until Lady Orwell appeared.

The young woman paused at some distance from Sinjin, reserved in her half-mourning, punctiliously courteous.

"Lady Charles is not at home, Lord Donnington," she said after the briefest of curtsies. "If you should care for tea…"

Sinjin felt as tongue-tied as a schoolboy. "Thank you, Lady Orwell. Can you tell me when Lady Charles is to return?"

"That I do not know." She gestured toward the stairs and led him to a door to what Sinjin presumed was the drawing room. He hesitated, seeing no reason to remain, but as he met Lady Orwell's grave gaze he began to wonder if he had had in some way misjudged her. *This* was not a woman expecting imminent engagement to a man she had been assiduously pursuing.

Had Melbyrne decided against courting her? Was this the face of a woman spurned, grieving for a lost love?

Guilt had already taken up residence in Sinjin's gut; it took little enough to add to its weight. He followed Lady Orwell into the drawing room, set his hat on the table and waited while the young woman excused herself with a murmur of apology.

Left alone in the room, Sinjin noted that it was strangely absent of any trinkets or decorations that suggested a woman's personal touch. It was clean and uncluttered, almost masculine...perhaps not so surprising when one remembered that Nuala had only been resident in London for a short while.

Unable to sit still, he rose and stalked around the room. By sheer chance he happened to glance behind one of the chairs near the mantelpiece. A painting leaned facedown against the wall.

Glancing toward the door, Sinjin lifted the painting away from the wall and turned it over. It was a portrait...a portrait of Nuala, recently painted but oddly anachronistic in style, as if it had been rendered centuries ago. Nuala's hair was bound up under a prim cap, and her dark dress bore a similarly prim, wide collar.

The clothing of another time. But Nuala's face was unchanged...solemn, her gaze looking out at the viewer with a deep and abiding sadness.

Sinjin closed his eyes, the image burning under his eyelids. There was something familiar about the gown Nuala had chosen to wear for the portrait. Something that drove him back to last night's inexplicable occurrence.

Fire. Fire and agony, a woman's triumphant face as she raised her arms and worked her black magic. Hatred beyond anything this world could contain...

Lady Orwell was just returning as Sinjin reached the door.

"I beg your pardon," he said, "but I must be going. I thank you for your hospitality."

She gazed at him with eyes that seemed far older than her years. "I shall tell Lady Charles that you called."

"I am grateful." Sinjin bowed shortly and strode for the front door. A woman was entering the house just as he reached the end of the hall. She was small and mousy, with unremarkable brown hair and eyes, but when she stopped to stare at Sinjin he was instantly aware that she was not as ordinary as she seemed.

Sinjin had had enough of extraordinary women. He tipped his hat and bowed, intending to continue on his way, but his feet refused to obey his will.

"Lord Donnington," the woman said, though they had not yet been introduced.

"Mrs. Summerhayes," Deborah said, coming to join them, "may I present Lord Donnington, the Earl of Donbridge. Lord Donnington, Mrs. Adolphus Summerhayes."

Sinjin bowed again. "Madam."

The young woman continued to stare with a strangely unconscious rudeness. "Have you come to see Nuala?"

Her frank question left Sinjin temporarily speechless. Lady Orwell stepped into the breach.

"I have informed Lord Donnington that Lady Charles is not at home," she said.

"Oh," Mrs. Summerhayes mumbled, as if her thoughts were far away. "You can't go on as you are, you know," she said to Sinjin. "There are too many things left undone."

"Lord Donnington was just leaving," Lady Orwell said quickly.

"It isn't over," Mrs. Summerhayes said, as if Lady Orwell hadn't spoken. "You must purge yourself, Lord Donnington, or he will ruin you both."

"What is she talking about?" Sinjin demanded of Lady Orwell, aware that he had begun to perspire. Deborah made no answer. He turned back to Mrs. Summerhayes. "To whom are you referring?"

She blinked. "Hasn't he told you?"

"Who?"

Her gaze focused again. "Forgive me," she said in a small voice. "It is not my place to interfere."

Sinjin's skin had gone icy cold. "*Who* wishes to ruin us?"

As if she had felt his chill, Mrs. Summerhayes shivered. "I cannot…see clearly," she murmured. "There is one who plagues you. One who speaks with your voice."

How could she possibly know? "Nuala…Nuala told you…."

Mrs. Summerhayes took a deep breath. "Is it your desire to know the truth, Lord Donnington?"

"For God's sake." Sinjin glanced again at Lady Orwell, but she had vanished. He could feel his knees begin to turn rubbery, his brain to fill with fog. "Make yourself plain, madam."

"I will help you," she said, "for Nuala's sake."

"Help me? Help me how?"

"I can draw him to you. Make him…speak."

"Who is he?"

But she had returned to her strange inner world. "Come to my house when you are ready. I shall do what I can."

"What *are* you?"

"I speak for those who can no longer speak for themselves."

Then she wandered away, into the shadows of the corridor that disappeared behind the staircase. Sinjin stared after her, laughed under his breath and slammed his hat more firmly on his head.

She was mad. As all the Widows were mad, in one fashion or another. But she knew things she shouldn't have known. She had looked into his soul. She had seen the...thing that had frightened Nuala.

I speak for those who can no longer speak for themselves.

Ludicrous. Beyond ridiculous.

Sinjin waved his carriage away and walked briskly back to his club. Male acquaintances tipped their hats as he passed; young women simpered and curtseyed. He paid them no heed nor noticed his surroundings until he nearly collided with Felix Melbyrne.

"I say!" Felix said. He backed away, removed his hat and played with the brim in a nervous manner, though his smile remained fixed in place. "How are you, Sin?"

Sinjin grunted, in no mood for conversation. Felix wasn't put off.

"I know I was a poor guest at Donbridge," he said slowly. "I couldn't bear to see Lady Charles... That is, I had reached the conclusion..." He swallowed. "Sin, I'm going to ask Deborah to marry me."

The declaration penetrated Sinjin's consciousness. "Marry her?"

"Yes. I love her." His smile became almost fierce. "You won't stop me, Sin. Not this time."

If it was outrage Felix wanted, he was to be disappointed. "Good luck," Sinjin said gruffly. "If you will excuse me…"

"You…you don't object?" Felix stammered.

"You are your own man, Felix. You may do as you choose."

"Then…have I your blessing?"

"If you require it, yes."

Melbyrne's grin became positively incandescent. "Thank you, Sin. I shan't forget this."

He was off before Sinjin thought to ask what had precipitated this sudden urge to propose. It didn't really matter. The boy had never been committed to the Forties in any case.

Sinjin took a few more steps, stopped again, glanced at his watch and looked back the way he had come.

Where the hell was Nuala? And what would he do when he found her again?

Destroy her.

Dragging his hand across his face, Sinjin banished the evil voice. He would keep it buried with enough whiskey to drown a whale.

Until she returned.

CHAPTER FOURTEEN

NUALA KNELT BEFORE the graves, head bowed.

The headstones were crumbling. They bore no names, no adornment; no one who did not know precisely where they were located could have found them.

That was how it had been meant to be, so no vengeful witch-finders could despoil the graves. Not that much had been left to bury, but at least some dignity had been granted the remains of the bodies left behind.

Mother. Nuala laid her palm on the grass that covered Mrs. Moran's resting place. Father, next to his beloved partner and wife.

There were others, nearly all of whom Nuala had known, worked beside, loved. Gregory, Sally, so many who had fallen.

The flowers Nuala had brought stirred in the wind. With barely a thought she sent the breeze away. She had been looking for peace here, some explanation for her returning powers, for what she had heard in Sinjin's voice and seen in his face. She had hoped for some gentle spirit to explain what she must do, how she might earn an end to the memories.

But the graves were silent. The rustling leaves in the nearby wood made no answer. The small animals who crept so near had no advice to give.

Slowly she rose, automatically brushing the soil and grass from her skirts. She wandered back along the barely visible path through the wood, beside several fields and into the village. It, too, was a quiet place, never touched by the witch-hunts. To these farmers and villagers, such horrible events might never have occurred.

Nuala retreated to her small room at the inn and lay on the bed, praying that a few hours' rest would bring some clarity to her mind. It did not. At dinner-time she descended to the dining parlor, prepared to eat another meal alone with her thoughts.

"Mind some company, gal?"

Nuala emerged from her brown study and glanced at the old woman in surprise. She hadn't seen the woman before; she might have been a fellow guest at the inn, or simply one of the villagers come in for a meal or a gossip with the innkeeper. Her appearance was unremarkable, her clothing very plain and patched, her skin weathered from much time spent out of doors. A straggle of thin, gray hair peeked out from beneath her bonnet.

"Please," Nuala said, indicating the chair next to hers.

The old woman sighed as she sank into the chair. "I see yow sittin' aloon here and thought ya might like a talk."

"That is very kind of you, Mrs...."

"Simkin." She signaled to the barmaid, with whom she was clearly acquainted, and grinned at Nuala. Her teeth were surprisingly white, and all seemed to be present.

"You've come a long way, haven't yow, gal?" Mrs. Simkin asked, meeting Nuala's gaze with watery blue eyes.

Nuala relaxed. In over two centuries, she'd had far more dealings with common folk than the Society of which she was now a part, and she was almost grateful to be called something other than "Lady Charles."

"I have, Mrs. Simkin," she said. "All the way from London."

"Huh." The old woman cocked her head. "More'n just from Lonnon, I think."

The air felt a little cold in spite of the warm weather. "We all make many journeys in life, do we not?"

Mrs. Simkin laughed. "Aye, that we do. Wise yow are, for such a fine lady."

Before Nuala could answer, the barmaid arrived with two pint glasses of ale. Mrs. Simkin immediately picked up her glass. Nuala left hers untouched.

"Come on, then, gal," Mrs. Simkin said. "Yer not too fine for a pint, or I ain't old enough to be yer granny."

Nuala couldn't help but smile. "It's been a very long time," she said.

The old woman set down her glass and studied Nuala with a grave air. "What is it, then?" she asked. "What's troublin' yow? It's him, innit?"

"I beg your pardon?"

"It's plain as day, gal. Yer runnin' away."

The ale exerted a suddenly powerful appeal. "What makes you assume such a thing, Mrs. Simkin?"

She shrugged. "Comes to me sometimes. Feelin's I get."

The old woman might have been talking about Nuala herself, of those long years when *feelings* had guided her in her work.

"We're both of us different, yow and me," Mrs. Simkin said. "That's why I have advice to give yow, unasked though it be." She finished her ale and stared pointedly at Nuala's glass. "Might be best if yow drink up, gal."

Nuala made no move to take it. Was it possible that she had found another witch, a survivor of the dark times? "What advice do you have for me, Mrs. Simkin?"

"There are things yet undone atween yow and this man. Runnin' away won't ease yer pain."

"I...I don't understand."

The blue eyes narrowed in their nests of wrinkles. "Lyin' don't suit yow, gal." She placed her hand at the small of her back and groaned, regarded her empty glass with disfavor and turned her unyielding gaze back to Nuala. "Yow understand well enough. Yow think yer afraid of him, but it's really yourself yow fear. That's why yow have to go back."

"Of course I intended to return. I only came to Suffolk—"

"—because yow thought the answers would be here. But they lie in yer own heart, gal."

Nuala stared at the nicks in the well-worn surface

of the table. The old woman was correct. She would not find answers here. What was there left to do but return and face Sinjin again?

"You are right, Mrs. Simkin," she said slowly. "I will find nothing more in Suffolk."

The old woman nodded, though she didn't smile. "Beware yer anger, gal. It lies at the root of the evil yow fight."

Her anger? Was that what the old woman had meant when she'd said that Nuala feared herself more than Sinjin? Hadn't she been angry with Sinjin from the beginning…angry that he'd held her to blame for Giles's death, angry that he had kept Felix Melbyrne from Deborah, angry that he had made her feel…

Nuala rose, making quite certain that she was steady on her feet before she let go of her chair. "Thank you for your advice, Mrs. Simkin," she said, laying several coins on the table. "I shall keep it in mind."

"There is something stronger than anger or hatred," the old woman said before she could walk away. "It is the one thing yow have lacked since the day of yer sin."

Nuala turned back, feeling faint. "Who *are* you?"

But the other woman got up and hobbled away without another word, never slowing until she was out the door.

Suppressing her impulse to follow the old seer, Nuala spoke to the innkeeper and arranged for a carriage to be brought round in two hours' time. She retraced her steps to the graveyard and knelt on the giving earth.

"I understand now," she said. "You sent me the answer I needed, even if it was not the one I hoped to hear."

Leaves swayed, and a mouse rattled through the grass. Nuala lowered her hand, and the tiny rodent scurried into her palm.

"Is that what I've been missing?" she whispered. "Is that why the price has not yet been paid?"

The mouse twitched its whiskers at her, leaped from her hand and scurried away. Nuala got up, touched each of the headstones in turn, and made her way back to the inn.

THE WRITING IN THE LETTER was as ugly as its sender.

Deborah laid the sheet of paper facedown on her desk and gazed out the window at the black, starless sky. She need never read it again; its contents were seared into her mind, misspelled scrawls that nevertheless made their meaning clear.

Bray had given her five days. Five days to pay the man before he released his "evidence" of her low birth to the gutter newspapers, those cheap and common scandal sheets whose editors had no compunctions about printing scurrilous items that might embarrass the nobs with their fancy carriages and palatial houses.

Strangely enough, Deborah hadn't been alarmed by the threat. She had told herself that the low papers were scarcely to be believed when it came to the most pernicious gossip. She knew that hardly anyone in Mayfair or Belgravia was likely to read them. And she had promised to wait for Ioan to confirm or deny the existence of the "witnesses" Bray had claimed he could produce as evidence of Deborah's shameful origins. She had placed her faith in Ioan's certainty of Bray's deception, and so she had not paid the blackguard a single penny.

But now she understood that such hopes and assumptions had been misplaced. The five days had passed, and Bray had made good on his threats. He had sent Deborah a copy of the testimony given by the "landlady" who had agreed to confirm his assertions. It was plain, unadorned and entirely convincing. There were others just like the landlady who were prepared to come forward, and not all of them could have been bribed or bullied into supporting Bray's story.

So it must be true. The sooner Deborah accepted the consequences of that truth, the better. The papers containing the sordid news might already have been released. In the best of all possible worlds, no one in Society would ever learn of the scandal.

But *she* would know. She could never forget.

Returning the papers to the desk drawer, Deborah found that her thoughts were strangely clear. The best thing she could do now was quietly leave London. Her parents—the only parents she had ever known—had left her a cottage at Baden. She might not merit the title she had received from Lawrence, but the cottage was hers by law. There she would be safe.

Nuala ought to be told. But she had gone out of town again, clearly preoccupied with troubles of her own—doubtless involving the earl of Donnington—and Deborah had no desire to add to them.

No; it would be wisest to escape the city while Nuala was away. Once Deborah had reached Baden, she would write to Nuala and explain everything. Felix would also have to be told, of course, when she was well settled. If Society determined that he was courting Lady Orwell and she had jilted him, surely no one would blame *him*. Any embarrassment he might suffer would be short-lived.

And Ioan wouldn't have to worry about her any longer.

Resolved on her course of action, Deborah entered her dressing room and began to consider which of her gowns she would take with her. She intended to live modestly; there would be no need for ball gowns or evening frocks. Two trunks would suffice for her journey; she would secure Stella another position before she left. There would doubtless be girls in Baden that Deborah could employ to help her in running her new household.

She was examining one of her half-mourning gowns when Stella's familiar knock sounded at the door. Deborah let her in, careful not to reveal any untoward emotion.

"Mr. Davies has come to see you, Lady Orwell," Stella said, a certain eager gleam in her eye. "He is waiting at the kitchen door."

Deborah studied Stella closely. The girl had known of Ioan's first visit, and doubtless servants' gossip had spread throughout the household. The world below stairs was a stratified one, in which the staff were very proud of their own ranks and the positions of their masters and mistresses, yet there was nothing but approval in Stella's manner. She quivered like a hound on the scent.

"No one will speak of it, your ladyship. I swear it."

Deborah believed her, but still she hesitated. Ioan had promised to return when he had proof that Bray's claims were either true or false. He would only be confirming what she already knew, and her shame would be complete.

But to say goodbye, and thank him again...that seemed the least she could do.

With Stella's aid, she dressed again and went downstairs. Ioan waited, cap in hand, his features picked out in moonlight and shadow. His solemn expression brightened when he saw her. Deborah's heart turned over.

"Lady Orwell," he said. "I have good news."

She tried not to look into his eyes, tried not to think of the strong, warm body under the worn and humble clothing. "Thank you for coming, Mr. Davies," she said.

He frowned a little, as if he were wondering why she seemed so uninterested in his "good news." "I have searched Whitechapel and talked with many people," he said. "There is no evidence that anything Bray said is true."

If only that were so. If only... Deborah took herself in hand and managed a smile.

"I am grateful for your efforts," she said. "You have put my mind at rest."

But she knew he didn't believe her. His frown, confined at first to his dark brows, reached his eyes.

"If you will forgive me, your mind is not at rest," he said.

How could she possibly tell him that she thought him to be lying, if only to protect her? "I have reason to believe that this...episode is not over," she said, feeling her way. "I have decided to leave London for a little while, until—"

"Leave London?" His quiet voice rose to an angry protest. "Why? You have no reason to do so. Not while I—"

He broke off. They stared at each other.

"You think I am lying to you," Ioan said.

"No! Not lying. It is just—"

"You've seen him again."

"No. Not since my last visit to Whitechapel."

He clenched and unclenched his fists. "I shall find him again. I shall do what I ought to have done in the beginning."

"No!" She began to walk toward him, stopped, tried to shake the confusion out of her head. "It has nothing to do with you, Mr. Davies. This is *my* concern. I have made my decision."

Never had Ioan Davies looked so close to violence. "And how will you explain this sudden departure to your own people?"

Her own people. The cream of Society, to which Ioan could never belong.

"Please understand, Ioan. Whether or not the story is true, I...need to return to the place I always considered my home."

"Where?"

"In Switzerland, at Baden. My... Sir Percival and Lady Shaw left me a cottage, and—"

"I will not let you go."

"We may be friends, Mr. Davies, but—"

He moved too swiftly. His arms closed around her, and his lips caught hers...firmly, decidedly, with all the leashed force of determined masculinity.

If she'd had any sense, she would have pushed him away. But she had none. She let him kiss her, and kissed him in return, captured by the joy of release.

Ioan broke off as quickly as he had begun. He held her a little away from him, breathing fast, his eyes afire with passion.

"You will not go," he said. "I will take on any man who speaks ill of you."

Deborah leaned her forehead against his chest. "Please, Ioan. Let me find my own way."

"Never." He cupped his work-roughened hand under her chin and forced her to meet his gaze. "If you must leave..." He swallowed. "Come with me, Deborah."

She couldn't move, couldn't think. "Come with you?"

Hot color washed his cheeks. "I can take care of you. I will find a good job. You will lack for nothing."

But his words were halting, almost clumsy. He

didn't believe what he was saying. He hadn't the faith in himself; he was poor and likely to remain so in a world with little sympathy for paupers.

And she, the bastard daughter of a whore…how could she ever be worthy of *him?*

His face burned under her fingertips. "Ioan, Ioan. If only things were different."

He broke away. "Forgive me, Lady Orwell. I forgot my place." He bowed stiffly. "If I may be of any further service to you, send word to the Bull and Thorn on Commercial Street."

"Ioan! You mustn't think…"

He didn't wait to hear her explanation. She began to follow, faltered, stopped. What would be the point? They both knew that he had spoken without thinking.

They both knew that feelings weren't enough. Not when she had rank and fortune, and he had his stubborn pride.

She went back into the servants' hall, her throat aching with grief. She must leave tomorrow, as early as possible. Finish packing tonight. No time for sleep…

"Lady Orwell!"

Stella was still in a state of high excitement, clutching her skirts and twisting the fabric between her hands.

"What is it, Stella?" Deborah asked wearily.

"There is another gentleman to see you, your ladyship."

Another gentleman? At this hour? "Send him away."

"But it's Mr. Melbyrne, your ladyship. He refuses to leave."

Yet another disaster in the making. Deborah

almost fled up to her room, knowing that Felix would have never risked such scandal if he did not have some vital reason for calling after midnight.

"Show him into the drawing room," she said.

The maid tripped away. Deborah followed more slowly, each step sucking her more deeply into despair.

Felix was on his feet when she entered the drawing room. His hat was very properly on the floor beside his chair, a concession to propriety almost laughable under the circumstances.

"Mr. Melbyrne," she said, remaining by the door. "It was unwise for you to come here. Lady Charles is not—"

"Hang Lady Charles," he exclaimed, his stare so wild as to be almost frightening. He made an aborted move toward her, shuffled his feet and suddenly dropped to one knee.

"My dear Deborah," he began, "my very dear girl…will you do me the profound honor…" His voice deepened. "Will you make me the very happiest of men, and consent to give me your hand in marriage?"

Deborah's knees buckled. She pushed Felix away when he would have helped her, and felt her way to the nearest chair.

"Forgive me," Felix breathed, pacing back and forth before her chair. "I have…I have done this very clumsily. I have spent the entire afternoon and evening…" He stopped. "I did not wish to alarm you. It is only that—"

"I am not alarmed," she said, forcing herself upright. "Only…I did not expect…"

"Surely you can never have doubted how much I adore you." Felix knelt again, his hands spread. "From the moment I saw you, I knew you must be mine."

Oh, disaster indeed. "We…we have hardly known each other—"

"We have known each other for eternity." He reached for her hand, and she was compelled to let him take it. "My dearest, I know how strenuously Lord Donnington has sought to keep us apart. He could not prevail upon me. I have left the Forties. You are all I require for my perfect happiness."

"Felix, I—"

"I have imposed upon you, I know. My love has got the best of me." He grinned indulgently. "I will leave you now and return tomorrow, when you have had time to consider. But I know that when we are together again—"

"I cannot marry you, Felix."

"It is only natural for you to hesitate. If you wish, I will wait another day. Even I can be patient with such a prize awaiting me."

Deborah moaned inwardly. She should tell him the truth. She owed him that much.

But what truth? That he didn't really know her at all? That he would surely turn his back on her if he knew of her true origins?

That she loved a man he would never see as anything but a poor, indigent commoner not fit to kiss her feet?

Courage or cowardice. She chose the latter. "It is too soon, Felix," she whispered. "I…require more time."

His mouth relaxed. "Of course! What an idiot I

have been. The incident at Whitechapel…it has disturbed you greatly." He bent toward her, worried creases between his brows. "You are ill. I shall send my physician. He is an excellent man, and has some experience with women's complaints."

"That will not be necessary, Felix. I am not ill."

"Of course you are. No woman should endure the experiences to which you have been exposed."

It was too much. Deborah stood, compelling Felix to rise and back away.

"You must believe me," she said as steadily as her trembling would allow. "I have no wish to marry. It has not been so long since Lawrence left me. I had never thought—"

He searched her eyes, and she witnessed the moment when he accepted that she was quite in earnest.

"Never thought?" he echoed. "You welcomed my attentions…and you never thought?"

"I thought we were friends."

"Friends!" He spun around, strode toward the far wall, and spun back again. "I shall not be content with 'friends,' Deborah." His anger dissolved into a proud sort of pleading. "I know you have money of your own, but I can give you so much more. We shall be the envy of London. I shall be the envy of the world."

"It…it just isn't possible, Felix."

He stood stock-still. "Are you… Can it be possible that you are refusing me?"

God help me.

"Yes. I must."

It seemed then that he might grasp her arms and shake her. Instead, he took several deliberate steps away from her, as if she had become a monster.

"You have misled me," he said hoarsely. "You have played me for a fool."

"No, Felix. You have never been a fool. I accept all blame for this misunderstanding. I ask your forgiveness."

He laughed. "Sinjin was right. He warned me not to be deceived by any woman. No, Lady Orwell, the misunderstanding was all mine."

"Felix, I—"

He bowed stiffly, effectively silencing her second apology. "I shall leave you, Lady Orwell. I trust you will soon recover from your recent ordeal."

With military precision he turned on his heel, snatched up his hat and marched out of the drawing room. The front door slammed. Deborah fell back into her chair.

It was over. A friendship she had treasured had ended, and it was all her fault.

But it would have come to an end in any case. Best that Felix feel fully justified in his rejection, and not be troubled by conflicting emotions over her past.

Deborah remained in the chair, listening to the long-case clock counting off the minutes. She knew she must have dozed, for when she opened her eyes morning sunlight was beginning to filter between the drapes. Some little time later she heard a carriage come to a stop outside, and Harold appeared to announce that Lady Charles had arrived.

Nuala came directly to her, unpinning her hat as she entered the drawing room.

"Deborah!" she exclaimed. "You look as though you have been up all night."

There was no question of telling Nuala the full truth of what had occurred, however much Deborah wished she might. "How was your holiday?" she asked.

Nuala took a seat and studied Deborah's face. "You are pale. What is wrong?"

"Nothing." She heard the anger in her voice and tried to calm herself. "I might ask why you so suddenly disappeared for the second time in less than a fortnight."

They stared at each other, both aware that a new tension had arisen between them. "I wished to visit my parents' graves," Nuala said without inflection.

Deborah flushed. "I am sorry. I had not meant—"

"I should have explained," Nuala said. "I have been thinking about my family a great deal these days."

As I have. "Yes," Deborah murmured. "I hope you are well?"

"Very well." Nuala hesitated. "Have you seen Mr. Melbyrne?"

It seemed futile to conceal Felix's visit, given that one of the servants would inform Nuala soon enough. "He called last night," Deborah said.

"Indeed?"

"I have not been out in several days. He was concerned."

"He called upon you at night merely to express concern?"

"Yes." Suddenly the secrecy was too much to bear. "I shall not be spending time with him in future. We both think it best that we avoid encouraging the rumors—"

"That you are destined to be married?" Nuala got up, her agitation plain in the abruptness of her movements. "But it has always been obvious that you and he—" She broke off and fixed Deborah with a probing stare. "You have quarreled. Why?"

"We had a slight disagreement...."

"*He* told you that he wished to scotch the rumors," Nuala said with some ferocity. "Lord Donnington—"

"Lord Donnington had nothing to do with it, Nuala. You must believe me."

But she wasn't listening. "It is my fault. I had thought... I had believed that Mr. Melbyrne had finally cast off the earl's pernicious influence," she said, her voice all frost and sleet. "It appears that I was mistaken."

"It was *my* decision," Deborah said, rising. "Mine alone."

She might as well have been speaking to a stone wall. Nuala strode from the drawing room, matching Felix outrage for outrage, and clumped up the stairs.

Deborah closed her eyes. In attempting to keep her friends from becoming involved in her troubles, she had done exactly the opposite. If she were not a coward, she would tell Nuala everything.

If she were not a coward, she would find Ioan and beg him to take her with him.

She was lying sleepless in bed when she heard

Nuala leave the house. Deborah could guess where she was going. There would be a terrible row between two people who truly did belong together.

And it would all be for nothing.

Deborah turned her face into her pillow and wept.

CHAPTER FIFTEEN

SINJIN WAS NOT AT HOME.

His butler was vague about his master's whereabouts, the old man's face revealing not the slightest surprise that a female caller should arrive, quite alone, at Lord Donnington's door in broad daylight. He was apologetic that he couldn't say when the earl might return, since Lord Donnington had an unpredictable schedule.

Nuala was not put off. Heedless of the rumor mill, she inquired at Sinjin's club only to find that he had not put in an appearance that day. She rode her mare in Hyde Park and saw neither Sinjin nor Melbyrne. Leo Erskine, whom she met on Rotten Row, admitted that he had not seen his friend for two days.

She could feel Erskine's stare peeling the skin from her back as she returned to Grosvenor Street. Let him speculate. Let all of Society think what it would.

There was one last place to look.

Dusk had fallen by the time Nuala called for the carriage. She banked her fury for the duration of the drive, trying to forget what Mrs. Simkin had told her.

"Beware yer anger, gal. It lies at the root of the evil you fight."

But her anger was justified. She had been mistaken in thinking that Sinjin's inexplicable behavior at their last meeting was a sort of madness he could not entirely control. It was all just a part of his game.

She had hoped their next encounter would be different. She had knelt before her parents' graves, the mouse in her hand, and thought she had found the answer at last.

She had been wrong.

The carriage rattled to a stop outside the cottage on Circus Road. A light burned in an upstairs window. Nuala instructed Bremner to wait and stormed up to the door.

Sinjin answered her knock. It was evident at once that he was in a state of inebriation. His feet were bare. His hair was a wild mane, his face was unshaven, his shirt unbuttoned. The dark shadows under his eyes betrayed sleepless nights.

"Nuala?" he croaked.

She pushed past him into the entrance hall. "You could not be content with humiliating me, could you?" she snapped. "You never intended to keep our bargain!"

Sinjin passed his hand over his face. "Nuala…"

"If you wished to continue to punish me, you could have done so without ruining Deborah's last chance at happiness."

He shook his head. "You're wrong. I never intended—"

"Stop." Tears gathered under her eyelids. "You succeeded in frightening me, Lord Donnington," she said. "I do not know how you devised such a method of doing so, but it was successful beyond your wildest dreams."

A strange expression crossed his haggard face, one she almost might have called distress. Then his mouth set in a grim line, and all traces of drunkenness vanished.

"You had better sit down, Nuala," he said.

"To what purpose? You have won. They have agreed to stop seeing each other."

He took her arm in an iron grip and pulled her toward the drawing room. "You are going to listen to me, even if I have to tie you down to a chair."

"If you try, Donnington, you will regret it."

His eyes glinted. "Don't test me, Lady Charles."

"Or you shall try to hurt me again?"

He winced, but he didn't let her go. He steered her into the room and set her firmly in a chair. "I have something to say to you, Nuala."

"If you think you can explain…"

"I can't. But I can apologize."

His words stopped her short. "Deborah and Felix—"

"Hang Deborah and Felix." He knelt before her, his hands gripping the armrests. "I did nothing to interfere with either of them. It's you I…" He glanced away. "What happened that night…I wasn't myself. You must believe that."

The anger drained out of her, leaving her hollow with shock. He was *apologizing* to her.

"I don't know what came over me," he continued, looking up into her eyes. "It was as if someone else were talking, doing things I…" He moved his hand over hers. "I don't have an explanation. My behavior was unforgivable. Unconscionable."

She remembered to breathe. "Are you saying… Do you wish to make me believe—"

"For God's sake, Nuala. I wanted you. I wouldn't have done anything to drive you away."

Surely he was playing with her again, attempting to win her trust before betraying it once more. Yet her heart insisted that he was sincere, that his eyes held a deep regret and tenderness that couldn't be feigned, even by such a practiced schemer.

But that other voice, that other face, so twisted with naked hate…

"Someone else?" she whispered.

"Maybe I *am* going mad." He pushed away and stood, his jaw working with emotion. "That was how I felt. Mad."

Nuala closed her eyes. Was it possible? Could Sinjin make himself so vulnerable and not mean what he said?

Was she going mad along with him?

"I would never harm you," he said. "Never."

"I don't understand," she whispered.

"Nuala." He knelt again, humble as he had never been humble before. "I don't ask you to understand. I only ask that you not despise me. I assure you…" He swallowed. "I assure you that I will discover the root of this madness and drive it out. I won't touch any woman until I can trust myself again."

Any woman. Of course. And why not? Their coming together had been strictly a matter of business.

"Has this happened before?" she asked in a still voice.

"No." He seemed even more distressed than he had a moment ago. "Not before we…met in London."

"Then some part of you must hate *me*."

His jaw set. "You are not being reasonable, Nuala."

"It seems we have both made mistakes," she said, rising. "You in attempting to defy your natural contempt for me, and I in hoping that there might be peace between us." She rose and walked swiftly toward the door.

Sinjin was there before her. "Don't go, Nuala."

His breath was warm on her face, his superbly masculine body too close, too powerful. "What is left to say?"

He lifted his hands, then let them fall. "What do *you* see when you look at me, Nuala? An enemy? Someone to hate?"

She raised her eyes to his face. "Do you truly care?"

"Haven't I made that clear enough?"

"Why?"

He continued to gaze at her with an earnestness and intensity that held her more surely captive than his body did. "Answer my question," he demanded softly.

"I don't hate you, Sinjin. Only what you can become."

"I swore that I would root out this…thing within me. Isn't that enough?"

How could she expect him to succeed in such a project when she had been unable to root out her own memories, her own anger? "We are not meant to be in one another's company," she said, fighting the urge to touch his haggard face. "I should never have come to London."

"Do you think I still blame you for what happened at Donbridge? I don't, Nuala. I admit my own responsibility in what happened to Giles. I was blinded by my…" He shook his head. "Will you accept that apology, at least?"

Nuala had to lean back against the door to stay on her feet. "No. *I* was arrogant. I made mistakes that cost a man his life and a woman her sanity."

"Are we to argue about it again? Can we not both admit that we are far from perfect?"

Nuala struggled to still the mad whirling of her thoughts. She no longer knew who the real Sinjin was: this quiet man who, against his nature, humbled himself to her, or the violent devil she had met six nights ago.

She wanted to believe he was *this* man, that the other had been a reflection of some darker part of himself that he would swiftly overcome.

Oh, how she wanted to believe.

"Are we really so different, you and I?" he asked, caressing her fingers. "Can we not come to some accommodation?"

"Even if you and I… Even if we reach this accommodation, Felix and Deborah will continue to suffer."

"I swear that I had nothing to do with their current separation. But if you are so certain that they belong together, I'll help in any way I can."

What came over her then had no explanation. She

kissed him. It was meant to be a simple kiss of gratitude and friendship, but it remained so only for the instant before Sinjin pulled her into his arms.

She told herself that she acted in defiance of her fear, and to prove that she was not ruled by anger and resentment. But when Sinjin took her hand and led her up the stairs, such rational convictions ceased to have any meaning. She was scarcely aware that he guided her to a different room this time, a room without a single exotic pillow. A place that was a refuge, a sanctuary, not the replica of a pasha's harem bedchamber.

Nuala was sensible of the supreme vulnerability he was displaying in bringing her to his private chambers. As if he realized how much he might reveal of himself in the spare furnishings and decoration, he hesitated inside the door and clasped his hands behind his back.

"We need not continue," he said very quietly. "You owe me nothing."

"I know." She drifted closer to him, touched his hand, his cheek. "No more negotiations, Sinjin. We meet here on equal terms."

Standing on her toes, she kissed him again. He closed his eyes, brushed her lips lightly with his. The bed was only a few steps away. Somehow they made their way there, though Nuala could not remember how she had come to cross the room. Sinjin breathed into her hair and then nuzzled her ear as he began to unfasten her bodice. His fingers were expert on the hooks, and she knew he had done this countless times before.

But those times would not be like this. They could never be like this.

He laid the bodice on a chair and returned, his eyes hot with desire. Her skirts came next. They fell into a pool at her feet. Sinjin put his hands around her waist and lifted her free of them. She felt light as down in his grasp. Because she had not expected to come to him tonight, she had worn her corset; he turned her about and smoothly unlaced it. It joined the bodice on the chair. He turned her round again, his hands resting just at the top of her hips.

"I want to see you naked," he whispered against her ear.

She was already growing wet, but his seductive voice brought on an ache that she was certain must match his own. She slid her hand down the front of his trousers and cupped it over the hard ridge beneath the wool. His hands tightened on her waist. She eased the buttons from their buttonholes and massaged him lightly.

Sinjin was having none of it. He pulled her hard against him and kissed her neck, sucking lightly on the skin until it began to tingle. Inch by inch he made his way down to the upper curve of her breasts. Nuala gasped in anticipation of feeling his mouth and tongue on her nipples. But he released her just long enough to pull the chemise over her head and toss it aside.

Nothing now stood between him and her naked flesh. He cupped her breasts in his palms, lifting them like ripe fruits to his lips. His tongue slid over her nipples with tantalizing slowness, tracing a path around the aureoles. Nuala heard her own breath catching in her throat, her low moan of pleasure as he sucked her into his mouth. With quick, hungry tugs he suckled her, first one breast and then the other, rolling his tongue around and around her nipples.

"Sinjin," she panted.

His mouth was too full to answer.

"I want…I don't want to wait."

He glanced up with a sly, secret smile. "You must be patient, my little witch."

It was an endearment this time, not a curse. He continued to lick and suckle her while he unfastened her drawers. They fell, and he kicked them aside. Then he knelt and removed her shoes. The act was every bit as sensual as anything he had done before. She expected him to dispose of her stockings, as well, but he left them alone. She barely had a moment to register the thought when his pressed his mouth between her thighs.

His tongue was agile. Oh, how agile. It found its way between her folds, teased and flicked, slid over the center of her need. She was afraid she was about to come then and there, but he stopped just in time, came to his feet, and lifted her onto the bed. Without pause he spread her legs wide, knelt again, and took up where he had left off.

If he had not been so skilled, she would have lost herself completely. But he knew just how to keep her on the edge without letting her fall. He explored every wet, swollen inch of her, licking up the hot liquid that spilled out of her, circling her entrance until she could think of nothing but having him fill her up. When he thrust his tongue inside her, she reached down for him and pulled him away.

"I need...I need all of you," she gasped.

"You'll have it," he murmured.

"But you...you must be—"

"Hush." But he rocked back, rose, and stripped off his shirt with an almost violent motion, never looking away from her face. He shed his trousers and drawers with equal alacrity.

He was...magnificent. There was simply no other word to describe his body: the broad shoulders, the well-defined muscle of his arms and chest, the lean waist and hips. And what displayed itself so boldly, arced high against his stomach. No, astonishing might be a better word.

"Do you like what you see?" he asked without an ounce of modesty.

"Oh...oh, yes. Do you?"

"I have never seen a woman like you."

She wet her lips. "That is quite a compliment."

"No." His voice had grown hoarse. "It is the truth." He moved to put his knee on the mattress, but she was faster. She swung her legs over the side of the bed, set her hands on his hips and took him into her mouth.

He stiffened and released a slow, harsh breath. He tangled his fingers in her hair as she kissed his silky head, slid her lips over it and curled her tongue over the remarkably smooth flesh. His breath hitched again when she took all of him into her mouth and suckled him, rendering him helpless under her caresses.

"Nuala…"

"Hmm?"

"I think you ought to…stop now."

She chose not to take his suggestion, but continued to explore with the greatest satisfaction. When he began to tremble with the effort to control his body's instinctive response, she withdrew with a final kiss.

"My God," he said roughly. He stood very still a moment longer, his eyes tightly closed, and then bent to gather her up, laying her on the bed.

"Do you know what you've done to me?" he asked, stretching out beside her.

"No more than you've done to me." She ran her palm over his muscular back.

He was clearly not satisfied with her answer. He trapped her mouth with his own, eased his body over hers, and settled between her parted thighs.

"I shall win this war," he murmured, licking her neck as his hard, hot shaft slid along the inside of her thigh. She swallowed, determined not to beg him again. He was intent on tormenting her, rubbing himself against her without allowing so much of the tip of his erection to touch her wetness.

Part of her was braced for that evil voice to condemn her again. But it was Sinjin's voice murmuring endearments, Sinjin's breath caressing her face as he eased into her…an inch, no more, teasing her until she could no longer silence her desperate cries.

With a sigh he slipped deeper, little by little, until he was fully inside her. Then he stopped, barely breathing, letting her feel him, reveling in her tight heat clasping him like a gentle fist. When he withdrew, Nuala gasped in protest.

Perhaps he decided to take pity then. Perhaps he could no longer bear the waiting himself. He lifted her bottom with one hand and plunged into her, so very fast and hard that she half rose from the bed with a cry of surprise. Then the rhythm took her, and she became a creature of pure sensation, feeling herself as much the possessor as the possessed.

Overcoming her shyness, Nuala watched Sinjin's face as he moved inside her. There was nothing of the sophisticated, cynical rake in him now. He met her gaze, and all she saw was tenderness, a vulnerability he had so seldom revealed to her before.

And though his body trembled with the effort, Sinjin held back, focused on her pleasure, giving way only when she began to throb with her own release. Then he began to move urgently, almost violently, thrusting impossibly deep until he stiffened and shuddered and found his completion.

He remained inside her for a time, his face pressed into her shoulder. Only after his breathing had slowed did he ease himself away and lie beside her, his hand trailing over her waist. Nuala savored the heat of his body against hers, the overwhelming feeling that she had found her home at last.

"Sinjin," she whispered. The words were so close, so very insistent. It would take so little effort to say them. So little courage, now that he had given her such a gift.

She turned toward him and lifted her hand to his

face. "Sinjin," she murmured. "There is so much…so much I would like to…"

He leaned up on his elbow, staring down into her face with an almost grave expression. She faltered and gathered her courage again.

"Sinjin—"

Abruptly he rolled off the bed, flung on his dressing gown, and turned his back on her.

Nuala sat up, pulling the sheets up to her shoulders. "Sinjin?"

He didn't turn. Nuala's elation melted away. Something had gone wrong, but not with Sinjin's behavior. He had been the perfect lover. Not once had that "other Sinjin" invaded their bliss.

It must be her. She had failed in some way she didn't comprehend. She had disappointed him. *She* had not been a perfect lover, not like the experienced women he was used to dealing with.

Or perhaps he had taken what he wanted and had no further use for her. Their bargain was complete.

Silently she slipped from the bed, pulling the sheets with her, and searched for the undergarments Sinjin had flung on the floor. She prayed he would keep his back turned long enough for her to dress, or at least until she had put on sufficient clothing to shield her nakedness from his gaze.

She had pulled on her chemise and had just fastened her drawers when Sinjin spun to face her.

"This cannot continue," he said roughly.

Nuala reached for the abandoned sheet. "I know."

"No. You don't." He started toward her. She looked for the stranger in his eyes, but it wasn't there.

"I realize that you have little regard for your reputation," he continued, "but someone must."

She nearly dropped the sheet. "When have you ever had regard for a woman's reputation?"

"I've never ruined any woman's good name," he said. "The ladies I've known have been mature, free-willed and capable of being discreet."

"As I haven't been." She draped the sheet over her shoulder and snatched up her petticoats. "Perhaps it is your own reputation you fear for."

He laughed, little more than a bark. "Oh, yes, I fear for it. Damn Erskine."

"What has Leo to do with—"

But he was moving again. He came to a halt within arm's reach and dropped to one knee.

"Marry me, Nuala."

CHAPTER SIXTEEN

THE SHOCK ON NUALA'S face was so profound that Sinjin was half-convinced she might actually swoon.

"Marry you?" she whispered. "Marry *you?*"

Heat rushed into his face. He rose, his heart a leaden weight beneath his ribs.

"Did I not make myself clear?" he asked. "I am asking you to be my wife."

Her gray eyes were all pupil, her skin pale enough to match the sheet she had dropped to the floor. "You don't know what you're saying."

"Don't I?" He attempted a smile. "Is the idea so repulsive to you?"

She stretched out her hands, found the hassock in front of his favorite chair and collapsed onto it. "Repulsive?" she echoed. Color flooded back into her skin. "You cannot have changed so much."

Pride was no easy thing to swallow. "Changed from our last meeting? Have I not proven—"

"You are…you were everything a woman could desire."

"Then what is it, Nuala?" He held her gaze, refusing to let her escape. "Are you still afraid of me?"

She trembled. "No."

"Do you doubt my sincerity?"

It was a question he should never have asked. The answer was plain in her eyes.

"Are you not the confirmed bachelor," she said, "sworn not to bind yourself to any woman until you pass the age of forty?"

This…this was not what he had expected. They had just shared a passion such as neither one of them had ever known, a perfect union indescribable in its power. And yet now she was mocking him, after he had humbled himself again and again. Mocking this appalling, overwhelming weakness, this bizarre compulsion, that had brought him to such a pass.

"Do you know what they're saying, Nuala?" he asked with far more heat than he had intended. "Have you heard the latest rumors?"

"Set yourself at ease, Lord Donnington. I knew the risks of coming to you. I take full responsibility for them."

"Do you take responsibility for the talk that you have been intent on trapping me into marriage since the moment we met?"

She started up. "I beg your pardon?"

"Erskine told me."

She fell back again. "Surely you can't believe—"

"I don't, but no denials from either of us will halt the rumors once they have taken root."

Her eyes filled with tears. "And this is the reason you wish to marry me?" She blinked, but the obvious effort to clear her eyes only spilled the tears over her cheeks. "Surely *you* have nothing to fear, if I am the one who is believed to be the pursuer. I have told you that you need not be concerned on *my* account. I can live with such rumors and worse. I am not alone in London. My friends will never desert me."

Every feeling insisted that Sinjin go to her, take her in his arms, but he seemed unable to move. "Do you refuse me because you fear the Widows' censure for breaking your vows?"

"No!" She took a breath. "No. But you have given me no good reason to…accede to your request."

How could he so want to strangle her one moment and kiss her senseless the next?

"I will give you a good reason," he said harshly. "We want each other. And we can have each other whenever we wish once we're married."

"We can have each other whenever we wish without the bonds of matrimony."

"Is that really what you want, Nuala?" he said, closing the space between them. "Sneaking about whenever we meet, or dispensing entirely with Society's approval by openly becoming my mistress?"

She wrapped her arms tightly around her chest. "Do you think I haven't the discipline to stay away?"

"I believe we have equal discipline in that regard…none whatsoever."

"You seem to have forgotten one vital point. I possess certain abilities that you despise."

"I hope that you can give them up."

She went very white, leaped up and held the petticoat to her hips with trembling hands. "So this proposal is about controlling me?"

A spark of that inexplicable rage coiled like a striking serpent in Sinjin's chest. "If you had sufficient reason…"

"Sufficient reason?" She stepped into the petticoat and wrenched it up around her waist. "I do not even know…I cannot control…" She flung fiery hair out of her face. "*You* have no power to make it stop."

"Are you so certain?" Sinjin struggled against the irrational anger. "Bloody— You won't need your damned magic once you're happily settled like any normal woman." He lifted his hand in a gesture of conciliation. "I can make you happy, Nuala."

Ignoring her corset and bustle, she turned her back and pulled on her overskirts. "We could never make each other happy."

A roaring started up behind Sinjin's ears, the voice of that *other* he had managed to hold at bay. He put more distance between himself and Nuala, half-afraid of what he might do.

"What if I've got you with child?" he asked.

"That is not your responsibility."

"Like hell it's not."

"There will be no child."

Sinjin felt as if he had been slapped by that same invisible hand she had used on him before. He didn't dare speak for fear that his only words would be curses, damning her to Hell.

"You are refusing me, then," he said.

"I must." She shrugged into her bodice, fastened

the hooks and gathered her shoes. "I do not believe you will regret my decision tomorrow." He heard her walk toward the door.

"Nuala."

The door handle turned. "I am sorry, Sinjin."

A vicious cruelty rose up in him, the black spectre of thwarted desires. "There is something you ought to know about your precious Lady Orwell."

She turned. "You claimed you did not interfere—"

"I did not." He opened the drawer to his bedside table and withdrew the folded newspaper. "One of my kitchen maids was perusing this paper this morning. My butler happened to find it in the servants' hall and brought it to me." He unfolded the paper. "It is only a gutter paper, not one that anyone in decent Society would ordinarily read. But its editors seem to rejoice in printing evil gossip about their betters."

Nuala stiffened. "What has this to do with Lady Orwell?"

"It seems the editors have come by certain information regarding the lady's birth."

"What information?"

"That she is the illegitimate daughter of a Whitechapel whore."

At first Nuala didn't believe him; her doubt was clearly written on her face. She strode to meet him, all but snatched the paper from his hands and began searching the columns until she found the portion Sinjin had marked.

"These are flagrant lies," she snapped. She threw the paper on the bed. "Who would say such evil things?"

"'An anonymous source,' according to the editor. But you're quite right…it is almost certainly a tissue of lies. Nevertheless, if my maid and butler are aware of the story, it will eventually spread to Society."

"Why…why would anyone do this? What possible motive…"

"You know Lady Orwell better than I. Has she enemies?"

"Enemies?" Nuala sat on the bed, pressing her hands together. "There has never been any question about her birth, her position…"

"She would hardly be the first by-blow to be raised as legitimate."

Nuala stared at him blankly, not even taking offense at his harsh words. "Melbyrne must have learned about this contemptible story. Perhaps that is why they—" She blanched. "She must have known about this for days. I knew she was keeping secrets. It explains so much…."

"Does it? What if Lady Orwell knew of it all along?"

"*You* are contemptible. Of course she did not know…even if it were true, which it is not."

"Then you still care about *her* reputation, even though you give no thought to your own."

Nuala attempted to rise, nearly lost her balance and fended him off when he attempted to assist her. "Don't touch me. Don't you dare touch me."

Sinjin braced himself for some hostile manifestation of her magic, but she strode to the door, flung it open and charged down the stairs. The front door slammed.

The room spun around Sinjin like a whirligig. The

unconscionable things he had said lay on his tongue like acid. He truly believed himself mad, just as he'd admitted to Nuala. But *why?* He'd never behaved like such a monster before. Until he'd met her again, he had never deliberately frightened a woman, cursed at a woman, taken pleasure in hurting a woman.

All of it—the voice, the dreams, the poisonous words—had come after he'd met Nuala. And he had asked her to *marry* him. Something he would never have done had he been in his right mind.

He'd thought twice before that she had bewitched him. Each time he'd dismissed the idea as nonsense. But he could no longer hide behind the shield of rationality. What other explanation could there be for his aberrant behavior?

He sat heavily on the bed and dropped his head into his hands. What purpose could she possibly have for bewitching him? She was not vicious; he would have recognized that much. It would be an elaborate scheme indeed for her to deliberately allow him to cause her pain and then turn about and compel him to propose.

She is a witch. She means to drive you mad indeed. To humiliate you, to steal away your soul.

Sinjin ground the heel of his palm into his forehead. *Be silent!*

But perhaps that angry voice knew better than he did. Perhaps it was only the more perceptive part of his mind, speaking out to protect him. A madness with reason.

Yet that supposition provided no real answers.

Had he done her such wrong in blaming her for Giles's death that she felt justified in destroying him? Why would she not have used her magic to overcome his opposition to Lady Orwell's relationship with Melbyrne from the very beginning? She needn't have made any kind of bargain with him at all, for her body or otherwise.

Unless…she didn't know what she did. She had been shocked when she'd wielded her magic against him. Had that all been a ploy, or had it been genuine, as he had believed at the time?

If he were to follow that line of reasoning, he would have to conclude that she was innocent of any deliberate influence on him…that she'd told him no less than the truth when she'd admitted that even she didn't fully understand what was happening to her.

If she does not, doesn't that make her all the more dangerous?

Once again Sinjin drove that "other" from his mind. The fact was that he had no answers, and no way of determining what was real and what was not.

"You can't go on as you are, you know," Mrs. Summerhayes had told him. *"There is one who plagues you. One who speaks with your voice. You must purge yourself, Lord Donnington, or he will ruin you both."*

Mad. Utterly insane. And yet there was something very wrong. As he had promised Nuala, he must get to the root of it. For his sake, and—if she were innocent—for hers.

IN A DAZE, NUALA instructed Bremner to drive her back to London at all speed. She had had two severe shocks this day, both so dizzying that even now she could scarcely comprehend them. What Bremner thought of her liaison with Lord Donnington was the least of her concerns.

Only one thing was important now. She must get to Deborah. She must learn how much the girl really knew, and help her to dispel these horrible rumors.

How could I have been such a fool?

Of all those who knew Deborah, no one should have been better equipped to recognize the extent of the young woman's distress. Nuala had attributed Deborah's desire for solitude to her unfortunate experience in Whitechapel; now she was certain that Deborah had been aware of the libel when they'd spoken last night. And she had not chosen to confide in Nuala.

Nor, Nuala suspected, had she confided in anyone else. How long *had* she known? Was it possible that there was some truth behind the story? *Could* Deborah have been born in Whitechapel and adopted by parents determined to conceal her true origins?

No. It wasn't possible. She would have known. And she would not have deceived Society or Lord Orwell; such deception on her part was not to be conceived of.

Who had done this thing, and why? Chewing on the bitter thought, Nuala stepped out from the carriage, entered the house and paused in the entrance hall, forcing herself to think.

What would she say to Deborah? Admit that she

knew the truth of what had been printed in the scandal sheet? Assure the girl that such rumor-mongering would never affect her reputation?

She could not make such promises.

Gathering her courage, Nuala started for the stairs and had just begun to climb when Jacques, the footman Deborah had brought from her former household, intercepted her.

"Lady Charles," he said, his face tight with strain.

Nuala's stomach rolled over. "What is it, Jacques?"

"We did not know how to find you, your ladyship. We did not know she had gone until—"

"Gone? Who is gone?"

"Lady Orwell, your ladyship." Jacques was pale, and he tugged over and over at his coat. "We…we suspected that her ladyship was not well. She had been in her rooms so long—" He hesitated, weighing the risks of speaking in so familiar a manner.

"It's all right, Jacques," she said, concealing her agitation. "You know that you can always speak freely."

He nodded nervously. "We have all been worried about Lady Orwell, your ladyship. She had dismissed Stella for the day, and no one had seen her for hours…." He went from white to red. "She took several trunks with her. I am sorry, your ladyship."

"It is not your fault," Nuala said, her mind already hard at work. "You could not have stopped her. Do you know where she has gone?"

"No, your ladyship." He swallowed. "We… didn't think…"

"How did she leave?"

"A carriage came for her."

Hired, no doubt, because Deborah didn't intend to return from wherever she was going.

"Did she leave anything for me?"

"Stella is still away, your ladyship. We did not enter Lady Orwell's rooms."

Then there might be something, though Nuala didn't dare hope too strongly. "Please ask the servants to come to the drawing room. I wish to collect as much information as I can."

"Yes, your ladyship."

She hurried up the stairs to Deborah's room. The bed had been carefully made up, and everything was in its place. The majority of her gowns still hung in the dressing room. She had taken very little.

As Nuala had feared, there was no note. She went to her own room. Nothing there, either. She descended to the morning room, in which Deborah had sometimes written letters. The table was bare.

Deborah had truly intended to disappear.

Nuala found the servants waiting in the drawing room. Their expressions ranged from openly worried to dispassionate, though Nuala suspected that none of them was unmoved.

Taking the nearest chair, Nuala tried to smile. "You need have no fear," she told them. "None of you are to blame for Lady Orwell's departure."

A few of the servants exchanged surreptitious glances, but quickly refocused their attention on Nuala.

"Please listen carefully," Nuala said, "and answer

as honestly as you can. Do any of you have an idea as to why Lady Orwell left so suddenly?"

The silence was too complete. One of the scullery maids seemed ready to speak, but quickly subsided. Nuala began to lose her patience.

I could make them speak.

The notion came into Nuala's head without warning, shocking her with its vehemence. Yes, she could use magic to make them speak. It would be yet another violation of her long-ago oath to do no harm with her abilities. It would most definitely step over that fine line between gray and black magic.

Deadly, deadly trap.

Nuala laced her fingers together tightly. "I believe that Lady Orwell may be acting against her own best interests and well-being," she said carefully. "Any information you can provide may help her avoid decisions she may regret."

The scullery maid shifted from foot to foot and bit her lip. "Your...your ladyship?"

"Ginny? Have you something to say?" Nuala leaned forward and smiled. "I will be grateful if can help me."

The girl's courage won out. "Your ladyship...I saw something today. Something awful."

"Something in the papers, perhaps?"

"Aye, your ladyship." The girl was on the verge of tears. "It was a story...a story about Lady Orwell."

Nuala nodded. "I know of this story. You were right to tell me." She looked from one tense face to the next. "Am I correct in assuming that many of you have also seen it?"

Uneasy glances gave the others away. Harold stepped forward.

"We didn't believe it, your ladyship," he said almost fiercely.

"Thank you, Harold. You all may go."

The servants filed from the room, backs hunched and heads lowered. Nuala waited a few moments longer, collecting her composure, and went directly to her room. There she began writing letters to each of the Widows, briefly explaining the situation and requesting their assistance. When she had sent the footmen to deliver the letters, she set down her pen and leaned her chin on her hand.

There would be no point in searching madly in all directions. First she must wait for the Widows to come, so that they could put their heads together and plan appropriately. Each of them had a circle of acquaintance that could be tapped for further aid.

Somehow they would find her. And then…

Nuala drifted away from the secretary and sat at her dressing table. Her mirror revealed a drawn, pale face that seemed to have aged ten years from her apparent age of twenty-five. It was not all because of her fear for Deborah.

"Marry me."

She should not be thinking of Sinjin. Not of his fantastic proposition, so incredibly out of character, nor of the unreasonable elation that had come over her before she had regained her senses.

They had parted for the last time. He had sworn to uncover the source of his madness, but she could not forgive his abominable behavior with regards to Deborah. It was as if that *other* side of him had reawakened at Nuala's refusal of his proposal.

"Marry me."

He had claimed to want to protect her—from rumors, from unfulfilled desire, from her own abilities. Perhaps he had even been sincere. But it had never occurred to him to suggest the one motive for marriage that she might actually have considered.

Nuala let down her hair, still disheveled after her hasty departure from Sinjin's cottage, and began to repin it. He had not offered that one inducement because he was not capable of the emotion that would make such a motive possible.

She let the pins fall and covered her eyes. What she felt now, so inexplicably, so unreasonably, was not enough. Not enough to breach the dark, looming wall of anger that had come between them. There was a danger here that went beyond her temptation to use questionable magic, or even Sinjin's bizarre transformations into a man she didn't recognize.

Whatever that danger was, it could not harm either one of them if they remained apart. If she never let him know she loved him.

Nuala picked up the pins and returned to her work.

CHAPTER SEVENTEEN

MRS. SUMMERHAYES'S HOUSE was not in a fashionable part of town, nor was it particularly large. To the contrary, it was modest to the point of obscurity, one among a number of terraced houses lining a nondescript street in Fulham.

Sinjin climbed the stairs, fingering his card. Perhaps she would not be at home. Perhaps she would not be inclined to see him, now that she had had time to reconsider her peculiar offer to a stranger.

He hoped that she would turn him away. Then he might admit to himself that he had been foolish to the point of imbecility to come here, as if the woman could actually help him.

But the door opened before he reached it. And there she stood, a mouse-brown young woman in a dress as unremarkable as her face and figure.

"I knew you would come," she said, and stood back.

Sinjin paused, looking beyond her into the entrance hall. It was well past dark, and there was little traffic on the street, but his calling might be misinterpreted should anyone see him enter her house alone.

"No one will see," Mrs. Summerhayes said with

a serenity Sinjin envied. "We are quite safe." She almost smiled, but the expression quickly transformed into one of grave sobriety. "Please, Lord Donnington, come in."

He did as she asked. The hall smelled musty, as if it had not been properly aired in months, and it was unreasonably dark. Mrs. Summerhayes seemed unperturbed by the prospect of poor first impressions. Sinjin searched in vain for a servant as she led him through a corridor behind the stairs and to a heavy oaken door.

"We are quite alone," she said, as if she had literally read his mind. "I have few servants, and I have given them the evening off."

"Madam," Sinjin said, "this is hardly proper...."

She didn't seem to hear him. She pushed open the door, which groaned on its hinges, and led him into an even darker space. Her skirts hissed as she moved about, lighting a single lamp.

Sinjin didn't know what he'd expected, but it was not what lay before him. The room was bare save for a round table and a number of chairs placed about it.

"This is where I work," Mrs. Summerhayes said. "I find it easier to concentrate without distractions."

He was about to ask what she must concentrate *on* when she gestured toward the table. "Shall we begin?"

Sinjin's jaw had begun to ache, and he realized that he had been clenching his teeth since he'd left the carriage. "I beg your pardon, Mrs. Summerhayes, but would you be so good to tell me why I am here?"

Her small, earnest face turned up to him. "You

have come to learn, to understand, to dispel," she said. "You have come to free yourself of the past."

He was one heartbeat away from walking out the door. "The past? If that has been your impression, madam, then I—"

"Do you trust me, Lord Donnington?"

The question stopped him cold. Trust her? He didn't know her, knew nothing about what she intended to do. He wondered briefly if she, like Nuala, was a witch, capable of twisting his thoughts.

But he suspected that she was something else entirely.

"You are a medium," he said.

She inclined her head. "That is a term favored by some."

A spiritualist. Hadn't she said that she spoke for those who couldn't speak for themselves?

"Do I understand that you intend to raise the dead?" he asked, hoping to overwhelm his unease with scorn.

"I do not raise the dead. I only listen."

"What have the dead to do with *me?*"

"Perhaps more than you can imagine." She gestured toward the table again. "Please."

Almost against his will, Sinjin followed her to the table. She pointed him to the chair at the opposite end from hers and settled herself with unexpected grace. With a flash of insight, Sinjin realized that, in this room, she was fully in her element. Out there she might be plain and unremarkable. Here she was a queen.

Mrs. Summerhayes placed her palms on the table. "Please, Lord Donnington. You must attempt to put all doubts from your mind as long as we remain in this room. I know it will not be easy for you, but you must do your best."

Sinjin didn't bridle at her calmly commanding tone. *He* was the supplicant now. He closed his eyes and let his hands rest on the table.

"You need do nothing else, Lord Donnington," she said, her voice growing more distant. "Simply allow yourself to relax. The other is ready to come to us."

"The oth—"

"Quiet your mind. And remember."

He didn't know quite how it happened. In a matter of seconds a severe chill raced over his skin, raising gooseflesh beneath his shirt. His heart began to race, and perspiration broke out on his forehead. He opened his mouth but did not remember how to shape the words.

"So you have come."

Sinjin jerked up his head. Mrs. Summerhayes still sat quietly at the other side of the table. Her head was slumped onto her chest.

"I have been waiting a very long time," the voice said, a deep rumble rising from the young woman's throat.

The ice in Sinjin's blood numbed his fingers. He recognized the voice, though it spoke in a higher pitch than the one he had heard inside his own head.

"Who are you?" he whispered.

A pale fog rose behind Mrs. Summerhayes, an

apparition that twisted and flowed and resolved into the shape of a man. Mrs. Summerhayes laughed softly. "I am one who has much to tell you, St. John Ware."

Sinjin tried to stand. His feet were welded to the floor.

"You need not fear me," the spectre said. "I am not your enemy."

As Mrs. Summerhayes spoke, the apparition darkened, gaining form and feature. The face was cut like a razor, with a sharp jaw and narrow nose. The eyes were hooded, their color concealed, but the brows were straight and dark. It wore equally dark clothing: a wide-collared doublet and breeches and buckled shoes, its head crowned by a wide-brimmed hat.

Sinjin clenched his fists. "I know you."

"Yes. You have seen my face before, have you not?"

God in Heaven. He *had* seen that face before, in his own mirror. Snarling, sneering. Filled with hatred.

This was the *other.*

"I see that I have little time, for the moment," the apparition said, his voice gradually smothering Mrs. Summerhayes's low tones. "She is strong, this little witch. She has paved the way, but I must walk the path."

"What have you done to me?" Sinjin demanded.

"Patience, cousin. All will be revealed." He lifted his hand, cuffed with white lace, and brushed at his doublet. "You took too much pleasure in your coupling. It was necessary to remind you of what she is."

The blood seemed to drain out of Sinjin's body. This creature *had* been with them, with him and Nuala, since her visit to Donbridge. *He,* whatever he was, had used Sinjin's voice, his will, to attack Nuala. The hatred Sinjin had felt for her...none of it had been real.

"Do not deceive yourself," the apparition said. "You despise her as much as I."

No. Sinjin pounded his fist on the table. "I don't believe in you," he snarled. "You're a creature built of my own imagination."

"Ah. If such were true, would it not be confirmation of your own hatred for the witch?"

"You're not real!"

The apparition gave a great sigh. "Watch, and learn."

The table's leg jolted against Sinjin's shin. The table itself began to heave, shuddering, rising inches from the floor.

"I could do much more," the apparition said mildly, "but too much might damage your mortal mind...as once mine was damaged by *her.*"

Sinjin looked at Mrs. Summerhayes. She had begun to tremble.

"Get out of her," he said.

"So you *do* believe." The apparition nodded as if in approval. "There is so much I must tell you. About the great evil that befell your kin. About the bitch you took such pleasure in bedding, and your fulfillment of the vow that will save you."

"What vow?" Sinjin concentrated all the strength he possessed and pushed up in the chair. This time he managed to stand. "What evil?"

"You know the answer, Sinjin Ware."

"She said you were out to ruin us."

"Ruin *you?* I intend to save you."

"From what? Damn you, what do you want?"

But something was happening, something even the apparition appeared unable to control. His form became unsubstantial, dissolving back into the mist from which he had come.

"You are cursed, Sinjin Ware," the ghost said, his voice receding with his body. "She is poison. She will steal your soul and leave nothing but ash."

Then the apparition was gone. Mrs. Summerhayes jerked violently. Sinjin jumped from his chair and rushed to her side.

"Mrs. Summerhayes!" he cried, not daring to touch her.

Her head lifted. Her eyes were rolled back in their sockets.

"Mrs. Summerhayes!"

With one final shudder, the young woman slumped in her seat. Sinjin gripped her shoulder. She stirred, straightened and met his gaze.

"Lord Donnington? Are you well?"

Laughter was hardly an appropriate response. "It is you who are ill. I'll send for a doctor immediately."

"That won't be necessary." She sighed and rubbed the skin between her brows. "It was not an easy passage, but I am quite well. Did he speak?"

"Didn't you hear?"

"I very seldom see or hear what occurs during a séance," she said. She frowned, searching his eyes with obvious worry. "I knew it could not be pleasant. It is still so unclear to me. Perhaps I was wrong to think I could help."

For a moment, just for a moment, Sinjin wondered if she had devised the whole episode as a ruse, as many spiritualists were said to do. But she had not asked for payment, and she had no reason to speak ill of Nuala. Quite the contrary.

"It...he came," Sinjin said thickly. "I never thought it possible that I would believe in ghosts. But he was real."

"Yes. Who was he?"

"I don't know." Sinjin leaned on the back of the chair next to hers, pushing the fog out of his brain. He couldn't bring himself to repeat what the apparition had said about Nuala. "It seems...I am being haunted."

Mrs. Summerhayes offered no reassuring disagreement. "It is rare for a spirit to haunt a person rather than a place. There must be a powerful bond linking you to him, whoever he may be."

"But you have no idea why?"

"I wish I might tell you. I only know that someone from the other side was attempting to contact you through me."

"The other side." He shook his head. "It is most certainly no benign spirit of the sort who makes floorboards creak and doors slam shut." He looked into her eyes. "You said I had to purge myself, or he would ruin us. What did you mean?"

"I can scarcely remember what I said," she murmured. "I am sorry."

He pulled in a deep breath. "I don't think he is finished with whatever he's doing."

"Yes." She closed her eyes. "I am sorry. So very sorry."

"But surely you can help me rid myself of him."

"If only I could. But there is a barrier, Lord Donnington. A force that prevents me from further interference." She looked up, and Sinjin saw tears in her eyes. "You must find the answers yourself. You must learn who and what he is, and by what means you can stop him from fulfilling his purpose."

A purpose she could not illuminate. A purpose that had something to do with a vow. And a curse.

"She is poison. She will steal your soul, and leave nothing but ash."

Sickened, Sinjin backed away from the table. "I am grateful, Mrs. Summerhayes," he said. "I regret that I have brought this trouble upon you."

She rose, leaning on the table, making clear with the attitude of her body that she didn't want his assistance. "Look to your heart, Lord Donnington," she said faintly. "I must leave you now."

Sinjin followed her to the door, afraid she might fall, but she moved resolutely to the staircase and began to climb, clutching the banister. He was left alone in the hall with his own churning thoughts. No answers, only questions far more disturbing than any he could have conceived when he had come.

Neck prickling, Sinjin went out to his carriage and instructed the coachman to take him home. He fell into bed, certain he would never be able to sleep.

He woke from dreams of fire and unspeakable torment.

His face was still his own when he stood before his looking glass; he dressed, forced himself to eat a few bites of breakfast and took Shaitan for a brisk ride in Hyde Park. He had hoped that the morning's routine would banish last night's visions, but a heaping dose of reality only made the ghost and its vile pronouncements seem all the more genuine.

Go to Nuala. Tell her what has happened. Prove to yourself that the spirit was wrong.

But he was afraid. Afraid to remind himself of Nuala's capabilities as a witch, of her refusal to be "controlled." Afraid of his own conviction that the ghost had not finished with him. That he might somehow put her in danger.

The worst was yet to come, and he knew in his soul that he could not escape it.

Putting aside all thoughts of calling on Mrs. Summerhayes again, Sinjin paced his room until his gaze fell on the newspaper he had left on his bed table. If he was not yet prepared to face Nuala, he might do something to atone for his mistreatment of another unfortunate lady.

He walked to his club, considering the possibilities. Either the story had as yet been undiscovered by polite Society, or it had already spread beyond the servants who were most likely to have read it. Nuala had suggested that something had come between Melbyrne and Lady Orwell. Did Melbyrne know?

The boy was at the club, sharing a drink with Breakspear and Nash.

"...highly unlikely to have a jot of truth in it, of course," Breakspear was saying. "Rubbish of the worst sort."

"But so little is really known about her," Nash said, accepting a glass from an attentive waiter. "Her parents and husband spent nearly all their time on the Continent."

"But blood will tell," Breakspear said, "and Lady Orwell has never proven herself to be anything *but* a lady. Isn't that so, Melbyrne?"

The boy shrugged. "I have never witnessed anything improper in Lady Orwell, but I have been mistaken before."

"It would not be the first time that a woman has set herself up as something other than she is," Nash said. "In fact, I remember—"

"I thought it was a gentleman's part never to speak ill of a lady in public," Sinjin said with a pleasant smile. "Or have I been mistaken my judgment of you, *gentlemen?*"

Melbyrne's shoulders went up in a defensive posture. Breakspear resembled a boy caught out with his hand on the biscuit tray. Nash lifted his glass to Sinjin.

"It is no secret," Nash said. "All of the club has heard the tale by now."

"From you?"

Nash frowned. "No. I merely—"

"It is rubbish," Sinjin said between his teeth, "as Breakspear said."

"Indeed," Breakspear murmured. He eyed Sinjin with a distinct air of caution. "The tattle will soon be proved false, I have no doubt."

"While Lady Orwell suffers the gossip you are so assiduously spreading."

"We did not spread it!" Melbyrne burst out. "It was Ferrer who showed us the paper. He was the one who—"

Sinjin caught Melbyrne neatly by his lapels, half lifting him from his feet. "You disappoint me, boy," he said softly.

"Sin, I—"

"Did you ask her to marry you?"

Dumbfounded, Nash and Breakspear stared at Melbyrne. He twitched in Sinjin's grip.

"She refused me," he said in a strangled whisper. "And now I have every reason to be grateful."

Sinjin let him drop, not gently. Melbyrne staggered and righted himself, jerking at his collar. Sinjin stared him down.

"You insult a woman you professed to love," he said. "I should like to find a suitable stable and horsewhip you."

Melbyrne went white. "But Sinjin, I—"

Turning his back on the boy, Sinjin strode out of the room, leaving a ripple of stunned whispers in his wake.

It was no good. He could do nothing for Lady Orwell. Oh, he might find Ferrer and give him a good thrashing, but it was too late to ameliorate the damage. Lady Orwell must suffer the humiliation of hearing her peers speculate as to the circumstances of her birth, knowing that even Melbyrne had betrayed her.

But Nuala would be by the girl's side. And *he* could defy the ghost and prove himself her friend by standing at hers...until he found the courage to tell her what he had seen.

If she truly meant to steal his soul, best to learn sooner rather than later.

THE UNASSUMING YOUNG MAN stood in the yard, cap in hand, speaking to Booth in hushed and urgent tones.

Ioan Davies. Nuala recognized him at once, though she could not begin to imagine why he was in Belgravia. She drew back from the window and hurried down to the servants' area.

Booth turned in surprise as Nuala entered the yard. She curtseyed and glanced at the young man, who bowed as prettily as a gentleman in spite of his well-worn workman's clothing.

"Your ladyship," Booth said nervously, "this man has come looking for Lady Orwell. I have told him she is not at home."

Nuala gestured for Booth to return to the servants' hall and confronted the young man. "Mr. Davies," she said. "This is quite a surprise."

"Yes, your ladyship." He met her gaze steadily. "I did not mean to intrude."

"Why do you wish to see Lady Orwell?"

If the boy were taken aback by her brusqueness, his calm expression didn't reveal it. "I beg your pardon, your ladyship," he said. "I will not trouble you further."

"Wait!" She reached for him as he began to turn away. He stopped, giving her a view of his grim profile, and faced her again.

"Perhaps you were not aware that I live here with Lady Orwell," she said.

He bowed again. "I did not, your ladyship, but I know you are Lady Orwell's friend."

"And you have come to see her."

"Aye, madam. But if she is not at home…"

Nuala was not about to let him escape, given the odd circumstances of the young man's visit. Why in the world would he wish to speak to Deborah, and come so far out of his way to do so? He had defended her in Whitechapel, to be sure…

And did not Frances say that he helped her again when I was away from London?

Every one of Nuala's well-honed instincts were on high alert. What had she been missing?

"Please, come into the house," Nuala said. She paused to make sure that he was following and led the way into the kitchen. He glanced around at the scrubbed worktables and cupboards, unease apparent beneath his dispassionate demeanor.

He would, Nuala decided, be even more ill at ease if she asked him into the drawing room. "Will you be seated, Mr. Davies?" She took her own seat at the large table in the center of the kitchen and waited for him to do the same. "I do not wish to invade your privacy, Mr. Davies, but it is quite important that I know why you have come." When he didn't answer at once, she prodded him. "Might it be because of the newspaper article?"

A man such as Mr. Davies would not be one to reveal undue emotion, but he flinched, and his mouth tightened in anger. "It is all lies, madam. I only wished... I hoped to..."

"Lady Orwell is not here, Mr. Davies. She has run away."

His chair scraped the floor as he shot up from the table. "That is not... If I had only... I must find her at once!"

Nuala closed her eyes. *How could I have been so blind? So terribly blind about so many things?*

"Compose yourself, Mr. Davies," she said, taking firm hold of her own emotions. "You must answer me honestly. Have you and Lady Orwell been seeing each other?"

"No." He flushed. "Yes, but you must not think—"

"I don't doubt your honor, Mr. Davies, or Deborah's. Do you love her?"

His astonishment was manifest. "I...I am only a common man, Lady Charles, hardly worthy of—"

"Do you love her?"

His chin came up. "Yes."

"And she loves you?"

"If she did, she would not have run away."

The pain in his voice cut Nuala to the quick. "I do not believe that even love could have stopped her. In fact, I think it was her love for her friends that sent her away."

"But I would never judge her, even if the things

they wrote…" A dangerous look flared in his eyes. "No one has the right."

"I agree, Mr. Davies. That is why I must know everything you know."

He gazed at her from under dark brows, weighing her sincerity, wondering if she could be trusted with something as precious as his feelings for Deborah—feelings of which she might very well disapprove. But as she met his gaze, something fell into place between them, a sudden and powerful bond of trust that required no magic or spoken vows.

"Did you know," he began slowly, "that Debo—Lady Orwell had been threatened?" he asked.

Nuala wanted to cry out at her stupidity. "How, Mr. Davies?"

"By the same man who accosted her when your ladyship was present in Whitechapel." He proceeded to explain the sequence of events that had occurred on Deborah's last visit to the rookeries. "I deceived her, madam," he said, his voice cracking. "I told Lady Orwell that I could not find any evidence that Bray was telling the truth about her supposed parentage. I thought I had silenced the bas—" He cleared his throat. "I did not expect he would ever dare go so far."

A fierce, hot anger sparked in Nuala's blood. "What was his motive? What did he hope to gain?"

"I do not know, your ladyship. Such men are generally in need of money."

Blackmail. Had Bray attempted to extort money from Deborah in exchange for maintaining his silence? Had she refused?

"I failed her," Davies said, clenching his fist on the table. "Now it is too late."

"Not too late," Nuala said. "I have sent word to friends who are discreetly making inquiries about her departure and possible destination. We shall find her, Mr. Davies. And we shall protect her from anyone who seeks to do her further harm."

They gazed at each other, in perfect accord. "There is still Bray to deal with," Ioan said. "I could not find him."

He didn't need to say what he would have done had he located the man. Nuala was glad he hadn't. She wanted to be there when the blackguard faced his just punishment.

"You know Bray's haunts," she said, "where he might be found?"

"Yes, madam. If he has not run away."

"Then I suggest we make another attempt to locate him."

Unexpectedly, Ioan Davies smiled. It was not a pretty expression. "I have not had the privilege of knowing your ladyship long," he said, "but I count the acquaintance a great honor." He sobered. "I will, of course, leave London once Lady Orwell is found."

"To preserve her reputation?" She leaned across the table, touching his hand. "If you hope to reassure me, Mr. Davies, you are going about it the wrong way. I care nothing for the difference in your stations or fortunes. If you love her, and she loves you... nothing in this world matters more."

"Your ladyship…" He swallowed. "You are very kind."

"I am not kind at all." She rose, and he quickly followed suit. "I shall be ten minutes, and then we will leave for Whitechapel."

"But madam…a lady such as yourself should not enter the places I must go."

"Rubbish. Mr. Davies, I have been looking after myself for far longer than you have been alive."

The quizzical lift of his dark brow told her that he didn't believe her. "Nevertheless…"

"It will do you no good to argue. You may wait for me in the mews." She returned to the house, sent Jacques to summon Bremner, and asked Booth to help her change into more appropriate dress. Ioan was pacing beside the coupé when she emerged from the house, while Bremner and the footmen looked on in bemusement.

Nuala wasted no time in instructing the coachman as to their destination. The carriage was just pulling into the street when someone shouted for Bremner to stop. Nuala stiffened as Sinjin's face appeared in the window. He was in the carriage before she could think to prevent him.

He cast a bemused glance at Ioan, who touched the brim of his cap, and sat beside Nuala.

"I must speak with you," he said.

She shivered at the furnace heat of his body. "I am otherwise engaged, Lord Donnington."

"With this gentleman?"

The sharpness of his tone might have seemed like

jealousy in another man. "Lord Donnington," she said coolly, "may I present Mr. Ioan Davies. Mr. Davies, Lord Donnington."

Sinjin took the younger man's measure with a searing stare. Mr. Davies met his gaze without humility.

"Mr. Davies and I are on our way to Whitechapel," Nuala said, withdrawing as far from Sinjin as she could without becoming too obvious in her desire to escape him.

"To Whitechapel?" Sinjin echoed. "Why?"

"I do not see that it is any of your business, Lord Donnington. If you would be so kind—"

"It has something to do with Lady Orwell."

"Why should you believe that, Lord Donnington? Have you information you did not share before?"

His expression tightened. "None."

Nuala signaled that Bremner should stop the carriage. "If you would be so kind as to leave us."

"Not until I know what you're up to."

Ioan straightened. "Lady Charles," he said, "do you require assistance?"

"No, Mr. Davies." She caught Sinjin's glare. "We intend to find the man who has done his best to ruin Lady Orwell."

"I know him," Sinjin growled. "His name is Ferrer, and he resides here in Belgravia."

"Mr. Ferrer, your good friend?"

"No friend of mine. He has been spreading rumors—"

"Whatever Mr. Ferrer may have done, he is not the one we seek."

"Who, then?"

"A man called Bray," Ioan said. "He is responsible for giving the story to the newspaper."

"I know nothing of this man. Why would he wish to hurt Lady Orwell?"

In brief, clipped phrases Nuala relayed what Ioan had told her, omitting any mention of his relationship to Deborah. By the end, Sinjin's outrage was unmistakable.

"By God," he said. "You are not going without me."

Sinjin's anger seemed quite genuine. It was as if he had come to regret his cruelty with regard to Lady Orwell and wished to make up for it.

Was that enough? Hope flared again, unwelcome and frightening. Could she trust him? There seemed little chance of dissuading him, and the time it would take to do so would impede her purpose and delay her pursuit of Bray.

"If you come with us," she said, "you must not interfere."

His eyes narrowed. "What do you intend to do?"

"Whatever is necessary to be certain that this man will never injure Deborah again."

"In that case, you will require my assistance."

"We will not, Lord Donnington," Ioan said in a low voice.

"You've no say in the matter, boy."

Ioan began to rise. "I have every—"

"That is enough, both of you," Nuala said. "Lord Donnington, you will either defer to me in this matter or leave."

He nodded curtly, though his eyes burned black. The three of them maintained a tense silence all the way to Whitechapel.

Sinjin was first out of the carriage, followed by Mr. Davies. Both men offered their hands to Nuala at once. She took Ioan's. She instructed Bremner to wait in a relatively secure location, and gestured for Ioan to take the lead.

Bray was not in any of the taverns or similar low dives Ioan recommended. The calculating smirks on the faces of the men who saw Nuala, a fine lady encroaching on their territory, quickly faded when they caught sight of Lord Donnington. Ioan looked like a panther about to spring.

But even had they not been with her, Nuala would have been perfectly safe. She felt the magic flowing through her body along with her blood, sparked into life as if it had never abandoned her. The wall that had held it captive had crumbled. Perhaps it was her conflict with Sinjin that had set the magic free. Perhaps it was her outrage over what Deborah had suffered. But it was with her, within her, and she knew it would answer her will, no matter what she required of it. Even the rough rookery denizens, blind to the unseen, felt her power and cringed when she turned to stare.

All but Sinjin and Ioan Davies, too focused on their hunt to notice.

By late afternoon they had dispensed with all the locations that Ioan had searched before, and Nuala knew that Bray would not be discovered in the usual way. She found an excuse to stand a little apart from the men and began to chant a spell of finding, drawing up the words from memory, allowing her power to infuse each syllable.

The spell was more successful than she could have hoped. She found the dull, cruel spark of the creature named Bray and reached a little further into her memory. She added phrases to the spell that she'd never dared use before, felt a peculiar grayness enter her mind.

Then it was done.

"I know where he is," she said.

CHAPTER EIGHTEEN

IOAN, HIS FACE DRAWN with exhaustion, stared at her with incomprehension. Sinjin's jaw was set. Perhaps he knew. Perhaps he had only guessed. But he would not try to stop her now.

The men followed Nuala, one to either side of her. She stopped at one of an endless row of half-fallen houses, rank with rot and rubbish. Sinjin moved ahead to stand before the door, which was nearly broken from its hinges.

"He is here," Nuala said.

"I'll fetch him out," Ioan said grimly.

"We shall go in together," Nuala said.

"He may be armed," Sinjin said.

"He will not be able to fight."

The men exchanged glances. In silent agreement, they pushed the door open.

"Upstairs," Nuala said, when Ioan would have searched the ground floor. He and Sinjin ran up the rickety stairs. A series of thumps and a faint cry echoed from an upstairs room. Nuala reached the landing and followed the sounds.

A woman in a much-mended red dress stood in

one corner of the room, her hands clutched at her nearly naked bosom. Bray crouched beside a sagging cot. His face was twisted with rage and fear, his body contorted as if he were fighting against invisible bonds.

Sinjin lifted him to his feet. Ioan raised a clenched fist. The man made no move to defend himself.

"Please," he whispered, his gaze darting to Nuala. "Please."

But the very concept of mercy was alien to Nuala then. She chanted a spell, and Bray's body went limp, then bounced up again like a marionette dancing on a string. In the space of a heartbeat he was flung across the room, striking the wall with a crack.

Sinjin turned to Nuala, expressionless. No, he would not stop her. Neither would Ioan, if he began to guess what was happening. They both wanted revenge. But *she* deserved to mete out Bray's punishment. *She* was responsible. *She* had failed Deborah, in every way.

No one struck a single blow, but when it was finished Bray's wrist hung at an unnatural angle, his face was dark with bruises and he had soiled his trousers. Nuala compelled herself to stop, though the darkness raging inside wanted nothing more than to silence him once and for all.

"You shall never trouble Lady Orwell again," she said.

Bray groaned through swollen lips.

"You shall go to the papers and retract everything you said about Lady Orwell," she said. "You shall see that an apology is tendered by the editors, or you shall suffer for your failure."

"Nuala," Sinjin said quietly.

"Do you understand?" she asked Bray.

He nodded, curling into the wall. Nuala glanced once at the nameless woman in warning, and left the room.

"*Duw,*" Ioan muttered as he fell in behind her. "I should not wish to be your ladyship's enemy."

Nuala paused on the staircase to lean over the banister, afraid she might be sick. A vast weakness had overcome her, and the room had begun to spin.

Strong arms lifted her and half carried her out of the house. Sinjin's string of curses was so much babble in Nuala's ears. Between them, Ioan and Sinjin got her to the carriage. She slumped on her seat, seeing nothing but gray.

Someone issued instructions to the coachman, and the carriage began to move. When they reached Nuala's house, only Sinjin was still with her.

In silence he helped her into the hall. She had an impression of shocked faces staring after as he carried her up to her room. She felt those strong hands lay her down on her bed, a voice calling for her maid. Immediately, Booth entered the room, and Sinjin retreated.

Some time passed, and Nuala's dizziness receded. Booth sat beside the bed, bathing Nuala's forehead with a cool, wet cloth; gradually the nausea eased, as well, and Nuala was able to open her eyes.

"Sinjin?"

He was still with her, standing in a corner well out of the way. "I'm here."

"Thank you."

He said nothing. His face was a stony mask, his disapproval—no, something much worse than that—hanging like a cloud in the room.

"Please help me sit up." Nuala asked Booth. The maid did as she asked, fluffing the pillows to provide a firm support for Nuala's back. "You may go, Booth. Please tell the others not to worry."

Booth shot a wary glance at Sinjin, clearly about to protest at the inadvisability of allowing an unmarried man of Sinjin's reputation to be alone with her mistress. But she accepted the inevitable defeat, curtseyed and left the room.

"You can speak freely now," Nuala said.

Sinjin moved to stand in front of the door. "You can't go on this way, Nuala," he said softly.

She had known this was coming, had tried to prepare herself while she was recovering under Booth's ministrations. But she was *not* prepared. The part of her that instinctively desired to explain, to apologize, was not nearly as strong as the part that rose to meet Sinjin's chastisement with defiance.

"You are not my husband," she said. "You have no right to tell me what to do."

"You're correct, of course. I have no right. But I can warn you, Nuala."

"Warn me? After the way you have acted?"

He was unmoved. "You've gone too far."

She sat up higher on the pillows. "Because I

wished to protect an innocent person from a fiend bent on her ruin?"

"Protect her? Is that what you think you were doing?"

"And how was what I was doing any different than what you would have done had you been in my place? Do not try to tell me that you and Ioan would have shaken the man's hand and asked him politely to leave Deborah alone."

The muscles in Sinjin's jaw flexed and released. "*One* of us would have done the job, and the blackguard would have had a chance to defend himself. It would have been a fair fight."

"He didn't deserve a fair fight." She swung her legs over the side of the bed, kicking her skirts out of the way. "He will heal eventually, but he'll not forget what can happen to him if doesn't heed my warnings."

His eyes were bleak. "Nuala, you might have killed him."

"But I did not." She glared at him with contempt. "I can see now that your former delight in Deborah's predicament was the more genuine emotion. You were never really interested in helping her at all."

"Do you think she'd welcome your kind of help?"

"She would rather suffer than defend herself because she doesn't wish to hurt her friends. Well, *I* shall speak for her. If anyone dares to mention these slanders again, I shall—"

"Thrash everyone in Society to within an inch of their lives?"

His voice was too still, too calm. Nuala tried to

catch her breath, recognizing that her anger was spi-raling out of control.

"Please understand, Sinjin," she said. "I must rely on my own judgment in these matters, just as I have all my life."

"Your judgment isn't sound. Not now."

"And *your* judgment is? I don't even know who you are, Sinjin. You are two different men, and I understand neither."

"I have been wrong, Nuala. At least I am trying to make out what is happening to me. You are refusing to look into your own heart."

She rose abruptly, finding that she could stand without suffering an assault of vertigo. "Perhaps you ought to go home. You may still bear me a grudge because I refused—"

"You were quite correct," he said. "I was wrong to have asked you."

"Then on one point, at least, we are in accord."

"Damn it, Nuala…" He ran his fingers through his hair. "Listen to me. This behavior can only lead to trouble even you cannot anticipate."

"Trouble from whom? *I* have no enemies."

"You'll be the one to suffer. Next time you might not be able to stop yourself."

"Please leave, Lord Donnington."

He turned his dark, unreadable gaze on her. "It can't end like this, Nuala. I won't permit it."

"You have no power to permit or not permit any-thing, Lord Donnington."

His mouth tightened, and Nuala was reminded

that this was a man who could be dangerous in ways she might have yet to learn. "You are making a bad mistake, Nuala," he said.

"That is no longer your concern. Good night, Lord Donnington."

With an almost unconscious thought she chanted a brief spell, and the door at Sinjin's back flew open. It was not easy to move him; his will was very strong. But in the end, her magic propelled him backward, forcing him to comply or fall. She slammed the door in his face.

There. He is gone and will never trouble you again. Gone.

Nausea flooded back into Nuala's throat. She sat down again, bracing her arms on the mattress. Defiance and anger vanished between one breath and the next.

What had come over her? She lay back and covered her eyes with her forearm. She had used her magic to attack and manipulate Sinjin as if he were a doll without volition of its own…as if he were a wretched beast like Bray. It was as if she, like him, were two persons in one body.

But if Sinjin's other self was cynical and cruel, even capable of violence, hers was reckless and vain and equally implacable. *He* had been willing to overcome his pride and darker impulses in order to help her find Deborah's tormentor…and to point out the perilous direction her magic was taking.

He knows nothing of magic. He had no means with which to judge what she did, or why. And yet…

Nuala rolled her face into the pillow. Whenever

they were together, it was as if the worst was aroused in each of them. But that "worst" had become something almost deadly.

Not long ago she had considered finding a way to rid herself of those small but dangerous abilities that could so easily be used for ill. Now those abilities were no longer small. If only she had some way to purge herself of these terrible temptations…

No!

She pounded her fists into the pillow, struggling to silence the voice that fought to entrap her mind. *You cannot live without magic. It is in your very nature. You have a right to that which has served so many.*

"But I've failed," Nuala whispered. "I failed at Donbridge, and I have failed Deborah. The elders were right when they taught us that a single slip could open the Black Gate, and once we passed through…"

As long as you work for the good, you will never fall through the Black Gate. It is your choice, and no one else's. Your power. Only yours.

Nuala rolled onto her back and sat up, a blanket of unnatural calm settling around her heart. For the good. There were so many things she might do now that her abilities had fully returned. First she would locate Deborah, and tell her that she was free to be with her young man. Then she would begin to seek out those hypocrites who so loudly condemned young women for any indiscretion or "moral" offense against Society when they themselves were guilty of the same behavior.

The Forties would make an excellent start. She would begin with Melbyrne, who had clearly injured

Deborah in some way before she had fled London. Then Ferrer, whom Sinjin had blamed for spreading the rumors, and Achilles Nash, who held such obvious contempt for the Widows. One by one each of the rakes, and others like them, would suffer for their treatment of the women who fell under their influence.

Nuala rose from the bed, a great wave of magic blowing over and through her like a fierce wind. Sinjin, too, must be punished. *He* was ultimately responsible for Deborah's unhappiness. *He* had the effrontery to think he could dictate to a witch of her blood.

Fire danced on Nuala's fingertips. She closed her eyes. With a gesture she set the bed alight. Flames rose, but did not touch her. She could not be hurt. Never again.

Her triumph shattered at the sound of someone pounding at her door.

"Your ladyship!" Harold burst through the door, staring in horror at the burning bed. He raced to Nuala, seizing her arm.

She flicked a finger. He cried out and snapped back his hand, staring in bewilderment at the red marks that banded his fingers.

Nuala blinked. "Harold?"

The footman recovered and bravely put his hand on her arm again. "We must go, your ladyship!"

She turned to stare at the fire she had created in her moment of insanity. In seconds it would spread to the walls and other furniture, and then quickly to the rest of the house. Someone might be hurt. Booth, Mrs. Addison, Jacques, Ginny…

Resisting Harold's tug, she reached again for her magic. The fire began to devour itself, shrinking inward until it was once more confined to the bed. Another word and it sputtered out, leaving the bedstead a blackened skeleton.

"Cor blimey," Harold whispered.

Nuala pushed past him and ran down the stairs. She rushed into the drawing room, snatched her portrait from behind the chair and threw it on the carpet.

When she was finished, all that remained of the portrait was a charred, twisted skeleton.

THE GHOST HAD BEEN RIGHT.

Sinjin walked blindly in the direction of his house, neglecting to tip his hat to the ladies and gentlemen he passed along the way.

She is poison.

He tripped over a bit of uneven pavement, clumsy as an infant. It was as if Nuala's spell still clung to him, forcing him to move against his will, robbing him of the last shreds of peace he possessed.

She will steal your soul.

A laugh died in his chest. Why else would he have been driven to pursue her, even after the apparition's warnings? Because he still hadn't completely believed. It had seemed so much fantasy, with no more substance than the spirit himself.

Now his doubts were all but vanquished. And yet…

The creature hates Nuala. He meant to injure her when she and I were together.

And how did that fact change anything? Whatever

the spirit may have done, Nuala *had* used her powers, not for good, but to harm…and not only to harm, but to come near to destroying a human life, however despicable that life might be.

And then she'd turned her powers on him, driving him before her as a wolf drives a sheep. Rejecting him completely, in every way.

You are cursed, Sinjin Ware.

The earth wobbled under Sinjin's shoes. He considered summoning a cab, but the thought of a bumpy ride through the congested London streets set his head to spinning.

He had to decide what to do. Nuala had been correct; he hadn't the strength to stop her if she chose to continue on her present course. Would she graduate to greater mischiefs? If she would go so far to protect a friend, how might she punish anyone she perceived as an enemy to others for whom she held affection?

If he could not influence her with logic or an appeal to her better nature…

The spirit will know.

Needles of ice pierced Sinjin's spine. The apparition was not yet done with him. It hated Nuala, to be sure. It could not be trusted. But it might provide Sinjin with valuable information, information that might enable him to find an answer to a problem for which he had found no solution.

Knowing at last what he must do, Sinjin made his way home. His butler examined him in alarm. His valet clearly wished to smother him with concern over his state of dishevelment, but Sinjin dismissed him. There was only one kind of help he needed now, and no mortal man could supply it.

He undressed, lay down on his bed and reached inside himself for the *other*. It was well past midnight when he felt the bone-deep chill settle over his skin. He sat up, threw off the sheets and stood naked in the middle of the room, listening. Gooseflesh covered his arms, and he knew he was no longer alone.

"I trust I have not disturbed you?"

Sinjin held his ground, though every human instinct recoiled in horror. The mist congealed before him, a formless cloud that gradually took on the shape he had seen in Mrs. Summerhayes's parlor.

"Of course I have not," the apparition said in a deep, mocking voice. "Can it be that you require my assistance?"

Sinjin stared into the spirit's hollow eyes. He could make out more detail now: the deep lines bracketing the spirit's mouth and creasing his forehead, marking him as a man of middle age; the reddish glint reflected in the hard, metallic gray eyes; the sharply cut bones that gave his cheeks and jaw a skeletal cast.

"Who are you?" Sinjin demanded.

"I am Martin Makepeace, and I was the first of the Wares, two hundred and forty-four years ago."

It seemed unlikely that anything could be quite so absurd as a ghost in his bedchamber, but the spirit's pronouncement left Sinjin almost breathless with laughter.

"The first of the Wares?" he repeated when he could breathe again.

The apparition—Martin Makepeace—stared at Sinjin in cold appraisal. "Yes," he said. "It was the name I chose to give my son when I had no further need of my own. And I have been watching over my family for those two hundred and forty years. Watching for one who will finally bring an end to my long quest."

Sinjin grabbed his dressing gown from the chair near the armoire and shrugged it over his shoulders. "You are a ghost. A spirit of the dead."

"If you like."

"And you've come to haunt me because I'm your descendant?" Sinjin found an unused cigar on a table and rolled it between his fingers. "I presume I am to feel honored by your attention."

The razor Sinjin had laid on the table beside the washstand suddenly flew from its place and clattered to the carpet inches from his bare foot.

"Do not mock me," Makepeace said softly. "I have but one purpose, and it will be fulfilled."

Sinjin bent to pick up the razor and turned it about in his hand. "And what would that be?" he asked with equal softness.

"To ensure the punishment of the witch Nuala, known to your world as Lady Charles."

"Punish her for what? Am I to infer that she has done you some personal injury?"

"I warn you, boy…"

"How can she have hurt a man who lived more then two centuries ago?"

"Ah." Makepeace closed his eyes, and his shape became more solid, until it seemed as if another living man stood in the room. "I told you it was not a story to be related in a moment."

Sinjin set down both razor and cigar, found a chair and dropped into it. "I surmise that you won't leave me alone until you have told it."

"Very astute, boy. As it was astute of you to discover the witch's true nature."

"How in God's name do you know what I've discovered?"

"Did I not say I was watching you?"

Sinjin gripped the arms of the chair. "How long?"

"Since you were a boy. As I watched your father, and your brother before you. The brother *she* killed."

"No." Sinjin started up, but that invisible force slammed him back into the chair. "Whatever she may have done to earn your hatred, she was no more responsible for Giles's death than I."

The apparition smiled. "Has she bewitched you so completely?" The windows rattled as if at a ferocious wind. "A few more days and I fear there would have been no saving you."

"I don't need saving."

"Then why have you summoned me?" Makepeace stroked the fine black wool of his doublet with a slender aesthetic's hand. "You believe yourself free, but you are not. She controls you, boy. I shall give you a chance to truly be rid of her."

Was that what Sinjin wanted? To be rid of her? Rid of the responsibility he felt for her actions, of the lust that could not be driven away by even the most rigorous discipline?

"What do you want of me?" he asked.

"Very good. We have made a beginning." Makepeace glanced about, selected a chair and sat, his half-translucent body blending with the chair's upholstery. "You shall be my instrument of justice."

"I'm no one's instrument. You've used me before, but that ends now."

"I did not use you in any way that did not reflect your own desires."

"Liar. You would have had me abuse her."

"As you, in your unbridled lust, would never have done."

"*No.* It was you. Only you."

There was something like approval in Makepeace's hooded gaze. "I see that your will is so much stronger than any of the others. That is why we shall succeed."

Sinjin leaned back in the chair, clenching his teeth to keep them from chattering. "We go no further until you explain why you wish to punish Nuala."

"That is a very simple matter, boy. I shall show you."

The room darkened. Sinjin braced himself.

And the fire came. It began at Sinjin's feet, eating through to bone, and licked up his legs. His dressing gown caught fire, but he was unaware of anything save the agony of his immolation.

"Feel it," Makepeace's distant voice intoned. "Feel what it is like to die."

CHAPTER NINETEEN

SINJIN FELT HIS BODY give way. The room vanished in a pall of acrid smoke.

"Do you feel what it was like for my father?" Makepeace said. "What it was like for him to burn, for his very organs to catch fire and be consumed within him while he yet lived?"

Unable to think, to see, to move his tongue, Sinjin could not answer. His lungs were white-hot coals in his chest, his heart a seething mass of melting tissue.

"*She* did this," Makepeace said, so close that he must surely be burning, as well. "Your witch used her foul sorcery to contrive the most terrible death any man could imagine."

"No," Sinjin croaked.

"How can you deny it, when you now suffer the very fate to which my father was condemned?"

"This…" Sinjin's felt his lips crack and peel away. "This is not real."

"So you said of me."

"You have…no power."

"Do I not?"

The already unbearable pain intensified. Sinjin's legs were naked bone now, and his ribs had begun to collapse into the empty cavity of his chest.

"You are right, Sinjin," Makepeace's voice murmured. "I have not the power to kill you here and now. Nor would I."

In an instant the flames vanished. The smoke lifted and was gone. The agony receded, and Sinjin felt the air seep back into his lungs, the frantic rhythm of his heart begin to slow. Carefully, he moved his arms, lifting his hands to his face.

It was whole. So were his legs, his chest, every part of him that had burned. Even his dressing gown was untouched.

He tried to focus on the figure that reclined so easily in his chair.

"Damn you," Sinjin whispered.

"Perhaps," Makepeace said. "But if I fall into the Pit, so shall she."

Sinjin dashed the sweat from his eyes. "Why?" he rasped. "Why have you done this?"

"To make you understand what she is capable of. Why she must be stopped."

"Nuala...Nuala would never—"

"You have seen what she can do." He leaned forward, staring into Sinjin's aching eyes. "Do you think I would be here in this world of sorrow if it were not necessary to preserve it against such evil as the witch can inflict?"

Sinjin bent his head. The memory of pain was still very fresh. But now that he could think again, he remembered seeing a face amid the smoke…a face he knew as well as his own.

Nuala.

"Yes," Makepeace said. "My father, Comfort Makepeace, was the witch's first victim."

"Her first victim? She is, at most, five-and-twenty. How do you propose that she achieved this… miracle?"

"Because she is not five-and-twenty. She is as old as I."

How many times, since the events at Donbridge four years ago, had Sinjin scoffed at fantastical proclamations such as these?

And how often had they proved to be true?

"Rubbish," he snapped.

Makepeace sighed. "Did she tell you of her tragic past? Of her brave, innocent people who were driven into exile?"

Sinjin's memories of his and Nuala's conversation at the garden party were very clear. "She said nothing about exile."

"Then she did not tell you why she was among the children of Satan when they were rightfully driven out for the most vile and wicked sorcery?"

"'Children of Satan?' You're mad."

"She killed my father because he would have prevented her and her kind from corrupting and destroying England."

"Destroying England?" Sinjin gathered his legs to rise. "I've heard enough."

"Sit yourself down!" A great weight ground into

Sinjin's shoulders. He fought it, and fell from the chair. The weight pressed him into the carpet as if he were a beetle being crushed under an enormous foot.

"They are not human!" Makepeace roared. "They have always despised our kind, and intended to rule us all in Satan's name. Had they succeeded, they would have begun a reign of terror surpassing the worst in human history!"

With a grunt of effort, Sinjin pushed himself up onto his hands and knees. "Three centuries ago," he grated, "people like you believed in demons and unicor—" He stopped, stunned by his own idiocy. Three hundred years ago, people had believed in unicorns. And fairies.

He had seen both.

"You have taken a witch to your bed," Makepeace said, sensing his weakness. "You stand on the very lip of Hell."

Sinjin rolled to sit with his back against the wall. "If such broad claims and illusions are all you have to offer as proof—"

Makepeace surged up from his chair. "Puppy," he snarled. "What must I do to convince you? How far must *she* go? Is it not enough that she has, in your very sight, used her powers to harm? That she killed your brother?"

"She would never have harmed Giles."

Makepeace sneered in disgust. He lifted his hand as if he would work some new mischief and then sank into his chair again. "You continue to deny that she had anything to do with your brother's death. Yet it was she who manipulated both him and Lady

Westlake so that the woman would shoot her lover. She made them both mad, by driving Lord Donnington to desperate lust for the girl Mariah and promoting the foulest jealousy in Lady Westlake's heart."

"Why? What possible purpose could she have for such acts?"

"Because she hates us. She hates the Wares, who once bore the name of Makepeace. It has been her purpose for the last two centuries to take the lives of every male in each generation. Only I have been able to salvage one heir in each family, to carry on our name and continue the battle."

The apparition's words made no sense until Sinjin cast his memory back to his father's generation, and *his* father's, and all the others about which he had learned as a boy.

In every family, several sons had been born. In each, all but one heir had died in young adulthood, childless, often after they had inherited the earldom, leaving it— as Giles had left his title—to a younger brother.

"Accidents," Makepeace said. "Was that not always the way of it? A fall from a horse, a shooting mishap, a drowning, a suicide. All coincidence, Sinjin?"

Of course they were. They must be. To believe that Nuala was over two hundred years old, that she could conceal such malice in her heart and yet lie in his arms, filling him with the kind of happiness he hadn't known for as long as he could remember...

"Think also on this, boy. Have you never wondered how the Earls of Donnington came by their great wealth? It was *I* who brought it about. I who advised my grandson beyond my own death, urging him to support Charles the Second during his exile in France. From King Charles he received the earldom and lands enough to make him rich. With every passing year, I have made the Wares more wealthy still."

"Then I am not the first to receive the signal honor of your 'advice?'"

"Not at all. I merely suggested…a whisper in your ancestors' ears when an opportunity for advancement arose. And you?" He smiled that skeletal smile. "I whispered in *your* ear when the witch came to you."

Sinjin clung to his composure, remembering his original purpose. Not to give in to the ghost's threats and blandishments, but to learn.

"Everything you have said is balanced upon the presumption that Nuala and all her kind are evil," he said.

"Would I be here, separated from Heaven, if she were innocent?" A deep weariness passed over Makepeace's face, and he closed his eyes. "I ask your help not only for myself and my murdered father, not only for the generations who have suffered, but for the sake of this new age, this new city. If you have any doubts about what the witch may do, what she has done to your family, then you must not shut me out."

Doubts. God, yes. He had doubts. Nuala was not innocent. Whether or not she had been ultimately responsible for Giles's death, as he had once believed, she was capable of violence against anyone who crossed her. She could not or would not control her abilities.

Perhaps Makepeace's father had deserved what

had become of him. Perhaps he had "driven out" a people who did not deserve such treatment. Sinjin had no way of knowing. But if he were to ask Nuala of her past, of her supposed age, of her alleged crime, would she ever admit to any of it? To *him*, whom she had so soundly rejected?

"Even if I were to accept anything that you have told me," Sinjin said, "I will not be your weapon of revenge. I will not harm Nuala."

"Harm her?" Makepeace leaned his head on his hand, and had he been a living man it would have seemed as if he were weeping. "I would punish her, yes. But I would not take her life." He looked up, the hollows in his face no more than wells of shadow. "It has been so long. So long. I have let my anger get the better of me. But I am no murderer."

Sinjin picked up the razor again. The sharpened edge cut a thin red line in his finger. "What would you have me do?"

"Complete the vow. Strip Nuala of her powers, so that she may never harm another living soul."

Strip her of her powers. What would that mean to a two-hundred-and-forty-four-year-old witch?

Salvation. Freedom from a cruel master she was incapable of defying. A normal life. The happiness Sinjin knew eluded her.

"How is such a thing to be achieved?" he asked thickly.

But Makepeace's shape, previously so solid in appearance, had begun to dissolve as if he were losing the power to hold himself in the mortal world.

"You must learn for yourself," he said, his voice growing faint. "Go to Donbridge. You will find a concealed door behind the paneling in the library. It contains a book written by my father."

"A book? What sort of book?"

"I cannot stay." Makepeace's shape became so transparent that the chair was fully visible through it. "You will find the means at Donbridge."

And then he was gone, only a trace of dark mist left behind.

Sinjin stood very still, waiting. Makepeace did not return. The room was deathly silent as Sinjin found his way back to his chair.

So he was to go to Donbridge and find a book that would explain how he was to put a stop to this madness. *If* he were to believe anything Makepeace had said. *If* he were to learn that this mysterious method of ending Nuala's power would do her no harm.

He knew there were things the ghost had not told him, things he had kept hidden. But what choice did Sinjin have?

Go to Nuala one last time. Speak with her. Ask her for the truth.

But she had closed her mind and her heart to him. It had gone too far.

He summoned his valet to help him pack.

"WE HAVE FOUND HER."

Nuala focused again on Clara's face. It was good news. The best. Deborah had been discovered at a country house in Kent, one of her late husband's properties previously unknown to the Widows. She had been persuaded to return to London…not by the Widows, who had assumed the work for which Nuala should have been responsible, but by Ioan Davies, who had insisted upon accompanying Clara, Frances and Julia Summerhayes on their sojourn to Kent.

"They cannot be separated," Clara said with an air of bemusement. "It is most definitely love, despite the barriers that ought to exist between them. Even Tameri has acquiesced to the inevitability of Deborah's downfall."

Inevitable, indeed. If Nuala required any further proof that her magic had become as wild and undependable as a Fane lordling's honor, Deborah's situation must have provided it. Nuala had been bent on putting Deborah and Melbyrne together, and she had been wrong. Blindly, inexorably wrong. Her path forward was now clear.

"Of course she will not stay in London," Clara continued. "It does not appear as if those ridiculous rumors will gain any further traction, but there would be the worst sort of talk once Deborah's relationship with young Davies became known. *She* might defy Society, but Davies will not permit it. I believe they mean to—" Clara cocked her head. "I should not tell you what Deborah will tell you herself. She, Julia and Mr. Davies should arrive by two."

So soon. It was nearly ten o'clock now, and Nuala knew she was in no fit state to speak to anyone.

"I…will not be here to see her," she said. "I am leaving London. I do not know when I shall return."

Clara leaned forward in her chair. "What nonsense is this?" Her eyes narrowed. "Has it something to do with Lord Donnington?"

"Nothing," Nuala said too quickly. "Whatever you may have heard...I have not been flinging myself at his head in the expectation of a proposal."

"A proposal?" Clara laughed. "What an astonishing thought. I have heard no such talk. But we *have* noticed that neither you nor Deborah have attended our gatherings in the past weeks, and you have been seen speaking intimately with Donnington on more than one occasion. Of course it had seemed that you had no liking for each other...." Her voice trailed off. "What goes on between you and the earl, Nuala? Has *he* been pursuing you?"

"Nothing of the kind. You are quite right—we despised each other from the moment we met. I...I knew him before I came to London, before my marriage. It was not a pleasant acquaintance."

"Ah."

"I knew I might see him again, but expected that we would avoid each other. Apparently, Lord Donnington's quarrelsome nature could not be denied."

"I see."

Clara did not see. A bee had found its way into her bonnet, and she had already drawn her own conclusions.

"I have been a poor friend to all of you," Nuala said. "But you need have no fear that I will follow Deborah's path. I have recently learned of certain holdings from my husband's estate in Scotland and

Northumberland. It is necessary for me to visit them before I can determine what must be done with them."

"But surely you can put this off until another day, when Deborah—"

"I cannot." Nuala rose. "Deborah is safe. She does not need me now, and I must finish preparing for my journey. Please give Deborah and Mr. Davies my very best wishes for their future happiness."

Clara stared, realized that she had been asked to leave, and got to her feet.

"Something is wrong," she said. "You are not yourself. *We* should be poor friends if we did not stand by you in your time of need."

"When I am in need, I shall tell you." Nuala broke for the drawing room door. "I shall send a letter from Northumberland when I reach my destination."

Blowing out her breath, Clara followed Nuala into the hall. She paused at the door, clearly prepared to continue her arguments. Without thinking or considering her actions, Nuala whispered the simplest of spells, and the older woman's face went blank. She murmured a goodbye and descended to her carriage.

Sickened by her sudden action against her friend, Nuala leaned against the wall, afraid she might not make it up the stairs to her room. It was so easy to work this shadow-magic to get her way. Second nature now, when for so many years even the whitest magic had been a careful practice, considered deliberately before the most rudimentary spell was spoken.

No longer. She was losing control of the very powers she had worked so hard to keep.

Working her way along the wall, Nuala reached the staircase. Within the hour she would be gone…north, just as she had told Clara. There was a man in Scotland, a witch who had been said to have relinquished his powers and become a monk. If he still lived, perhaps he could show Nuala the way to relinquish her own.

There was grave danger in such a purging, a chance that she might not survive the process. But she was prepared to pay that price.

It was her last hope.

Nuala climbed to the first-floor landing and braced herself on the banister. One way or another, this must end. She would end it.

But not without saying goodbye to Sinjin.

DONBRIDGE WAS AS QUIET as the grave.

Only a handful of servants remained during the Season, and they maintained a strict state of efficient invisibility that suggested they were keenly aware of their master's mood. The moment he arrived, Sinjin changed his clothes, raided the kitchen for a sandwich to stave off insistent hunger, and went directly to the library.

He found the hidden cupboard door after only a few minutes of searching. The cracks in the paneling were almost invisible; he was not surprised that he hadn't noticed them before, having spent little time in the room since his accession to the title.

His hands shook as he found the catch and the door swung open. The dank smell of mildewed paper filled his nostrils. The book he found was small and bound in red-dyed leather, its pages threatening to crumble before Sinjin had turned the first page.

He sat behind the desk and laid the book before him. The cover was blank, but the frontispiece displayed a primitive illustration of a woman, half-naked and leering, her hands raised as if she would attack the reader with weapons spun of air.

The woman looked like Nuala.

Sinjin turned the page with such haste that he nearly tore it in two. He ignored the damage and continued past the Scriptural verse on the next page to the first chapter.

Of Witches, the title said. By Comfort Makepeace. Dense, crabbed writing crowded the paper, words shaped in antique script and an Old English dialect. Sinjin bent over the book, translating the language as best he could.

It was obvious that Comfort Makepeace had despised the women—and men—he named witches. Line after line described the evil they had worked among men since the days of Christ, how they were not bound by God's law, or Man's. They poisoned wells and struck down livestock merely to display their power; they killed those who dared attempt to expose them for the tools of Satan they were.

Sinjin closed the book, his eyes aching. Such extreme accusations could not be rational or true. They smacked of fanaticism. Just as had Martin Makepeace's threats and warnings.

Rising quickly, Sinjin scanned the bookshelves. Few of the volumes had been touched in years; Giles had not been a great reader, and Sinjin kept his own personal favorites in his rooms. But after a time he found a history of England wedged between Gibbon's *The Decline and Fall of the Roman Empire* and a well-worn copy of *Tom Jones.*

The section on the English witch-hunts was no more than a few paragraphs, but it was enough. Sinjin closed the cover and returned the book to its place.

He had been an utter fool. How had he not seen it from the first? Perhaps Comfort Makepeace had not been a witch-finder himself, but the man had clearly hated them enough to be such a monster.

Returning to the desk, Sinjin thumbed through the old tome's fragile pages, pausing at each illustration. Most were crude wood-block prints of various witches performing wicked magic on innocent, terrified men, women and children. Not one depicted a hanging, a flogging, or any other overt act of violence against the loathed creatures.

Yet Sinjin's gaze was caught on a sequence of illustrations near the end of the book, as primitive as the rest, but even more sickeningly evocative. In the first illustration, naked woman stood facing a man in the same dark, sober clothing worn by Martin Makepeace. Her hands were bound, and her hair flowed loose about her shoulders.

In the second illustration, the woman lay on her back on the ground, and the man crouched between her thighs. In the third, he was stretched out on top of her. And in the last, the woman knelt with bowed head, defeated. Clumsy though the illustrator was, he had managed to convey a terrible sense of despair in the woman's body.

Sinjin swallowed and read the text beneath the pictures. It was very explicit, both in the description of the physical act and the words that must be spoken as it was done. The cantrip was more effective if the witch were willing, but her cooperation in the coupling was not required.

Shutting the book, Sinjin dropped it to the carpet. It was obscene. Yet *this* was what Martin Makepeace had intended that he should find, the instructions he was meant to follow.

He walked out of the library and slammed the door, as breathless as if he had run several miles. He couldn't do it. Not at any price.

The familiar, icy chill returned, running along his limbs and spine.

"Makepeace," Sinjin said hoarsely.

The ghost didn't appear, not even in the form of the mist that always presaged his materialization. But Sinjin heard the apparition's voice just the same.

"Do you still doubt?"

"Did your father hang witches?"

"He tried to halt their evil, but he did not kill them."

"He merely raped them."

"Reciting the cantrip in the act of coupling is the only means of breaking their power."

"Then you've got the wrong man to do your dirty work."

"I have the right man. A man who is the last of his line, and will die without issue should he fail."

"You expect me to believe that Nuala would kill me?"

"Or make certain that you have no sons of your own. She knows who you are, boy. She has always known."

"I don't believe you."

"Then believe this. She will not realize what you have done. You may guide her, teach her to be a good, humble woman. And she will be well when it is finished. She may yet earn salvation."

"And you? What will become of you?"

He waited for Makepeace's answer, but none came. The chill passed away.

Dizzy with shock, Sinjin wandered up to his room. She *couldn't* have deceived him for so long. She couldn't have pretended their passion, the bond that had grown between them. She couldn't be over two hundred years old. She couldn't have killed Giles, or his father's brothers, or all those sons of previous generations.

Yet there were unicorns, and fairies and ghosts. Ghosts who remained attached to this world for the sole purpose of securing what they believed to be justice.

Sinjin sat numbly on the bed and considered the worst. If Nuala really were what Makepeace had claimed, then Sinjin had but two choices: do as the book instructed, or let her continue on her path of wanton rage. Anything she might tell him must be presumed to be a lie. If she were wholly innocent of the crimes of which Makepeace had accused her… she might suffer a little while, but in the end she would be well again.

You may guide her, teach her to be a good, humble woman. She would need *him,* turn to him for comfort. Be with him.

No. I do this for her. For those she might harm. Not for myself.

Good God. He was seriously considering it. She would never forgive him. Never.

"Your lordship?"

The footman's voice was muffled through the door, but it held a note of urgency. Sinjin got up and let the man in.

"I beg your pardon, your lordship, but there is a lady to see you."

Black premonition bit at Sinjin's heart. "Did she give her name?"

The footman handed him the card. Sinjin crumpled it in his fist.

"Conduct her to the drawing room and inform the servants that they are to have the rest of the day off."

The footman bowed and retreated. Sinjin took a deep breath and prepared himself to meet her again.

Nuala was waiting in the drawing room, her gaze fixed on a portrait of Sinjin and Giles with their father. It had been painted when Giles was ten and Sinjin eight; they had looked very much alike then.

"Sinjin."

She didn't smile as she turned to face him. There were hollows under her eyes, and her skin was pale.

Two hundred and forty-four years, Sinjin thought. He imagined he could see it now, an ancient sorrow in her gaze, a weight of decades and centuries.

"I was not sure if you would see me," she said.

He didn't ask her to sit. There would be no lengthy conversation. "If you have come to explain…"

"No explanation could be sufficient. I can only ask you to forgive me as best you can. We shall not…" She hesitated, her throat working. "I shall be leaving London for a time. It is likely that we shall not meet again for many months."

Her words came as a shock. It wasn't that Sinjin hadn't considered that a separation might relieve him of an untenable choice; if Nuala were simply to vanish, he could take no action against her.

But he felt no relief. "Where are you going?" he demanded.

"To Scotland. I believe it would be better for me to leave London and remain in solitude."

"Solitude?"

"Yes. Perhaps, in time, I may learn to be quite ordinary again."

In spite of her solemnity—even in light of all that had happened—Sinjin could barely stand to be near her without taking her in his arms. "You wish to be rid of your magic?"

"If it is possible." Abruptly she moved toward the door. "I only came to say goodbye."

He caught her before she reached the door. She melted into his arms. He kissed her, and she returned the kiss with fire and hunger and desperation.

CHAPTER TWENTY

SINJIN BARELY HAD TIME to close the door before Nuala had unfastened her skirt and began working on her petticoats. In a fever equal to hers, Sinjin helped her shed the garment and stripped away her drawers. She needed no spells to drive him mad with lust.

He kissed her frantically as he lifted her and carried her to the largest chair in the room. With trembling fingers he unbuttoned his trousers, lifted her bottom and spread her thighs apart. She was already wet and swollen, pink lips begging for his caresses. But he could not wait. Bracing his knees on the chair seat and his hands on the back, he entered her with one smooth thrust.

Nuala was no longer thinking of apologies, of the journey ahead, of the monk who might cure her of her particular madness. She was only aware of the feel of Sinjin as he moved inside her, his breath catching with each motion. There was nothing gentle in the taking, nor did she want gentleness. She locked her legs around his waist, urging him on, begging him to drive as deep as her body would allow.

Only at the end, when they were both near the

glory of completion, did she hear him begin to speak, in a low and rhythmic chant. She recognized the words and their fell purpose, and her mind detached itself from her quivering body.

He doesn't know what he is doing. He couldn't. But as the cantrip began to do its work, and his thrusts became more insistent, she felt the words' power begin to work through her, reaching their climax as Sinjin released his seed inside her. As her helpless body followed his, she heard cruel laughter. Not from Sinjin, who collapsed to his knees and pressed his face into the hollow beneath her ribs, but from the one who had used him as a tool of vengeance.

She had not understood. She hadn't guessed, even when she had puzzled and worried over Sinjin's inexplicable behavior. How long had Makepeace been with them? How had he reached Sinjin and taught him to use the spell?

Don't you know, witch?

The old, terrible memories returned, and with them the knowledge she had hidden from herself, from the very senses that should have revealed the truth from the moment of her arrival at Donbridge over four years ago.

She closed her eyes and let her hands rest gently on Sinjin's hair. He must have learned the truth of his heritage. She couldn't know how long he had been aware of it, but she was certain he'd been ignorant of his descent, and of Makepeace, when she had worked as a maid at Donbridge. Surely he'd still been ignorant when they'd met again in London, or he would have taken action long before now.

Yet it really didn't matter. Makepeace, whatever he had become, must have deceived Sinjin and convinced him that Nuala should be stripped of her magic. How much had he lied to achieve his ends? Had Sinjin taken her in hate?

No. There was no hatred in his eyes as he lifted his head and met her gaze, only a great sorrow and regret.

"I'm sorry, Nuala," he said, his voice raw with emotion.

"Why?" she asked, stroking the disheveled hair away from his forehead. "I wanted it, too."

He rose and backed away, his walk unsteady, and fetched the coat he'd tossed over the sofa. He covered her from waist to knees and retreated again.

"Do you… Are you well?" he asked.

"How could I not be?"

He swallowed. "Nuala…I know the truth."

She sat up, pulling the coat with her. "About what, Sinjin?"

"That you were alive two hundred and forty years ago."

She didn't insult him with a denial. "It is true," she said. "I could never find a way to tell you."

"I wouldn't have believed you." He turned away, dragging his hand over his mouth. "Martin Makepeace came to me," he said. "Do you remember him?"

If only she could laugh. "Yes."

"Did you know that it was possible for a man to return from the dead?"

"Yes."

"I did not. But after all I've seen…" He shook his

head with a sharp jerk. "He told me that I was the last of a line his grandson had founded in the seventeenth century. He spoke of my ancestors, about why so many of the male line have died since the first Ware was ennobled. He told me what you did to his father." He glanced toward her, the lines etched between his brows drawn tight. "Did you kill Comfort Makepeace?"

"Yes."

He leaned over the sofa, his face so white that Nuala feared he would be ill. "Why? Did he hurt you? For God's sake, tell me!"

Nuala was silent. To reveal the full truth would destroy him. He had enacted the spell because he'd assumed that she had committed a heinous act of murder. The guilt of knowing he had been deceived...

"He claimed you and your kind were evil," Sinjin said, "and that Comfort only wanted to stop you from hurting others."

"He did attempt to stop us."

"Did you...kill members of my family?"

She could not let him believe such a thing, though she knew her weakness to be despicable. "No, Sinjin. I did not."

"Have you killed others?"

Her body was growing numb. "No. No others."

His breath shuddered out. "I had to make sure of you," he said, his face a mask of anguish. "I never believed you were evil, only that your abilities...the temptation... You were turning into someone I didn't recognize...so much anger..."

He was right, of course. She had intended to put

an end to the temptation herself, even at the possible
cost of her life. Now there would be no journey to
Scotland, no seeking of a man who might or might
not be able to cure her.

"I know, Sinjin," she said. "I know what you have
done. And I do not blame you."

"God!" He slammed his fist into the sofa's back.
"If only you'd been honest with me from the beginning. If only you'd explained…"

"You wouldn't have listened."

It did not seem possible that his expression could
hold any more anguish. "If there'd only been another
way. Any other way."

She was amazed to find herself capable of smiling.
"I do not hate you, Sinjin. I am relieved that I am no
longer…beset by temptation. You have taken that
burden from me."

He returned to her chair and dropped to his knees.
"I would care for you for the rest of my life, if you
would accept. But I know that is impossible."

"Yes," she said. "I am afraid it is." She felt the
weakness collecting in her legs. "I must go."

He bounded up again. "I can't let you," he said,
his voice sharp with panic. "You're ill."

With exquisite care she levered herself out of the
chair, still clutching his coat to her waist. "I am perfectly well." She reached for her discarded petticoats.
"Please, let me go."

"I won't—"

The room spun around her. Sinjin caught her
before she fell.

"Nuala!" He gathered her in his arms and carried her to the sofa. She felt his hands in her hair, on her face. "What in God's name have I done?"

She was afraid to open her eyes. "It will pass."

"Tell me what to do." His voice was raw with panic. "How can I help you?"

"Don't worry." She reached for him, traced his dear, tormented face with her fingertips. "It is only temporary."

And it was. The dizziness passed and left in its stead a peaceful lassitude. A part of her knew she should leave Donbridge before the spell took its full effect. But her body was no longer hers to command. Somehow she must make Sinjin understand that it was not his fault. Somehow she must...

The lassitude overwhelmed her, and she sank into a dream of her family. And of Christian, whom she had mourned so long. He would not blame her that she'd given her heart to another. They would all greet her soon. She had finally paid her debt. She had won her redemption at last.

"RIDE HARD," SINJIN told the stable boy, pressing the note into the young man's hand. "Change horses if you find it necessary. This message must reach Mrs. Summerhayes before sunset."

The boy touched his forehead. "I will, your lordship."

He left on Shaitan, bursting away at a gallop. The stallion could not endure the pace indefinitely, but there would be fresh horses for hire at nearly every village between here and Cambridge, where the boy would wire the message to London.

Nothing more could be done. Sinjin ran back into the house, found the doctor descending the stairs and accosted him.

"How is she?"

The doctor's grave expression gave his answer even before he spoke. "She is very ill," he said, "but I can find no cause. Are you quite certain, Lord Donnington, that you have provided every detail of how this came about?"

Every detail. As if this man would ever believe, let alone find a way to reverse what had happened in the drawing room.

"You must help her," Sinjin said. "Money is no object. If you must call in specialists, assistance of any kind…"

"I can certainly do so, Lord Donnington, but I can promise no different result. I have seen no case like it before. Lady Charles is…" He turned his face aside. "Have you called for her family?"

Sinjin braced his legs against a wave of terror. "I have wired her nearest relations in London," he said. "Only tell me who else to send for, and I'll see it done."

With an almost imperceptible shake of his head, the doctor jotted down several names and handed the note to Sinjin. In minutes Sinjin had sent two more riders, a second to Cambridge and the other to Huntingdon. He had already arranged for the doctor to remain at Donnington for as long as necessary. Until Nuala recovered.

She *must* recover.

As night fell, he sat by Nuala's bedside and prayed. Nuala didn't hear him; she lay in a near-coma, eyes closed, skin drained of color, her breath frighteningly shallow. Sinjin held her cold hand, trying futilely to chafe some warmth back into it. After several hours the doctor returned and insisted he leave the patient to her rest.

There was nowhere for Sinjin to go, nothing more he could do. He walked into the park, past the folly where, not so long ago, he had learned that entire worlds existed beyond the one he knew.

He stood under the bright moon and flung back his head.

"Where are you?" he shouted. "Show yourself, you lying bastard!"

Makepeace, if he heard, chose not to respond. Sinjin shouted himself hoarse, but he might as well have been speaking to the mice and foxes.

He dropped to his knees, beyond despair. A moment later he had himself in hand again. He got up and trudged back to the house. The doctor, half-asleep in his chair, started awake again and shook his head. Nuala's condition had not changed.

It was midmorning when the Widows drove into the lane. The dowager Duchess of Vardon, Ladies John Pickering and Riordan, Mrs. Summerhayes, Lady Selfridge—all had come. They did not need to know precisely what had happened to hold Sinjin responsible.

Only Mrs. Summerhayes revealed no overt emotion. When Sinjin showed the ladies into the drawing room, she gazed at him without reproach or anger, only a quiet sort of waiting. As each of the widows went upstairs in turn, Mrs. Summerhayes remained quietly in her chair. After an hour Sinjin couldn't bear it any longer.

As if she'd anticipated his request, she rose and followed Sinjin into the library.

"You must help me," Sinjin said. "Help me to save her."

The young woman turned to gaze at the fireplace where the charred fragments of Martin Makepeace's book lay scattered among the ashes. "I speak for the dead," she whispered. "I do not control them."

"I don't believe that. You knew I needed help the moment we met."

"But I did fail to warn you. I didn't recognize the danger. I...I am to blame."

Sinjin seized her arm. "Our mistakes are irrelevant now. There must be a way to undo what I have done."

She met his gaze. Her eyes were wet with tears. "What did you do?"

Sinjin told her. She listened without comment until he had completed the entire sordid story.

"You did not know what you were doing," she said at last.

"No. God help me. I didn't know she would be..."

He couldn't finish the sentence. He had no defense, even had he wished to offer one. He had let himself accept just enough of what Makepeace had told him because the ghost's apparent desires had meshed so well with his. He had fallen prey to his own gnawing doubts. All because he had become afraid of Nuala's power, and what it might do to them both.

"I will pay any price to save her," he said.

Mrs. Summerhayes sat abruptly, the tears spilling onto her cheeks. "If I knew the price, I would tell you."

"Summon the ghost. Make him speak."

"I will try. Please, sit down."

He obeyed, every muscle taut with fear. Mrs. Summerhayes closed her eyes, resting her hands on her lap. Her breathing deepened. For an instant her face took on the expression he had seen in her parlor before the apparition had appeared. Then the expression was gone, and Mrs. Summerhayes opened her eyes.

"I cannot," she said. "This house prevents me. *His* influence is too powerful."

"Then we'll go somewhere else," he said. "There must be a place…"

"I am sorry. He is beyond my reach."

"For God's sake, there must be a way!"

"I do not know it."

He surged to his feet and strode to the door.

"Lord Donnington."

Hope stilled his heart. "What is it?"

"Part of what the spirit told you is true. I believe that Nuala did kill Comfort Makepeace. But not for the reasons he claims."

Sinjin pounded the door with his fist. Of course Nuala had had a reason, but she had refused to defend herself. It was as if she had *wanted* to die.

She wasn't fighting. She had given up.

He entered the entrance hall just as a maid was con-

ducting new guests into the house: Lady Orwell and
Ioan Davies. Deborah was clearly distraught, Davies
hollow-eyed. They stopped when they saw Sinjin.

"How is she?" Deborah asked anxiously. "We
came as quickly as we could...."

"She is very ill," Lady John said as she descended
the stairs. "I will take you to her."

Deborah flew up the stairs. Ioan remained behind
with Sinjin.

"Is there anything I can do?" he asked.

"No. Nothing." Sinjin started for the stairs.

"If you will permit Lady Orwell to stay with Lady
Charles, I will take a room at the village inn."

"I have rooms enough for you both."

"I thank you, Lord Donnington."

Sinjin had no more time to waste on the boy. He
followed Lady Orwell up the stairs and stood outside
Nuala's door, listening to the soft drone of Deborah's
voice. Begging Nuala to come back, just as he had
done. Speaking of the Widows, and how eager they
were to have her return to them.

Only let her live, and I'll never see her again.

Deborah emerged an hour later, bumping into the
doorjamb as she half stumbled through the door.
"Lord Donnington," she said in a choked voice.

"Did she—" he began. "Was there any sign..."

She shook her head, picked up her skirts and rushed
past him. He didn't go after her. There was nothing
he could do to help her. He couldn't help anyone.

He went into the room and locked the door. The
rasp of Nuala's breathing was like the grinding of a

saw on coffin wood. He sat beside her, stroked the hair away from her face, murmured the same apologies he had offered again and again.

Nothing. She was dying. He could think the word and know it to be true.

He laid his head on her waist, choking on his own silent tears. Her heartbeat was slow, fading.

Take my life. Mine, not hers. Let the name of Ware die with me.

"But it is not your life I want, boy."

Carefully Sinjin raised his head, smoothing Nuala's nightdress with a gentle palm. "Makepeace."

"You do not sound pleased to see me." Makepeace materialized beside the fireplace, stretching his arm casually cross the mantelpiece.

Sinjin rose from the bedside, amazed at his own composure. "You lied to me."

Makepeace shrugged. "I told what you were ready to hear."

"You always intended for me to kill her."

"You were my last hope of justice."

"Justice? What justice requires an innocent woman's death?"

"No woman is innocent." He smiled, and Sinjin wondered how it was possible that he had failed to see the unadulterated evil in Makepeace's eyes. "Since what was done cannot be undone, I see no reason why you should not know. My father hanged the witch's sorcerous consort for acts against Man and God."

"Then you were a witch-finder," Sinjin said, his stomach heaving.

"My father and I helped rid the world of Satan's spawn," Makepeace said. "They could never be saved. Scripture is clear. 'Thou shalt not suffer a witch to live.'"

"And that is why you hanged them," Sinjin said. "Not because they hurt anyone else, but because of your own fanatical hatred of something you couldn't understand."

"They bespelled innocent villagers into believing that they had done good works, healing the sick and aiding in the growing of corn and livestock. But such acts are the province of God alone. He does not permit Himself to be mocked."

Sinjin remembered what Nuala had told him of her people at the dowager's garden party. Perhaps they had made mistakes, as she had. Perhaps they had sometimes misused their magic, as she had. But now Sinjin understood that they were not gods, only people with abilities as natural to them as spinning was to a weaver or fashioning coats to a tailor.

"*You* made a mockery of God," Sinjin said. "Nuala never harmed any of my family, did she?"

"It was her doing. I was forced to punish my descendents when they failed to keep the vow to destroy her."

So Makepeace had been the one to arrange for the "accidents" that had befallen so many Ware heirs. "My brother?" Sinjin asked.

"I never made myself known to him. He brought about his own death."

Not Makepeace, not Nuala, not Sinjin himself. Giles had died of his own fatal misjudgment.

"You knew that Nuala was at Donbridge," Sinjin said. "Why didn't you approach me then?"

"The time was not right. You were bound to another lover. But when you met the witch again in London…"

The attraction had been immediate, though Sinjin had been too blind with anger and resentment to recognize his own desire for her, or hers for him.

"You became helpless under her spell," Makepeace said. "I saved you, and you fulfilled the vow. Now it is over."

Sinjin fell to his knees. "Let her live. I will keep her close. She'll never harm anyone again."

"*You* will keep her?" Makepeace sneered. "No mortal man could hold her. Find yourself a humble, God-fearing woman, boy, and know that you have done your sacred duty. Let that comfort you to the end of your days."

Sinjin was moving before he realized that his knees had left the floor. He threw himself at Makepeace, felt the shock of cold envelop him, the shudder of astonishment as Makepeace absorbed the attack.

The room turned end-over-end. Sinjin's brain seemed to shatter inside his skull, his bones turn to powder.

He found himself in a village square, standing among men in sober dress. Behind him, a crowd of villagers, eager and apprehensive, watched for the witch-finder's next move. Before him stood a gallows, made to hang several men or women at once but now bearing only a single victim.

Comfort Makepeace spoke briefly to the good,

upstanding men who had worked alongside him to bring the fiends to justice. The condemned prisoner shifted on the scaffold, perhaps attempting to free himself of his bonds. He had been a handsome man, Christian Starling, before the interrogation.

Martin glanced about the square. *She* had not come. He had wanted her to see what came of defying him, of denying him what he had wanted so badly.

No. You have broken her spell. He was no longer in her thrall. She had already lost many of those she called family. Now she must feel her consort's pain and know that her vile seduction had been exposed for the evil it was.

Comfort Makepeace bowed his head and led a prayer of thanksgiving and benediction. When the last words were spoken, Comfort nodded to the mayor, who in turn signaled to the hangman.

Starling did not weep. He didn't beg for mercy as they positioned him above the trap door and fitted the noose around his neck.

Comfort watched, smiling. His back was turned to the alley when Nuala emerged, her face flushed, her hands raised as she chanted her spell.

The scream came not from Starling's throat, but from the man who had condemned him. Martin felt hot liquid gush down his thigh. He couldn't move, even as the flames consumed his father from the inside, even as Comfort turned to meet his son's gaze and pleaded for his life. In minutes it was over, and nothing remained of a great man save ash and bone.

Martin cried out, cursing Heaven itself. He knelt

beside his father, weeping uncontrollably, mingling his tears with his father's remains.

The sober Puritans stared in shock, frozen, useless. Martin got to his feet, swaying like a man sotted with drink.

"Seize her," he snarled.

Several young men started reluctantly toward Nuala. She made no move to escape. She cast her gaze over the astonished observers, glanced at Makepeace and looked at last on Sinjin.

That was when Sinjin knew he had entered some kind of shared dream, not merely a memory brought to life by Makepeace's enduring hatred. Sinjin stood apart, an observer, and yet his body was solid, real.

"You must go," Nuala cried out to him as the men drew slowly closer. "Leave this place. Forget you ever knew me."

"Leave you? Never." He tried to go to her, but his limbs were heavy and useless. "Run, Nuala! For God's sake, save yourself!"

Martin Makepeace turned to stare at him. "Do you think you can save her?" he mocked. "She escaped me once, but now it is too late."

"No!" Sinjin fought for mastery of his legs and lunged toward Nuala. The young men reached her first. They seized her limbs and beat her down, dragged her unresisting toward the gibbet. Sinjin spun and ran at Makepeace, who languidly raised his arm. Sinjin fell, his muscles so rigid that his bones threatened to snap.

"Sinjin!" Nuala screamed. "Sinjin!"

"Perhaps you wish to die together," Makepeace said to Sinjin, ignoring her. "Would that suit you, boy?"

Sinjin fought his unseen bonds until his joints began to pull free of their sockets. "You wanted her," he gasped. "It wasn't just your father's death that made you hate her. You desired her, and she rejected you."

The witch-finder's mouth had become a pit of blackness, his eyes empty sockets. "She was Delilah, Jezebel, Lilith. She was female evil incarnate. She was—"

"A woman you could not have. Did you threaten her family, Makepeace? Tell her you'd kill them, kill her husband, if she didn't give herself to you?"

"They deserved to die!" He sliced his hand downward as if to sever any remaining ties between him and his many-times grandson. "You are of no further use to me. I will see you hang before another of our name falls to Satan's whore."

"I will not let you," Nuala said as the men struggled to force a gag over her mouth. "You will not have him!"

"You have no power to enforce your will," Makepeace said. "Your lover saw to that."

"Take me!" Sinjin rasped. "She can do you no harm. Let her go!"

"Let her go? When I have waited so long for this moment? When I gave my life to studying the blackest arts, turned my back on all I believed, for the sole purpose of destroying her?" He nodded toward the waiting crowd. Three villagers approached Sinjin, their faces hard and grim. "Take him to the gallows."

"No!" Bright, flickering light rose in an aura about Nuala's head, and her captors fell back. "I say *no!*"

Makepeace blanched. "It isn't possible! The spell—"

"You have forgotten the one thing that can overcome the blackest of magic." She drove the men away with a blast of flame. "Let him go, or I will do to you as I did to your father!"

Sinjin fought to lift his head from the earth where he had fallen. "No, Nuala! The first time nearly destroyed you. This time you will lose your soul!"

"It is worth it." She gazed at him from across the clearing, her eyes so awash with love that Sinjin could scarcely catch his breath. "If *you* will live…"

With a great roar of rage and despair, Sinjin leaped up, scattering the three strong villagers like bowling pins. His feet never touched the ground as he ran to Nuala, grasped her hands, held her still.

"No," he said gently, pressing his forehead to hers. "I will hold Makepeace while you escape." She began to shake her head, but he caught it between his hands. "You must, for I cannot live knowing you have sacrificed your soul."

They gazed at each other, so bound in the moment that the world stopped its spinning. "I…" Nuala gasped and closed her eyes. "We have only a little time, Sinjin."

"I know." He stroked her hair, kissed her brow, her cheek, her lips. "Go." He turned her toward the wood. "Go back. I will always be with you."

Her eyes snapped open. Her hair burst into flame. And then she collapsed into his arms.

Makepeace laughed.

Sinjin lifted Nuala and faced the witch-finder. "You haven't won. Not so long as there is breath in my—"

An icy wind struck his face and blew through him, whipping at the heavy folds of Nuala's skirt. He staggered, and the ground gave way beneath him.

He landed on his feet, the walls of his own room closing in around him. Nuala was no longer in his arms. He fell back, struggling to force air into lungs crushed by the vast weight on his chest. Makepeace's body, restored to its ghostly form, wavered and shimmered before him.

"Nuala!" Sinjin cried. He spun toward the bed. Nuala lay there, unchanged, beneath a blanket that had not been disturbed.

"Nothing has been altered," Makepeace said with a skull's naked grin. "She is as she was. If you had permitted her, she might have saved you both."

"Not at the price she would have paid," Sinjin said, letting the tears fall unchecked. "She has atoned for what she did so many years ago. You've lost that chance forever."

With a high wail of madness the ghost sprang at Sinjin. The impact stunned him, weakening him at the exact moment that Makepeace seized control of his body. He felt his limbs go numb, his head fill with thoughts not his own.

We will finish this together.

The ghost jerked him toward the bed. Nuala had not stirred. She seemed strangely at peace, as if she had anticipated and accepted this end.

Sinjin leaned over the bed, extending hands he no

longer recognized. His fingers reached Nuala's slender throat. *She would die at his hands. He would feel the life leave her, feel her soul shrink to nothing as her beautiful, wicked body drew its last breath....*

Deep inside his mind, Sinjin fought. He regained mastery of some tiny piece of himself, a spark of will Makepeace could not break. And he realized, as the spark caught and began to grow, that Makepeace had made a fatal mistake.

"You have forgotten the one thing that can overcome the blackest of magic."

With a wrench that seemed to split Sinjin's flesh in a hundred places, Makepeace broke free. "Yes," he hissed. "There is but one key to her survival, and you do not possess it. You are like me, Sinjin Ware. You will never possess it!"

"I can do one thing, you filthy bastard. I can send you to Hell."

"You have not the power. You—"

Sinjin plunged his fist into the mist of Makepeace's flickering form and closed his fingers. He felt something solid, something that gave as he tightened his grip. Eyes bulged in the withered mask of Makepeace's face.

"You...you cannot—"

The slender cord in Sinjin's hand snapped. Makepeace screamed. His face thinned and lengthened like pulled taffy and dwindled to nothing. The mist funneled inward in ever-tightening spirals, draining like some dark liquid into Sinjin's fist. Makepeace's dreadful cry grew faint, begging mercy of someone

Sinjin couldn't see. When Sinjin opened his fingers, his hand was empty.

Sinjin rushed to Nuala's side. The pulse in her throat had slowed almost to invisibility. Sinjin bent over her and kissed her.

It wasn't enough. Sinjin had known it wouldn't be enough. *"There is but one key to her salvation, and you do not possess it."*

He had never possessed it, even when he had believed his heart lost to Lady Westlake. His heart had never been in danger. He had wanted Nuala. He had desired her, admired her, wished to protect her. But that last, essential element was missing. He was like Giles, like his father, incapable of the one vital emotion that could change the world.

Sinjin pressed his mouth to Nuala's, breathing into her, willing her his life, everything he was or ever could be.

Nuala's breath hitched, ceased. Her heart slowed and stopped. Sinjin caught her up in his arms and spoke the words, the words he had never uttered before, as if they could be true.

"I love you."

Nuala jerked, gasping, eyelids fluttering. Her heart drummed wildly and then settled into a slow but steady rhythm. She breathed deeply. Her fingers drifted across the sheets and found Sinjin's face.

"Sinjin?"

Thank God. Thank God. He cradled her head against his shoulder. "I'm here, beloved."

"I had a beautiful dream."

Sinjin rocked her, letting the tears fall where they would. "What was it?" he whispered.

"I dreamed that you loved me."

"It was not a dream."

She wriggled in his arms, pulling free just enough to look into his eyes. "I was...gone, wasn't I?"

"I would never have let you leave me."

"You saved my life."

He encircled her face with his hands. "You *are* my life."

Her fingertips brushed his cheeks. "You saved my soul, as well."

"You had already saved it yourself."

"No." She dropped her hand and covered her eyes. "How can you love me? For so many years I sought to atone for what I'd done. But I fell so far. I betrayed my family, everything in which I believed. I have done so much wrong...."

"And I have done worse. In my profound ignorance, I believed I had the right to judge you." He took her hand and pressed his lips to her palm. "Can you forgive me?"

"There is nothing to forgive." She looked beyond him, darkness lingering in her eyes. "You sent him away, didn't you?"

"Makepeace is gone. I do not believe he will return."

She closed her eyes. "I have lived so long in the past. My hatred never truly left me, even when I sought to help others."

"I know about Christian," Sinjin said. "You loved him, and you saw him die. Who wouldn't hate the man who did it?" He stroked her hair. "You acted as anyone might have done."

"But have I learned anything? Would I have done things differently, if I could go back?"

"You can only go forward now, beloved."

She gripped his hand. "Strange. I hardly feel as if my magic is gone. Yet I am grateful. I can never abuse it again."

He pulled her close. "There must have been another way."

"I have no regrets." She laid her check on his chest. "But now I must decide what I can do with my life as it is. The life you have given back to me."

Sinjin tensed. "You said you had a beautiful dream."

"That you loved me."

"You…" He swallowed. "You do not share the sentiment."

"Sinjin, I am over two hundred and forty years old. Does that mean nothing to you?"

"You don't look a day over twenty-five." He loosened his hold. "Is it because of Christian? Because you loved him so deeply?"

She drew back again, her face solemn with sadness. "I did love him. And I loved Charles, too, in a different way. I have lost the only two men I cared for, before…"

Hope eased the fist gripping Sinjin's heart. "Do you think you can lose me, Nuala?"

"I don't know. I'm afraid."

"But you care for me."

"Oh, Sinjin. Yes. I always have."

He desperately wanted to kiss her, to seal her lips

before she could retract her words. "Is it that you don't wish to marry?"

"You have a duty to continue your line, to have an heir to the earldom. I do not know if I can ever—"

"Hang my line. I'd rather it had never existed."

"If it had not, *you* would not exist." She brushed his hair behind his ear. "Even if I can bear children, I do not know how much longer I will live. I believed it to be part of my punishment to survive so long, but everything has changed. My time may run out tomorrow, in ten years, in a hundred."

Sinjin understood. He might grow old while she remained young and beautiful. The loss of her magic might take an unknown toll.

"No," he said, catching her hands in his. "We won't count the hours or the days. We won't spend our time yearning after children who may or may not come to us. We will be together, Nuala. That is all I want of life. If you will have me."

"And what if my magic returns?"

"Do you think that likely?" he asked quietly.

"I don't know. I will not be sure until the day I die."

He kissed her fingertips. "We will face that challenge if and when it occurs."

"You'll be the laughingstock of London. The Forties will never see you again."

"What a pity." He ran his thumb along her lower lip. "Then you will marry me, rogue though I have been?"

She smiled almost demurely, though the emotion in her eyes gave her away. "Isn't it customary to ask a woman's father or guardian for her hand?"

He stared at her. "Your father? But—"

"Or guardian." She put on a prim expression. "Guardians, as the case may be."

"You don't mean… You don't intend that I should go to those dragons, and ask their permission?"

"Those 'dragons' are my friends," she said. "Surely you aren't afraid of a few retiring widows?"

He snorted, feigning far more confidence than he felt. "If that is what you wish…"

"I do."

He leaped up. "I shall see to it immediately. And you are to rest."

"Yes, of course."

"I shall send a maid to sit with you."

"If you insist."

"I do."

She lay back meekly, permitting him to fuss with the blankets and pillows until he was quite certain that she was comfortable and safe. He lingered by the door, afraid to leave her, disgusted with his own reluctance to beard the lionesses who waited below. After all he and Nuala had been through…

He nodded sharply, turned on his heel and walked out the door. The doctor stood immediately without, poised on his toes as if he were prepared to break the door down.

"Lord Donnington!" he cried. "What has happened?"

Sinjin wondered briefly how much of his battle with Makepeace had been audible to those outside the room. "Lady Charles has recovered," he said.

"Recovered? But that is… How…?"

"You may see her if you wish." Sinjin stood aside, and the doctor hurried into the room. Sinjin sent one of the maids to Nuala's chamber with water and plain biscuits, took a deep breath and descended the stairs.

The Widows and Ioan Davies were gathered in the drawing room, sitting or standing in tense silence. They started when they saw him. Deborah rushed forward.

"What in God's name has been going on?" Lady Selfridge demanded. The dowager duchess stood at her shoulder like a forbidding goddess, and the others circled Sinjin in the manner of a wolf pack eager to bring down its prey.

"Everything is all right," Sinjin assured them. "Lady Charles is fully recovered."

The women murmured in disbelief and amazement. "How can that be?" Lady Orwell cried. "She was so very ill…."

"Nevertheless, she is no longer in any danger. The doctor is with her. If you would all be so good as to be seated…."

None of them moved. Sinjin clenched his teeth.

"There is a matter I must discuss with you," he said.

"What matter?" Lady John Pickering asked. "We are all ready to assist Lady Charles in anything she may—"

"I beg your pardon," Sinjin said. "I have chosen an inopportune moment. Rooms have been prepared for all of you, and a simple dinner will be served at eight." He bowed and was ready to flee when the former Duchess of Vardon called out behind him.

"You had something to say, Lord Donnington."

He turned. "Nothing that cannot wait, Your Grace."

"I think you ought to say it," Julia Summerhayes offered from her place at the rear of the gathering.

Sinjin gave her a long look. The young woman was serene, almost smiling.

Damn it.

"Very well," he said. "I wish…I wish to ask…" He met the women's gazes one by one. "It is my intention to marry Lady Charles."

Someone, perhaps Lady Meadows, squeaked a giggle. Lady John raised her brows. Lady Selfridge made a moue of disgust, and Lady Orwell clasped her hands in an attitude of beatific joy.

"What makes you think you are good enough for her?" Lady Selfridge asked.

"We have seen no indication that you have done anything but make her life a misery," the dowager duchess said.

"She wasn't ill until she came here," Lady Riordan murmured with a distracted air.

"But how could Lord Donnington make her ill?" Lady Meadows trilled.

"Lord Donnington is not to blame," Mrs. Summerhayes said, drawing all attention to her. "It is not for us to determine how someone should be happy."

No one spoke, though many glances were exchanged. The resistance was palpable.

"We will speak to her," the duchess pronounced, "when she is well enough."

"I am well enough now."

Everyone looked toward the door. Nuala stood on the threshold in her dressing gown, vitally alive, her face aglow with good health and unmistakable happiness.

She stepped forward and stood beside Sinjin, though she didn't touch him. "As you see," she said, "I am quite far from death's door."

Deborah held out her hands. "Oh, Nuala! I am so glad!"

"As am I, Lady Charles," Ioan said, genuine pleasure on his usually sober face.

As one, the widows crowded round, exclaiming and examining Nuala from top to bottom.

"Ladies," Sinjin said, "she must not be overtaxed."

The women fell back with obvious reluctance. Lady Selfridge fixed her intimidating stare on Sinjin again.

"Lady Charles," she said, "Lord Donnington has said he wishes to marry you."

"And I," Nuala said, "wish to marry him."

"How wonderful!" Lady Orwell exclaimed.

"How very interesting," Lady John said.

"I shall provide the flowers for the wedding!" Lady Meadows gushed.

"And I shall want to paint you both," Lady Riordan said, pushing wild ginger hair out of her eyes.

The dowager duchess merely looked down her nose at Sinjin, while Lady Selfridge continued to glare.

"Are you quite certain, Nuala?" she said. "After all he has done... His reputation..."

"You can't imagine what I've done to provoke him," Nuala said.

"Someday you must tell us the whole story," Lady John said.

"Yes," Nuala said. "Someday." She looked up into Sinjin's face, nudging him with her arm.

Sinjin cleared his throat. "Am I... May I assume I have your permission?" he asked, addressing the room at large.

"We must put it to a vote," the dowager said. At an unspoken signal, the ladies clustered in the corner of the room, speaking in hushed voices and casting frequent glances in Sinjin's direction. He found that his palms were wet when the women finally broke apart and formed a line facing him, standing shoulder to shoulder like the Trojans at Thermopylae.

"We have decided..." Lady Selfridge began. Her grim expression eased. "We have decided to bestow our blessing."

Nuala linked her arm through Sinjin's and smiled broadly. "You see?" she murmured. "I told you they were my friends. Perhaps, someday, you may prove yourself worthy to be their friend, as well."

Sinjin cleared his throat. He bowed to the ladies. "Thank you," he said. "And now I think it best that Lady Charles return to her bed. My house is yours as long as you choose to remain."

He bustled Nuala from the room before his nerve broke entirely.

"You have won the battle," Nuala said. "Two battles. You have been very brave, my love."

"Hardly brave. After what I did to you…"

"We can only go forward, Sinjin, remember?"

"If I could give back what I have taken…"

She stood on her toes and kissed the side of his mouth. "Perhaps you can. Perhaps a time will come when some part of my magic will return. And you will help me to use it wisely."

"When have I ever been wise?"

"We are all of us fools, Sin. The question is whether or not we can learn from our mistakes."

His throat tightened. "You really ought to go to bed, my dear."

"Only if you come with me."

"You're not…"

She silenced him with a most passionate kiss, and he knew then that this was one spell he had no hope of breaking.

Cast of Characters

The Widows' Club

Nuala, Lady Charles, wife of the late Lord Charles
    Parkhill. Formerly known as the maid "Nola."
Deborah, Lady Orwell, wife of the late Lawrence,
    Viscount Orwell
Tameri, Dowager Duchess of Vardon
Frances, Lady Selfridge
Lillian, Lady Meadows
Margaret "Maggie," Lady Riordan
Julia Summerhayes
Clara, Lady John Pickering

Related Characters

Victoria, Dowager Marchioness of Oxenham, Nuala's
    mother-in-law
Christian Starling, Nuala's first husband
Ioan Davies, a Welshman, Deborah's friend from
    Whitechapel
Bray, a Whitechapel troublemaker
Mrs. Simkin, a wisewoman of Suffolk

The Forties

St. John (Sinjin Ware), Earl of Donnington
Felix Melbyrne, Sinjin's protégé

Lord Peter Breakspear
Harrison, Lord Waybury
Achilles Nash
Sir Harry Ferrer
Ivar, Lord Reddick

Related Characters

Leo Erskine, second son of the Earl of Elston, Sinjin's
   best friend
Adele Chaplin, Sinjin's mistress
Jennie Tissier, Felix's potential mistress

Various Ladies Sinjin Considers "available"

Mrs. Laidlaw
Lady Winthrop
Lady Andrew

Various Gentlemen at Lady Oxenham's Ball

Lord Manwaring
Mr. Hepburn
Mr. Keaton
Mr. Roaman
Lieutenant Richard Osbourne

Other Ladies

Lady Rush
Lady Bensham

Mrs. Eccleston, matchmaking mama
Miss Laetitia Eccleston, unfortunate daughter of
Mrs. Eccleston

Servants

Bremner, Nuala's coachman
Stella, Deborah's maid
Booth, Nuala's maid
Harold, Nuala's footman
Jacques, Deborah's footman
Hedley, Sinjin's butler
Babu, Tameri's footman
Shenti, Tameri's footman
Ginny, a scullery maid

Characters from the Past

Pamela, Lady Westlake, Sinjin's late lover
Lady Shaw & Sir Percival Shaw, Deborah's late parents

Aunt and Uncle Turner, Nuala's late aunt and uncle
Sally, Nuala's late cousin
Comfort Makepeace, a witch-finder
Martin Makepeace, his son

Mariah Marron, former Countess of Donnington
    (*Lord of Legends*)
Ashton Cornell, also known as Arion, King of the
    Unicorns (*Lord of Legends*)

Giles, late Earl of Donnington, Sinjin's elder brother
   (*Lord of Legends*)
Cairbre, a lord of the Fane (*Lord of Legends*)

Brief Glossary:

Aesthetic: Movement of the late 19th century, dedicated to the arts, literature, decoration, and architecture. Aesthetic dress was unstructured, flowing and light, dispensing with stays, bustles and other encumbrances.

Donbridge: Principal estate of the Earls of Donnington, in Cambridgeshire

Fane: A race of immortal Faerie-folk, also known as the Fair Folk

Gladstone: British Liberal Party statesman and four-time Prime Minister

Salisbury: British Conservative Party statesman and three-time Prime Minister

Tir-na-Nog: Home of the Fane, the Blessed Land

REQUEST YOUR FREE BOOKS!

2 FREE NOVELS FROM THE ROMANCE/SUSPENSE COLLECTION PLUS 2 FREE GIFTS!

YES! Please send me 2 FREE novels from the Romance/Suspense Collection and my 2 FREE gifts (gifts are worth about $10). After receiving them, if I don't wish to receive any more books, I can return the shipping statement marked "cancel." If I don't cancel, I will receive 4 brand-new novels every month and be billed just $5.74 per book in the U.S. or $6.24 per book in Canada. That's a savings of at least 28% off the cover price. It's quite a bargain! Shipping and handling is just 50¢ per book.* I understand that accepting the 2 free books and gifts places me under no obligation to buy anything. I can always return a shipment and cancel at any time. Even if I never buy another book from the Reader Service, the two free books and gifts are mine to keep forever.

185 MDN EYNQ 385 MDN EYN2

Name	(PLEASE PRINT)	
Address		Apt. #
City	State/Prov.	Zip/Postal Code

Signature (if under 18, a parent or guardian must sign)

Mail to **The Reader Service:**
IN U.S.A.: P.O. Box 1867, Buffalo, NY 14240-1867
IN CANADA: P.O. Box 609, Fort Erie, Ontario L2A 5X3

Not valid to current subscribers of the Romance Collection,
the Suspense Collection or the Romance/Suspense Collection.

Want to try two free books from another line?
Call 1-800-873-8635 or visit www.morefreebooks.com.

* Terms and prices subject to change without notice. Prices do not include applicable taxes. Sales tax applicable in N.Y. Canadian residents will be charged applicable provincial taxes and GST. Offer not valid in Quebec. This offer is limited to one order per household. All orders subject to approval. Credit or debit balances in a customer's account(s) may be offset by any other outstanding balance owed by or to the customer. Please allow 4 to 6 weeks for delivery. Offer available while quantities last.

Your Privacy: Harlequin is committed to protecting your privacy. Our Privacy Policy is available online at www.eHarlequin.com or upon request from the Reader Service. From time to time we make our lists of customers available to reputable third parties who may have a product or service of interest to you. If you would prefer we not share your name and address, please check here. ☐

BOB09

SUSAN KRINARD

77365	LORD OF LEGENDS	___ $6.99 U.S.	___ $6.99 CAN.
77315	COME THE NIGHT	___ $6.99 U.S.	___ $6.99 CAN.
77258	DARK OF THE MOON	___ $6.99 U.S.	___ $8.50 CAN.

(limited quantities available)

TOTAL AMOUNT	$ _____
POSTAGE & HANDLING	$ _____
($1.00 FOR 1 BOOK, 50¢ for each additional)	
APPLICABLE TAXES*	$ _____
TOTAL PAYABLE	$ _____

(check or money order—please do not send cash)

To order, complete this form and send it, along with a check or money order for the total above, payable to HQN Books, to: **In the U.S.:** 3010 Walden Avenue, P.O. Box 9077, Buffalo, NY 14269-9077; **In Canada:** P.O. Box 636, Fort Erie, Ontario, L2A 5X3.

Name: _____
Address: _____ City: _____
State/Prov.: _____ Zip/Postal Code: _____
Account Number (if applicable): _____

075 CSAS

*New York residents remit applicable sales taxes.
*Canadian residents remit applicable GST and provincial taxes.

HQN™

We *are* romance™

www.HQNBooks.com

PHSK0909BL